WAKE OF THE WHALE

a tale of the Pacific Coast

by

LARRY L. BAILEY

Wake of the Whale

A DDP Literary Press Book

Published by
Double Dragon Publishing
PO Box 54016
1-5762 Highway 7 East
Markham, Ontario L3P 7Y4 Canada

http://www.double-dragon-ebooks.com

ISBN: 1-894841-83-2

A DDP First Edition September 12, 2002
Photo of Larry Bailey by Anne Hilling, Hilling Design

for MARIA

For Susan

Some day I'll write our adventure.

A sailor sat in the shrouds one night,
The wind was piping free;
Now bright, now dimmed, was the moonlight pale
And the phosphor gleamed in the wake of the whale,
As it floundered on the sea.

---Elizabeth Oakes Smith

PROLOGUE

They call me Lucky. A while ago, in a time not so distant in years as in spirit, I left my heart's home in the high mountain fastness of Stehekin, bound for the coast. The mountains are the Holy Land, God's Country, a crystalline evanescence of the Great Mother herself. But unprepared, without food or shelter, in the winter I would die. November was the limit, the edge of the abyss. Beyond November I was doomed. I must go down.

High altitudes and high latitudes test humans. Whenever there is trouble and hardship or when fear and weakness prevail, we descend. Inertia, or gravity, or some other force causes us, like water, to flow downhill.

Children who grow up in the mountains are told, "If you need to find people, follow a stream downhill." The further down you go, the more people you find. Eventually we'll all be lined up on the world's beaches, a mile deep, jostling each other towards the sea.

The relative number of people who live in the high lands is an index of a society's health. As their civilizations crumbled, Romans and Greeks and Babylonians and Mayans and all the rest, collected into ever-larger cities at ever-lower sites. Only the monks and the book-savers stayed in the high places and kept the faith for us all.

Your great-grandfather would never have built his house on a flood plain. Today, suburbs sprawl across the valleys and tide flats where they are regularly inundated to everyone's surprise. Even in Paleolithic times humans lived on more of the planet than now. Many ancient archeological sites are too high in altitude or latitude to be considered habitable now. And while the rich were not nearly so well off then, the average person lived better and worked less.

If you travel the mountains in any part of the US, you will find deserted homesteads, whole ghost towns, in areas now uninhabited, which were home to your revered pioneer ancestors. As the native peoples of the far north and the mountains lose their indigenous cultures, they move into lowland towns.

Life always looks easier down the hill. If you look up a slope, objects are enlarged, exaggerated, loom in threat. Look down and everything seems diminutive, controllable. So down we go.

Down, of course, is the wrong way. Everyone knows it. We are all supposed to strive for higher things, to climb the mountain of success, to hold the high ground. There are summit meetings and high councils and messages from on high. We do not descend into heaven or work our way down through the ranks. Even our musical scale progresses upward, (although I read in some old book that to the ancient Greeks the natural musical progression was down.)

The Bible says "Lift up thine eyes unto the hills, for therein lieth thy salvation." We all know that the right direction is up. But this is an age when the flame of human spirit flickers low and the dark pull of that other force draws us ever downward.

Usually my anti-gravity gland is very active. When my mind is clear, my body sound, my spirit true, I can let go the darkness and float upwards. From the time my Grandfather took me for a summer on the Stehekin and talked to me of the old days, I have naturally sought the high lands.

The only thing that always affects my a-g gland is hunger. By the time I admitted to myself that my partner, Snake, had gone south, I knew I was in trouble. Winter was hard upon me and I had no money, no food, and no feed for the horses.

There is a kind of relief when all the money's gone. It clarifies things, begins a new cycle. But the problem that year was deeper than money. I knew I could ride the horses sixty miles down the lake to Chelan, work in the orchards, prune with the Mexicans, and lay up at Granny's. I'd done that before. And I fit right in with the Mexicans, dark and silent. I knew I could go home and read all winter. Granny would like that.

She didn't care for the line of business I was in at that time, and I thought she would take the butcher knife to Snake the second she saw him. But if I read all winter, stayed out of trouble and worked every day, I could get on her good side. Not that she could have helped much in any financial way, it's just important to me to stay on Granny's good side.

But books were not going to do it. I had what Granny would call a hankerin' for somethin' real. Too many books. Writers had gone from writing about each other writing to writing about themselves writing. The books were full of hysterical characters doing implausible things in alien landscapes.

The last straw was a best seller from a couple of years before that time by Robin Thomas called Even Honkies Sing the Blues. Snake had bought the paperback at the lodge in Stehekin on one of his Saturday tourist ogling trips. He read it in a couple of days, laughed his ass off. I couldn't get half way through it.

First music, now literature. It was all disco - kind of catchy, anyone could dance to it, but you never could remember the words. This could be you and your friends looked at downhill. Nothing serious, no loomings or forebodings.

Granny raised me on a different sort of literature. The classics, she called them. Old books. Granny figured that if a book was a hundred years old or more, it had done all the damage it was likely to do and was safe for a child to read. She made me a deal. I could read all I wanted, but for every book I chose to read, she would choose one for me.

The first one I remember was a Bobb's-Merrill condensation of Greek, Roman and Norse myths. It was hot, better than the comic books I sneaked when I could. I sailed with the Argonauts, hid from Cyclops and had horny fantasies about the Sirens. I read in the shade of the great tree at Asgard and rode with the Valkyrie on my paint pony. I chose Tarzan of the Apes and read it in two days. She chose a condensed Gulliver's Travels. I read Riders of the Purple Sage, she picked Huckleberry Finn. Next turn she picked Robinson Crusoe, then started throwing short stories and poems at me - Poe and Hawthorne and Coleridge.

When I was twelve we had worked our way up to Moby Dick. I read somewhere that Ernest Hemingway said that all American Literature went back to one great book, Huckleberry Finn. It seems to me that Brother Ernest was remiss in his reading, or he lied. Among all our Leviathan books there is one that looms above them all, one grand hooded phantom, like a snow hill in the air.

I liked the book so much, I wanted to find out what sort of man wrote it. Granny showed me a picture, in her Lives of American Writers. I was shocked. It didn't seem that an old man with a white beard and watery eyes should be able to talk so young and alive as he did in that book. For a long while after, I would have this weird dream. The white whale would attack. Then, there was old man Melville, the broken Pequod in his teeth, with a kind of wild laughter in his eyes and a great foaming wake streaming from his hair and beard.

Granny worked at the library five days a week, so it was easy for her to keep an eye on me there. My Grandfather died when I was ten so there was only her and me. If I was not in school, I went where she went. Every day after school and all summer long, that was the library. Sometimes in that old building I felt like a barbarian at Alexandria.

But if I couldn't go off into the wilderness, my second choice was to go off into a book. I will admit to indiscriminate reading. I read whatever I found interesting. Sometimes it would be the classics; as often, the heretics. Mostly it seemed that the heretics made more sense.

Granny was a heretic. That's what Brother Devon Lee, the evangelist, said when he came to hold meetings for two weeks the summer I was fourteen. But Brother Broughton took him aside and talked to him for a while and he never repeated it.

Granny had been speaking in tongues again, and Interpreting it herself. Usually one of the old ladies would speak the message in a strange language, all weepy and swaying under the spirit. Then another old lady, out of nowhere, would start the interpretation, voice clear as a bell, speaking King James English pretty as you please.

Their messages were usually about avoiding sin, particularly fornication and adultery, and how you better read the book and understand it clear or Jehovah would burn your butt in hell until you could say the whole book backwards and forwards.

But Granny's messages were different. Her messages condemned bad stewards of the Earth and declared that it was easier for a camel to pass through the eye of a needle than for rich people to get into heaven. Brother Lee didn't like it. He explained that "The Eye of the Needle" was a gate in the wall of Jerusalem and that small camels passed through it quite easily.

Brother Broughton told him not to worry about it; no one would pay attention to a crazy old lady anyway. What could you expect from someone who'd married a half-wild Indian?

Brother Lee said it was very irregular, how could you be sure it wasn't the devil talking such strange stuff?

Granny knew what Snake and I were up to the second we talked about spending the summer on the Stehekin.

"You stay out of trouble," she said to me when Snake went outside, "and stay away from that Snake. He looks like an addict to me."

She'd accused me of being an addict since I smoked my first joint. But then, who ain't an addict? Whether it's drugs, or alcohol, or power, or money, or sex, or fame, or knowledge, or truth, or God, everyone is stuck on something they can't get enough of. Something that will kill them in the end. The whole civilization is addicted to petroleum and power and greed and violence. We all are helpless, hopeless addicts.

I suppose it was my addictions that led me away from Granny, down to the coast that November. That and the dreams. Some might call it fate, but what is fate besides the sum of our dreams and addictions?

These dreams were different. Power dreams. I recognized the signs immediately. I hadn't had a power dream since that last summer on the Stehekin with my Grandfather. But then it had been a bear.

There was no bear in these dreams, but a whale, black and white with great gleaming teeth. She did not loom above me, but came up from below, rolled against me and beckoned me down, into the sightless sea.

Night after night she came to the camp where we waited for the plants to grow. Night after night she tried every scam, every wile to draw me into her world. Every night I resisted, but my curiosity grew. I knew some night I would let go, there in the darkness, and follow her into the depths.

I did not go to seek adventure. Adventure finds me often enough on it's own. My Grandfather said that only white men seek adventure, and that is because the Great Mother made them with holes in their souls which they try to fill with adventure or gold or sex or violence. I try to ignore the three-quarters of me that is white.

And I did not go to write a book. Granny tried to get me interested in writing when I was a kid. It seemed like a trap to me. If I spent my time writing, I would have no life to write about. I decided I would rather live than write.

But some stories demand their telling. Besides, I had to tell this story myself, since no one else was likely to get it right. My part was minor, but I did see some things closer than anyone else now alive.

I don't pretend to be some great writer. Granny did shame me into a couple of quarters of junior college in Wenatchee, and I did all right. But I've spent too much of my life among real people who speak a live language to be very comfortable with the language lawyers and professors speak. It seems to me their words mostly refer to other words. I always try to refer my words to real things. When you get the hang of it, it's a hard habit to break.

The Poet always told us to avoid anything that could be

misconstrued as a moral or message or meaning in any poem or work of fiction. When I tried some to novelize this story, no matter how hard I tried to shape and twist it, meaning kept rearing it's ugly head. I guess my only choice is to tell it the way it happened.

They say that to write a book anyone will read anymore you have to grab your reader by the throat, with no warning, right on the first page, and drag them through the story so fast they don't have time to realize they'd rather watch television. You have to get your characters into bed before they've even been properly introduced, as if you could begin to weave before you strung your loom.

Well, I figure anyone who has to be gone at that way will never understand this story in the first place. So if it's literary assault and battery you want, you may as well put this one down.

Immediacy. That's what they say you must have. And suspense. Well, this story happened, as I say, some time back, and there is no mystery as to the outcome; it was all over the news.

Maybe you will understand it all. I don't. But some stories demand their telling. So like some ancient mariner or skid row bum, I grab your arm. "Hey, man! Hey, hey, listen to my story!"

CHAPTER I

I knew I would die there, drown like a bear cub swept out to sea. My raft hit something. Air hissed, then bubbled as the gash sank below the surface. The raft whirled. I could see the sharp beak of a snag just above the water as it ripped another hole.

The raft caught and tilted steeply. All my gear slid down the pine planks, almost dragged me under. I struggled free and grabbed for the snag. It was slippery but solid. Then one of the waterbed mattresses I'd used for pontoons wrapped slickly around me, as much good now as a ripped condom. I slid it up over my head, felt it pull loose and go with the tide.

I gasped air into my lungs and yelled. In the black fog, my voice died a few feet away. No chance my cry would be heard, or heard, be answered. Whatever happens on November nights in the murky channels of the Skagit Delta is better left uninvestigated.

I could hear my heartbeat, faint but distinct, beneath the icy water. I knew it would not beat long before the cold slowed it inexorably to a stop. It might be better to drown. The glacial current dragged at me steadily. I pulled myself to the slimy snag and felt the large log it protruded from. I was able to get one leg over, as if I mounted a horse, and sat above water from the waist up.

The log was a deadhead, had floated just beneath the surface until it hung up on the sandbar. When the tide flowed it would rise again. If I was then still alive I could ride this ungainly mount back upriver. But the cold stabbed at my groin, numbed my legs, told me that only my grinning corpse would take that final ride.

The top of the log was just out of the water. The seaward current slackened, turned and slowly the water rose. The heartbeat was louder now, seemed faster. I concentrated my will in my hands, clamped them onto the snag. I had no sensation from the waist down. In the liquid darkness I did not know if my eyelids were open or closed, but I could not move them.

The heartbeat enfolded me, mechanical in its mad rhythm. I tried to focus on something else. But the beat pounded into my ears. Then it was a voice. "The end," I thought, "Hallucinations begin."

"What in hell?" I could not tell if it was male or female, but the 'hell' reference seemed clear enough. Well, the hell with them. I would hang onto this goddamned snag until hell froze.....

"Damn you, let go," the voice said. I tried to grip harder. I would hold on until the last beat.

I could feel something pound on my hands, rip at my fingers. I knew I would lose my grip, but I fought on. Then I was loose, on my back in the water. Someone dragged me up the side of a boat. Charon, I thought. Then I was dumped in the bottom like a hooked salmon and I waited for the club to the back of my head.

"Jesus Christ," the voice said, shrieked with unearthly laughter, "You are a hard bastard to save."

I was rolled over, then a face grinned in mine, a black, tattooed face that could only belong to a devil.

"What kind of a strange fish did I fish up this time?" the voice asked and I was poked in the sore ribs, hard. "Here, drink this." I tried to raise my hand, but it was frozen into a kind of claw. I felt a hand under my head, a cup against my lips. I sipped and it burned me, tasted bitter. I spit, blew hot liquid over my chest.

The devil laughed again, that shriek. I would not drink some witches' brew no matter what they did to me. The light was faint and we rocked drunkenly. I didn't know they had boats in hell.

"Drink it." I felt the cup again, clamped my lips. "Are you stubborn, or stupid?"

I tried to talk, felt my mouth move, but there was only a hoarse croak.

That laugh again, maddening, not male, not female. Just as a devil would be. I sat up, banged my head, fell back.

"You're not going anywhere," the voice said. "You're mine, I caught you."

A chill wave came over me, my body shook. Maybe I should rest for a while, get my strength.

I didn't move or open my eyes. I wanted to clear my head first. I could hear someone move around, hum bits of some melody. I could sense no threat, despite the weird memories I had of the recent past. I hurt too much to be dead. Each breath tore my chest; each heartbeat stabbed my temples. The way the boat rocked we must be tied up.

I tried to open my hands. It seemed they moved slightly, but I would have to look at them to be sure. I wondered if I would have permanent claws. Well, if I did, I would grow the nails long and learn to live like a bear. My Grandfather would have done it.

"There's a natural mystic flowing through the air," the voice sang in a clear tenor. "If you listen carefully now you will hear. This could be the first trumpet, might as well be the last. Many more will have to suffer; many more will have to die. Don't ask me why."

I risked one eye slightly open, but could see only the edge of the bunk. I moved the other lid slowly. There was a dark movement and my eye slowly focused. Long twisted locks sparkled like fine black wool. Two feathers dangled, one raven, one eagle. Broad shoulders, muscled arms, a deep waist above a wide flair of hips. Brown really, not black. Strong, smooth legs tapered into high-heeled boots. The devil turned and her mystery was revealed.

She pulled on a tiny bikini bottom as she looked at me. The tattoos went far beyond her face. Some kind of scaly animal coiled up out of the buckskin G-string, it's wing tips arched over each breast. The creature's head was hidden in the shadows of her throat. A snake crawled up each thigh. Small flowers and bright insects scattered around.

Her face had been permanently shaded to increase the prominence of the cheekbones, enlarge the eye sockets, make the full lips even fuller. She smiled and it was exaggerated, mask-like. Sharp white teeth glistened.

"Well, Jonah, are you back among the living?"

I tried to raise myself, croaked.

She laughed and her dark nipples shook. "You're lucky the Wigit spit you out. Usually they just swallow you up. Strong medicine to be a friend of Wigit. There must be a purpose." The smile frowned, great concern. "How do you feel? You wouldn't drink the tea. It would have been easier with the tea. You want some now?"

I felt yes but couldn't say it.

She raised my head, tipped the cup. It was too hot, and bitter, but the first swallow glowed life through my body. I sipped greedily and it burned. I clawed at her arm with my useless hand.

"Be cool," she said. "Sleep some more, I'll be back before morning. The Wigit will rock you to sleep."

Light pained my eyes. A hatch creaked, closed, and what had been blinding white was fathomless black.

"Ah, Jonah. You live." A soft light wavered in the blackness. The flame flickered, then steadied as she set down the lamp. "We need to get you moving. You'll be sore as hell anyway."

She touched my hand, stroked it softly. The skin jerked in pain. She smiled that great mother's smile. "It will feel better, soon," she said. "I brought you something to help it."

She took off a long, dark, mannish coat and kicked off the high-heeled boots. She wore only the G-string. She pulled back the blanket and I realized I was naked. I felt small, shriveled, but I could not move to cover myself.

She took the feathers from her hair and stroked my body from head to foot. My skin quivered as from an electric shock. After a few passes she hung the feathers above a round mirror. She went to a small stove mounted on gimbals, lit it with a wooden match and heated water in a copper kettle.

She put leaves and flowers in two mason jars and then poured boiling water over them. She hummed a little and I wished she would sing again. She strained the tea into large white mugs with Coast Guard insignia and blue stripes.

"I need something to wake me up and you need something so the pain is less."

She tipped one mug to my mouth. It scalded my lips, but she insisted. After a few gulps she lowered my head and sipped her own tea. By the second time she raised my head the tea was cooler and I barely felt it. I barely felt anything. I was not asleep, but paralyzed with relaxation. After a third time, the cup was empty and I drooled the last of the tea down my chin.

She laughed softly. "You're some sight, sailor." She began a slow massage, first my hands then my forearms. I knew they relaxed, but I could not move them.

"You sure had a death grip on that Wigit," she said and went to my feet and rubbed them briskly, then my legs and chest and upper arms. She pressed my temples and the remainder of the headache evaporated.

She kneaded my belly and I distantly felt an erection.

"Good," she said, "now I know you'll make it."

She began to stroke me slowly, then faster. In a couple of minutes I knew I was coming. She slowed her stroke, finally stopped, wiped my belly with a towel.

"Sleep some more if you can," she said. "I need to." She took off the G-string and climbed in beside me, pushed me to the back of the bunk.

CHAPTER 2

The whale came for me again. It was as if she knew I was close, within reach. She rolled against me languidly, in supplication. I could hear her enormous heart beat its wild rhythm so near me. I could feel adventure in the rush of her spout.

That same tenor voice, or another like it, repeated a chorus. "They've got so much things to say right now, so much things to say." I struggled, drowning, saw faint light and rose towards it. That was too close.

"Good morning, Jonah." She lowered the music, turned to me. "You look better."

"I feel better," I said, still hoarse.

"I was afraid I would have to catch your soul," she said. "And I do not know your relatives so I could give it to them to be reborn." She handed me a mug of tea. Again it scalded my mouth, glowed through my body. "Where do you come from, sailor?"

I stared at her. Jeans hid most of her tattoos and a sweatshirt printed with a tomahawk and the words, "Custer had it coming." We might get along. But that face would have been strong enough without the tattooed shading. I thought of a totem pole, of wild dancing.

I started to sit up, remembered I was naked. "My clothes," I croaked.

She handed them to me, freshly washed, turned her back. I dressed painfully, wobbled to my feet.

"Boots?" I asked.

"No boots," she said. "You were barefoot, sailor. All you had was a library card." She handed me the laminated card. "How come you're riding a Wigit at midnight in the middle of the delta? Barefoot." She was nearly as tall as I was; her shoulders might be wider. Her Kabuki face probed mine.

"Wigit? I was on a raft, it hit the snag."

Her wide eyes widened. "Raft? A rubber raft? What were you doing?"

"No. I made it. Up in the mountains. With boards. And some waterbed mattresses."

"I thought you looked crazy," she said. "I fished up a crazy man."

I found it hard to deny. "We used them to feed our drip lines," I explained. "We filled them with a portable pump." I could see it only sounded crazier. "Where are we? I need to go."

"We're in LaConner. You can't go. You're mine, remember. I fished you up." Sharp white teeth grinned.

I wasn't eager to fight her. "Look, I have to find someone. A guy named Snake. He stole all my money."

"I know a Snake," she said. "He was at the club. Last Saturday. He comes in every Saturday. Spends a lot of money and tries to hustle the young girls."

It did sound like the same Snake. "What's he look like?"

"A cracker," she said. "Taller than you, but thin, kind of stooped. Crooked teeth and a mustache. Baggy pants. And he always wears a black baseball cap with a long bill."

Got him. That easy. Let's hope he didn't change his nasty habits. "What club? What day is this? Wednesday? Must be Thursday."

"Friday," she said, "You've been asleep a while."

Tomorrow night, then, I would grab Snake's skinny neck and squeeze it until he shit my half of the money from the summer's crop. "Where's the club?"

"On the reservation," she said. "Across the channel. It's a dangerous place."

"I want Snake," I said.

"Just remember when the rain falls, it don't fall on one man's house." She sang with the stereo as she turned, lit the stove.

I looked at my feet, splayed wide from years spent barefoot. I didn't like to have people see my feet. I wondered how I could come up with money for boots. Maybe she would trust me, loan me some money.

"I need boots," I started.

"I'll get some," she said. "What size?"

"Ten and a half, triple E," I said. "Boots. Not shoes. Western boots."

"Cowboy boots? Okay, sailor." One large eye winked.

What she brought me were some hippy boots with a strap across the instep and square toes, supposed to look like the Civil War or something. I would cut the straps off when I got a chance. They were narrow, pinched my feet.

"Let's go eat breakfast," she said as I struggled with the boots. "There's a restaurant called Pisces, a hippy place with good Mexican food."

"I'm not Mexican," I said.

"I didn't say you were. I like Mexican food. You can eat whatever you want."

"No. I don't have any money."

"I guessed that," she said, pulled me up. "Maybe they'll take that library card."

I tottered along the dock. She led me north, up the main street. Everyone stared. I wished I had a comb or a hat, my coarse hair must look like a butchered Afro. My hands still resembled claws. I looked over at her twisted locks and permanent stage makeup and realized that we probably looked like old friends, even lovers. It was a sober thought. I hoped there were no little white children on our route. They surely would be terrified.

Huevos Rancheros with lots of salsa. Frijoles with white tortillas. Starbuck's Coffee. The LaConner fog lifted and the gulls cheered. Even the hippies stared at us, a couple of animated Kachinas.

Her name was Cree and she was Canadian. Bella Coola. I'd heard of it, up the coast, on a fjord off the Queen Charlottes. Bentinck Arm, I remembered from something I'd read.

"North Bentinck Arm", she said. "In the old days they called it Rascals Village. I guess they didn't get along with the Hudson's Bay agent. The Americans always paid more for the furs, but it was illegal to sell to them. We smuggled them."

Her mother's father had been a Haitian seaman on a South African ship, an old square-rigger, with a severe Dutch captain. He jumped ship in Vancouver, stole a fishing boat and worked his way up the coast to Bella Coola. That was in the twenties. During prohibition he used the fishing boat to smuggle rum into Port Townsend and made enough to build a store and a few rental cabins up the shore from Bella Coola.

He loved and married a Haida girl from Skedans and they still lived at the store, guided hunters, fueled fishing boats. Cree's mother helped the old couple still and sold the baskets and blankets she made. Cree's father had been a fisherman, lost at sea. "Probably a Wigit got him," she said. Her boat was called Wigit, too.

"What's a Wigit?" I asked her.

"The Sea Grizzly," she said. "The Snag-on-a-Sandbar. Half orca, half Bear. Powerful medicine. Dangerous."

The Wigit was her home. "The other fishermen call this old boat my coffin," she said with a fierce grin, "but it's the Ark to me. As long as I have the Wigit, I can live by myself, anywhere around the Great Ocean. I could be in any water, anywhere, any time. The whole world is mine. It's the land that is divided and separated, not the water. When land people get to the water, they stop. When I get to the land, I just go around or through it. Water is everywhere."

We walked around a little, but too many people noticed us. I'd had people look at me suspiciously, but this was new. We might as well have been a couple of cannibals out for lunch.

LaConner had turned from a rowdy fishing village into an artist's colony. All the stores and motels had been phonied up with fake Victorian trim and the prices tripled. Artistic looking hippies and beatniks cluttered the place. Every second car was a Volvo or a Saab.

We went into a bookstore called Logos. It was full of slick, expensive paperbacks. Most promised to save you from yourself. There was the I Ching and The Sacred Tarot. Linda Goodman's Sun Signs and What You Always Wanted to Know about Sex and Then Some. There was Psychic Light and The Ministry of Healing. Communication Between Man and Dolphin, Voices from the Stars and Shakespeare's Revelations by the Spirit of Shakespeare. Back to Eden, and Ehret's Mucousless Diet Healing System. I didn't see how you could read all that, sort it out, and still have time to save yourself.

When the clerk wasn't looking I slipped a small spiral notebook under my shirt. There were some things I wanted to write down.

Cree bought a thin, cheap paperback of the Tao Te Ching. "This is more my size," she said.

She heated some beans and rice for a late lunch and fried some leftover corn tortillas. I could taste rose hips and lemon grass in the tea she made. We sat on the deck and she worked on a net. She lit a joint and we passed it. I told her about Granny and my Grandfather. She told me some of her grandfather's adventures as a smuggler.

I fell asleep in the wan afternoon sun. When I awoke, the sun was gone and the fog gathered. Cree sang softly from below.

I listened to her for a while. The melody caught me, but I could not hear the words. I went down into the cabin. She sat on the bunk, worked at the splice on a thick hemp line. I got a butcher knife from the galley and cut the straps off my boots. They had bothered me all day.

She watched me, smiled. "You like Marley?" she asked and turned the stereo on, the tape started in the middle of a song.

"... and I don't expect to be justified, no, not by the laws of man."

"You know, 'Bob Marley and the Wailers?'"

"I know," I said. "I've heard of them. Never paid much attention."

"You need to pay more attention," she said. "I have to get across the channel. I dance tonight. It's expensive to keep a crazy fish like you."

"I'll pay you back," I said. "As soon as I find Snake. I'm not always broke."

"No," she said, "You're mine. I'll feed you." She started the engine and went up to cast off.

In less than half an hour she tied the boat to a small dilapidated dock on the Swinomish Reservation. There were two other fishing boats, deserted and rusting. No one was around.

"Do you cross the channel every day?" I asked her.

"Sure," she said. "I don't like to sleep over here. Too many crazy people."

"So I've been spending the night over here?" A chill raised my neck hair.

She laughed that crazy laugh. "Just the first night," she said. "I was off last night. The Wigit wouldn't let anyone hurt you. Not while you are weak. You have a purpose."

"Right," I said.

She laughed again. "Last night we went to Anacortes."

"Why Anacortes?"

"Just some business," she said. "Had to keep a fisherman happy."

She took off her clothes and folded them, put on the G-string and coat. "Stay on the Wigit," she said, "And stay quiet. There's lots of tapes, mostly Reggae, no hippy music."

"I don't like hippy music," I said.

She handed me the Tao Te Ching. "There're some more books, too." She showed me where they were in the cabinet.

"Keep the curtains closed," she said, and slipped out into the growing fog.

CHAPTER 3

I was not afraid to leave the boat, but I didn't want to defy Cree. I watched out a porthole for a while. Nothing moved in the dark woods but a couple of frantic squirrels. I smoked half a joint Cree had left for me. I decided to try a tape, keep it low. There was one lying on top of the others. PETER TOSH/BUSH DOCTOR. On the cover was a wild man, Medusa dreadlocks flying before a flaming sky.

I slipped it in the deck, turned it on. The first song was a plea to legalize marijuana in Jamaica. A noble enough sentiment, but it seemed a little distant from my current situation. I listened to a couple more songs, but I began to have trouble with the words. I turned it down to a murmur, picked up the book.

Mystic gibberish at first, then the fourth line broke through my fog, reverberated. "Existence is the mother of all things." I read on. I couldn't understand it all, even with the footnotes. What I did understand seemed obvious. But, if you thought about it, it made you think about other stuff, then some more. It sounded like my Grandfather, just in a different language. It made me think of summer on the Stehekin. "Chasing and hunting will drive a man wild."

I was sleepy and lay down on the bunk. The lamp burned low, flickered out. The tape started over for the second or third time, but I was too tired to turn it off.

"Live clean, let your works be seen, my brothers.
Stand firm or you're gonna feed worms."

I tried to block the sound with my arm.

"...another one come tell I say,
if you want to be saved, son,
you've got to go to the grave, son.
Pack of bullshit, that is bullshit, I say.

I sat up in the bunk. The red light of the tape deck shone in the darkness like a beacon. I found it, turned it up.

"Now that you waited,
until your back is against the wall.
One step to progress, my brother,
you know Jah will help you all."

Jah, the face of God as Wisdom to the Rosicrucians I remembered from one of the strange books I'd read.

A new song began.

"Jah is my keeper.
Jah is my light and my salvation,
so whom should I fear?"

Jah, the Tao. I was afraid to sleep. If the whale came, in this state of mind I probably would follow her.

The wind rose and the Wigit began to rock and bump into the dock, a knocking as if something wanted in. I tried to ignore the music, but I didn't want to turn it off. It was better than no company.

I lit the lamp and flipped through the pages of Lao Tzu's little book. Wherever I stopped the words grabbed at me.
"A good traveler leaves no track...He who knows others is wise. He who knows himself is enlightened...He who knows where to stop can never be perishable...There is no greater crime than seeking what men desire...By non action everything can be done...To keep to what is weak is called power...The female always conquers the male by

quietude...He who makes easy promises will seldom keep his word...Thinking that one knows when one does not know is sickness...He who speaks does not know."

The boat rocked violently; the lamp in its gimbals stayed straight and true, but the shadows danced and swayed around me so that it was hard to read.

I put the book down and Peter Tosh sang,

"All you've got to do
is live clean, let your works be seen, my brother.
Stand firm or you're gonna feed worms."

The wind whipped the cedar and fir trees along the shore. A branch broke loose and cracked into the side of the boat. The boat reared and strained at the bow line, knocked me to my knees. The lamp flared and went out. Peter Tosh sang on.

I heard a great splash towards the open water, then another. I braced myself against the bunk and looked out the porthole on that side, saw nothing but blackness. The Wigit shivered and jerked and I was sure the lines would give way. The splashes seemed closer, almost upon me.

I huddled on the cabin floor, protected my head with my arms as I was tossed about. It was impossible to move with this crazy rhythm as you could with a bucking horse. Nothing was predictable. Just when I thought I had it right some quick sideways motion would knock my head into the side of the bunk.

Inland there was a crash as a tree went down. That seemed to stir up the black wind even more and it shrieked and howled.

On the tape thunder crashed.

"If it's life that you're running from,
there is no hiding place.
They're problems,
just your problems,
nobody else's problems.
You've gotta walk and don't look back."

I let go, went limp on the floor and let the Wigit roll me about. Close to the center of gravity the motion was much less. The tape played madly, over and over. The great splashes offshore came intermittently, somehow soothed me. I fell into a near sleep and waited.

Cree shook me sometime later. "Wake up, sailor. You aren't as well as I thought."

"I'm fine," I mumbled, tried to push away her hand.

She felt through my hair.

"Good," she said as if to herself. "I thought you were past danger.

"What?" I said. "Leave me alone."

"Wake up." She shook me by my hair. "You will turn into a Gagid and follow the whales."

"What is that?" I asked her. "Gagid?"

"A sea monster," she said. "Sometimes when a person almost drowns, gets too close, they change." She searched my hair again.

I jerked my head away. "What are you looking for?"

"Spines," she said. "That's the first sign. Sea urchin spines on your head."

I felt my own head. It seemed normal. I stared at her, wondered if I could get past her.

"You need medicine," she said. "Right now. I'll make some tea."

"No," I said, sat up. "No medicine."

"I'll tie you up if I have to," she said.

I looked at her, felt her strong hand on my arm. "You're the boss," I said.

CHAPTER 4

Great blackened girders arched over a dark, undefined space, which we entered down a long narrow stairway. The dim ray of light, which shone through the wide door at the top, seemed to die a few feet away. There was the faint stench of rotten fish. As we descended I could see a single smoky lamp flicker on a far table. Several people sat there and the distant murmur of their voices was the only sound besides the echoes of our footsteps.

Cree led me through a maze of tables grouped around large inverted wooden barrels, which served the dancers for stages. We approached the lamplit table and a male voice said, "Hey, Cree. Want a line? Who's your friend?"

"Lucky," she said. "He's staying with me for a while." Then she turned to me. "Want a hit? Aaron has good coke."

I looked at the glittering white powder stretched almost across the glass-covered table and thought of the gunpowder trails my Grandfather used for fuses when he blasted stumps. Aaron offered me a tightly rolled hundred-dollar bill.

I was afraid not to take it. My hand was stiff yet and I had trouble holding the bill. I leaned over the table and sucked a couple of inches of the line into my right nostril. The coke exploded in my sinuses and my head jerked back. I could hear a ripple of laughter.

I started to return the bill to Aaron but he said, "Better even it out or you'll be lopsided all night."

"No," Cree said. "That's enough. He's been sick."

"It's okay," I said and took an equal hit on the left side. That time I was ready and did not jerk my head.

"Whew," a plump blonde woman at the table said. "Hardcore."

"So how was your trip to Anacortes?" Aaron asked Cree. "Did you get that taken care of?" Something in his eyes did not match the dark smile on his face.

"Yeah," she said. "No problem. They loved it. I told you fishermen had better taste than hippies." She handed him some folded money with a hundred on the outside. "They say thanks, come back again."

"Good," Aaron said.

Someone pulled another table over and added two chairs. We sat down. My heart raced as it had that night on the sandbar and I felt like my head was a balloon, would pull free of my body. Cree looked at me. "You okay?"

"Sure," I said. "Great."

I leaned back, out of the circle of light, and looked at them. There was Aaron, full beard, long hair, but he didn't look like a hippy, maybe someone who pretended to be a hippy.

On one side of him was a skinny little guy, very nervous, often looked at the closed door. Stringy blond hair fell over his wire-rimmed glasses and he repeatedly tossed his head so he could see. In the lamplight I could just discern the outline of a swastika tattooed on his left hand.

Next to him was a fat guy with a studious look in a tweed jacket and new bell-bottom jeans. He could not find a comfortable position in his chair.

On Aaron's other side was the blonde, pretty in a way, but well used, hardness in her fleshy face. Her jeans were tight, her blue silk blouse half open. Clinging to her was a slim woman whose red hair fell to her waist over an antique fur coat, which nearly swallowed her.

They each took a hit off the line, apparently in honor of our arrival. "Cut us another line, Gerard," Aaron said to the skinny one. Gerard took out a leather pouch and dumped some rocks and powder on the table and started to work at it with a razor blade.

The fat guy tried to see my face in the shadow. "I better go,

Aaron," he said, shifted in his chair. "But the fact of the matter is," he paused for attention, "is we could all profit from it. We have a lot of people signed up who would pay good money. We'd split it half-and-half. What you do the rest of the time is your business."

"Yeah." Aaron said. "I'll think about it."

No one else acknowledged the fat guy as he got up and slowly worked his way to the stairs. He bumped into a table and everyone laughed loud enough for him to hear.

"Who's he?" Cree asked.

"Some professor," the blonde woman said. "Wants Aaron to use his boat to take tourists out to watch whales or something."

"He's a creep," her skinny friend said. "Kept looking at Lila's nipples."

"Lighten up, Morganne," Aaron said. "Everyone looks at Lila's nipples."

"He probably wants to watch whales fuck," Morganne said.

"Edward Randé," Aaron answered Cree. "They call him Eddie. He's a friend of the Poet's."

"It figures," Cree said. "Where's Lance?"

"He went down to Seattle with some Product. He'll be back later." Aaron counted the money Cree had given him and put it in an inside pocket of his down parka. It was all hundreds. "You need some more?"

"No," Cree said. "Not yet. Have to get the pump primed."

"Patrick and Pancho will be here," Aaron said. "They should be on the eight o'clock ferry from PT."

The door at the top of the stairs briefly opened, silhouetted a tall figure in a western hat and a long, tan duster like a movie cowboy. "Oh, god," Morganne said, "The Poet. Now we have to listen to his bullshit all night."

"No," Aaron said, "He's taking some Product to his reading. In Port Townsend. Lee's flying them over."

"Good," Morganne said. "Maybe they'll crash. He doesn't know what he's doing. Probably get us all busted."

"He's not that bad," Aaron said. "Just gets a little excited."

"He's an asshole," Morganne said, obviously wanted him to hear.

"Who?" the Poet asked, shuffled from one foot to the other at the end of the table. "Share water, brother," he said. "Aaron, got my coke?"

"Sit down," Aaron said, pointed to the chair the fat guy had vacated. "Want a hit?"

"Sure." The Poet grinned and turned the chair backwards, straddled it. Morganne glared at him.

"Hi, Morganne," he said and laughed as he took a big section of the line. He wiped his nose with the back of his hand and powder scattered across the table. He tipped back his hat, thin red hair fell over his pink forehead. "Robin might come tonight," he said and scratched his ragged beard. "He wants some coke. He has some girls over."

"Twelve-year-olds?" Morganne asked. The Poet glared at her. "Maybe thirteen," she continued. "Black, I'll bet. One of these days one of them will cut his balls off."

"You don't grok it, Lila," the Poet said. "He's a celebrity. He can do whatever he wants. His new book's another best seller. He says he's going to write a book about me."

Morganne rolled her eyes.

"How's the boat?" the Poet asked Aaron and everyone looked at him. "Oops, sorry. Who's this guy?" He looked at me as if he'd just seen me.

"Lucky," Aaron said. "He's Cree's friend."

"You in the business?" he asked me.

"What business?" I asked, gave him no expression.

"I guess not," he said. "Did I blow it?" He shrugged at Aaron.

"Don't worry about it," Aaron said. "Let's take a walk." The two of them moved to a far corner and talked in low tones.

"It's nearly time to open," Cree said. "You ready, Lila?"

"As ready as ever," Lila said, took a big hit off the line.

The door opened several times and people scattered around the place. Someone set up the bar in the dark not far from us.

Aaron and the Poet came back. The Poet patted the pocket of his duster and winked at Aaron. "I'll be back before closing," he said. "We'll read 'em a few poems, sell 'em some coke and fly back."

He started away, stopped, turned and made some hand sign. "Thou art God," he said. As he moved towards the door, his small head bobbed clumsily as if it wasn't quite connected to his large body. The brim of the hat flapped in a broken rhythm. He reminded me of some ungainly bird, like a crane.

"What is this 'Thou art God'" bullshit," Lila asked Aaron.

"The Church of All Worlds," Aaron said. "It's from a book by Robert Heinlein, Stranger in a Strange Land."

"That's an old book," Lila said. "That's the one where some Martian messiah comes to earth and teaches everybody to fuck everybody."

"And they call each other 'water brothers'", Morganne said, "and 'grok' things and live in 'nests.'"

"Some people started a religion based on it," Aaron said. "The Poet claims he's a member."

"I can see why it would appeal to him," Lila said.

"He says he's on a new path, now," Aaron said.

"I think he got his directions crossed," Lila said.

Suddenly music crashed from many speakers simultaneously, too loud to identify, and lights came up all over, focused on the stages. A topless woman danced on each stage as if she had been there all along. Colors flashed and swirled. Cree and Lila were gone. Aaron, Gerard and Morganne remained at the table with me.

There were only a few customers, all men, who sat near the stages, absorbed in the dancers. But more came down the stairs every few minutes.

The four of us finished the line and Aaron wiped the table. At the end of each song the girls rotated to new areas and whoever went on the main stage punched up her song on an ornate antique jukebox.

It was mostly run-of-the-mill disco and California Cowboy until I saw Cree select her song. As she stepped onto the stage and the opening chord blared from the speakers several of the other dancers groaned and one whined, "How am I supposed to dance to this shit?"

"If it's life that you're running from, there is no hiding place," Peter Tosh sang. "They're your problems, no one else's problems...." All eyes were on Cree although she looked at no one. She hardly danced at all, just moved sinuously. Her hands reminded me of the Hula; told some story no one could understand. It was hard to see her beautiful body as sexual, the tattoos and her hands protected her, made you see something you hadn't come there for.

She was followed by Lila who danced to the Doobie Brothers' "Taking it to the Streets." Her overweight body came alive, as sexy as Cree was distant. Lila had every move, made eye contact with everyone, assured each man that she was there just for him. Morganne watched each table react to Lila, her face immovable as a mask.

When Lila's eyes came to our table, something changed. As she looked at Aaron I was sure it was not a tease, that she was there just for him. Her eyes met mine and she winked almost imperceptibly, made me smile. Then she teased Gerard, licked her lips and stroked her breasts. I could see he was consumed with lust for her. Then her eyes were gone, played with someone else.

When Lila left the stage Aaron touched my arm and nodded towards the stairway. I followed him up to the deserted processing floor and out a small side doorway. We leaned against a rusted railing in the light of the full moon. He lit a joint and passed it to me. I drew in a deep hit and it calmed the raging coke a little.

"What's your plan?" he asked me.

"What plan?" I evaded.

"Why are you here?"

"Accident," I said. "I'm looking for my partner. Guy named Snake. He stole my money."

"I know Snake," Aaron said. "He's staying with a guy I know in PT. Buys a lot of coke. Sells it to college kids mostly. Bad news."

"Tell me about it," I said. "He owes me for fifty pounds."

"Of coke?" I could see Aaron's eyes widen.

"No," I laughed. "Weed. We grew it in the mountains."

"So you're the one." He looked at me carefully. "He brags about ripping you off. Says you'll never find him. He sold it for twelve hundred a pound. Good shit."

"I'll find him."

"It won't be hard," Aaron said. "He's coming over here tonight. Wants to buy some Product."

"Good," I said. "I hope he brings a lot of cash."

"Probably ten grand," Aaron said. "He wants a quarter of a pound." Aaron looked in my eyes as he passed the joint. "So then what?"

"I don't know," I said. "Drift along, I guess. Back to the mountains."

"Cree likes you a lot," he said. "She wants you to stay around. Besides, she owns you." He grinned.

I wasn't sure if he was serious. "Too many people here," I said. "Assholes like Snake."

"You can get away from them," he said. "On the water. You want to do something interesting? Make some real money?"

"What's something interesting?" I asked casually.

"I've got a boat," he said, "a schooner, an old one, called the Quest. My partner from Santa Cruz has it down South. They're due in Monterey Bay in April. I need a crew to sail it up here and get the product off. Cree's in on it."

"I'm no sailor," I said. "I fit better on a horse."

"We can teach you to sail," he said. "I need people I can trust."

"What makes you think you can trust me?" I asked him.

"Cree," he said. "If she trusts you, I trust you."

"What makes you think she trusts me?"

"She wouldn't have brought you here if she didn't," he said. "Besides, we talked about it. Last night."

I didn't like to have people decide things for me. "No," I

said. "Thanks a lot. I left some horses up on the Skagit. I need to get back to them."

"Well, think about it," he said. He held out a little bronze colored bottle and a tiny silver spoon.

"No," I said. "I'm going fast enough."

When we got back to the table Cree was on break, sat there in her overcoat. I sat down beside her.

"Well?" she asked.

"I don't think so," I said. "Sounds risky."

She laughed. "Compared to growing weed in the National Forest? Aaron's in The Brotherhood. They take care of their people."

"I'll think about it," I said to get her off the subject.

About midnight there was a commotion on the stairway, several people talked loudly and shoved each other. Out of the fray burst the Poet and a guy in a gray flight jacket with pilot's wings. They laughed and slapped each other on the back as they came to the table.

"Told you I'd be back," the Poet said loud enough to be heard over the music. "Here's your money." He handed Aaron a roll. Aaron quickly put it away. "They loved the poems. This bastard almost killed me, though. Doing barrel rolls and loops in the Seattle-Vancouver corridor. The controllers gave him a bunch of shit on the radio. Never figured out who we were though."

"It was your fault," the pilot said, steadied himself against the table edge. "Pouring all that coke down me. Shee-it. Then daring me to do it. After all that brandy at the reading. You fuckers are crazy."

"Poets are supposed to be crazy," the Poet said. "Like Rimbaud. We see the future. And it's fucked."

"You're fucked," Morganne said.

"Fuck you, bitch," the Poet said, reached for her breast. She slapped him very hard. "Cunt," he said and lunged for her.

Aaron grabbed him, pushed him back in his chair. "It's time to leave," he said.

The Poet started to laugh, but when he looked in Aaron's eyes he sobered. "Okay," he said. "I'll deal with this pussy later. She can't admit she wants it."

"Leave," Aaron said.

The Poet lurched a few steps away, turned and gave us a drunken salute. "Shhhhare water," he said.

A little while after they left, Aaron tapped on the table to get my attention then looked hard towards the stairway. I looked and there came Snake with two other guys. I slid my chair back into the shadows and waited.

The three of them came over and sat at the next table. There was a tall guy with long blond hair. He looked like an athlete, but soft, out of training. The other was shorter and wiry, dressed like a Mexican in a serape and flat crowned leather hat, but he had light brown hair and light eyes.

"Hi, Patrick," Morganne said to the tall one. He smiled at her. "Hey, Pancho," she said to the other one. He looked at her with no expression. She ignored Snake.

Snake beckoned to Aaron, wanted to do business. Aaron moved over to his table. They talked in low tones for a few minutes then Aaron said loudly, "There's a friend of yours here, Snake," and nodded towards me. I stood up.

Snake looked like he had seen his grandma's ghost. He started to get up as I walked towards him. I pushed him down in his chair. "Where's my money, son-of-a-bitch?"

"Shit," he said, "I was goin' to bring it to you. I wanted to turn it over a few times, make it into some real money."

"Bullshit," I said and sat down beside him, very close. "You're a liar and a thief. If you don't come up with the money I'll take you back to Stehekin and tie you to a tree for the winter." I could see that he remembered the traditional way for dealing with his kind in my country.

"It's only been a couple of weeks," he said. "I was coming back. Ask Patrick. I told him."

Patrick made a neutral gesture.

"Well, ask Aaron, or Cree." He looked around frantically. "I wasn't gonna rip you off. I know better than that."

"You got that right," I said. "It's your head that'll get ripped off."

"I don't have no money," he said. "I mean not here. It's all in PT. You can come over there."

"Sure," I said. "I've gone stupid. Empty your pockets."

"Do it," Aaron said. "I'll front you the product. You can pay me next week."

Snake pulled a roll out of his pocket. "It's ten grand," he said. "I only got five hundred a pound. Lots of mold."

"You're a lying bastard," I said. "I know how much you got. This is a down payment. You better come up with the rest, fast."

"I'll try," he said. "But I lost a bunch on some bad coke. I been tryin' to make it back." Behind him I could see Aaron shake his head then wink.

"I'll be in Port Townsend tomorrow," I said. "You better have another twenty grand."

"Tomorrow?" he whined. "I can't have it by tomorrow. It's all in Product. You don't want Product."

"Sure," I said. "Why not? I can get off the Product. Better than nothing. I'll see you tomorrow."

I went outside to calm down. Cree came out a few minutes later. "Let's go," she said. "I got the rest of the night off."

Back on the Wigit, while Cree crossed the channel, I counted the money. It was $9,800. He had intended to beat Aaron for $200

CHAPTER 5

She was there again, that great black and white smile. "Follow me," she seemed to say, "I won't hurt you." With a great leap she thundered against the water, insisted. My resistance weakened in the warm, womb-like waves. I could just let go.

I floated, rocked in the twilight. There was a faint smell of spices and tropical flowers. Thunder sounded in the distance, birds welcomed the rain. Peter Tosh sang, "Jah is my keeper, so whom shall I fear?" My mooring line barely reached the shore. I felt breath in my face, opened my eyes.

"Good morning, sailor," Cree said. "I have tea for you."

I sat up and took the steaming cup. Her brew washed away the coke and weed, cleared my head. I hadn't felt so good in a while. She sat next to me on the bunk, pressed her bare leg against mine. I looked at the beauty she hid behind the tattoos and the mannish airs, and I wanted her badly.

The dim dawn had become pale midmorning when we relaxed with another cup of tea. The radio was on a Bellingham station that played jazz. A news bulletin caught our attention.

"There are reports from Jonestown, Guyana that California Congressman Leo Ryan, a news team and several associates have been shot and killed by unknown assailants as their airplane prepared to take off from the airport there. Ryan had gone to Guyana to investigate a self-sufficient religious community sponsored by the Peoples' Temple of San Francisco, alleged to be a cult, which refused to allow members to leave. The shooting occurred late yesterday at the airport in Jonestown."

"Lila and Morganne know those people," Cree said as the music returned. "I've heard them talk about Peoples' Temple. Some preacher named Jim Jones. Morganne was a member I think."

"I need to get to Port Townsend," I said. "Can you take me?"

"Not on the Wigit," she said. "We'd have to go all the way around the island. Too far for one day. I have to work tonight."

"I better get on it," I said, put on my boots. "Before that bastard disappears."

"Lee would fly you down," she said. It would only cost about fifty bucks to go down and back."

"I don't know," I said. "The way he looked last night isn't my idea of a pilot."

"He's a good pilot," she said. "He only gets that way when he's with the Poet. I had him fly me to Bella Coola a couple of times."

"He'll do it on Sunday?" I asked her.

"Lee will fly anytime," she said.

"Where do we find him?"

"Bayview," she said. "It's just a few miles, up by Highway 20."

We walked to the Pisces restaurant and Cree called Lee at home and he agreed to meet us at the Bayview airstrip. Then she called Lila. Lila and Morganne came in before we finished breakfast. We headed for the airport in Lila's old red Mustang.

"Did you hear about Peoples' Temple?" Cree asked them.

"No," Morganne said. "What?"

"Some congressman got shot down in Guyana."

"Shit," Morganne said and killed the tape, looked for news on the radio.

"...unconfirmed reports of hundreds dead at the Peoples Temple Compound. Survivors tell of a mass suicide and murder orgy under the direction of the Reverend Jim Jones of San Francisco. Local authorities say that Congressman Leo Ryan and his entourage were caught and murdered at the Jonestown airport as they tried to leave with several defectors from the congregation."

Morganne's face turned ashen and she and Lila looked at each other. "That bastard," Morganne said. "I knew some shit would come down. He's fucking crazy." She turned the radio off. "All those people," she said. "All those beautiful people."

We drove on in silence.

Lila and Morganne wanted to go with us. Lee agreed to take us all for sixty dollars. He was very professional, not at all the belligerent drunk who had been with the Poet the night before.

He flew over the narrow channel of Deception Pass where houses clung to the cliff above the angry surge of constricted water. He crossed the narrow neck of Whidbey Island and swung the plane several miles out over the choppy water of the straits to the west.

In less than half an hour we landed at a narrow strip just outside Port Townsend. "I'll go call Patrick," Lila said and headed for the phone booth beside a small block building. We found shelter from the wind next to a metal hangar until she came back.

"Patrick's still asleep," Lila said. "With some teeny bopper, no doubt. I talked to Pancho; he'll come get us. I didn't tell him you were here," she said to me.

"Good," I said.

Pancho appeared in a gray Range Rover and we all piled in. He gave me a long look before he started the engine.

I had never seen such a posh four wheeler. "Nice rig," I said to him.

"Not mine," he said. "It's Patrick's. His parents bought it for him when he was on the ski team. Then he decided he wanted to sail in the America's Cup so they bought him a cigarette boat. So he could get out to the sailboat, I guess."

The radio was on and the music was interrupted by another report on what they now called the Jonestown Massacre.

"Perhaps as many as a thousand people including many women and children have been found dead at the compound. There are reports that one of the bodies is that of cult founder Jim Jones, but that has not been confirmed by authorities. Most of the deaths appear to have been the result of cyanide laced Kool-Aid. Survivors say parents forced their own children to drink the poison before partaking themselves...."

"Turn that shit off," Morganne screamed at him. Lila reached over and turned off the radio.

We pulled up in front of a three story Victorian house that overlooked most of Port Townsend. "How did Snake get a house like this?" I asked Cree.

"It's Patrick's," Lila answered. "Belonged to his grandparents. They owned a big sawmill, logged a lot of the Olympics."

The inside of the house was full of expensive antique furniture and Oriental carpets. Clothes, records and drug paraphernalia littered the place. A young girl asleep on a window seat raised up and stared at us.

"Snake's room is upstairs," Lila said. "Next to Patrick's."

We went up the broad staircase, made no sound on the deep Chinese carpet. Lila turned to the left on the second floor. The third door stood open. "In here," she said.

The room was empty except for a stack of Hustler magazines and a lot of stems and seeds scattered around. Morganne opened the heavy drapes. It was a large room with another beautiful carpet. There were the marks of heavy furniture recently gone and the obvious impression of a waterbed in the center.

"Are you sure this is it?" I asked Lila.

"Yeah," she said. "The bastard's gone. I'll go ask Patrick."

In a few minutes I heard Patrick's groggy voice from across the hall. "Leave me alone, bitch. Go fuck someone else."

"Where's Snake," Lila asked him.

"Gone," Patrick mumbled. "This morning. He bailed out of here in a U-Haul with that runaway kid that follows him around."

"Where'd he go?" Lila asked.

"California, I think. He has some people in San Francisco. I don't know. I'm not his mama."

"Go to hell," Lila said.

Pancho took us to the airstrip and Lee flew us back to Bayview. The sun nearly was down when Lila dropped us at the Wigit. "You work tonight?" she asked Cree.

"Yes," Cree said. "Then I'm off for two days."

"You coming?" Lila asked me.

"I don't know," I said. "I don't care much for the place." Then I remembered my last night alone on the Wigit. "Yeah," I said, "I'll be there."

"Good," she said. "I'll see you later."

When we got to the Club, only a couple of the dancers were around. The lamp at Aaron's table was dark. Cree lit it and asked what I wanted to drink.

"A cola or something," I said. "No alcohol."

"I'll bring you some Perrier," she said. "It helps with the acid in the coke. Want a hit?"

"Sure," I said. "Sounds good." She handed me a tiny bottle and a carved ivory spoon.

The coke seemed to clear my head. Cree punched up some Bob Marley on the jukebox and turned it down so you could hear the words. "You're running and you're running and you're running away. You're running and you're running and you're running away...from yourself."

Lila came in and sat down. "Hi, Lucky."

"Hello," I said. She wanted something.

"Want a hit?" she asked me.

"Sure," I said. "A little." She handed me what looked like a Vick's inhaler. I couldn't make it work and she showed me how to turn it to drop one hit into the chamber at a time.

"Well, I better get ready. You keep this." She handed back the inhaler and went behind the bar to the room where the dancers changed.

Aaron and Lance came in a few minutes later. They said hello but obviously were involved in something private so I went outside through the side door Aaron had shown me. The wind was cold so I moved around to the lee side of the building.

I saw the glow of a cigarette down the catwalk. Whoever it was seemed startled, quickly flipped the cigarette and I heard it hiss in the water below. I moved towards the figure and it retreated.

There was no outlet on that end of the catwalk so I waited. After a few minutes the figure shuffled towards me. It was a small man, stooped and shaky like an alcoholic. He pulled a fisherman's cap down and turned his face as he passed me.

I heard the music come up down below so I went back in. Aaron beckoned me over to his table. Morganne was there, peered at me from deep in the ancient mink coat. Her face showed tiredness and strain.

In the near silence between songs Aaron turned to me. "Well?" he asked. "Are you in? I'll help you find Snake in San Francisco."

"Sure," I heard myself say. "I'm in. What the hell."

"Good." His smile reminded me of the whale's. "Four percent. Of the profit. It may not sound like much, but this is a big load. You could make a hundred grand."

"Fine," I said. "Just help me find Snake."

I saw Aaron wink at Cree when she came by the table. She stopped and leaned over me. "So, you'll do it?"

"Yeah," I said. "Why not?"

"Good," she said.

About midnight Cree came over for a break. The cocaine raged in my head and the music irritated me. "Let's go outside," I said. "Get some air we can breathe."

The catwalk looked deserted. We leaned close together and Cree pulled out a joint. I struck a match and as it flared I saw the fisherman's cap a few feet away. His eyes peered out like some furtive animal's.

"You, again," I said.

"Yeah, just me." he said almost imperceptibly, "I was gonna talk to you. About Aaron."

Cree turned towards him. "Hello, Woody. What about Aaron."

"Nothing," he whined. "I just thought you should know," he said to me.

"Know what?" I stepped towards him to hear better and he flinched back as if I threatened him. "Easy," I said, opened my hands in a peaceful gesture.

He had stepped into the moonlight and I could see that he still looked at me suspiciously. His voice quavered, I thought he would cry.

"You're not him are you?" He looked at me with unfocused eyes. "I mean in a different skin? No, of course not. Just a little tweaky, I guess. But listen, man. That Aaron is bad news. Makes you do things you never would do."

"What did he make you do?" I asked him.

"Nothing." He paused. "Not that I want to talk about.

"What don't you want to talk about?" I took another step towards him.

"Nothing," he said, backed away further. "Not a thing. Or think about it either." He swayed, steadied himself against the railing. "But he works at you, at your mind kind of. And then you offer, no, you beg, to do something you never would do."

"Like what? Damn it," I said, "what is this bullshit?" Cree touched my arm, calmed me.

"Like anything." His voice steadied a little and he stepped forward, put a skinny hand on my arm. "Think of something you never would do, imagine it ten times worse, and before he's done with you, you'll do it. He can make you ask questions you don't want answers to. Make you go places you don't want to see."

"Well, no one makes me do anything I don't intend to do." I said.

"Right," he shook his head and it started his whole body trembling, "that's what I said. He's just a man. What can he do to me? But maybe he ain't a man." His voice dropped to a whisper. "Maybe he's the devil." He waited to see my reaction. "Jesus Christ," he said, "I don't know what he is, but if I was you I wouldn't sail with him. Not from here to LaConner. Why man, that could take years. Bring you back an old man. A year with Aaron can seem a lifetime."

"You better go," I said. "This is gettin' on my nerves."

"Just you wait until HE gets on your nerves." He cackled, had to brace himself. "It won't be long."

I raised my fist as if to hit him. He ducked and bobbed, then leaned close to me, filled my face with his. "Just remember, I warned you."

Cree took my arm, led me towards the door. The apparition melted back into the shadows.

"What the fuck was that?" I asked her.

"His name's Woody," she said. "He used to be an engineer at Boeing. Then he got strung out on heroin and coke. Speedballs. He was Aaron's partner for a while, a few years ago. He follows Aaron around now, tries to keep people away from him. Aaron bailed him out of jail in Seattle a couple of weeks ago."

"Weird," I said.

CHAPTER 6

I worried about my horses. There had been a few days feed where I'd left them, but then they would have to move down. Someone might take them or they might cross the river and wander onto the highway. Winter approached and it looked like a hard one. My Grandfather would never forgive me if I just deserted them.

I had stashed the saddles and other tack when I made my raft and then turned loose the four horses and Flea, the pack mule, in a meadow along the river. The two geldings I'd helped Snake buy at the Okanogan auction didn't mean much to me, but I'd raised my two mares from foals, cared more for them than I did for most people. And old Flea had been with my Grandfather and me that last summer on the Stehekin. He was family.

I talked to Cree, told her I had to go take care of them.

She said, "Let's get Lee to fly us up there. Maybe you can find someone to keep them until spring."

It sounded like a plan. We ate breakfast at Pisces and she called Bayview. Lee was busy for the day but agreed to do it the next morning.

A gusty wind pushed the little plane around and drifts of rain slapped against the windows. The upper Skagit coiled like a muddy green snake down through the North Cascades. Lee banked into a turn just above Marblemount and I soon spotted the little meadow. It was empty. He flew very low and I searched the trees nearby to see if they'd taken shelter there. Nothing.

Lee flew a slow spiral while Cree and I looked for them. Finally I saw horses, more than a dozen, nearly three miles down the river. They were in a smooth field near an old farmhouse where smoke curled from a stone chimney.

I didn't recognize mine at first, but then I saw Flea, off by himself. The other horses in the pasture dwarfed my Appaloosa mares. They were draft horses, Percherons I thought.

They all galloped to the far side except for Flea who just looked at us. "Where can we land?" I asked Lee.

"How about that road?" He pointed to a gravel track along one edge of the field.

"Sure," I said, but I was not sure. It didn't look like a place to land a dragonfly.

I braced myself as mud splattered up the sides of the plane. Lee crowded the side next to the field so his other wing would miss the trees. He braked to a stop and shut off the engine. "Here we are," he said.

Cree followed me into the pasture while Lee wiped the mud from the windows. The horses watched us suspiciously. I whistled the two tones I'd always used to call them and the mares put their ears forward. I whistled again and Flea started for me. The mares saw him move and followed. Cree dropped back as I walked towards them.

Honey, the tall dun, still wasn't sure, hung back. But my sweetheart, Freya, the stocky blue roan who'd carried me over the mountains only a week before, had no doubt. She stepped towards me, greeted me with a soft whinny. I put my arm around her neck and Honey came up on the other side. Flea stood back a little, patient as always. Snake's geldings stayed with the others, they'd forgotten me already.

I went up on Freya's back, guided her with my legs and took Honey's halter with my right hand. Flea followed us over to Cree. "Do you ride?" I asked her.

"Sure," she said and was on Honey's back in a smooth motion.

We rode them over near the airplane.

"We'll ride up to the house," I called to Lee. He nodded.

As we rode I saw a man come out of the house. He was old, moved slowly, seemed to sink further into the mud with each step. The draft horses surrounded him, escorted him towards us. We met in the middle of the field.

"Howdy," he said. "I see you belong to these horses."

"Yes," I said. "Sorry if they've caused you any trouble."

"No trouble," he said. "But you might have a foal or two if they stay here. They seem to like my big old stud, Mike. Nearly broke down the fence to get to him."

He looked closely at Cree. She sat the horse easily, two feathers flying in the wind. Out here her exaggerated features seemed at home. "You're not from around here are you?" he asked her.

She smiled at him. "No," she said. "I'm from Canada."

"I see," he said. He turned back to me. "Name's Corkindale," he reached up to shake my hand. His damp hand was knobby and strong like the roots of the trees.

"They call me Lucky," I said.

"Pleased to meet you," he said. "What can I do for you, Lucky?"

"I need a place to leave these horses. Until next fall. I have some business on the coast. I can pay you for it."

"The mares are fine," he said. "And this old guy," he nodded at Flea. "But them two geldin's are sorta crazy."

"I don't care about the geldings," I said. "Can them if you want to. Keep the money. They belong to a guy I used to know."

"I've got a little pasture over the hill I could put the geldin's in," he said. "They should be okay. And I've got more hay than I need. You want to get them before foalin' time though. I'm gettin' kinda old to be tryin' to take care of a bunch of babies."

"No problem," I said. "I'll be back long before then."

"I'd need fifty dollars a month, and some for hay when the snow's on," he apologized.

"No problem," I said. "I'll pay in advance." I pulled out the roll I'd taken from Snake.

He watched closely as I counted out a thousand dollars. "That's a lot of money, son," he said. "I hope it doesn't cause you any trouble."

"No trouble," I said. "Just a down payment on a debt."

We followed him to the house and I borrowed some tools, pulled the horses' shoes and trimmed their hooves close. They seemed to know I was leaving, were all over me. I told Corkindale where I'd left the saddles and he said he'd get them the next day, keep them safe for me.

It rained hard as Lee took off down the muddy road. I asked him to circle the field once so I could look at them again.

"No way to land," Lee said. "Not in this wind."

"Shit," the Poet said. "What a waste of time."

"I can see what I need to see," Aaron said from the front. "Make a couple of low passes."

Eddie shifted his bulk, tried to see out the fogged window.

From the jump seat in what was usually the luggage compartment I mostly saw the backs of their heads. I wasn't sure why Aaron had asked me to come along. Ballast maybe, although Eddie should have been enough weight.

"How deep is the water next to the dock?" Aaron asked.

"I don't know," Eddie answered.

"Find out," Aaron said. "Probably too shallow. We'd have to anchor out a ways. It is pretty sheltered, though. The house looks big enough. Who's living there now?"

"Some country and western band from California," Eddie said. "Tim lets them use it for rehearsals before they tour. They're called 'Route One' or something."

The engine screamed and I could tell we were very low. As Lee banked hard to the right I could see a Tudor style brick mansion surrounded by a huge lawn. There was a dock in a little cove with a speedboat tied up. Then all I could see was gray sky with torn clouds and torrents of water.

"There's room for all of us," the Poet said. "Aaron and Maria, me and Linda, Lila and Morganne, Eddic and what's-her-name."

"Suzette," Eddie said.

"I don't know," Aaron said. "I need Cree close. And Lance. We'd need his boat to get back and forth to the mainland. Are there any other houses?"

"Just that old caretaker's place," Eddie said. "It isn't really livable."

"We could do domes," the Poet said, "Or yurts. Linda used to live in a yurt in that commune in Michigan."

"I don't think Tim would let us build anything," Eddie said. "He wants to keep the island the way it is. That's why he bought it. He probably wouldn't even want that many people here."

"We won't tell him," the Poet said. "You said he never comes up here."

"Somebody would tell him," Eddie said. "Besides he flies over just to check on it every couple of months. He isn't stupid.

"Excuse me," the Poet said.

"I'll think about it," Aaron said.

"Defoe Island," Cree said. "I know that island. The English called it Destruction Island because the natives killed a boat full of sailors there - some captain named Berkeley. They blamed it on the Haidas, but it's too far south."

"It's a big house," I said. "Looks like room enough for all of us."

"I'm not living in some big old spooky house," she said. "I'll stay on the Wigit. You can live there if you want to."

"Aaron wants me to," I said.

"Aaron needs friends," she said. "He tries to do too much."

"He'll help me find Snake," I said. "Help me get the rest of my money."

"If anyone can do it, Aaron can," she said.

"Defoe Island?" Lila asked. "Where the hell is that?"

"In the San Juans," Aaron said. "No one else lives on the island. We would have it to ourselves."

"Who's ourselves?" she asked suspiciously.

"You and Morganne, Me and Maria, Lucky and Cree, Lance, Linda and the Poet..."

"No fucking way," Lila said. "Not the Poet. He makes me crazy. How about Eddie?"

"Yeah," Aaron said. "Eddie and Suzette or whatever her name is. He has a grant to start a biological journal called PREDATOR. And it's a good place for his whale research.

Lila nodded. "But the Poet," she said. "He has no god damned sense. He'll get us all busted."

"He's learning," Aaron said. "He says he'll do whatever we say."

"Sure," Lila said. "He'd say anything."

"I'll put Lance on his ass," Aaron said. "Give him a little basic training."

"I'd like to give him some basic training," Lila said.

"Take it easy," Aaron said. "What do you say?"

"I'll talk to Morganne," Lila said.

"Defoe Island," Lance said. "Sure, I know Defoe Island. I dodged the Coast Guard there once. There's a little cove that faces south and this big brick house, looks like an asylum or something."

"That's it," Aaron said. "The perfect place for us. There's a generator for power. We can anchor about a hundred yards out."

"Sounds good to me," Lance said, stood, stretched his powerful body as if he would go there right then.

"The band starts their tour a week before Christmas, we can move in then," Aaron said.

"I'll be ready," Lance said.

The Eagles' "Take it Easy" blared from a large set of speakers.

The Poet danced his bird-like mating dance in the empty livingroom. Linda sat in the corner on the floor, watched him with no expression. He grinned, swept a bow with his hat as we came in.

Aaron turned the stereo down. "You'll have to move that upstairs," he said. "This floor is for everyone. We need to keep it a little quiet."

"We need music," the Poet said, took a hit out of his stash bottle.

"Upstairs," Aaron said. "Lance will help you move it."

"I need more room," Eddie said. "I can't do research in a closet." He crossed the broad hardwood floor and looked out across Rosario Strait. "The view is okay, but I need room for my computers and a layout area for the journal. Two rooms won't do it."

"Okay," Aaron said. "Lance can move up to the third floor. He can see better from there anyway."

"Good," Eddie said. "He makes Suzette nervous. Never says anything. Makes me wonder what he did in Viet Nam."

"He doesn't talk unless he has something to say," Aaron said. "But don't worry, the Poet will talk your ass off."

"The third floor," Morganne said. "Who else is going to be up there?"

"Just you and Lila and Lance. He'll be at the other end. It's a huge loft. We can hang some curtains or screens."

"How about Gerard?" Lila asked.

"He's going to stay in the basement when he's here," Aaron said. "He'll mostly be at the lab in Seattle. Too dangerous to move the lab here."

"How about Cree and Lucky?" she asked, looked at me.

"Cree wants to stay on her boat," he said. "There's a small room next to me and Maria on the second floor if Lucky wants it."

She sat quietly on the floor, dark, beautiful and very pregnant. She didn't look more than eighteen. Bright colored bits of material were scattered around her. She looked up from her needle and gave me a friendly smile. "You must be Lucky."

"Yeah," I said and crossed over to her. "You must be Maria."

She nodded, continued sewing. "I'm making a quilt. For the baby." She adjusted her position, took a deep breath. "I have to be ready."

I looked at her work. There was a brown island with evergreen trees and the orange sun set behind brilliant clouds. In the foreground a bold black and white orca breached.

"It's a dream," she said. "All my quilts are dream quilts."

CHAPTER 7

Three Hare Krishnas surrounded us as we came out of the concourse past security. Their shaved heads bobbed to some drum only they could hear. Aaron walked straight ahead and the one who'd tried to block him dodged out of the way.

"Peace, brother," he said, tried to hand Aaron a pamphlet. It didn't work, so they turned on me.

"Peace, brother."

"Piece of ass," I said, looked as fierce as possible.

A smile floated across the eyes of the closest one but he kept his face rigid. "Spare change," he whined.

"Change your diaper," I said.

"Well, Krishna bless you," he said, retreated.

"And God damn you," I said.

Aaron chuckled as we went down to baggage claim. "At least we missed the flower girls," he said. "The Moonies, they're the worst. They'll grab you, figure you won't hurt a woman."

Aaron took his leather duffel bag off the carousel. All I had was a new backpack and I'd carried it on in spite of the flight attendant's frown. I didn't like strangers handling my stuff.

We got in a cab in front of the terminal. "Holiday Inn at Fisherman's Wharf," Aaron said. "Take the Bayshore through to Van Ness."

"Sure," the driver grinned. "You don't want the scenic route."

"We're not tourists," Aaron said.

It was clear on top but as we descended towards North Beach

the fog grew thicker until we barely could see the garlands of Christmas lights on the near houses. The traffic was slow and muffled, the cries of the gulls muted. In front of the hotel a Salvation Army bellringer pulled his uniform coat tightly around him and gave his bell a perfunctory shake, did not look at us.

After we checked in, Aaron got on the telephone, made several calls to people called JJ and Rocks and the Bird Man. I assumed they were from the Brotherhood. He asked each about a scruffy looking dude with some teeth missing, came from Arkansas, wears a baseball cap, might call himself Snake.

Aaron broke out his stash bottle and we waited. One call came, a negative.

"Don't worry," Aaron said. "He won't buy or sell any coke in North Beach or the Haight without running into my people." He went back to his book, something called WHERE THE WASTELAND ENDS. After a few minutes he looked up.

"Why don't you go for a walk, get to know the area?"

I started to say no. I didn't want to go back into the chill.

"You might run into Snake," he insisted. "Just be back by five. I want to beat the dinner crowd to Alioto's."

I wandered around the waterfront, watched the few tourists on the tinseled cable cars. I drank some espresso in an empty old beatnik coffee shop called Queequeg which made me think of Granny and all the books I could read snug in my old room on the sunny side of her house.

I'd seen the Poet and some of the others with a book called ADVENTURES OF A RED SEA SMUGGLER so I found a copy in a dark little bookstore and sat on a bench under a dripping overhang on the dock and tried to read it, but it was too long ago and far away.

I let myself back into the room just before five.

Aaron put the book down and grinned. "It'll be a few minutes," he said. "I should get another call anytime now with an address."

We did a line on the dresser top and he turned on the KRON news. It was all about money. The economy was on the rebound from the worst week in Wall Street history in October thanks to the 19.7

billion-dollar tax cut and airline deregulation. Even though the dollar was still near record lows and interest rates at record highs we could all expect the golden age any minute. This was indeed a Christmas season to be thankful.

Before we could digest this wonderful news the telephone rang.

"Yes," Aaron said, then, "Hey, man. Good to hear from you, haven't seen you since the last Sky River Rock Festival...Yeah, I agree, festivals are dead, need to move on...." He picked up the hotel pad and pen and wrote something down. "You're sure he's there?...All right, man, I owe you. You get up our way, you come and see me."

He put the phone down. "Got 'im," he said, waved the pad. "Tonight."

The maitre'd recognized Aaron, gave us a good table with a view of the deserted docks. The Mexican waiter treated us like we were a prince and his retainer traveling incognito. Aaron insisted I try the bouillabaisse and it was good. Some tourists stared and asked the waiter what we ate that was full of shells.

When Aaron paid the waiter he included a little folded bindle made of Christmas paper which the waiter slipped into his pocket. "Thank you, sir," he said loudly with a wink. "Come again soon, sir." The tourists shook their heads and muttered in disbelief.

"We'll wait until it's good and dark," Aaron said and opened the drapes, peered out into the fog. "This is a night job."

He read and I fidgeted. Granny always said I didn't belong indoors, couldn't sit still for five minutes. I tried again to read the smuggler book, but could make no headway.

"Turn the radio on," Aaron said. "There's a reggae station at about ninety-one.

I found it and Peter Tosh sang, "I don't like soon-come..." It made me laugh, settled me down. In just a short time Aaron called a cab.

He gave the driver the address and directions. "That's kind of a rough area," the driver said. "I won't wait for you, not in this slop."

"No problem," Aaron said. "We'll call another cab when we're ready."

"You won't find one that'll pick you up there, if it's very late," the driver said.

"We can handle it," Aaron said.

In the headlights of the cab, it didn't look like a rough area. Rows of Victorian townhouses stepped down the street with tiny garages cut into each one. Small rivulets cascaded over retaining walls. Faint lights shone from windows and pale pools collected under streetlights. Occasional soggy holiday decorations struggled to give a sense of normalcy. The driver dropped us at an intersection and Aaron paid him, included one of the bindles.

As we climbed the slippery sidewalk, Aaron checked his pocket. No one else was on the street. Some of the garages had house numbers on the street side; others bore scars where numbers had been removed. In the middle of the block, Aaron stopped, looked back at the marker on the previous garage then said, "This must be it."

We climbed mossy steps. The house was dark except for a single light in an upstairs window. Aaron knocked loudly on the faded door. The house was silent. He knocked again, then stepped back to look at the windows. The light was off. He hammered on the door, tried the handle, shook it, hammered again.

Finally there was a faint female voice, "Who is it?"

"Where's Snake?" Aaron asked.

"Who?"

"Snake."

She said something we couldn't understand.

"Open the door," Aaron said, "Or we will." He hit the door with his shoulder and it shivered.

"Just a minute."

The door opened a crack; Aaron blocked it with his foot.

"What do you want?"

"Snake," Aaron said.

"I don't know no Snake."

"I do. JJ told me he was here. He owes me money." Aaron forced the door open a little more.

"Hey man, don't push. Snake's not here. He went to Santa Cruz."

Aaron pushed the door further open, wedged his shoulders through. "We'll wait," he said.

She let it go and I followed Aaron in. Her voice quavered, "He won't be back until Thursday."

Aaron found the light switch, turned on a bare green bulb in the center of the room. She had wire rimmed glasses and worn jeans barely clung to her skinny body, her face was raw from acne. She could have been thirteen or thirty.

"Freebase," Aaron said. "I can smell it. Is that dumb bastard freebasing?"

"We like to smoke," she said, her hands shook. "It goes further."

"You'll go further, too," Aaron said. "Further to hell. Tell that bastard to come down or I'm going up to get him." He was loud, knocked over a chair.

"I told you to get rid of them," Snake's nasal voice whined at the top of the stairs. "I'm not sellin' anymore tonight."

"You better come down," she said. "These guys aren't here to buy."

"Who the fuck is it?"

"I don't know," she said, backed away from Aaron and started for the stairs.

"Get your ass down here, Snake," Aaron growled.

As Snake's bare feet stumbled down the stairs Aaron motioned me into the shadow of the hallway and he slipped to the other side. Halfway down Snake stopped. "Aaron?"

I could see he had something small and dark in his hand. I moved further into the hallway and said, "No, back here," and made noise with my boots, hoped Aaron had seen the gun.

"Lucky?" Snake said.

I backed into a doorway, the door creaked.

"Where the fuck are you?" He was in the hallway.

Then Aaron said, "Far enough Snake, I'll blow your ass off."

"Shit," Snake said, "I thought you were rip-offs. You scared the shit out of me."

"Just put the gun down," Aaron said.

"I won't shoot you," Snake said.

"Put the gun down," Aaron said.

Snake laid the gun on the floor and I stepped out of the doorway, picked it up.

"What do you fuckers want?" Snake asked.

"Money," Aaron said. "A bunch of money."

"I don't have any money," Snake said. "You took all my money."

"Bullshit," I said.

Aaron stepped into the light. He had a nickel plated automatic. "Call your girlfriend," he said. "Have her bring all the money and Product in the house."

"You bastards," Snake said. "Why don't you leave me alone."

"We will," Aaron said. "As soon as we get our money."

Her hands shook badly as she piled it all on the cheap coffee table. There were a few rolls of hundreds, not nearly what he owed me, and some baggies of some kind of rocks that didn't really look like cocaine. I picked one up and looked at it.

"Freebase," Aaron said. "Garbage. Gerard can turn it back into Product. At least it won't smell so much on the plane this way."

Snake sat on the floor, glared at us. "Okay," he said. "You have it. Now get out of my house."

"Oh no," Aaron said. "Not yet. Lucky, go take a look around. See how bad they're holding out on us. Go with him," he said to the woman.

I found another large bag of the rocks under a waterbed upstairs. A small waterpipe made of lab glass and a propane torch were still hot on the nightstand. There was also another roll of hundreds she'd stuck in the toilet tank in a zip-loc. Her eyes widened when I found it and she ducked when I turned towards her.

"I won't hit you," I said. "Snake might be another story."

"Just look over your shoulder," Aaron said. "We'll be back."

"Leave my gun," Snake whined. "I need to protect myself."

"Talk to JJ," Aaron said. "I'll leave it with him. He can give it to you if he thinks you should have it."

He dialed the phone, waited. "JJ. Hey man, we need a ride.... From Snake's pad.... Yeah, thanks, we took what he has. It's not much.... You know he's freebasing?...Yeah, him and this lady are all fucked up.... Okay, we'll watch for you."

"Leave me a little product," Snake begged. "Just enough until tomorrow, I can get more then."

"Fuck you," Aaron said. "Do you good to get your head straight for a few minutes. You might wake up."

"Just a little," Snake begged. For Bonnie. She needs it bad."

"Shut up," Aaron said.

JJ was a black guy in a powder blue Eldorado convertible that pulled up in front of Snake's. He didn't fit my picture of the Brotherhood. I had thought they were all hippies and didn't go in for show, put lots of money into causes, against the war and saving whales and such. JJ's main cause seemed to be JJ. When he dropped us at the terminal, Aaron gave him Snake's gun and the one he'd carried.

"Next time," Aaron said.

SF International was full of people on last minute trips home for Christmas, salesmen, students, GIs and other vagabonds. As we walked up the concourse a Happy Holidays banner had come loose at one end and trailed nearly to the floor, waved feebly in the gusts from the automatic doors as we waited on my backpack to come through the x-ray machine.

The blonde attendant at the gate had on a little plastic holly pin and Aaron asked her if it was mistletoe.

She smiled seductively and said, "No, but we could find some."

He slipped one of his holiday bindles in her palm and she winked and slid it between the buttons of her white uniform blouse into her bra.

"It'll be safe there," she said, "In case you want it back."

"I just might," he said. "Next trip."

"I'll be here," she said."

I was glad to get onto the plane. My boots were stuffed so full of money and freebase that I walked with a limp. Aaron said it gave me character. He carried as much as I did but didn't seem to notice it at all. As soon as we were seated he slipped me an inhaler like Lila's.

"This'll clear your sinuses," he said. It did.

"Welcome aboard ladies and gentlemen," the pilot said. "We should be above this weather in a few minutes and it looks like clear sailing up the coast." We soon broke through into brilliant sunshine under a deep blue sky. The clouds far below seemed as remote as another planet.

CHAPTER 8

There was a metallic glow, dark blue fire in ice, which crackled into a rainbow as I approached. It made me almost afraid, an unwilling reverence. It was arranged on a piece of black velvet the way some pagan god might arrange a holy place. A blunt translucent pyramid shone in a ring of smaller rocks amidst delicate drifts of powder.

The central crystal pulled my eye into its frozen depths, fractured the flow of light to create the illusion of endlessness. What had seemed blue, then rainbow, was no color at all, and when my shadow fell across it, was nearly invisible. It seemed to hover on the edge of non-substance, more energy than matter.

Gerard smiled like a proud father and tossed his hair out of his face. "One hundred percent pure cocaine hydrochloride," he said. "It gets no better. Not even from Merck and Merck. I call it Northern Lights."

"It's yours," Aaron said to me.

I looked at him. "Why mine?"

"It's that garbage we took from Snake. All cleaned up."

"More like transformed," Gerard said. "From a base to an acid."

"But why is it mine?" I looked at Aaron. "You took it."

"No," he said. "We took it. For you, to pay back what he owes you. It's only four ounces, there was a lot of crap in it and Gerard gets ten percent for cleaning it up."

"Snake owes you money too," I said.

"Not that much." He laughed. "I'll get mine."

"We can split it," I offered.

"No you keep it," he said. "Some day I'll need your help. That's how it works. Karma. With the thirty-eight hundred dollars we got, it's a total of about twelve thousand. He still owes you eight grand."

"We'll never see him again," I said.

"Don't count on it," he said.

You may think I am an advocate for cocaine use. I am not. I no longer use any drugs, legal or illegal. But I told you, this was another time. I didn't know many then who didn't use illegal drugs although most of them would deny it now.

Besides, our whole civilization depends on drugs. Whether or not they are legal depends on who makes the money. I still don't see a meaningful difference between Bonnie and her crack habit in the Haight and the sorority girl at Stanford with her diet pills and tranquilizers. The only difference is that the sorority girl can afford her habits and her doctor and the drug corporations make the money. Both are out of their minds on drugs.

Back then, even the Surgeon General assured us that cocaine was not addictive and less dangerous than marijuana. A judge in Massachusetts threw out a possession case, declared the drug not a narcotic.

It was snorted at all the best parties and it energized corporate board meetings. State legislators were seen in Capitol restrooms with crystal vials and tiny silver spoons. The mayor hardly raised an eyebrow at the long white lines stretched across banquet tables.

Those of us in "the business" were heroes to athletes and cab drivers, students and fishermen. Our money was welcome in trendy restaurants, the finest clothing stores and the political campaigns of both parties. The best weddings were not complete without a finely etched crystal mirror laced with pure white garlands of our Product.

By the time of the events that I relate, cocaine hydrochloride had become the soma of the sophisticate, the Blessed Sacrament of the affluent. A whole industry sprang up to provide us the chemicals and test equipment we needed. "Paraphernalia" alone added a hundred million dollars a year to the nation's economy.

Movie stars were pictured with platinum razor blades on gold chains around their necks. It was estimated that twenty percent of the population used cocaine regularly.

It began to interest Big Business. Defense attorneys wanted a piece of the action instead of a fee. Some airlines were known to overlook obvious smugglers. Junior executives found better returns on investments with their friendly dealer than they could get from Wall Street. Real Estate Brokers were happy to deposit stacks of hundreds into their trust accounts for large purchases, especially if an ounce or two was thrown in to sweeten the deal. Power is power whether it comes from whale oil, crude oil, or cocaine.

In the war on drugs, cocaine held noncombatant status. While freebase in the ghettos was good for a few headlines, most of the coke business was considered to be pretty genteel. Police departments had no time to chase blow-heads, particularly if they were white. Besides, there was nothing quite like a toot of the white lady to get you through those long night patrols.

Cocaine was a drug the ruling class could understand. Marijuana inhibits the ego and allows the threat of instinctual behavior to surface. LSD dissolves the ego into the even greater threat of universal identification and the power of the group. But cocaine enhances the ego, creates the illusion of individual power. Anyone could relate to that.

So, wherever we went the Product was welcome, whether it was the Pink Flame of Peru, the sulky amber fire of Bolivian or the crystalline purity of Gerard's Northern Lights. We were crusaders just back from the Holy Land with strange tales and exotic spices. We were Marco Polo, Cortez and Captain Cook. We were the crew of a southern whale ship just docked in Nantucket with our hold full of the finest spermaceti.

We sailed before a sharp wind, rigged in the way Patrick had taught us was wing and wing, that is the main on one side, the jib on the other, headed out into the Strait of Juan de Fuca for another day of practice.

Patrick loved it, ordered us around like so many deck monkeys on the Bounty. He hassled me about my boots the first day out, said I should get some deck shoes and rubber boots like a proper sailor.

I told him to go take a look at any illustration of real sailors in the age of iron men and wooden ships and he'd see that all of them wore boots about like mine. He said this was the real world, not a painting. He didn't mention my boots again.

Once we were well out Patrick had us shorten the sails on the sleek ocean racer so that it behaved more like the schooner would. Then we took endless turns at each station while we tacked at every angle to the wind.

He taught us to steer close hauled, as tight to the wind as possible until the sails began to luff, then ease off, then back again like a ponderous pendulum. We had learned to jump at his "Ready about," and not get caught by the boom as it swept across the deck.

We had to climb into the rigging to untangle lines and walk out on the boom to reef in sail. I had more trouble than I expected getting used to it. I'd done some risky things on a horse, but in every case not too far below me was solid ground. Here there was nothing solid or still.

After several days of practice, Patrick said we were to the point where we could be considered a beginner crew. We took that as a compliment. Even the Poet had been subdued by the task. It was hard to work as we did and run a smart mouth too.

I enjoyed the work; I hate to sit around. The Poet claimed that you could get the same effect if you did enough coke - adrenaline rushes, elevated heart rate, heavy sweat and heightened awareness. There was no need to work out. He was there only for the nautical experience, as an artist.

The spray stung my face, chilled me like no mountain winter had. The surge and leap of the bow reminded me of a horse as it bucked in slow motion. I straddled the post at the prow, both hands on the rail, and let my body move with the flow. Not a bad ride, but I would rather have had the smell of horse sweat and acrid Okanogan dust in my nostrils.

I felt the shapes at first. They coursed along on either side as dark as the waves, but like the boat, they cut through the water. Unlike the boat they made no sound.

I started to tell the others, but was entranced. I tried to estimate how close they were, but realized I did not know their true size. Against the fractal seascape I had no perspective. They could be ten feet long or a hundred.

One was close enough to see white underneath and near the head. Orcas. We had seen pods at a distance twice but never this close. They paced along beside us, completely aware of us, and yet no one else on the boat knew they were there. And I hadn't known a few minutes before. More than a dozen powerful intelligences swam a few feet from our heads and we did not know it.

I watched them and felt them watch me.

"Ease the helm," I heard Patrick call. Then, as we lost momentum, "Ready about." The deck tilted and I could hear lines hum and winches chatter, felt the swing of the boom. As we turned, the orcas turned, in effortless precision. I leaned with the boat and felt a part of their tribe. It was as though we sailed on a mirror as they knifed through the fluid of the sea and the boat through the fluid of the air.

After a few minutes, bored or busy, they turned away, followed the tremendous leap of one who burst into the air with no warning, briefly shared our element, then arched back into the water and was gone.

I moved aft to take my next turn on the wheel. "What the hell was that splash?" the Poet asked.

"Nothing," I answered.

"Nothing important," Patrick said. "Go ahead and take the wheel, Lucky. Poet, go take the bow lookout."

CHAPTER 9

"I knew there were bad souls here," Maria said. "I feel them."

"The Spanish named it La Isla de Dolores," Eddie said. "I found it in Hazlitt's history of British Columbia. A boatload of Spaniards came ashore for water and all of them were massacred."

"They probably blamed the Haidas, too," Cree said.

"They had armor," Maria said. "Like steel vests. And helmets." She had started labor but refused Aaron's suggestion that she might be more comfortable upstairs. She was very animated. "They were surprised."

"I'll bet," Aaron said.

"No, really," she insisted. "They were just walking along and men, Indians, slipped up behind them and cut their throats. They were very quiet."

"Welcome to the New World, motherfucker." The Poet slid his finger across his throat.

"Well, it's what they learned from the Spanish," Cree said. "And the English."

"Fuck 'em if they can't take a joke," the Poet said. He crossed the living room, peered out the window. "Where's Linda? She needs to watch this so she knows what to do when her time comes."

"It's pretty choppy, Lance will take it easy," Aaron said.

"I need a boat so we don't have to go everywhere with Lance." The Poet made steering motions in the air.

"You'd drown yourself," Aaron said. "Relax, she'll get here."

Maria had a contraction, grimaced, then smiled as it eased. Her dark face reminded me of my mother, Native and white marbled into mestizo cafe au lait.

My mother had hated her color as she suffered through grade school roles as Pocahontas and Sacajawea. To me she had been as beautiful as the earth itself.

"You're the color we'll all be, soon," my Grandfather would say to her. "We lighten, the whites darken. One day we'll look around and there won't be a difference. We'll all have golden skin."

But not soon enough for my mother. After high school, when all the boys came home from World War II, she fell for a P-51 pilot turned spray plane maniac who was my father. But he flew into a power line when I was six and she found out how her old schoolmates treated a mixed blood widow. She grew tired of blond farm boys and husky loggers but not before one took her on a vacation to Hawaii. She never really came back, except to pick up her clothes, but I was with my grandparents long before that.

"Lucky," Cree called.

I went up the stairs and into Aaron and Maria's room. There were only candles for light. The bed was a large pad on the floor covered with batik sheets. Maria sat with her back against a cushion that was propped against the wall. She was nude and largely dilated.

Cree motioned me to sit with Lila and Morganne beside the bed. "Push when you're ready," she said to Maria.

Aaron was at Maria's side, stroked her back.

"Don't touch me," she said. "Not now." Then she smiled at him. Sweat ran from her face.

We watched quietly as she strained through two more contractions. The baby's head was visible, sticky black hair over a red scalp.

"It's crowning," Cree said, "Just a few more minutes. You're doing great." She wiped Maria's forehead with a cool towel.

Maria pushed twice again, then there was a lull. She relaxed and sat up, looked around in surprise. Then, "Oh, God," she said, "here it comes." She leaned forward; veins throbbed in her face from the effort.

The baby's head suddenly slipped through and there was a new face among us, dark and, I was sure, female. Another contraction birthed the shoulders and Cree gently pulled the child free, placed it dripping on Maria's chest. The umbilical cord pulsed thickly, took on a faint blue overlay. It was definitely a girl.

Lila poured small glasses of champagne, passed them around and started to chop a line on a mirror etched with a naked goddess striding beneath a glittering Ursa Major. Maria only touched the wine to her lips as we drank but she looked hungrily at the cocaine.

"After we cut the cord," Cree said. "You've been a good girl for a long time."

"What's her name," Morganne asked.

"Dolores," Maria said. "My own little island of sorrows." Her eyes looked into the distance.

"You blew it," the Poet said to Linda as she came through the door. "It was born two hours ago. They didn't even tell me."

"Sorry," Linda said. "It was really rough. Lance had to zigzag so we didn't take the waves head on. He sure can handle that boat."

"Too bad he didn't handle it a little sooner," the Poet said.

"That was my fault," she said. "I was looking for something for the baby." She took a box wrapped in hand made rainbow striped paper out of a shopping bag. "It's a serape, from Guatemala, baby size. I hope it's a girl."

"It is," the Poet said. "Dolores. Kind of a weird name."

"It's nice," Linda said.

The plane paused just long enough for the heavy man to step onto the pontoon and jump to the dock, then Lee swung it around and gunned the engine, took off into the stiff wind. The gray suit and red tie looked out of place, and the glasses and bald head. What kind of party was this?

Lance had brought a boatload and Cree was due with more. Patrick and Pancho had brought four girls from Port Townsend. I'd been sent to guide the suit in.

"Hello," he said, extended his hand, "Frank Lewis."

"Lucky," I said, briefly took his hand. "Aaron's inside."

"Good," he said. "I need a drink." His pants cuffs were soaked, flapped against the low cut street shoes. He labored across the slippery lawn and climbed the broad brick steps.

He stopped to breathe patted one of the porch columns, "Nice place I've heard about it. Tim supported me in the last election. We were supposed to have an event up here but I couldn't make it." He got control of his breathing. "I need to play more racquetball, get in shape."

Several of the other guests stared at him as he crossed the floor to shake hands with Aaron. He looked down at the line stretched across a wood framed mirror. "I don't know you're doing that," he said. "Got any Scotch?"

"I think so," Aaron said. He opened a cabinet beside the fireplace and took out a bottle of Cutty Sark. "Just cheap shit," he said. "Rocks?"

"No," Lewis said, "just get it in a glass." He gulped some. "Better," he said, "That was some flight. Where do you find these wild men?"

"They usually find me," Aaron said. "Glad you could come."

"Have to meet my constituents," Lewis said. He laughed. "I guess most of these people aren't in my district."

The Poet saw the Scotch bottle, came over with a water glass. "Just what I need," he said, shuddered as he took a big drink. "Take the edge off this coke. Sneaky shit, what is it?"

"Northern Lights," Aaron said.

"Never heard of it," the Poet said. "Share water, brother." He raised his glass in toast.

Lewis saw Maria come down the stairs with the baby, met her at the foot, gave her a kiss on the cheek. "How's our baby?" He pulled back the blanket, stuck his finger in the baby's face.

"She's fine," Maria said.

"Dolores," he said. "Where did you get that?"

"From the island," she said. "The island named her."

"Whatever you say," he said, put his arm around her. "Are you going to name me godfather? After all, I'm the reason it happened."

"I don't know," she said. "I don't know if Aaron wants a godfather."

"Sure he does," Lewis said. "Come on, we'll tell him." He led her over to Aaron. "Maria and I decided I'm to be Dolores' godfather."

"We'll see," Aaron said, "hadn't really thought about it."

"You wouldn't have had a chance to make a baby if I hadn't pulled some strings." Lewis smiled, but there was hardness to it. "If something happens to you, I'll take care of them." He drew Maria close and she pulled away.

"I have to change Dolores," she said.

"I'll see you later," Lewis said. "At least you owe me a dance."

"What kind of magic?" the Poet asked.

"Real magic," said the fleshy man who wore an embroidered smoking jacket with wide sleeves. He flourished a tiny silver wand with a cut crystal on the end.

The Poet ducked. "Like Merlin?"

"Surely. Like Merlin or the Fisher King or Aleister Crowley. 'Do what thou wilt shall be the whole of the law.'" The sleeves fluttered as he spread his arms wide and gazed upwards.

"But I mean like flying or making things disappear."

"It can be done," the magician said in a mysterious tone.

"How?" the Poet asked. "Can I learn it?"

"You must expand your ego until it stands with the gods." The magician drew himself up, thrust out his chest and touched the Poet's head with his wand.

Morganne rolled her eyes at Lila. "Wouldn't you know it? Miller running his trip on the Poet."

"Perfect," Lila said. "I'll bet he has him out in the woods before morning."

"Who is he?" I asked them.

"Miller Richards." Lila said the name as if it were a nasty secret. "The famous author and teacher of magic."

"I never heard of him."

"Good," Morganne said. "I like you better all the time."

"He's a witch," Lila said. "The church of Wiccan. A friend of ours was in his coven."

"His harem, you mean." Morganne drew the fur coat more tightly around her.

"What's a coven," I asked.

"A group that does magic together," Lila said. "Sexual magic."

"Sexual bullshit," Morganne said. "He thinks an epiphany is a good blow job."

Miller and the Poet sat together in a corner. The magician talked persuasively, but I couldn't hear most of it. I did hear that Wicca was "the Craft of the Wise," and initiates could bend, shape and change reality.

"Twist it, at least," Morganne said.

"Change in conformity with will," I heard Miller say several times before we went out on the porch to hear the band better. The Poet was mesmerized.

The band was "Fuzzy Crook and Friends." Fuzzy had played guitar in several big time rock bands before they made it. But when it was record contract time he invariably was dropped in favor of someone a little taller, a little more handsome. Agents said he just didn't have that between-the-legs appeal.

He and an assortment of itinerant musicians played the Puget Sound bar circuit, did covers of popular country rock and had some good songs of their own. He was a friend of Aaron's. He liked the Product. As Morganne said, he had his head clear in the bag. They played this party for half an ounce of Northern Lights Aaron had bought from me. And for Maria. Fuzzy had a well-known crush on her.

The porch was jammed and a large group stood in the light

rain on the lawn. A few danced, but it was half hearted. This was a band to listen to. Fuzzy sang "Midnight Rider," even threw in a few Gregg Allman mannerisms. Then they did some Eagles' songs.

When Aaron and Maria came out on the porch, Fuzzy introduced her and Dolores, called the baby "Our little Do." He paused for a full minute, then, "This next one's for you, darling," he said. He looked into Maria's eyes the whole time as he sang "Rainbow Lady."

I went back inside to look for Cree. Linda and Lance sat close together, talked with a dark little man who wore a white robe-like shirt covered with Egyptian hieroglyphs. Dark eyes laughed through gold rimmed glasses.

"It all comes from the wisdom of Egypt," he said with a British accent. "And before that, Atlantis. When they sent out the ships bearing the twelve, the Warrior, the Physician, the Architect, the Farmer and so on. The purest form remains in Egypt." There was a hint of effeminacy in his movements but just enough to compel attention.

"But how about the Maya?" Linda asked him.

"Yes. They received the knowledge also," he admitted. "But they did not keep it true. They degenerated into superstition and human sacrifice."

Cree appeared out of the kitchen with a cup of tea. "That's just Spanish propaganda," she said. "An excuse to slaughter them. They had larger cities and a higher standard of living than Europe at the time. The only sacrifices were volunteers."

"Sacrifices are always volunteers," I said.

"Want some tea?" Cree asked me. "It's to ward off evil spirits. The house is full of them."

"No," I said. We went out onto the side porch. "Who's the Egyptian?" I asked her.

"That's Suras," she said. "He's a chiropractor in Bellevue. He's another friend of the Poet's."

I was puzzled. "The Poet said Suras was from India."

"No," she shook her head. "His family is from India. He was

born in South Africa, went to school in England. I doubt if he ever saw Egypt."

She sat on the bottom stair with her tea. I sat beside her. "Want to go for a ride?" she asked me. "To LaConner? I'm supposed to pick up Robin Thomas."

"Tonight?"

She nodded. "He had company, some big time literary agent. He couldn't leave until the guy went back to Seattle."

"Sure," I said, "I'll go."

Lila caught us, made us do a line before we left. Runabouts and small cruisers were tied to every foot of the dock and other boats were tied to those. There were a few people around but most were up at the house. Cree had moved the Wigit out and tied it with a long line to a tree at the mouth of the cove so there would be more room for guests. We pushed off in an orange two-man rubber raft and paddled out to it. I did not like the feel of being on the water in anything inflatable.

There was little wind, no whitecaps. Even Deception Pass was smooth. A silver sliver of moon slid across Skagit Bay as we passed the LaConner breakwater. We tied up behind a little Victorian house built on pilings, hung half over the water. Cree found a chunk of oyster shell, threw it against a window. It opened and a small head stuck out. It took him a while to see us.

"It's the Defoe Express," Cree called up to him.

"What? Oh, yeah, the Poet's party," he said.

"Aaron and Maria's party," Cree corrected him.

"Okay, whatever," he said. "I'll be right down."

We waited several minutes then Cree said, "We'd better go get him." We pulled ourselves to the top of the sea wall and went up a narrow steel stairway to a kind of catwalk along the side of the house. Cree knocked on a narrow door but there was no response. She opened it and I followed her in.

Robin was on the couch making-out with a dark skinned girl.

He looked up angrily, "I said I would be right out."

"I'm no cab driver, baby," Cree said softly. "The boat's leaving."

"Okay, okay," he said, helped the girl button her blouse. He grabbed a bottle of wine off the table. "Did you bring any coke?"

"No," Cree answered.

"Fuck," he said. "Well, let's do it. I promised Celine some good coke. I hope there's some at this party."

"Aaron always has good coke," Cree said.

I had noticed before we left to get Robin that some furtive guest hunched in a corner and scribbled on a pad similar to mine. When we came in with Robin and the girl, this person suddenly came alive. He stared through thick Clark Kent glasses, which enlarged his eyes, made him seem closer than he was. His limp blond hair was cut punk style, like a brush. Robin glared at him, made a point to avoid him. The guy turned, jerked back and forth as he walked away, reminded me of the south end of a northbound goose.

I found Lila, pointed him out. "Who's the geek?"

"Walt Gann, cub reporter," she said.

"Newspaper reporter?" I asked her.

"Freelance," she said. "Whoever will pay him."

"Like who?" I asked.

"Northern Sun, once in a while if it's juicy. Some of the co-op papers, High Times. Rolling Stone bought a filler from him once so he bills himself as 'published in Rolling Stone.' He used to own the Seattle Standard, but he took it down. Blew it bad."

"How'd he blow it?" I asked.

"He published an interview with D.B. Cooper, you know, the hijacker? Walt hyped up the whole country, told everyone how he had been blindfolded and taken to some cabin on the islands. Everybody was waiting for the interview. But it was a scam, some guy from Oregon conned him, charged him three thousand dollars for a phony interview. Turned out they had run the same scam on two little podunk newspapers on the coast, too. Everyone laughed the Standard out of town."

"How'd he get here?" I asked her.

"God knows," she said. "I don't know half these people and I don't think Aaron does."

Aaron did seem nervous, moved from group to group and looked out the window often. The band played again but it didn't seem as tight as before and Fuzzy's voice didn't quite get the high notes.

"It isn't 'Fiddler on the Roof'," Frank Lewis said. He led Maria in a clumsy dance, which pretty much cleared the living room.

Robin Thomas stood at the head of the dining room table. His girl slept on the chair in front of him; the Poet sat to his right. Several other guests gave him their rapt attention.

"I hate typewriters," he said to them. "My thumbs get caught in the keys." He made a goosing motion with long, skinny thumbs.

They all laughed.

I went on into the kitchen, but it was jammed. Aaron squeezed through, motioned for me to follow. The press of people stopped us behind Robin Thomas.

Aaron turned, talked quietly. "There's a reporter here," he began.

"I know," I said. "I asked Lila about him."

"Good," Aaron said, "I was right about you."

A couple passed by, bumped us towards Robin. He turned, his face angry, looked up at Aaron. "Why the hell are you looming over me?" he demanded.

Aaron looked down at him, said nothing.

"Don't try to intimidate me," Robin screamed. "I know where all this money comes from."

There was a general hush and the sound of footsteps as everyone tried to get a better vantage point. Aaron still said nothing.

"You can't ignore me," Robin said, "just because you're way up there. The bigger they are, the harder they fall."

"Cree," Aaron said softly, "Mr. Thomas is ready to go home."

Robin shook the girl. "Let's get out of here," he said.

Cree had squeezed between Aaron and Robin, and looked down at him. "Let's sail," she said.

"I warned you, boss," the Poet complained when they were gone. "Robin doesn't like tall people. They make him nervous. I always sit down when I'm around him."

"He should invest in some stilts," Aaron said.

"Or a penis extension," Lila said. Everyone laughed.

The party began to change in spirit. Small groups drew in on themselves, stared suspiciously at outsiders. Private stash came out and there was much sniffling and coughing. I looked out the front window and saw several blankets partly covering groups of two to four busily engaged bodies. The band packed up their equipment and made Aaron feed them a fat line.

I was about to go upstairs when the reporter approached me. "Hey, man, what was the hassle?" he asked as he came too close.

I stepped back. "Who are you?"

"Wally," he said. He started some kind of hippy handshake that I couldn't follow. I pulled my hand away.

"What was the question?" I asked him.

"The hassle," he said. "Between Robin Thomas and that guy, Adam, or whatever."

"Aaron," I said. "I didn't see any hassle."

"You were right there," he said. "I couldn't see anything from where I was."

"I didn't notice anything," I said. "Why?"

"Just curious, " he said.

"I saw you writing in a pad all night," I said.

"Just notes," he said.

"What kind of notes?" I stepped towards him, blew him back.

"I'm not a cop," he said.

"You brought it up," I said.

"No, man, I'm a writer," he said. "I'm doing an article on Robin Thomas."

"That's why he doesn't like you," I said.

"People never like reporters," he said.

"I know the feeling," I said.

"So who is this Adam...Aaron? You seem to know him pretty well."

"Just met him," I said. "A friend of a friend."

"I don't believe you," he said. "I saw how you were together, like you were his shadow."

"You're hallucinating," I said. "Better get some sleep."

"I could pay you for an interview," he said. "A hundred dollars."

"That's a lot of money," I said, "but I didn't see a thing."

The Poet had disappeared with Miller the Magician. "Making magic in the moonlight," Morganne had said, ran her tongue over her lips while Lila giggled.

It was hard to sleep with all the drunken yells and boats roaring and a pile of cocaine loose in my head. Cree had gone with one load and would have to take another. Linda went with Lance on his boat to take a group to Bellingham.

After a while it was quieter. Someone knocked on my door. "Yes," I said, tried to sound sleepy.

"Lucky, you awake?" It was Morganne.

"Yeah."

She came in. "Want to smoke a joint?"

"Sure," I said, sat up.

We smoked for a while and it eased the rush, but my hand still shook.

"Want some wine?" Morganne asked. "I'll get it."

"No," I said. "Alcohol doesn't agree with me."

She leaned against me. "I know what you need." She rubbed me through the blanket. "Me too."

I kissed her and she let her robe fall open. Her body was slender to the point of emaciation. Tiny nipples barely stood out from her chest. I touched her and she responded frantically.

"Let's make some magic," she said.

When I awoke, she was gone, and the pale January sun sent gray morning through my window. I looked out and there were only two strange boats left. Lance's speedboat was not there, but the Wigit was tied to the end of the dock as usual and smoke came from the galley stove's tin stack.

A flute melody floated up from below with the smell of coffee. I pulled on jeans and a sweatshirt and went downstairs barefoot.

I found the coffee on the stove and poured a cup. As I took a drink, the flute sounded again, came from the breakfast nook off the kitchen. I moved to where I could see. A very dark man swayed with a wooden flute as though he charmed a snake. I nodded to him. He smiled, did not miss a note of his intricate melody. The smile would not let me go.

I leaned against the cabinet and listened for a few minutes. Then he laid the flute down.

"Mornin'," he said.

"Want a cup?" I asked, indicated the coffee.

He shook his head. "I don't use no white man's rocket fuel. Makes me sick." He stretched, muscles rippled on his bare torso. "Any rum around here? That's a good wake-up, rum with lots of Tabasco." He licked his lips. "I do like the white lady, though. That was some fine shit at the party."

"Mine," I said. "Northern Lights."

"That's what they called it. Where'd you get such righteous blow?"

"A guy made it for me. Out of some bad freebase."

He looked at me doubtfully. "Now, that would be some magic, to turn ice back into pure snow. Where'd you get it?"

"Really," I said. "A guy made it, or cleaned it up. A friend of Aaron's, a chemist."

"Aaron has some strange friends," he said. "Like me."

"Or me," I said and we laughed together.

"Can I buy some?" he asked.

"Sure," I said. "How much you want?"

"A spoon," he said. "You call it a gram. How much?"

"A hundred bucks."

"Woo-ee," he said, "that is some rich shit." He paused, considered. "Okay," he said, "I got to have some."

I went upstairs for a gram bindle and dumped a little from my stash bottle onto a white china plate. I needed a wake-up, too. The coffee didn't get the job done.

He paid me with twenties then started to open the bindle. "No," I said. "I brought breakfast." I cut out two small lines, handed him the plate and a hundred rolled into a straw.

He took the coke in tiny little blasts, savored each one, then picked up the plate and took another. I wished I had taken mine first. Finally he handed the plate and straw back and I quickly cut another line, took half in one side, half in the other.

"Damn, you're a regular Hoover," he said.

I laughed. "Not compared to the people here."

"No," he said. "Everybody here has their nose pretty well open for her. She's too rich a bitch for me. I don't like to sell it. I'm a filmmaker. They call me Akbar."

"What kind of films?" I asked him.

"Documentaries," he said. He studied me for a minute. "Ghetto films, nigger films. What white folks don't like to see. The truth."

I cut two more lines, took mine first. When he finished he played his flute again and I looked out the window, watched the gulls fight over scraps from the party. I felt a heavy step in the kitchen, saw the Poet come around the corner.

"Hey, I want some," he said, pointed to the plate.

I cut him a small line. He sucked it up then took a hit in the other nostril from the pile that remained. He ran his hands through his hair, left it straight up, then shook his head. His face was shadowed in red from a two-day stubble; his eyes were bloodshot and wouldn't focus. He gulped coffee and stared at the pile of cocaine.

Akbar put down his flute and looked at him. "You're the devil, man," he said softly.

"What?" The Poet stared at him. "What the fuck did you say?"

"You're the devil, man. The Holy Koran says the devil has red hair and blue eyes. You must be the devil."

"Fuck you," the Poet said, "and the horse you rode in on."

Akbar winked at me and played his flute again.

The Poet muttered his way upstairs. I split what was left on the plate, did my half and left the rest with Akbar.

Outside, I blinked at the bright sunshine and chewed a grass stem. The smell of Cree's hot-as-hell omelets wafted from the Wigit. I was suddenly hungry, drifted down to the dock like some cartoon bear on the scent of honey.

"Good morning," Cree said. "Breakfast?"

"Yeah, I need it."

"I thought you would," she said, grinned at me. "How was Morganne?"

I looked at her. "How did you know about that?"

"We talked," she said. "Last night before I left."

CHAPTER 10

Aaron went to Santa Cruz with Maria on a Product run the Tuesday after the party. I had only a couple of grams left of the Northern Lights. Most of it had been bought and used on the island. No one wanted to run out.

Lance watched the house. Gerard was in Seattle, engaged in some alchemy in his lab. Eddie and Suzette were too good for manual labor; they had to do research. That left the Poet and Linda, Lila and Morganne, Pancho and me as apprentice sailors for another week of practice. Cree went out with us one day, then refused to go again. She knew as much about the water as Patrick ever would.

Aaron and Maria and baby Do got back Friday evening and the spirit flowed free. Part of the Product had traveled in a huge baby powder can, the balance in a large roll amongst the dirty diapers.

The Poet agitated for another party, but was badly outvoted. He took off with an ounce to see Robin Thomas, left Linda with Lance for three days. They got pretty close.

Eddie and Suzette went to a Whale Conference in Massachusetts. Eddie had a paper ready on "Predatory Mating Patterns of the Orca, or Killer Whale, and was sure to be a star. Suzette had gone to Seattle for some new clothes". Lance ran them to Bellingham to catch their flight, took Linda along.

That morning, a Gulf of Alaska storm hit the coast and tore through the sound. Lance and Linda were shaken when they got in. Lance asked for help to pull his boat on shore above the high water line.

The storm built overnight and the next day the waves in our sheltered cove broke over the dock. Cree moved the Wigit to the more sheltered side and tied up with an extra line. She dropped over several more bumpers.

Lila and Morganne and I hung out, did our share of the Product and took care of everyday stuff like meals until the storm passed.

The Poet flew in with Lee on Wednesday afternoon, told us that the Hood Canal floating bridge had gone down in hundred mile-an-hour winds. He said he had waited for two days for the weather to clear.

Patrick and Pancho showed up that evening. Patrick said it was time to go for a cruise around Vancouver Island to see if we were ready. His brother needed his boat back in about a month for the Victoria to Maui race. He planned be in Hawaii with Ted Turner for the five-hundredth anniversary of Captain Cook's arrival. I wondered if they would re-enact bashing the great Captain's head in on the beach a few years later.

Patrick's announcement about a ten-day cruise was not a welcome interruption. He insisted that Cree come along to get used to working with us. We asked him for a week to get ready and he split it his way at three days. We each packed the small duffel bag he'd allowed us and sneaked aboard whatever extra shit we could. Everybody had a full stash bottle.

When the storm passed, the weather was good for late February, bright and what passes for dry on the coast. We sailed in broken fog with almost no wind the first morning out. About noon a westerly stirred and we beat into it on short tacks once we'd cleared Lopez Island. As we entered the strait off Victoria we couldn't make much progress so we hove-to a mile off Dungeness Point and had a line. No one really wanted to go on so Patrick finally agreed to drop the anchor.

The wind was a little more from the north by morning and we had to work ever tighter into it as the island coast trended northwards. Patrick relented short of the open ocean and found an anchorage across from Neah Bay.

The next two days were measured by long tacks in the Pacific, each leg ten miles or more with long breaks for the crew. The unfettered southwest wind drove us on.

The sea was completely different from the sound and the straits. There was no boundary marker but it smelled different, tasted different. The water had a deeper glitter, a darker hue. Mountainous swells came in herds, rolled us this way and that and were gone. The watery shadows of Philippine typhoons and nameless North Pacific gales passed under us to expire against empty beaches on the edge of the continent.

I had sudden rushes of nausea twice and had to run for the rail. I wasn't the only one. But by the second day the long elevator rides seemed normal and the way we had begun to walk, in a partial crouch, legs bowed out, you would have known we were sailors or cowboys.

We rounded Cape Scott early on the sixth day. A fresh wind from the west-northwest drove us inside the small islands off the cape and we burst into Queen Charlotte Strait.

"Not bad time for the season," Patrick said, "but for perspective a good racing crew would have been disappointed with three days."

Cree said, "Bullshit."

Queen Charlotte Strait was a dream. The wind was behind us and in the wide channel we rarely changed course. Everyone but the helm and the bow lookout could lay back and play tourist most of the time. We saw several orca pods but none as close as the pod I'd watched.

Cree was hyper. "Right up there," she said more than once. "Just up McHugh Sound and then Bentinck. I need to visit my mother."

"Why the hell don't you just go?" the Poet finally asked her.

"I will," she said, her magnified eyes stared northwards. "Next winter, for sure next winter."

We followed the ferry route through the narrow channels above Campbell River. Even with the good wind it was hard work. Mile and a half legs at best, then, "Ready about," and set the sails for the new tack. By the time we laid up each night no one wanted more than some soup, a line, and some sleep. Even with the coke there were no insomniacs.

The open water of the Strait of Georgia had the same gray color as Puget Sound and we felt at home. A good blow came up and we flew past Texada Island. We would bound off the tops of the swells and dive so deep into the troughs that it seemed impossible that we could ever mount the next swell which seemed to tower over the mast. At times we rocked wildly from side to side and Patrick would have us trim sails until we steadied. Cree muttered that we'd probably take our last dive before evening.

Patrick was determined to get back a day early. He was bored. He was tired of ordering us around and he had taught us most of what he knew. He hadn't bothered to teach us to navigate, not necessary for our purposes, he said.

One more day of up early and work like hell all day got us down through the traffic off Vancouver. There was a total eclipse of the sun, the last this century, that afternoon. Morganne wanted Patrick to lighten up so we could watch it, but he refused. If anything he drove us harder as the sun slowly dimmed, then finally brightened again.

Patrick had me at the wheel. He randomly assigned people according to his own unchallenged wisdom, and I had noticed that when he really wanted to make time, he liked to have me at the helm. I was more interested at the effects of the changed light on the sea and the land, than I was in trying to look at the sun.

Shadows doubled and reflections dimmed in the fractured light. Birds started up in great confused flocks and would not settle. I looked into the binnacle, half expected to see it spinning wildly, but the needle held constant. I adjusted a few spokes and the needle nudged over.

As soon as the light was normal, Patrick called everyone forwards to set the spinnaker so we could make even better time. We left behind a few people out to fish or cruise who will not soon forget a close encounter with us. When Cree was bow look-out, on close passes she would lean out over the bowsprit, posed like a figurehead, then turn at the last minute with a wide smile and a wave.

Patrick hardly paused at the dock on Defoe, then with Pancho as a one-man crew, headed for Port Townsend. Cree silently went aboard the Wigit, obviously wanted to be alone. Lila and Morganne collapsed in their room. I wanted food. Anything but soup.

The Poet wanted me to fix him something too. Linda had been sick the last three days, was nearly seven months pregnant. She was under orders to have the baby in time to help sail Aaron's boat up from Monterey Bay.

"But what will we do with the baby?" she asked him.

"You can leave it with your mother," he said. "It's only for a couple of weeks."

I had not told anyone that it was my birthday. I hated celebrations with people to whom my birth really meant nothing. Morganne had asked when I was born and I had told her early April.

She said that made no sense, that I didn't seem like an Aries at all.

I told her it was all relative. The truth is, I was born the end of February, but it was such a hard winter and my mother so tired, that she did not leave her bed to take me out until April, which I have always considered was my true birth into the world of the sun.

I scrambled some eggs with onions and mushrooms, found some salsa and added some cayenne. Linda looked in the skillet, made a gagging sound, said she didn't want any and went upstairs. I split off a small serving for the Poet, added a generous shake of Tabasco before I called him.

He howled and ran to the sink for water which only made it worse. I silently ate and watched his performance. He got himself worked up good, threatened to sue me. Linda came down, asked what was up.

"He tried to poison me," he accused me. "He can't do it with coke, so he put something in my eggs." He showed Linda the plate.

"Same eggs I'm eating," I said, shook some more Tabasco on mine.

She looked at his eggs, smelled them, then looked at mine. I offered the plate to her and she gagged again. I shrugged and continued eating. She calmed him down and took him upstairs.

I went up to my room, marveled at the quiet. I had learned that sailing was a very noisy business with almost no privacy, like living with distant relatives you'd never met. I was used to spending a lot of time alone.

CHAPTER II

During the last few days of the cruise I'd learned that most of my shipmates now dreamed of whales. I'd kept my nighttime visitor to myself, but within three days, four of the others reported whale dreams.

Cree was first. "Orcas in my head all night," she said the morning before we turned back southeast from the tip of the island. "They call me home."

The next morning we overheard Lila and Morganne discover that they'd had almost identical dreams of travel with a nomadic pod. My own dream that night was suspiciously similar but I didn't admit it. Cree gave me a significant look.

Linda said nothing, but she was too interested every time Lila and Morganne mentioned their common dream. The Poet said dreams were just a bunch of weird shit and he never could remember his anyway.

Our first day back Maria started to describe the now familiar wandering pod. "It was beautiful," she said. "We all traveled together and it felt like one mind and you couldn't be sure where your mind stopped and the others started."

No one said anything but each of us strained for the next words she said.

"There were too many people, so we just left, swam north and north, towards a star, until there was no one but us."

"In the ice," Morganne said. "Crystals everywhere, glittered in the sun. But we were warm and had plenty to eat."

"And Do was there," Maria said. "And we all swam so fast they could never catch us."

"Pretty fucking weird," the Poet said. "I haven't had any damned whale dreams. Have you had any weird whale dreams?" he asked Linda.

"Well, sort of," she said. "I mean, I had some dreams I can kind of remember. There were whales."

He stared at her. "You, too? You mean you think you had the same stupid dream they did?"

"Well, maybe," she said carefully. "Similar."

"Why don't I have this fucking dream? If everyone has it, why don't I." He looked for someone to accuse.

"Maybe you will," Linda said. "Maybe if you don't do so much coke before we go to bed...." She stopped herself.

"You just don't want me to fuck you all night," he said.

Aaron was in Santa Cruz for resupply. He'd gone alone and everyone was anxious. I sent three thousand dollars with him for two ounces. I'd found I could turn a nice profit on grams just to people who lived at the house on Defoe or visited us there. Aaron didn't like small deals - more danger, less profit. Everyone always ran out and I was the only store on the island.

Gerard assured me he could extract the pure substance from anything with cocaine in it, although with some products it might mean a fifty- percent loss. At the price Aaron let me have ounces, even with Gerard's ten percent, the numbers worked. I was determined to sell nothing but Northern Lights.

The Poet was my best customer when he was stranded on Defoe, but when he could get a ride to the mainland, he always came back with something he was sure was better and would argue with everyone for a few days.

Lila and Morganne mostly used what was left around and what they could clean off equipment. They always volunteered when anything needed to be cleaned.

Maria spent most of her time alone with Do. Sometimes at

meals she would not say a word, just smiled when anyone spoke to her.

Lance hung around Maria whenever she came out, offered to do anything she might need. She didn't talk to him, but sometimes she would look deep into his eyes as if she had a message she could not speak. He took it for love.

Lila and Morganne tried to head him off, but he'd scented the quarry, was not about to give up the chase. He'd kept his private life private, but from the swagger and the limp lines he tried on Maria, I was sure he was king of the taverns in Marysville or Burien.

Maria began to have her meals alone at odd times. If Lance appeared she would withdraw. He always tried to make some physical contact, brushed against her or put his hand on her waist. She shrank from it, but he saw only his own design. When the Poet teased her about Lance's lance, she grew very red and embarrassed. He took it as proof of his suspicions.

Cree finally called Lance on it, the afternoon before Aaron was due back. "You need to leave her alone," she said. "You're just bothering her."

"She likes me," Lance said. "I can see it in her eyes. She's just afraid of Aaron."

"Those two have been through things you can't imagine," Cree said. "She's been to hell for him. She loves him. Leave her alone."

He did leave Maria alone after that, but he would glare at Cree and comment that people should mind their own business. She ignored it.

Gerard got enough out of my two ounces to give me one ounce clear. Pretty rich stuff, but I could get one seventy-five a gram now with no complaints. So I could keep my own nose happy and clear fifteen hundred. I still held on to a few thousand as a reserve. It was a nice, regular business.

I saw Aaron and Patrick and Lance go through half a gram apiece in an all-nighter, but I couldn't begin to do that much. The two grams I took from each turnover kept me happy for a month. There was always plenty of weed to smoke. It just seemed to appear as lots of five or ten pounds passed through. No one had much interest in pot as a business; it was done as a favor.

I knew that what we waited on from the south was over five tons of weed and I wondered how they expected to move that much when they didn't do it as a regular business.

"Don't worry," Aaron assured me. "Hippies will buy it all day and all night, then beg for more." There was a twist to the way he said "hippies."

Everyone but the Poet continued to have the dreams. We usually didn't talk about it when he was around. He said they weren't dreams, but hallucinations, probably caused by whatever Gerard put in the coke. He claimed Northern Lights must be stepped on heavy because it was too mellow, didn't have that jagged edge he thrived on. He said his friends on the mainland agreed and none of them had any bizarre whale dreams.

At this point even Lance claimed regular late night orca visitations, but I had my doubts. Lila and Morganne, Maria, Cree and I talked openly about it. Cree didn't think it unusual. Aaron wouldn't say much but he listened closely. Maria was into it the most. The more we talked about it, the more she led us.

It felt to me as if each night after we all eventually went to bed, made love, watched the stars, or whatever we did to relax, as sleep approached, our minds merged, connected across the moonlit spaces by strands of ectoplasm or electrical fields or sub-real particles we will not discover for a thousand years. Then the orcas would come and give us a ride.

Images and strange, liquid sounds tumbled through our brains. Memories, maybe, someone's memories. Maybe our own if the biologists are right that once we were fish. Mostly it was just flashes of shorelines seen from the water or long murky stretches when the eyes were of no use and they had senses we didn't. And always there was the star, beckoning as though we could swim right off the planet.

My old friend who'd first come for me in camp was there, but now she was a part of something larger. Maybe the others had always been with her and I just hadn't been able to sense them.

We left behind the dark treed, fog bound coasts we saw every day and went north, into the ice. We saw glaciers and silver suns, fiery skies and pearly seas, visited hideous wrecks at the bottom of brown gulfs. There were languid sunlit baskings in crystal lagoons among violet mists, steaming and free.

At dark, the polar aurora glittered down, reflected cryptic patterns across the heave of the tide. It could have been a future time or one long past, but the water tasted clean and felt smooth on the skin.

Those were the nights I remember. The others, full of interminable thrashings about underwater, I tried to forget. It wasn't frightening or painful, just didn't seem to relate much to my present situation. It was alien, distant, the unwanted underside of our own flat world, with depths and denizens beyond our senses.

Aaron went south again, took Lance. They were supposed to go lean on Snake if they could find him. Maria spent more time with us. She did very little coke, was afraid it could harm the baby through her breast milk. She smoked a lot of good bud that Aaron had brought her last trip.

Eddie and Suzette triumphantly returned from the whale symposium with promises of articles to be contributed to PREDATOR by renowned experts they'd met. They both headed for the oak framed mirror, which lay on the end of the dining table and cut themselves two fat lines apiece.

I was sold out, so the Poet called Lee to come and fly him to Bellingham where a young widow he'd met at a reading would pick him up and take care of his problems. Linda was more depressed each hour he was gone, but no one else missed him.

After two days he landed with a whoop at the end of the dock and waved a handful of bindles over his head. It was some crappy

Product full of ephedrine and procaine, but he was wired tight. No one would buy it but he managed to give most of it away, lost a gram, and ended up trying to wheedle me out of part of my personal stash of Northern Lights. Mine was mine.

Aaron got hung up down south. Lila and Morganne wanted to go to Seattle for a few days so Cree took them to LaConner. Then she would visit her friends at the club and maybe fish a day or two if there was enough weather for cover, bring us back some steelhead or sea bass. She said the people at the club missed her reasonably-priced fresh fish and she needed to recapitalize her life.

The longer he'd had his nose dry, the more sullen the Poet got. He made pot after pot of coffee, smoked weed endlessly, fell asleep randomly. Linda coped with her eighth month and stayed out of his way. I wished the others would get back so I didn't have to spend so much time avoiding him.

He forced a cup of his dreadful coffee on me one morning. His hands shook as he tried a mischievous smile and he said, "I had one of your whale dreams."

"Not my whale dreams," I said.

"Maria's dreams," he said. "I think she makes you all have them. She's a weird little piece."

"Dreams are nothing," I said. "Not in the light of day. Just something to talk about."

"You didn't really have the dreams, did you?" He grinned and touched his fist to his nose a couple of times the way some white men do to indicate camaraderie. "You're just going along with it."

"No," I said. "But I don't pay much attention to it."

"You'd pay attention to the one I had." He shuddered and ran his thin fingers through his straggled hair. "Blood all over the place. Terrible sounds. Those things explode right in them, the blood floods into their lungs."

"What explodes?"

"The harpoons. They have these killer ships that run them down and blast them with harpoon guns."

"Not in my dreams," I said.

"Over and over," he said. "They do it over and over."

Aaron wanted to be picked up at Sea-Tac so he didn't have to turn in another rental car in Bellingham. I took Lance's boat to LaConner, and drove down in Aaron's old BMW 2000.

Lance jammed into the back seat and Aaron wanted me to drive back. They had some highly acid, damp Product that hurt like hell in your nose, then just sort of tickled the lower reaches of your mind.

"We should have bought the weed," Lance said, "Drove it back."

"There's still more money in this," Aaron said. "Once Gerard gets through with it."

We went by Gerard's lab, but Gerard was paranoid, didn't want to work there for a while. He collected a bunch of beakers and Bunsen burners and tubing and some big jugs of anhydrous ether and hydrochloric acid. Aaron wrapped them in a blanket, put them in the trunk, and Gerard climbed in the back with Lance.

Gerard was wired on speed or something and ran off at the mouth on most subjects new since the Bronze Age. I drove fast for LaConner. I put Bush Doctor on the tape deck but halfway through the first side Gerard threatened to go psycho if I didn't turn it off. He was up for some old Led Zeppelin or Canned Heat. I wondered how he would be if he was psycho.

I slept most of the way across the channel, shivered in a windy corner of the cockpit. Aaron and Gerard sat with their heads close together. Occasional bits of conspiratorial talk blew past my ears, but I made no sense of it. The full moon played tag with us through the clouds, made a white line across the water which followed us like a spotlight.

The Wigit was at the end of the dock and I nearly ran to it. Cree was happy to see me and I stayed with her on the boat.

A couple of hours before dawn we awakened to a brightly lit

sky and shouts from the front porch of the house. Something burned there like fireworks or a magnesium flare, lit the underside of the trees like an inverse sun. Giant shadows crossed and recrossed.

We got to the porch in time to see Lance jam down a massive pottery platter on top of a large beaker that spouted flame. A red circle glowed through the plate then Lance was blown back, shook his hands in pain.

Gerard appeared with a large fire extinguisher, shook his head sadly and sprayed the flame. "There's a kilo of Product in there," Lance screamed.

"That's why I don't want it to burn up," Gerard said as the flame sagged then flared. He hit it again with the foam. "I told you to watch it," he said to Lance.

"I didn't know what to watch for," Lance said. "What the hell can we do with that mess?" He leaned over gingerly, looked into the smoking beaker. Liquid the color and density of dirty wash water steamed and flecks of brown foam dribbled over the sides.

"I'll have to clean it up." Gerard said.

"How can you clean that slop up?" Lance still sounded hysterical.

"No problem," Gerard said. "It'll just take a while."

Lance looked doubtful.

"I just need the right solvents for each chemical," Gerard explained. "I need some reagents and my books. I better just take this shit down there. Someone has to take me to Seattle." He used a funnel to pour the slop from the beaker into three empty ether bottles and taped the stoppers on.

I begged off the trip. Lance could do it, it was his boat. Aaron gave Lance the BMW keys and I was relieved that I didn't have to go. I saw them get into Lance's stash bottle before they left the dock.

Lila called, found out Aaron was back and asked Cree to meet her in LaConner. She'd find Morganne and be there the next morning, she said. Aaron seemed happy to have the problems somewhere else and talked long hours to Maria, spent more time with the rest of us than he had for a while. Eddie and Suzette hung around, waited for the mirror to come out, then back to their research.

After Aaron fixed the Poet's nose problem his dreams stopped. He looked less of an entranced dervish. He called Lee and flew to the mainland.

He told us that Robin wanted some Product and had lined up a couple of readings. I was sure he meant a couple of girls. He told us again that Robin's new book was about him. He was puzzled, though, the title was Landscape with Flamingo. "I never really thought of myself as a flamingo," he said. "I thought I was a red-tailed hawk." He flapped his arms and made a chicken motion with his head. His bright serape floated out from his shoulders, made his head seem even smaller.

CHAPTER 12

Gerard recovered about a third of the original Product from the bottles of chemical stew. There were several days of apprehension before he called to say he was drying the last batch. It came out fine and everyone was happy. The loss tripled the price, but it was a dry spell so we managed to survive. Aaron had to sell his in small lots.

Gerard gave Aaron a Product tester some friends of his had made. It was a foot long rosewood box, which contained a tiny thermostatic heat block. The dial was marked with the melting point of cocaine and several well-known cuts. Gerard had Aaron write down the melt points of some other possible contaminates. We played with it and it seemed to work pretty well. Northern Lights melted clean, right on the mark.

He was quickly down to a couple of ounces, so Aaron had Lance run him to LaConner. He called south from a pay phone, but no one in Santa Cruz had anything worthwhile. He got hold of JJ who said sure, plenty of the white girl around, but nothing under a hundred thousand. That was two and a half keys. A bunch of shit to walk past security.

Besides that was just about all the money Aaron had to work with and he wouldn't put it all on something uncertain. He needed partners.

Patrick and Pancho made the run over from Port Townsend, but they just wanted some stash. All their money was out or in Product and they'd partied too hard to collect the cash yet. Patrick's customers were all country club types and well known athletes so he was sure they'd pay when he caught up to them.

Eddie scraped together a few thousand from friends and fronted the cash for the next issue of PREDATOR. Suzette pitched a fit at first but she had developed quite a habit and Eddie promised her a steady supply.

The Poet reappeared. A flamingo pin glared pink on his hatband. He found out what was up and swore he had the answer to Aaron's problems. The widow he'd told us about had asked him to help her collect her recent departed's life insurance. The company had held out on the $100,000, claimed suicide.

The Poet was convinced that he could get the money for her. She'd offered him ten percent but he was going to hold out for twenty-five. Then he and Aaron could be partners.

He spent the night with Linda, but next morning he dressed in his vagabond poet finest and called Lee to fly him out.

Aaron made several trips to call potential investors, made a little progress, but it was slow. Old contacts were gone. There was a lot of good product around; some Colombians were in town, selling it cheap. Good, fresh shit was the rumor, knock your head off.

The Poet called Linda, first from Bellingham then two days later from Minneapolis where he'd gone with the widow to shake down the insurance company. He was depressed, the company had said no. He'd yelled at them and tried the 'sympathy for the blonde widow' bit but nothing worked.

Then he called again the next afternoon and he was ecstatic. The widow had convinced him they should go to a lawyer. The lawyer had made one telephone call and they had the check. He'd be back on the next flight. We didn't need to worry about money anymore, he said.

The Poet wanted to make the run with Aaron. He had put in twenty-five thousand so he had the right to watch his money, he said. Lila and Morganne had been lobbying for a while to make a run.

Aaron said okay, as long as they traveled separately, as mules. It was still a lot to carry, so Aaron asked me to go, too.

I would rather have waited for my two ounces on the island, but I decided I should help the cause. Lila and Aaron each called and made reservations at the North Beach Holiday Inn. They managed to get rooms on the same floor.

The day we left, Linda came downstairs to tell the Poet goodbye. He cavorted around in his cowboy hat and serape until Aaron saw him and made him change.

"If I'm a smuggler, I want to look like a smuggler," he complained.

"A good smuggler looks like my Aunt Thelma," Aaron said.

We drove to Sea-Tac jammed into the BMW. Gerard was supposed to meet Aaron there with five thousand and didn't show. It wasn't a lot of money, but it was a commitment. Aaron decided to wait.

I was to go ahead with the Poet and get the room but Lila talked him into keeping me back. "I wish you wouldn't do so much alone," she said to him. "It's not smart."

The Poet left with a swagger. Lila and Morganne were booked on the next flight. "Call Gerard again," Lila said to Aaron. "It's probably just a stall."

He called and came back to the bar. "I think you're right," he said. "He's still trying to raise the money."

There were seats available on Lila and Morganne's flight so we all checked in. They moved into two empty seats across the aisle from us soon after the plane took off. A flight attendant came over to say something, but Lila pulled out her stash bottle and solved the problem. Coke was a great solvent.

The Poet met us outside security at San Francisco International. He was proud of himself. He had the serape on and Aaron frowned at it. "Hey, man, it's cold down here," he said. "I forgot to bring a coat. Besides, what difference does it make? I'm not going through security."

Lila put the back of her wrist to her forehead in a fake faint. Morganne giggled.

"Let me take that, boss," the Poet said, indicated Aaron's leather bag. "I've got a cab out front."

"No thanks," Aaron said. "And get rid of the cab. Never use the same cab both ways. We'll ride the bus. It goes right to the Holiday Inn."

"You can't," the Poet said. "I changed the rooms."

Aaron was angry; everyone else stared in disbelief.

"To this Chinese place," the Poet said quickly. "A perfect smuggler's den. I thought we should stay in Chinatown. They have steam baths and masseuses."

"And extra cops," Lila said.

"Whose name did you use?" Aaron asked him.

"Mine," the Poet said. "They wanted a credit card. No one knows me, boss."

"They will soon," Morganne said.

"In the joint," Lila said.

"Fucking bitches," the Poet said.

"Go cancel it," Aaron said.

"I already paid for the rooms," the Poet said. "With the card. You'll have to pay me back."

"How much?"

"Two hundred for each room They connect. Plus fifty each for the steam baths." The Poet saw Aaron hesitate. "Come on, boss, loosen up a little. What's the point of this shit if you can't enjoy yourself?"

Aaron had Lila call the Holiday Inn, but the rooms were already taken and they had nothing else.

"Okay," Aaron said after he and Lila had talked privately around the corner of the concourse. "We'll try this Chinese place once. But you better not ever change a reservation of mine again."

The Poet hung his head.

"And get that ridiculous costume off. Now," Aaron said.

"Anything," the Poet said, pulled the serape over his head

and wrapped it around his hat, carried the bundle under his arm. "Anything you say. You're the boss."

We had to walk twelve blocks to the hotel from the closest airporter stop. For our worn bodies, the Chinatown hills were steep. I used to float up hills steeper than this on the Stehekin. Morganne worked up a good sweat, carried the fur coat most of the way. Lila was flushed, gasped.

The entrance was a revolving door, which isolated each of us for an instant. We quickly re formed our group. Three Chinese men were at the desk. They glanced our way and the youngest disappeared into the back. The other two kept their eyes on us as the Poet gave them a careless salute and a broad smile. One of them said something to the other. They clearly remembered him.

"Shit," Morganne whispered.

Aaron stopped, let the Poet get the keys. The silent attendant on the elevator checked both keys twice, stopped at the eighth floor and escorted us to our rooms.

"For go out, call desk for elevator." was his only advice.

The steam bath turned out to be steel cabinet, just big enough to squeeze one large or two small people into, with a steam generator underneath. There were long instructions in Chinese, then bad English.

Aaron wanted Lila to go out with him, try to look normal. They called for the elevator and in about ten minutes the attendant came for them. When they left, the Poet said, "Great," and turned on the steam bath in our room. While he waited for it to heat, he opened the door to Lila and Morganne's room. I watched Morganne give him an angry look.

"Come on, Morganne," he nagged. "Take a steam bath with me. It'll be great." He took his shirt off.

"There's not room in there for both of us. Maybe I'll do it with Lila, later." She read on, ignored him.

"You always do it with Lila," he said. "Give me a try."

"Fuck you," she said.

"Just for a while?" He whined like a toddler.

Morganne just glared at him.

He took his pants off. His skin was very white, unreal, and he was soft everywhere. He had on loud Andy Warhol boxers. "Hey, Morganne," he said, made sure she saw him.

When he turned she made a gagging face.

He went in the alcove and loudly climbed into the steam cabinet. "Holy shit," he yelled, "this is hot."

"Maybe it'll burn his balls off," Morganne said quietly from the other room, made me laugh.

Aaron and Lila came back but weren't interested in steam baths. JJ's contact had put on the stall, wanted to do just a pound for now, then wait at least twenty-four hours before they let go of the rest of it. Aaron was supposed to meet the investors from Seattle the next day at Gerard's.

Lila argued with him. "It's stupid," she said. "He'll fuck it up."

I hoped they weren't talking about me.

"I'll have Lance meet him," Aaron said. "At the airport. Watch every move."

"He'll fuck it up," Lila repeated.

"I'll fuck what up?" the Poet asked as he came from the bath. He showed pink through his towel. His red hair was plastered to his head, his nose inflamed by the steam.

"I need you to take half a pound to Seattle in the morning. First flight. Lance will pick you up at Sea-Tac and take you to Gerard's. He knows who it belongs to."

"Hey, I can handle it," the Poet said. "I need some of mine, too, to sell. At least a couple of ounces. I won't go back up there without any."

Aaron agreed to that and in a while he called for the elevator again.

"It's like China," Lila told Morganne. "They escort you to the elevator, on the elevator, to the desk to deposit your key, then bow at door. All the while they stare at you like you might suddenly turn into a space alien."

In about two hours they were back. Aaron tipped the attendant who looked in and around the room. He closed the door and Lila said, "we've got to get out of here. They'll call the cops."

"I think it's okay," Aaron said. "But I don't like it."

The Poet was dozing on his bed. "Cops." he said, brushed back his tangled half-dry hair. He came fully awake, eyes wide. "Cops?" He got up, pulled on his pants. Morganne looked in, giggled furiously. Lila shut her up.

"Relax," Aaron said and the Poet sat down, struggled with his shirt.

"He'll lose it right in the lobby or some shit," Lila said, looked disgusted.

"Did you get some coke?" the Poet asked Aaron.

Aaron looked at him. "No," he said. "We didn't. You're right Lila. We have to get out of here."

It was a long time before the soft triple knock that by now was familiar. He opened the door without invitation. It should have been locked.

"Elevator is here," he said.

We crowded behind him onto the elevator. "You have bags," he said without expression.

"We're gonna blow this popsicle stand," the Poet said, tried a guffaw.

The attendant looked at him all the way to the lobby. The keys made a loud clink when Aaron dropped them. He started to turn.

"Must sign papers," the desk clerk said. I find Mr. Lee." The young man who'd disappeared earlier stepped out of the back to watch us while the desk clerk was gone.

Mr. Lee didn't hurry.

"The rooms were not satisfactory?" He asked Aaron. "You have early business, I see."

"No, they were fine." Aaron said. He started to pay with cash.

"No," Mr. Lee said. "I have your friend's card." He held up a gold card.

The Poet was stricken with fear. He reached for the card but Mr. Lee deftly moved back just in time.

"Take the cash," The Poet said. "Let me have my card."

"We prefer no cash this late at night," Mr. Lee said. "And we must verify ownership on all cards." He started to make a call.

"What is this shit," the Poet attempted belligerence, but his voice shook. "You have to take cash. It's legal tender."

"We prefer not," Mr. Lee said. He stepped around the corner, out of sight when his party came on the line.

Lila pulled on Aaron's arm. "Let's go," she said. "Let him deal with it."

"If you bastards run out on me, I'll go psycho before you get to the door," the Poet whispered loudly. "Don't leave me here for the cops." His red stubble was slick with sweat.

"Quiet," Aaron said. His look reminded us of the young man who now dialed his own call.

"I'm going," Lila said. Morganne was set to follow her.

Mr. Lee smiled around the corner, hung up the phone. "Very good, sir," he said to the Poet. "No problem. If you will just sign."

The Poet scrawled his name. Any graphologist could see he was stoned or stark raving mad.

Mr. Lee himself unlocked the door, gave it a spin to test it. "Thank you very much," he said, bowed slightly. "Please stay with us again"

"When pigs fly," the Poet said.

"Don't talk about pigs," Morganne said. It was good to hear her giggle again.

CHAPTER 13

We had to walk about a mile from Chinatown before we got a cab. It felt good just to be outside. Even the Poet's antics didn't irritate me as much. Aaron asked the driver if he knew of any hotel close to Fishermen's Wharf with a vacancy.

"Full up," the driver said. "If you want downtown or North Beach. Lawyers or Prosecutors or something, convention. Rooms at the airport. The Hilton had lots of room a couple of hours ago."

"We don't need to be out by the airport," Aaron said. "We have business in North Beach."

"I'll bet you do," the driver said. "I can't help you, buddy. Just the Hilton."

"Okay," Aaron said. "The Hilton."

We checked in without a hitch. "Nice to be back in America," Lila said.

"Or planet Earth," Morganne added.

"Get some sleep," Aaron said to the Poet. "You have to check in at seven-twenty."

"It's after midnight," the Poet said. "Just give me some coke, I'll stay up. You said you didn't get any. How can I go without it?"

"It'll be ready," Aaron said. "if you get some sleep."

We took one room. The Hilton didn't give a shit; they were used to parties. They figured we would wind up at least three to a bed anyway. The Poet soon snored. Aaron pulled off his boots, dumped out several taped plastic bags.

"You got it," Morganne said.

"One kilo plus a pound," Lila said. "It's nice. I tested it."

"Well aren't you proud of yourself," Morganne said.

"How much is he going to carry?" Lila asked Aaron.

"Ten ounces," Aaron said. "The half pound they're waiting on and two ounces of his."

"He'll blow it," Lila said.

"He'll be okay," Aaron said. "Lance will pick him up at the airport."

"I'm going with him," Lila said. "He'll freak out and flush it down the toilet on the plane or something."

"Maybe you should," Aaron said. "I'd feel better."

"I'm not going," Morganne said.

"I didn't ask you to," Lila said.

Aaron got out the melt tester. He chopped some powder, placed it in a small pile as directed. As the needle went up, something burned brown but the temperature wasn't on Aaron's list. At the mark for cocaine, there was a quick melt of most of the pile, then a fragile white smoke. A sweet smell like bubblegum or root beer filled the room.

"That smell is strong," Morganne said. "They might notice it in the hall."

"No one notices any more," Lila said.

Aaron switched off the box. "Gerard will figure out what that was that burned early when we get home," he said.

The Poet seemed fairly straight when Aaron woke him up. He got on the airporter with Lila, didn't complain that she was along. The Product was in the Poet's boots.

"I want to do it right," he said.

Lila watched him like a mother hen watches a snake.

Aaron, Morganne and I had most of the day to kill. We ate breakfast in the coffee shop, wandered around for a while. Back in the room Aaron cut us each a line and the world came back into balance.

Morganne wanted to go with him on the second buy.

He said no.

"You took Lila," she said. "You're supposed to have someone with you."

"Lila has more experience," Aaron said. "Besides, I've been through this one once."

"It's pretty weird to have to wait twenty-four hours for the second half. They should want to get your money and get you out of town," Morganne said.

"They said it was for security," Aaron said. "To see if anything came down. And they wanted to check the hundreds against the hot list."

"Sounds suspicious," Morganne said.

"Yeah," Aaron said. "I think they needed my money to buy the other half."

"They might rip you this time," she said. She could fill in for Lila perfectly well.

"No," Aaron said. "JJ knows them. I've known JJ a long time."

"In the Brotherhood?" Morganne asked.

"What Brotherhood?" he replied.

Aaron was more than two hours late. Morganne called the airline and managed to get new flight reservations when it was clear he wouldn't make it.

"A god damned DC-10," she said. "Flying tin can."

"What's wrong with DC-10s?" I asked.

"They just crash all the time," she said.

Aaron was wired when he got back. He'd tested it himself. They'd tried to put him over the edge, and he'd had to contest it.

"You've got a nose full," Morganne said. "Are you going to melt it?"

"No," he said. "It's the same Product. Better than seventy percent."

They had a package of zip bags so we broke the Product down

into roughly quarter pound lots, double bagged it and wrapped the bags in a tough, colored cellophane that kept down the smell.

Aaron and I stuffed our boots and he had a chest pad designed to hold flat, four-ounce bags. Morganne had sewed some pockets into the lining of the baggy fur coat and it swallowed several packages. "Slick," Aaron said.

I put my backpack on the conveyor and went through the metal detector. Aaron had carried his leather bag because we were too late to check it. I turned, saw Aaron give the x-ray operator a long, deep look. I looked down at the screen as his bag went through. Under some faint shadows of clothes lay the tester with its wires and dials and switches like a cartoon of a terrorist's bomb. It was bumped from the screen by the next bag. The operator smiled into Aaron's eyes until he picked up the bag.

"Thank you, sir," she said.

The flight attendants hurried us on board. It was the last West Coast commuter that day and they wanted to get it over with. They did their "just before we all die" routine with the oxygen masks, claimed the seats would float. I thought of suddenly floating in the North Pacific. I wasn't dressed for it.

The captain assured us we'd stay at thirty some thousand feet. I liked his version.

The airplane seemed to vibrate a lot, a frequency that got to your fillings and assaulted your inner ear. Morganne held her head and looked miserable. Aaron was between us. He slipped me his little inhaler. He had a wonderful sense of timing.

Morganne refused it, so I knew she must hurt pretty badly. We hit some turbulence; one of the attendants fell into a guy's lap. The "Fasten Seat Belts" light flashed on. I definitely didn't feel good. The vibration drilled at me and downdrafts bounced me between the seat and the seat belt. On some particularly sharp bumps, a loud creak came from beneath our feet. I thought about the high March swell down below. Aaron seemed pale.

The best I could do looking out the window was to see myself dimly, distorted and doubled by the layered glass. Most of the mirrors

I'd looked into recently had lain flat. I brought down the shade, left just a niche through which I might glimpse a star or city lights if it cleared.

Morganne fell asleep, her coat gaped open. Behind one frail shoulder I could see the shine of a plastic bag. I nudged Aaron, showed him. He woke her and had her change places with me. She laid her head against his arm and went back to sleep.

Aaron began to sweat profusely from the heavy insulation of the vest. He had to pull it off where he sat and I got down his bag from the overhead rack and we slipped the Product in it. Aaron cooled down some and drank a couple of bottles of Perrier one of the attendants brought him. She thought he was airsick.

The pilot bounced about eight times when we landed, just to keep the theme.

The pain in my head was all I could think of as we looked for the BMW at Sea-Tac. None of us could remember the garage layout. We finally found the car and fell into it.

Lila met us at the door of Gerard's lab. "We've got trouble," she said.

"I need to sleep," Aaron said.

"You need to talk to some pissed-off people," Lila said.

"About what?" Aaron asked.

"The Product," Lila said. "They say it's been walked all over, full of procaine and ephedrine."

"I'm going to die," Morganne said, she sat on the floor and hung her head, huddled in her coat.

"Where's Gerard?" Aaron asked. "He can talk to them. Just until morning."

"He tried," Lila said. "He went to get two ounces back from his biker friends. He's paying them out of his own pocket. They're hot."

"That Product was fine," Aaron said. "You were there. You're the one who tested it."

"We melted it, remember," she reminded him.

"Yeah," he said. "Sorry."

"I think the Poet cut it," she said. "He got away. Just for a couple of hours. Ditched me at the airport, went in the john and disappeared."

"Where was Lance?" Aaron asked her.

"With me," she said.

"Trying to get in your pants," Aaron said. "Where'd Lance go now?"

"He went with Gerard," she said. "The bikers told Gerard they'd castrate him. They both took guns."

"Sounds like dealing with bikers," Aaron said. "Who else is mad?"

"Those professors," she said, "and that basketball player, Tom Davis. And Miller Richards. I talked to him. I think he knows what the Poet was up to. He was on his way to the island."

"Why was he going to the island?" Aaron asked.

"He said the Poet was throwing a party," she said.

"Fuck," Aaron said. "I'll call Maria." He went into Gerard's plywood cubicle bedroom.

"Fucking bastard," Lila said. She rubbed Morganne's head and neck, cut her a line.

I lay down on the old couch by the door and tried not to hear anything. Sounds were worse than the airplane vibrations. Voices stabbed at my mind. I remember angry arguments, saw Aaron count out stacks of hundreds. Lance pushed my feet off the couch and sat for a while, then left, took money to someone. Gerard played with test tubes and a melt block.

The cyclical pain in my head eased after a while and I slept too deeply for memories. When I awoke I could see no one. I found Lila and Morganne slumped against the wall, heads close together. Aaron and Gerard were face down on Gerard's waterbed, motionless. I watched closely, saw Aaron breathe.

I sat on the couch. The late winter sun broke above the stately homes across 15th Avenue from the lab. Aaron and Gerard snored almost in unison. Lila and Morganne slept in each other's arms, used Aaron's bag for a pillow.

Gerard's little scanner squawked with police band traffic a foot from his head. I slipped over and turned it off. He woke, glared at me, but fell back asleep before he could say anything.

I turned on the radio. There was a frantic report of a nuclear accident some place in Pennsylvania, Three Mile Island. I'd never heard of it. They didn't seem sure if it was a complete melt down or not. Someone from the government came on and assured us it was all under control. I searched the dial for some Reggae.

The old BMW overheated south of Conway, so we took the exit, stopped along the dike and dipped some water out of the slough in Perrier bottles. I poured a bottle over my head, shook my hair dry and squeezed back into the back seat. Lila and Morganne jammed in on either side. The brief coolness of the water yielded again to the headache.

On the radio, Peter Tosh preached, "Live clean, let your works be seen, my brother. Stand firm or you're gonna feed some worms."

Then there was another report on what they now called the "nuclear incident" back east. "...Radiation release is estimated to be minimal outside the containment vessel."

"Just a few million people with cancer," Lila said.

"Just a few thousand animals dead," Morganne said.

Aaron found Lance in the tavern across the street from the dock. As we ran against the chop through Deception Pass, I dreamed of a few days not being bumped about the surface of the earth in some mechanical contraption.

Maria was rested and happy. She smiled at everyone.

Aaron hugged her, kissed Do. "Did the police come around?" he asked her.

"No," she answered. "They can't. I knew no one would come."

"Why not."

"Guardians," she said. "There are guardians here. Lance saw them." Lance looked away. "Nothing can hurt us," she said. "They're always there, but you can see them at night."

Aaron just held her, said nothing.

Cree came in from the Wigit, hugged me and rubbed my butt. Linda came downstairs, painfully pregnant. She was relieved that we hadn't seen the Poet. We all ate dinner together, listened to the horror stories about last night's party.

Soon after dark Maria said, "They're here. Look at the trees." She led us to the window. "All around the trees. See the light, like sparkles? They come every night. No one can hurt us."

The eastern trees were backlighted by the moon, which gave them a faint aura, but everything looked normal to me.

"There are smaller ones in the bushes," Maria said. "See the glow. Especially the lilacs. They like lilacs."

No one argued with her.

CHAPTER 14

I awakened suddenly, uneasy. The light from the window was very faint. Fog clung to the damp trees. I could barely see the Wigit as it tugged against the lines at the end of the dock. The white shape beyond seemed part of the fog; my eyes could not find the edge. It made no sound or movement.

After a few minutes a breeze briefly stirred and for an instant I could see the words firmly painted in black, US COAST GUARD. They were close, surely watched us. I moved quietly, as though they might hear me.

I knocked softly on Aaron's door. "Yes," he responded immediately.

I opened the door. "Look out the window."

"I know," he said. "They came about an hour ago."

"What should we do?"

"Nothing," he said. "We don't have anything but personal stash."

"I'll go tell Cree," I said.

"She knows." He smiled. "She gave me a wave a while ago."

"How about the others?" I asked him.

"Let them sleep," he answered. "They'd just get paranoid. They'll be gone in a while. Just a scare."

I went down to the living room and watched out the window. After a few minutes Cree slowly walked up the dock and across the lawn. She swung her hips, bent to examine something. A real sight for their binoculars. I opened the door for her to stride through. She laughed a quiet, fierce laugh.

Lila stumbled down and put coffee on. She couldn't have seen it from her room. In a few minutes she came in with the pot and cups. Aaron pointed.

She looked. "I was afraid of that," she said.

Linda came out, bleary eyed, held her stomach. "What are you looking at?" she asked.

Cree motioned her over, showed her the white shadow behind the fog. It seemed to settle Linda, like the end of a long wait, a focus for her anxiety. She grew animated, wanted to know what she should do.

"Nothing," Aaron said. "They'll go away."

"This time," Lila said.

The fog thinned to a faint haze. The cutter sat, framed in the oak window, like a model ship on a painted ocean.

"No fucking coffee," the Poet grumbled from the kitchen. "Linda."

"I'll make it," she said.

He came in, tried to sit between Lila and Morganne. Morganne jabbed him with a thumbnail.

"Don't park your big ass here," she said. "This lot's full."

He sat on the floor, groaned as he crossed his legs. "Hey, boss, I need a toot."

"Not right now," Aaron said.

"I'll go get mine." He started to get up.

"Not right now," Aaron said.

His tone made the Poet stop. He looked around at all of us like he'd just noticed we were there. "What are you all looking at?" He strained to focus out the window. "Oh, shit," he said. "This is it, isn't it? And you all just sit there. Let's do something." He was on his feet, pulled at his hair in thought. "We've got to get out of here."

Morganne swallowed a giggle.

"Why do you always cackle at me, you bitch?" He looked out the window, looked back at us. We hadn't moved. "You turned me in, didn't you," he said to someone. "They came to get me. You can't do it, boss, I've been a good soldier."

Lila went off. "You stupid piece of shit. Sit down. We're all in this together. If they come, they come. Then you fight it in court."

"I'll call my lawyer," he said, started to dial.

"The phone's tapped," Morganne said.

His blood pressure started back up. "How long?" He slammed down the phone. "When did you know? You didn't tell me. Oh, fuck, I said all kinds of shit. Why didn't you tell me?"

"You always assume a phone's tapped," Aaron said.

"You should have told me," the Poet said.

"I was just teasing," Morganne said.

"Bitch," the Poet said.

Lance was for firearms. The enemy was out there and he had guns. He planned the defense. Aaron vetoed that. When the sun was well up he asked Cree if she would head out on the Wigit, take one of her usual routes and see how the cutter reacted.

"If you get out okay," he said, "call me from LaConner, talk usual business, groceries and stuff."

The Coast Guard seemed to ignore Cree but twenty minutes after she left the cutter moved, headed north fast. Aaron sent Lance to follow them in the speedboat, see where they went then make a decoy run to Bellingham.

The days grew warm as the sun returned from the south. A week after the equinox passed, early ducks bobbed in the shallows. Tribes of geese circled above us bound for the Skagit Delta and points north. There were reports of gray whales inside the straits.

Eddie was excited. Researchers on the East Coast saw few marine mammals, they'd all been exterminated one way or the other. He'd promised a bunch of them all the orcas and grays they could watch.

He could definitely deliver on orcas. And even a glimpse of a gray, at that time, brought scholarly distinction. He made deals with

Cree and Lance to take people out. He had a friend from Bellingham with a forty-foot trimaran who could squeeze on a dozen for a day trip.

"Wish you had your boat up here," he said to Aaron. "The thing is, is we could split five thousand a day for a while."

I'll think about it," Aaron said.

People came and went for a couple of weeks. Academic types, mostly male, with a few well-painted female assistants. Lee made a lot of money, sometimes flew eight flights in a day. Several of Eddie's graduate students set up camp in a tipi back in the woods and worked as guides or whatever.

Eddie presided. He shook hands, slapped backs, drank lots of scotch and white wine. A few of the younger men and several of the ladies got a tour of the house, complete with a surreptitious line on the heavy mirror he used as a dissection table. Lance took Suzette to Anacortes every two days to bank the checks.

I stayed in my room, or Morganne and Lila's. I had several books I wanted to read, so I spent as much time as I could at that. We "kept the mirror warm," as Lila put it and listened to lots of music. Morganne and I explored each other quite a little.

Upstairs was supposed to be off limits, but now and then someone would wander up to use the bathroom or stumble into one of our rooms. Eddie finally found the room keys for us and we started keeping our doors locked.

By the end of the second week, I had to get out of there. My first thought was to have Lee fly me across the mountains. I'd drop in on Granny, give her a thousand dollars. But I could hear her questions, about the money, about my inhaler, about the white stuff that surrounded me, dusted from my clothes. I could go dry for a few days, but I didn't want to go without it that long.

"You need a sweat," Cree said one morning. "You'll get strung out, be a slave like the others."

"No," I said. "I'll be careful."

"I'll make a sweat," she said.

I forgot about it, but the next day she said, "It's ready."

"What's ready," I asked?

"The sweat," she said, beckoned me. "I went across the island, found some willows by a spring."

"Not today," I said. "I'm tired."

"You'll just hide in here from the tourists and suck on your inhaler."

I couldn't argue. A few hours away from the house sounded good. And I hadn't had a real sweat since my Grandfather died. As long as we could get away from the whale people.

"Are any of them over there?" I asked her.

She laughed. "There aren't any of them a hundred feet from the house. Except the students, but they stay on the path."

I put some stuff in my backpack.

"Leave your bottle," she said. "You won't need it."

I put it back but I had a half-gram bindle in my pocket. Lila said you could shove it up your nose with a stick if you had to.

We could hear the trimaran leaving with today's research group. Eddie shouted orders. I didn't look back. The voices faded as we topped the ridge and started down a gentler slope. I followed Cree. She was certain of the path.

With the house out of sight, it was hard to believe it was there. Tightly packed Douglas Firs cooled the ground. Thick stands of Oregon grape and patches of salal interrupted the muddy gray slope. Birds stopped singing, called their challenges to our intrusion.

We climbed again, broke out into small trees scattered around large stumps. Cree followed a high ridge that curved to the west then southwest and I struggled to keep up.

Her sweat was beside a spring, just above the western beach, at the foot of a steep bank. Four live saplings were bound together into a low dome, covered with layers of sailcloth.

She'd made a hearth nearby between two interlaced cedars, banked a fire and covered it with mud and seaweed. The faint wisp of smoke drifted unseen up through the cedar branches. She dug into the fire, threw on some shavings and coaxed the flame.

"Strip," she said, the way a doctor might.

I left on my briefs. She guided me in and had me sit on a folded navy blanket in the back of the shelter. She dug hot stones out of the hearth and piled them in the middle. It rapidly warmed up.

"It's a start," she said. "As soon as the fire is hot, we'll have some red ones." She stripped to the skin and sat across from me, closed the flap.

Within minutes it was uncomfortably hot. My head hurt. She was between me and the opening, probably wouldn't let me out. I started to sweat and felt cold for a while.

She brought in some hotter rocks and my head pounded again. Just when I thought I couldn't stand more, she splashed water on the stones. Steam built up at the top, slowly seared its way zone by zone down my body. Even my feet poured sweat.

There was a hiss and another wave of moist heat. Cross-legged, I dropped my head near the floor where it was slightly less hot.

Cree opened the flap and I cooled rapidly, my wet hair became ice on my back. She closed the flap and the heat pressed my head down again. More splashes and steam. Then again. I tried to lie down but she prodded me up.

"Quickly, now," she said after several hot and cold cycles. "Into the water." She dragged me down the beach.

I was sure the water hissed around my ankles as I stumbled in. Just above knee deep she tripped me into a wave. I expected cold, but it wasn't. Balanced against my body's extra heat, it was about right.

I rolled over, my head was clear. I floated like an otter at play. I combed my beard and mustache with my fingers. Several cool waves lapped over me. I felt good.

I hadn't forgotten anything, but problems had not followed me here. When I went back I could handle it. Move out maybe, meet the crew in Santa Cruz when the boat arrived. I could be myself again. The waves felt colder and I stood.

Cree got to her feet slowly, looked at me. "So?"

"Much better," I said. "Kill or cure."

"You don't look dead," she said. "But it's not the cure. You're the cure. Stay away from that stash bottle."

"I know," I said. "I have to do that."

"It's not easy," she said.

We walked up the beach. I started to shiver even though the low sun was bright.

"Get those ridiculous shorts off," Cree said, "they'll freeze you." She led me back into the shelter, left the flap open. Sunlight streamed in, steam escaped. Cree spread out the blankets, had me lay down.

I had missed those wonderful hands, those sharp fingers to prod out every soreness, that strength to dissolve the tension. She worked on one extremity then another, slowly circled in. She finished with her mouth, left me limp and unconscious.

It was dark when she woke me, gave me some tea. She encouraged me to gulp it down. It soon laid me out again. I remember a fat full moon that glowed through the canvas and Cree's wiry body all over mine.

CHAPTER 15

The sun roused me early. Cree had covered me with her blanket. She squatted by the fire in her overcoat, stirred something in a pot. More tea, I thought. But it was soup. Mussels and clams and roots, some leaves that looked familiar.

"All native," she said. "Came from right here."

"What tastes like potatoes?" I asked.

"Potatoes." She grinned at me. "They're native, after all. Potatoes were definitely here before white men."

"Where?" I asked her.

"I found them down the beach about a mile, an old campsite," she said. "They're all around a spring. I just started digging."

"They're from last year, they'd be rotten," I insisted.

"Not these," she said. "My mother's people just leave them in the ground, dig them when they need them. They're different, whites call them finger potatoes." She showed me a handful.

They were six inches long and almost as slender as a carrot, but otherwise looked like white potatoes. I took one; it smelled like a potato.

"I brought these to plant here," she said. "Then if we are ever hungry here, we can eat them."

That seemed like a longshot.

"Potatoes are important," she said. "They saved the poor people in Europe more than once."

She dug near the spring with a dry stick, buried individual tubers several inches down. She surrounded each one with several fist-sized rocks.

"Keeps the moles and gophers out," she explained. "Once the potatoes get started there will be plenty for them too."

I finished the soup.

Cree rinsed the bowl and spoon in the spring. "I have to go," she said. "I have a research group to take for a ride." She grinned, "I need to stock up on barf bags and condoms." She pumped twice with her pelvis. "Whales must be an aphrodisiac. Power is supposed to be the best. Whales got power." She tied the bowl and the utensils into a piece of sailcloth.

"Have they seen many whales?" I asked.

"Lots of orcas," she said, "and we saw grays three days ago, this side of Port Angeles. We watched them blow three times. Lone cows with no calves."

"So what do they do? Just watch them?" I asked her.

"Take pictures, talk into tape recorders. A couple of them just talk out loud and the assistant writes it down in shorthand. You know what this one bitch said? One of the assistants? She said, 'We came all this way and spent all this money, and the whales act like they don't even know we're here.'"

She threw her pack bag over one shoulder and started to climb the bank.

"I'm ready," I said, started to get my coat and boots.

"You stay," she said. "You need it. Spend the day. You know how to get back. Once you're on top, be sure to follow the ridge that circles northeast. In the end it's the best. Don't try to cut across."

It was a command, and she was gone. I sat down in the sun. A jay chattered at me, took me to Stehekin. For a while the sunlight streamed through pines and the smell of sage from down Lake Chelan rose to meet it. A band of fog drifted in off the straits, broke the spell.

I went down to the beach barefoot, let my feet feel the gravel and shells and seaweed. Sand dollars lay all around. The breathing holes of clams showed abundant life just beneath me. Tangled ropes of seaweed wrapped my ankles, and in the backwash tried to pull me in. It felt good to strain against them.

I was cold, but the fog bank gradually burned away. I found some bright bits of shell and several sea worn quartz pebbles. The pebbles were familiar, might have tumbled down the Skagit from the high country as I had. The shell fragments were cool and cryptic. I wondered at their origins and put them all in my pocket, felt peace.

I thought I might stay the night after all. I followed the tide, dodged small waves or let them surge over my feet. Gulls kept me company, squawked and snatched food from the foam.

I heard a great splash offshore and looked in time to see a boiling dive wake a hundred yards out. I thought I saw flukes, the dark double scimitar of an orca, but it may have been a shadow. I wondered why I hadn't seen the dream whale for several weeks. Too busy.

She'd left a kind of vacancy that hadn't been there before. I needed something. I left the tide, scrambled up the low bluff above. I put my boots on and wandered south but soon was cut off where steep rocks protruded into deep water. I skirted tide pools back up the beach, searched for more stones and shells.

Cool passed over me. The light dimmed as another band of fog drifted in, grew dense as if it would stay. I hurried along towards the sweat. Cold, wet jeans clung to my calves. I needed my coat, something else. The calls of the gulls were damped and distant.

I got my coat from the shelter, pulled it tightly around me. I squatted to scratch at the fire, see if there were coals. There were. I stirred it to a blaze and felt a lump in my coat pocket. The bindle. I carefully opened it. The Product was finely flaked Northern Lights. I loosened the compacted pile with a fingernail. I spilled a little as I poured a crude line in my palm, lost some more as I inhaled. But enough got in.

I felt comfortable. It was just the thing to finish the mood, drive the chill from the fog. Cree had left some firewood and I coaxed the blaze higher. My fingers were stiff. I wondered if it was from that long ago night on the snag. I straightened my dirty hands over the fire, wiped the sand from my knuckles. The tattoo still was there, one letter on each finger of my left hand.

It made me think of the school, the nuns with alcohol breath wielding rulers, the dreary hours not reading the books they gave me.

My cousin Antonio from Kelowna got me to go with him. Granny said that Antonio had a case of misery-loves-company, because he had to go anyway.

She finally said okay, but if I went I stayed the term. My grandfather had been dead three years and I hadn't gotten to the reservation more than twice. A school full of Native kids sounded good to me.

The boys at the school were split into two groups, each devoted to the force that guided their lives. One group, about a third of them, had tattooed L-O-V-E across their knuckles. They didn't mean the brotherly kind. It was the kind they would demand from their girlfriends as soon as they got back home.

The other two thirds of the boys had cut H-A-T-E into their fingers. It was how they felt about the nuns and most of the rest of the world. If the nuns noticed a fresh tattoo they would smack the culprit's hands with a wooden ruler. The nuns didn't discriminate between LOVE and HATE.

The boys pressured me to join one group or the other. Antonio was a HATE, but I wasn't sure. I finally decided to start my own group of one, and carved L-I-F-E into my own left hand. That pissed-off all of them, but I didn't plan to come back the next year anyway.

I hadn't thought of Holy Cross Mission in a long time. I hated that year. Antonio went there as if it was some weird game, a challenge he could meet. I hadn't known that humans could treat other humans the way they treated the boys.

I had learned to be invisible to Father George. Every boy knew the deal. Each Sunday, Father George would pick out the best boy for that week to have lunch with him and to experience a few minutes of priestly worship of his body as a reward. In turn, the boy was asked to worship Christ through the medium of the priest's own sanctified self.

This union of priest's body and boy's body, he taught them, was exactly like the union between Christ and his Church. After all, Christ was male and the church was male although it served a female function. Some of the ways he wanted to worship the boys' bodies didn't please all of them, but others said you could learn to like it.

Some boys tried very hard to be the best. Some boys could be the best without trying. Best was a matter of changing definition. My great achievement that term was the avoidance of that particular honor.

I opened the bindle, started to pour another line of Northern Lights in my hand. A gust caught the paper and tossed it into the fire. I tried to get it out, burned my fingers and dropped it again. Flames burst through and the coke was gone in a thin strand of smoke. I licked the few flakes of Northern Lights that clung to my hand, cooled my blisters in the spring.

The wind scattered sparks that sizzled against the damp earth. The sailcloth on the shelter flapped. Fog obscured even the low branches. Now I had to get back to the house.

I didn't know what time it was. I had forgotten the angle of the sun before the fog came. I used a piece of the canvas to carry water, stirred the fire into mud with a stick. I hadn't brought anything to forget, so I turned and climbed the bank and angled across the long slope above.

From the top, a logged tract fell gently to the east, broken only by a few second growth firs and clumps of weedy alder. The bottom of the slope was lost in fog. A quarter mile north I knew the broad hilltop would narrow into the ridge I was to follow.

It was late and the circle to the north, then east, was a long detour. I could not believe that there was anything impassible between me and the house if I took the direct route, not for someone used to the woods. I angled down the slope. It wouldn't hurt to try it for a ways.

Soon I was far enough down that it would have been a long climb back to the ridge. I turned directly east, moved fast through scattered alder and madrona. Deep beds of Oregon grape cushioned the way; the heavy air stilled the sound of my passing. I was knocked off course by occasional thickets of tall salal intergrown with blackberry canes, but each time I corrected my course, just as we did when sailing.

At the bottom was a small north flowing stream. The opposed slope was steep and streaked with small mudslides. The stream trended slightly eastward, so I followed, hoped to find an easier ascent.

The curve of the streambed continued until I was sure it headed straight for the house. This would be as easy as the ridge and more direct. I found a parallel deer path and moved quickly.

I'd gone about half a mile, to a place where the little valley steepened and narrowed, when the path left the stream and started a gradual climb towards the ridge Cree had recommended. I left the path and fought through the thick growth along the creek. Rocks obstructed the stream and several two-hundred-foot Douglas Firs stood among them as gate posts or sentinels.

I had to wade to squeeze between the last two boulders. I burst through, scrambled down a muddy slope and nearly lost my footing. A tiny cascade poured between the rocks, rippled down the slope and collected in a shallow pool. The coke had dried me out, so I knelt and scooped handfuls of the water. It tasted of green moss and peat, quenched my thirst.

The general course of the stream was the way I wanted to go so I followed, put up with its twists and turns to gain the main objective. The island was less than three miles wide west of the house, so it couldn't take more than another hour even if I had to climb or detour. This was definitely better than the ridge.

I thought I must be close to beach level again as I considered how far down the stream had dropped. It was odd that a stream would run completely across the island, rather than from the interior to the beach as most island streams. I would need to look at it on a map.

The steep descent continued, the water seemed willful, anxious. I was below the fog now, could see further ahead. In spite of the gray light, it was a pleasant valley, not overgrown, and I saw no scars of logging.

The stream passed the face of a small bluff with a spring at its base. I knelt for more water. I felt eyes on my back and moved carefully, surreptitiously scanned the bluff.

It was easy to see him. Native, for sure, at least mixed, very dark. He watched me without expression. I looked away then whirled, stared at him.

He made a small movement and I saw two black feathers trail from some sort of headband.

Someone sent to watch Aaron, I thought. I decided to find out. I walked briskly downstream until I knew I couldn't be seen, then followed a deer path that switched back his direction. The narrow path joined a larger well-worn trail. The angle was right to bring me out above him. I took off my boots, carried them. I pressed my feet into the dark mud, moved silently.

At just the right point, a firm path turned towards the edge of the bluff where I'd seen him. I set my boots in the salal near the junction so I wouldn't miss it or them. I crouched forward to surprise him.

The path dipped out of sight near the rim, so I dropped and crawled until I could just see over. I saw nothing, at first. Then he moved. I saw the feathers, then his profile, sharp beaked and serious as he gazed down on the spring. It was as though he hadn't seen me. He waited for something that was to come down that path.

I got to my knees, sat back on my heels so that he couldn't help but see me from where he squatted just twenty feet below. He did not react, continued to search with silent eyes. I stood, moved forward a step.

With a startled squawk he jumped from his perch, became a raven that swooped across the clearing at the foot of the bluff and landed on a fir snag beyond the spring. He eyed me and called again, stepped from one foot to the other.

I moved down to the perch, sat and looked over the clearing. All seemed normal. Just a damned raven. I needed to get home. But then what or who had worn the path? Deer don't keep lookouts. I looked for footprints, saw none but my own.

I went back up the path, looked for my boots. Somehow I missed them. I had gone too far for the cross path, so I backtracked, but still didn't find the boots. I did find a path that seemed to be the one I'd left but there were no boots. Someone must have taken them; I'd been fooled.

I searched a little more but the sun seemed far down behind the low overcast. I could do it barefoot. It couldn't be a mile from where I was. I slid down through the molded leaves to the little stream. The water still flowed eastward so I followed, struggled through waist high salal.

I was sure to break out onto the beach around the next bend. The raven flapped along from tree to tree, did his nervous dance and called. His voice was the only sound.

I had to use brush for handholds as the downslope steepened. The water silently rushed beside me. The overcast lowered, became fog again. This should be the final drop to the beach. But I heard no waves, smelled no seawater. My feet bled but were too cold to feel.

There was a last low bank. I couldn't see the beach for the fog. I jumped anyway. It was only a five-foot drop, then the sand slope. My feet were grateful. Now along the beach to the house.

But the sand was dry and trees grew from it. I'd lost sight of the stream. I backtracked, didn't find it. I found what must be my original tracks, used them for a bearing. Eventually I would reach the water.

There was nothing green in this pathless wood. From the dry sand poked weeds that were just sticks, and evergreen trunks whose tops were too far up into the fog to be seen. I couldn't be sure if the trees were alive or dead. Large poison galls swelled like boils from the withered bark.

My sore feet stumbled against scattered stones. I saw mushrooms, knarled and shaggy, dusted over with fine gray silt. There were no colors, only shades, and the light was drained as though it had come through smoke or water.

The slope began to rise. I must have circled. I turned downward but soon ran into my own recent tracks, already filling with sand.

It must be some kind of dune I had to cross to reach the beach. The leafless scrub was thick and tough; it grabbed at me as I climbed. I clambered along on all fours for a time, but still didn't reach the top. And the slope grew ever steeper.

I sat with my back against a dry trunk. The raven landed and shrieked from a branch on one of the strange trees. I had forgotten the raven. It could lead me somewhere. I'd wait until it flew away then follow it.

Apparently it intended to wait for me. This could take a while. Well, my thrashing around in the woods hadn't helped. I tried to reconstruct the terrain I'd covered. That really didn't make sense. A stream that ran from the edge to the center and disappeared, elevations that had to be far below sea level. To account for it, I had to be on an upside down island with all the slopes reversed, a subterranean reflection.

The raven flapped and flew and I got up. It fluttered in a circle and sat on its perch. I sat down. A few minutes later it flapped again. I waited. It settled on the snag and watched me, one eye then the other turned towards me. Dark came as I waited.

The raven's squawk woke me soon after sunrise. My head was full of dreams; dead trees wailed and pitch, thick and dark as blood, dripped from the branch stumps. I shook my head; the sun drove out the last foggy remnants.

My hands were curled with cramps and my arms were asleep from the elbow down. My feet were wooden and distant. I tried to raise my hand, whacked myself in the face. I brought it back up slowly, rubbed it like a stick against my chin. Some feeling returned and it began to move. After a few minutes I could use that hand to rub the other.

The raven called repeatedly, exercised its wings. It flapped away, then back. I got up weakly, started up the path. The bird called and again turned the other way. I stopped. The morning sun came from behind me as though I faced west. Unless this was evening. But... I was sure it was morning.

I turned and followed him. The way seemed different, no longer tangled and overgrown. The sun filtered through a tangle of maple branches swollen green with buds. The earth warmed and I began to feel my feet. I seemed to be on a broad ridge, which curved northeast. The raven flew from tree to tree, urged me on.

There was dew on the brush and the air smelled of salt water. The gentle ridge widened to a small treed plain and the path ran straight. The raven flew further and further ahead.

I saw the house framed in green by the lawn as the slope broke down towards the sound. The path branched, one way to the dock, the other to the north porch and our dining room. The raven scolded me from the gable.

I went around the back, in through the kitchen and up the back staircase. I fell on my bed.

Lila and Morganne knocked on the door and came in. "All the tourists are gone," Morganne said. "Until next week." She opened the drapes for light, looked at me. "You're a fucking mess," she said. "Been wrasslin' bears?"

"No," I said. "I took a short cut."

CHAPTER 16

"This is more like it," the Poet said. "Marrakesh or Casa Blanca."

"A little too far north," Aaron said. "And not a camel in sight." He went into the cramped office to register.

I sat on the wrought iron bench and eased my new boots off, let my feet stretch. The boots weren't that bad, but there were zippers up the inside which irritated me, and as usual, they were too narrow.

The Poet squinted against the low sun; his brushy eyebrows flamed orange. "Kind of a dump," he said, "when you really look at it."

Aaron came out, gave me a key. I put on my boots and followed him up the walk. We stood on the bridge, which crossed into town and looked back at our new home.

The tinted stucco cabins were crowded into one corner of the little cove where Soquel Creek enters Monterey Bay. "The Venetian" was etched into a wooden sign in an Italian script.

The back walls of the streetside units buttressed the low bluff above the beach. High tide lapped a low seawall below the balconies on the seaside units. Altogether there were thirty or so small apartments, in several rows, that had served summer refugees since the thirties.

As in an old fresco, the Mediterranean light of sun on plaster reflected onto painted Etruscan tiles set into Adriatic balustrades. Tendrils of smoke and music coiled through the narrow alleyways. Batik curtains ballooned from sharp shadowed windows and the ambiguous cries of children or gulls echoed in the bright courtyards.

The creek below us carried the scent of Redwoods on inland hills as it spread across the warm sand and rippled into the soft waves that came off the bay. In the forgottenness of the off season, no one was around except for the kids at play. If we had to hole up somewhere until the Quest came in, this looked okay to me.

The Poet followed us. "I don't want to be across the street," he complained. "I'm never where the action is."

"There is no action," Aaron said. "Just business."

"But I'm part of the crew, boss." He ducked his head, puffed out his lip.

"So when the boat comes in, you'll have a job," Aaron said. "You need to go back tomorrow, stay with Linda."

"Tomorrow! I can't go tomorrow." He looked at Aaron in disbelief. "We just got here."

"You wanted to see the place." Aaron's gesture directed our eyes around the cove. "This is it. Now go back and take care of Linda. It'll be at least two weeks."

"But this is the fun part," the Poet said. "The fun is always the anticipation."

"You can anticipate back on Defoe," Aaron said.

"I'm not going back to that rock," the Poet shook his head decisively. "Not with all of you gone."

"Cree will be there," Aaron said.

"I'm not comfortable with cannibals," the Poet joked with fear in his eyes.

"Linda needs you," Aaron said.

"I'll take her to Bellingham," the Poet said. "With her folks. They're close to the hospital."

"She doesn't need a hospital," Aaron said. "She needs you. Cree can handle the birth."

"She needs her mama," the Poet said, "Not me. I need to be down here with you, boss. I want to be in on the business."

"Maybe next time, if you hang onto some money," Aaron said. "This time you're just a sailor."

"Excuuse me, Admiral, sir," the Poet said, gave Aaron a limp salute. "I'll be on about my own business then, sir." His eyes looked like he would cry.

When the Poet was across the street Aaron grinned at me and said, "He sure is poetic tonight." He leaned against the banister of the bridge, watched some ducks swim under. "He'll have plenty of time for the baby to come, it will probably be a month. Pete ties up in the daytime, moves at night or when there's fog for cover."

"So we just sit here for a month?" I was ready to go back, too.

"You can't have a new crew show up, then disappear in a couple of days," Aaron said. "Too noticeable. Get to know the area. Lila and Morganne will be here tomorrow, they know their way around down here. Be a familiar face to everyone. We have lots of friends here."

"I'm glad Aaron sent him back," Morganne said. "I'll be glad when Linda has the baby. He's too horny."

"She's not too pregnant for Lance," Lila said. "And they don't try to hide it anymore."

"They'll probably kill each other," Morganne said. "I hope Linda can handle it."

"Cree will be there. She'll take care of Linda," Lila said. She turned to me. "Say something, Lucky."

"Too much sand here," I said. "I need to see trees, let's go for a drive."

Lila had the top down on her Mustang and stopped to tie a scarf over her hair just before the freeway. Morganne wrapped the fur coat around herself and ducked down. At eighty-five, I had to gasp for air, but in about three minutes we circled Santa Cruz and Lila slowed to take a rough, narrow road marked "Felton 6, Boulder Creek 13."

Almost immediately we were among trees. Not palms or even oaks and maples, but evergreens, with ruddy-scaled trunks and frond-like needles that reminded me of cedar. And there were large pines with spread tops and delicate blue-green needles. The road switched through several turns and we climbed rapidly.

Felton wasn't much of a town, hardly slowed Lila's dash into the mountains. Morganne crouched in the front unwilling to look out.

"There's no cliff here," Lila said, "You can look now."

"You're trying to kill me," Morganne said, would not lift her head.

"Look at that guy's butt," Lila said and whistled.

"Where?" Morganne's head came out of the fur coat like a turtle's.

"Sucker!" Lila laughed and swerved.

"Bitch," Morganne said, withdrew her head. "Tell me when we get there."

The Redwoods were all second-growth, but they were as big as old growth Ponderosas at home. I'd seen original Douglas Firs as big, but these were just youngsters, yearlings, that grew amidst the stumps of their parents. The ground was dry beneath them, without much undergrowth except in the shadowed swales.

Lila watched me in her mirror. "What are you staring at?"

"Trees," I said. "I'm a forest animal. All that sand and water gets to me after a while."

"Me, too," she said. "You should swim in the creek, back at The Venetian. It helps. That cool, sweet water runs over you smelling like the woods."

"How many times have you been here?" I asked her.

"I used to live in Capitola," she said. "When it was real. Right after Morganne left People's Temple. We hid from them down here, dyed our hair and dressed like hippies."

"Hid from who?" I asked her.

"Jim Jones's goons," she said.

"Murdering bastards," Morganne said. She slid up in the seat. "Most of them are dead now. And a lot of good people with them."

"What did you do to them?" I asked her.

"I left," she said. "And I knew things. He was afraid I'd talk to a reporter or something."

"He was really a weird fucker," Lila said. "He was Director of the Housing Authority in San Francisco, hung out with Nixon and Reagan. People thought he was God."

"He did too," Morganne said, "He used to spit on the Bible and call Jehovah a crazy sky god, say it was time for new gods. We all knew what he meant."

"You really knew him? I mean like close?" I asked her.

"I was one of his girls," Morganne said, "on the Planning Council. We could get away with anything. Once he picked you, you were queen for a day every day."

"You mean like his wives?" I asked.

"He thought so," she said. "There were too many for him to fuck us all. The trick was to be in the group but not let him notice you too much. And don't fuck anyone he was jealous of, someone taller or something."

"But then he noticed her," Lila said. "She was his hot Holy Grail for a while."

"They all shunned me when I wouldn't do it," Morganne said. "Most of them didn't even know why, they just knew Big Jim wanted me shunned."

"So you left?" I asked.

"They caught me once," she said. "I had money and everything, but he put a black guy to watch me. I tried to run so the goon grabbed me and beat me. With a coat hanger, like I was a whore."

"So she called her old high school smoking buddy," Lila said. "And I busted her out."

"It took me a week to get alone with a phone," Morganne said. "Lila came to a meeting, brought me some different clothes. I changed in the bathroom."

"And we flew away on this red magic carpet I'm driving right now," Lila said.

"And I thought then I'd escaped just so you could kill me on the streets of San Francisco," Morganne said. "Instead you're going to kill me now." She cringed into the corner.

"I'm only going thirty-five miles an hour," Lila said.

"But this isn't a road," Morganne said. "Some kind of wagon track."

"This is State Highway Nine," Lila said. "It isn't like you haven't been here before."

"I never did like it," Morganne said.

"I didn't even go back to my job," Lila said to me. "Not even for my paycheck. They must have wondered what the hell happened to me."

"The goons would have caught her if she went back," Morganne said. "They had connections everywhere and they knew who she was. She'd been to meetings before." Morganne posed flirtatiously, "Just to see me."

Lila stuck out her tongue at Morganne. "So we just came down here," she said. "And I got a connection and started selling lids of pot. To hippies. Twenty-five dollars an ounce. I paid two hundred for pounds, doubled my money. Pete, you know, Aaron's partner? He fronted me my first pound. From there on I could buy my own. The Brotherhood did that for people in need. Kind of a welfare system."

"It saved us," Morganne said. "Here I was selling dope to strangers and I hadn't even smoked it."

"It took me six months to get her to try it," Lila said. "She was sure it would ruin her chromosomes."

"Speaking of that," Morganne said, "Aaron gave me a joint of Thai Stick." She lit it. The resinous smell cut through the pine and redwood. "Mmm," she said. "The good old days. We used to get half a ton of this a week."

"She used to bitch about having to bag it," Lila said. "We always sold quarter ounce bags, from what Aaron and Pete didn't wholesale. We always had all we wanted."

Boulder Creek, the sign said. A couple of bars, a couple of hippy restaurants, a couple of gas stations and a bunch of antique stores strung along a muddy, pot-holed street. The background was dark evergreens. I felt at home.

We wandered around, had lunch at "Frodo's Place." Morganne wanted to spend some more time in the antique stores but Lila and I were burnt out. We already had watched Morganne run her hands over most of the used merchandise in town. The older something was, the longer it took her to commune with it.

"Just another hour," she begged. "You guys don't have to come with me. Have a drink, go for a drive."

Lila looked at me and I shrugged. "Okay," she said. "One hour. Meet us right here."

Morganne was delighted.

CHAPTER 17

"You have your bottle?" Lila asked me in the car.

"No," I said, "I haven't been doing any. Clear my head up."

"You were pretty strung out," she said.

"No, I wasn't," I insisted. "I couldn't have stopped if I was."

"It'll get you," she said. "It gets everyone. Everyone with a soul. It's pure spirit, too strong for humans."

"Not for me," I said. "But I'm just going to do it when I really feel like it."

"I always feel like it," Lila said. "That gives me an idea."

The house clung to a cliff on a crumbled hill above Ben Lomond. The wooden stairway swayed like a rope ladder. I didn't look down. At the top, Lila pushed open the door and I followed her into a half-full storage room. Another narrow stairway led up through a trap door.

At the end of that climb was the kitchen and next to it a large dining room with stained glass windows. I could see no one, but the air was alive with the smell of fresh spices. On top of a green enamel Monarch cookstove, residual steam rose from a copper teakettle. I wondered how they'd gotten the several hundred pounds of cast iron stove up here.

"Wait here," Lila said. "I'll go find Josie." She went up the stairs softly, for surprise.

There were shrieks and laughter from female voices, a pause, a male voice, the sound of footsteps.

"Lucky," Lila called. "Come up here."

I climbed the stairs, followed the voice and the smell of the tea through a door.

"This is Lucky," Lila said. "He's on Aaron's crew, too."

My eyes adjusted slowly to the dimness. Josie was a tiny woman with blonde hair, wrapped in a blanket. Lila hugged her. The male voice was a very dark man with a Caribbean accent.

"Darrel," he said and shook my hand. Then he buttoned his pants.

He lit a stone pipe and handed it to me. "The best ganja," he said. "Brotherhood ganja."

I smoked and passed it to Lila. She sipped, did not inhale. "Do you have any blow?" she asked Josie, passed her the pipe.

"No," Josie said. "Not here. I can get some. My neighbor has grams. How much?"

"Couple of grams," Lila said. "We have to pick up Morganne, so we can't wait."

"No problem," Josie said. "It's just up the road. Five minutes."

"Very nice blow," Darrel said, flashed his teeth.

"What's the price?" Lila asked.

"Hundred dollars a gram," Josie said. "Aren't prices fuckin' crazy?"

Lila counted out twenties. "We're spoiled," Lila said. "Remember Aaron? Pete's partner? He's big-time, has this chemist who can make pure out of anything with coke in it."

"I thought the Brotherhood didn't do blow, bad Karma. Just hash and good weed like Thai Stick," Josie said.

"Not Aaron," Lila said. "He's the prodigal brother or something."

Josie stretched and the blanket fell from her breasts. "I'm surprised Pete still does business with him. He's Mr. Holier-Than-Thou. Won't touch anything but weed."

"They go way back," Lila said. "Before the dawn of time, I think."

"I miss the old days," Josie said. She tossed the blanket and stood nude, slowly put on jeans and a sweatshirt with a Grateful Dead decal.

"Weed will save the world," Lila said. "Remember? Not many believers in that anymore. Just businessmen."

"And Colombians," Josie said. "Do you have Colombians up there?"

"No," Lila said, "Not yet. But everyone says don't trust them."

"They kill people," Josie said. "They killed three freaks in L.A. and some black guy in Phoenix that I know of."

"People who owed them money?" Lila asked.

"The black guy did, but the freaks just wouldn't buy from them," Josie answered. "It's a warning. All the freaks on the West Coast know about it. Jimmy's going to stop dealing, except for weed, and get a straight gig. He's scared."

"You still with Jimmy?" Lila asked. "Where is he?" She shook her head, grinned at Josie. "Had one in the bush, huh?"

Josie was offended. "Jimmy left him here. He went to the Bay Area to look for blow. He told Darrel to watch the place and protect me."

"Good protection," Lila said. "You suppose he'd protect me?"

Darrel winked. "If I must," he said with a minute bow.

"Jimmy knows," Josie said. "He says better Darrel than some stranger. This way he knows I'm safe. He's really freaked, about the Colombians. He says the government helps them, doesn't try to catch them. I think he's paranoid."

"Colombian dealers are bad people," Darrel said. "In my country we are very careful of them. They are bullies. They have lots of connections and lots of guns. American guns. Freaks better get lots of guns, too."

"What is your country?" Lila asked.

"Belize," He said.

"Where's that?" Lila asked. "Africa?"

"It used to be British Honduras," he said. Lila was still blank. "Central America. Between Guatemala and Honduras," he explained. "Many of the Mayan ruins are in my country."

"Close to Yucatan? I went to Yucatan to buy pot with my old boyfriend," Lila said.

"Yes, the southwest corner of the Yucatan. We have our independence only a few years," Darrel said. "We are no longer colonials. Now we have our own small government for a very small country."

"How small?" Lila asked.

"Less than nine thousand square miles," he said. "A quarter of a percent of the United States. A little smaller than New Hampshire or Vermont."

"This could go on," Josie said. "I'll go get your nose candy."

"Such a small country must be very crowded," Lila said.

Darrel laughed. "Less than a hundred and fifty thousand people. California has almost ten times as many per square mile. It's less dense than Oregon."

"Must be a fucking jungle or something," Lila said.

There is some jungle," Darrel said. "Very beautiful jungle that people come from all over the world to study. And that's where the Mayan places mostly are. We have white sand beaches, the second longest barrier reef on the planet, the best scuba diving in the Western Hemisphere." He caught his breath. "Not to mention perfect weather all year."

"Except for hurricanes, I'll bet," Lila said.

"You get used to them," Darrel said, "Like earthquakes."

"So what is the government like. God, Santa Cruz County has more people than that."

"Everyone is pretty laid back," Darrel said. "There aren't many jobs, but it isn't hard to live."

"Sounds like paradise," Lila said.

"A very boring paradise," Darrel said. "Beautiful and boring. I want some more tea. Would you like some tea?"

"Sure," Lila said.

We had several cups of tea and a lot more ganja. Darrel put on a Jimmy Cliff tape, then some Burning Spear. In the window on the west, the afternoon sun flowed through a stained glass mandala where a circle of dolphins danced in a ring and an orca and a grey whale intertwined as yin and yang.

"How about Morganne?" I asked Lila. "It's been more than an hour."

"Where the hell is Josie?" Lila asked no one.

"We could go get her and come back," I said.

"I don't want to drive up here twice," Lila said. "I want a line. Darrel do you have any?"

"No," he said. "Too rich for me. Only on very special occasions."

"This is a special occasion," Lila said.

"Sorry," he said. "This will ease the pain." He handed her the pipe.

"No thanks," she sputtered. "It will just fuck up the rush when I get my shit. If I get it."

"You'll get it," Darrel said. "Josie is very reliable."

"A few minutes, she said," Lila reminded him.

"Soon come," Darrel said, barely audible.

"I don't like soon-come," Lila said, almost grinned.

"Any woods around here?" I asked. "Some place I could walk?"

"Not until you get up to Big Basin," Darrel said. "There's a State Park."

"Why don't you go get Morganne," Lila said. "Go somewhere. Pick me up tomorrow. Darrel can protect me." She tossed me the keys, fanned her face with her hand. "It's hot in here. I need to get out of these clothes."

Morganne was furious. "Where the hell have you been? Where's Lila?"

"I murdered her and stole the car," I said.

She laughed. "I suppose I'm next."

"I was going to eat you," I said.

She got in, put a large framed print into the back seat. "Let's not go back," she said. "To Capitola."

"How about Aaron?"

"We'll call him," she said. "He's not our father."

"Sometimes I wonder," I said. I drove downhill, towards Santa Cruz. "What do you want to do?"

"Go to San Francisco," she said. "See a concert or a movie. It only takes a couple of hours."

"Not me," I said. "Santa Cruz is too big for me. Besides, we'd have to wait until tomorrow to get gas. We have the wrong license number for today."

"I hate rationing." She made a face of disgust. "Let's go sleep on the beach," she said. "I know a great spot, down at Sunset Beach. It's a State Park. No one goes there in March. We can take our blankets from The Venetian and tell Aaron."

"We'd freeze our butts off."

"We'll build a fire," she said. "I just want to get away for a while. It's too intense around Aaron right now."

"Because the boat's late?"

"Boats are always late," she said. "You just hold people off until it gets in. Everybody knows it happens when it happens." She shook her head. "No, Pete's friends are on Aaron about coke. They're terrified of the Colombians. Half of them say they're going into some straight business or something, leave the life. I can't believe it."

"I trust Aaron," I said. "He's taken good care of us."

"What if he quits?" She sounded like a little girl. "What will we do?"

"I'll go back to Chelan and pick apples," I said.

"I mean me," she said. "And Lila and Lance and Patrick and Pancho."

"Don't worry about Patrick," I said. "And you don't even like Lance."

"I just don't want things to change," she said. "We've all been together so long. Friends are important."

"You can still be friends."

"Not if everyone is working here and there." She paused, looked at me. "Lila's talking about leaving the country."

"Where would she go?"

"She says Canada if she has to, but she'd rather go south. Where it's warm all the time." She looked away. "I don't want to leave the country."

"It's just lines on a map," I said. "I went to school in Canada for a term with my cousin. It was okay. The country, I mean, friendly."

"What if she goes to Fiji or somewhere?" Morganne asked.

"You'd be okay," I said. "You don't need Lila."

"I don't need her," Morganne said almost in tears. "I want her. I don't want a life with just what I need. How about what I want?"

"You can't always get what you want," I sang.

"I want a line," she said. She punched me in the ribs. "Then I want you."

Aaron fixed the first problem for her and I think he envied us as we loaded the Mustang. I don't think he'd had a night on the beach for a while.

Before we left, Morganne hung the print on her wall. "Maxfield Parrish," she said. "'Contentment.' Why can't the world really be this way?"

I looked at the faded old print. The placid lake with massive peaks above sun driven morning mist reminded me of Lake Chelan. "I know a place like this," I said.

"Where?" She asked.

"Stehekin. Where I spend my summers. For winters I go to the other end of the lake, to Chelan where the orchards are. My Granny lives there."

"What are you doing here?"

"I've lost my mind," I said. "Or my soul."

"Take me there." She said softly.

"Okay," I said. "When we get this trip over."

"This trip will never be over," she said.

Morganne's "great spot" was a narrow grassy cove, which held a shallow tide pool that reflected the full moon as it rose. Above the steep beach was a mound of sand, which hid a small, soft depression. A lone cypress slanted away from the wind in the center. Underneath its low boughs we nearly were invisible.

We gathered driftwood and picked up some bits of abalone shell. We sat on the rim of our tiny sanctuary and gazed out over Monterey Bay until our cove focused the final rays of the sunset.

Eddie had told us that just offshore was one of the deepest underwater trenches on the planet, an alien world full of strange creatures who occasionally washed up on shore. From the oceanic depths the unseen canyon sliced into the foundation of the continent between Santa Cruz and Monterey, just beyond the shallows, a tentacle from out of the heart of the planet, a conduit to the beginnings.

You sure couldn't see it from here.

I built a small fire just outside the cypress roof. Heat and light reflected from the sand, was trapped under the tree. We laid out our blankets and took our time.

Deep in the dark the fire subsided. In the west the moon slid down the sky, was quenched in the sea. Above us stars winked through the breeze stirred branches. We clung to each other until morning.

CHAPTER 18

"Aaron got a call from Pete," Lila said. "The Quest will be here in a week."

"Right," Morganne said. "I'll go pack."

"I'm ready," I said. "I haven't made a dime since I've been down here. Spent a bunch of money."

"I'm glad Aaron pays the rent," Lila said. "But he can't do that forever. It's the middle of April."

"I sure can't afford any rent," I said, "unless I make some money soon."

"You always have money stashed away," Morganne said. "Don't try to tell me you're broke."

"Closer than I like to be," I said.

"He probably has five thousand dollars," Morganne said to Lila. She was just a little low.

"We could sell some Product down here," Lila said. "I know enough people. Josie says it's hard to get, right now."

"No," I said. "Aaron doesn't want us to deal down here."

"It would be stupid to risk heat over a quarter ounce or something," Morganne said.

"Maybe I should take some up north," I said.

"I want to go with you," Morganne said. "I'm sick of California."

"California Dreamin'," Lila said.

"North Cascades Dreamin,'" I said. "Chelan's probably warmer than Santa Cruz today."

Even at mid afternoon, the guttural sea lion barks from under the dock were softened and distanced by fog. Through the mist, the sun shone flat and white and there were no shadows.

"It could stay like this for a month," Lila said.

"It's how the Redwoods get their water," Morganne said. "There's not nearly enough rain here for trees that big. The Redwoods drink the fog."

"We need to do something," Lila said. "I'll be glad when Cree gets here. She always knows what to do."

"Day after tomorrow," I said. "Come with me to pick her up."

"We could drive down to Big Sur again," Morganne said. "I love to look out over the cliffs and the surf."

"You wouldn't see much today," Lila said.

"We could eat at La Ventana," Morganne said. "You liked their abalone."

"We can get abalone at Smuggler's Cove," I said. "We can walk there."

"We need an adventure," Morganne said.

"This is an adventure," Lila said. "Adventures are mostly boring."

"We need a fun adventure, like in a book or a movie," Morganne said. "Let's make our own movie, without cameras. Everyone else is in our movie."

"My movie would be different from yours," Lila said.

"Sure," Morganne said. "It would be cynical and dirty, probably black and white with some of that machine head jazz in the background."

"Right," Lila said. "And yours would be all misty and perfumed and star little furry animals singing Neal Diamond songs." They laughed until they had to hold each other up.

"What would Lucky's be?" Morganne studied my face.

"A silent movie," Lila said. "Just pictures full of tiny little details that no one else notices."

"No," Morganne said, "I know him better. It would be a Western full of horses and Indians and desperados."

"And damsels in distress," Lila said. She looked at me. "What kind of movie would you make, Lucky?"

"I wouldn't," I said. "I'd write a book."

"A book?" Lila said. "What do you know about books?"

"I read one once," I said.

"So that's why you're always writing in that notebook." Lila looked at me, tried to see if I was serious about it.

"Just adding up my profits," I said.

"Let's go up to the city and stay until Cree gets in." Morganne said.

"Too expensive," I said.

"Everything is too expensive for you," she said.

"Let's buy an ounce and go on a run," Lila said.

"Not me," I said. "The best way to pass the time is sleep."

"We can sleep for three days after the run," Morganne said. "Or something."

"We have to get Cree," I said.

"We'll pick her up. Day after tomorrow we'll just hit our stride. Let's do it. Aaron can get ounces for fifteen hundred. If we promise not to sell any."

"I don't know," Lila said. "I might get horny and rape someone. Darrel kind of got me going."

"Rape Lucky," Morganne said. "He's easy."

"You're getting kinky now," Lila said.

"You were kinky long before I met you," Morganne said.

Morganne cut the first line. "It's Bolivian," she said. "About eighty percent pure." She sniffed the bag. "See, smells like cat piss."

Gerard had told me that most of the smell was hydrochloric acid. He'd said most Bolivian that hadn't been reworked or cut way down was too acid, tore up your sinuses. Morganne used her etched gold straw to hit the line with each nostril, handed it to me.

I hadn't done much cocaine in a while, just an occasional sociable snort with Aaron. I took a small hit, rubbed my nose until the sting subsided, took another.

Lila took a healthy piece of the line and shuddered as if it was strong whisky. "Mmmm," she said, "Tasty. It'll be speedy, Bolivian's always speedy." She took another big hit.

It was clear that to get my five hundred dollars worth would be a challenge. "My turn," I said. "That was just a sample." I took a bigger hit in each side.

It numbed my nose and upper lip. I could feel my face flush as the blood flowed strong from my stimulated heart. My sight cleared although I had not been aware that it was not clear. I could hear traffic across the bridge in town. Voices murmured all around me, from the beach, from the apartment next door, from the courtyards nearer the water.

Disparate threads of music wove an aural tapestry. Distantly, on the horizon between real and not, I heard the Jamaican preacher, "If it's problems that you're runnin' from, there is no hidin' place."

"Where'd you go?" Morganne asked me.

"Runnin' away," I said.

"That's a Bob Marley song," she said. "'You're runnin' and you're runnin' and you're runnin' away. But you can't run away from yourself,'" her thin voice sang the melody perfectly.

"Mine was Peter Tosh," I said. "Same idea."

"Let's go over to Aaron's," Morganne said, "I want to see Maria and the baby."

"I've hardly seen Maria," Lila said.

"She just stays with the baby or walks into town by herself," I said. "Even if you're there you don't see her."

"I'll get her to come out," Morganne said. "Let's do it."

Aaron's unit was across the courtyard and down a level. It had two bedrooms and a regular living and dining room. A balcony hung out into the seaward mist.

Aaron had been reading, still held the book, Divine Horsemen, by someone named Deren. "How'd you like the Product?" he asked us. "I think it's a little hot, even for Bolivian."

"Too bad Gerard's not here," Lila said. "Probably save me a nosebleed before this is over."

"It's got me wired," Morganne said.

I gave a thumb's up.

"Linda had the baby," Aaron said. "Last night. The Poet just called. He wants to bring them down. I told him no."

"I hope so," Lila said.

"Where's Maria," Morganne asked.

"In her room," Aaron said. "Sewing quilts and staring out the window."

"I'll go get her," Morganne said.

"Go for it," Aaron said.

Morganne knocked on the door and went in. Aaron cut a line on the glass coffee table. In a few minutes Morganne came back with baby Do in her arms and Maria close behind. Maria gave us all an embarrassed smile and her eyes did not quite focus.

Morganne sat on the couch and Maria shivered beside her. They tickled Do and cooed at her and she smiled and gurgled. Lila leaned across the table and touched Maria's hand, offered her the straw. "How're you doing?"

"I'm okay," Maria said. "I've been sewing. And taking care of Do." She took a hit from the line. "Aaron took me to Monterey. So I could get this." She dropped the neck of her sweatshirt over her left shoulder, exposed the curve of her breast and removed a two-inch bandage. An angry red swelling was splotched with colors and covered with a thin scab.

"Look," she said, leaned across the table, pushed up her breast so we could see. A tiny, tattooed, crimson heart, pierced with a black thorn, bled a bright blue teardrop.

We all looked at Aaron. He shook his head. "Ask her," he said. "I argued with her for two days, then gave up."

"I had to do it," Maria said. "For the whales. And all the others. The babies." She looked out towards the bay.

"She's been having whale dreams," Aaron said.

"They talk to me," she said. "They protect us. This is a bad place, but they take care of us."

"Santa Cruz is beautiful," Lila said. "Lot's of good people here."

"Not anymore," Maria said. "The bad spirits have come. You either do what they want or leave."

Lila shook her head. "Well, I'll be glad to get home, too," she said.

"That's a beautiful skirt," Morganne said and spread out a section of Maria's patchwork skirt.

"I made it," Maria said. "Out of some old jeans from the Salvation Army in Monterey. See, here's Do on DeFoe." She pointed to a rag doll baby under a cut-out fir tree on a denim bluff above the paisley sea. All in shades of blue. She had appliquéd dark tears down the baby's cheek.

"It's beautiful," Morganne said. "What else is there?"

"One is Aaron," Maria said, pulled the skirt around. From the triangular panel, as if through parted curtains, a giant's face looked out. Thick corduroy hair and a sun bleached beard framed deep Indigo eyes and full satin lips. The velvet nose beaked sideways like a shadow. In the stone-washed whites of his eyes she had embroidered a swarm of sperm with golden tails. Morganne ran her fingers across the embroidery.

"It makes me think of babies when I look in his eyes," Maria said. "When we were on the run, I couldn't wait until it was all settled so we could have babies."

"What's the third panel?" Morganne asked her.

"It's for me," Maria said. "But it's still blank. I don't know what to do about me."

"Let's go out for dinner," Morganne said. "All of us."

"I couldn't go," Maria said and patted Do.

"You could get a sitter," Lila said, "There's an agency."

"Let's go somewhere Do can go," Morganne said.

"Like where?" Lila asked. "The Royal Fork?"

"There's a good Mexican place in Santa Cruz," Aaron said. "They like babies."

"I'll go get the car," Morganne said, held out her hand to Lila for the keys.

"Why not," Lila said. "As long as they have Margaritas. This

Bolivian needs some Tequila to take the edge off."

"Margaritas by the pitcher," Aaron said.

Late sun rebounded from painted stucco window arches. Banks of ferns and sweet begonias trailed from the tops of plywood columns. Smoky red strings of chilis and thick garlic braids festooned the walls. Faded Castilian coats of arms watched from the shadowed niches above each table. Delicate wrought iron screens separated the booths and beaten brass scuppers held candles against the onset of darkness.

Our back corner could have used an extra candle. The first pitcher of Margaritas hardly made it around the table. Lila passed her inhaler and only Maria declined.

The Mexican waiter noticed and came over for a turn. He urged the crab enchiladas on us, "Very good crab," he said. "From up north, Dung-e-ness."

"Dungeness, that's what I want," Morganne said. "Food from home." We all agreed.

"You're from Dungeness?" the waiter asked.

"Very close," Aaron said, "Across the straits."

The enchiladas were tender, the rice and beans perfect. There was salsa so hot it brought tears to my eyes and a warm glow to my belly. The icy Margaritas chased it all.

"This is the best food I've had in weeks," Morganne said. "I was starving."

"Me, too," Lila said. "Are you okay?" she asked Maria. "You hardly ate anything."

"I haven't been hungry," Maria said.

"You need to eat," Lila said, "For you and the baby."

"I try," Maria said.

"There's Patrick," Morganne said. "And Pancho."

We all watched them come in and sit down three booths up from us. Patrick had a red bandanna for a headband, wore white bell-bottoms and sandals. Pancho, as always, wore dark leather that blended with the shadows and a soft brimmed suede hat hid his eyes.

"They weren't supposed to come down until next week," Aaron said, "Too many people down here know them."

"I know that girl," Maria said. "She was with me in The Ark."

"The red head?" Morganne asked.

"Uh-uh," Maria said. "She was always in a lot of trouble."

"I thought they weren't supposed to bring anyone down here," Lila said.

"They weren't," Aaron shook his head. "Sometimes I think I'm just a baby sitter."

Patrick and the red head kissed and she giggled. Pancho leaned over to kiss his girl, but she quietly turned away. She had intense dark eyes and long straight hair. It seemed to me he'd gotten the best of the deal.

After ten minutes, they still had not seen us. "I'll go flip him some shit," Lila said.

"I want to hear his excuse," Aaron said.

Lila swung her hips and winked at Patrick as she approached him. He suddenly realized who she was and stopped in mid smile. He twisted one side of his mustache, which he'd let grow out to somewhere between a pirate and Fu Manchu.

"Hey, sailor," Lila said.

Patrick leaned out of the booth to look past her, see whom she'd been with. He saw Aaron and waved.

"Who's your friend," Lila asked.

"Um, ah, Cherry," Patrick said. "Cherry," he caught her arm, interrupted her chatter, "This is Lila, you know, I told you about her, she's from SEATTLE."

"Oh, hi," Cherry said. "Glad to meet you." She thought for a moment. "I'm from.... San Jose."

"What part?" Lila asked her. "I grew up in San Jose."

"Uh, well, you know, the other side of town," Cherry said.

"Which side is that?" Lila stopped smiling.

"On the Santa Clara side," Patrick said. "I met her at the airport. She was picking up her brother."

"Yeah, my brother," Cherry echoed.

"Right," Lila said. "Aaron wants to talk to you," she stared at Patrick. "I'll keep Cherry company."

Patrick put on a broad smile. "Sure," he said. He couldn't hold his eyes steady as he approached us.

"Who's Aaron?" I heard Cherry ask Lila as she sat down.

"Patrick's fairy godmother," Lila said. "What's your address... in San Jose? We might have mutual friends."

Cherry looked desperately at Patrick for help. He put his finger to his lips, turned back to Aaron.

"When did you get here?" Aaron asked him.

"Today, this morning," Patrick said. "I was going to call you."

"You drove overnight?" Aaron asked.

"Yeah, well, we wanted to drive straight through," Patrick explained.

"There wasn't any hurry," Aaron said. "You're too early. You need to lay low. And send the red head back to Seattle."

"She's from San Jose, over..."

"Bullshit," Aaron said. "Maria knows her."

"She just moved down here," Patrick continued.

"Get rid of her," Aaron said. "Where are you staying?"

"The Dream Inn," Patrick said.

"Kind of high profile," Aaron said.

"We're cool," Patrick said. "I found a berth for my boat a few blocks away. I told the guy I was here for trials on a secret America's Cup boat of Ted Turner's. That will explain everything."

"Sure will," Aaron said. "Including the boatload of reporters who'll follow you around every time you go near the water. I think you need to go back up north and start over. And leave the jailbait home."

"Hey, I'm not going anywhere," Patrick said. "I want to be here when the Quest gets here. I've got an investment, too."

"It will be two weeks, at least," Aaron said.

"It's way late," Patrick said. "Everyone is getting nervous."

"Who?" Aaron wanted to know.

"Well, me," Patrick said, "and Pancho, and Gerard's people."

"I talked to Gerard," Aaron said. "They're cool."

"The Poet is going to go nuts," Patrick said. "He isn't used to this."

"He doesn't even have any money in it," Aaron said.

"He gets wired and blows his mouth to everyone," Patrick said. "Lance and Linda do everything but fuck in front of him."

"I'll call Lance," Aaron said, "Bring him down here."

"Gerard's been talking to some black dude with Colombian connections." Patrick said. "Drives a gold Eldorado pimpmobile."

"I know him," Aaron said. "Name's James. He's a gambler. Bad Jones."

"Well, I don't want to deal with Colombians," Patrick said.

"We won't," Aaron said, "but you need to go back north."

"I'm going to stay," Patrick said. "But I'll get rid of Cherry. She drives me crazy anyway. I swear I didn't know she was from Seattle."

Aaron didn't let the tension relax until Patrick was back at his table.

"That little bitch," Lila said when she sat down with us again. "She's too dumb to lie."

The night was cold and there were pockets of fog in the low spots. Maria clung to Do in the back seat of the Mustang between Aaron and me. She talked to Do as if we weren't there, recited everything that had happened that evening. I could see concern in Aaron's face as he watched.

Back at The Venetian, no one was interested in a three day run any longer. Aaron and Maria went to their place. Lila and Morganne came to mine for a good night toot.

"Why doesn't he take her to a shrink or something?" Morganne asked.

"Maria?" Lila shook her head. "He can't do that. She hates shrinks. She might go off and hit one. She was raised by her aunt, some German Holy Roller bitch who used to lock Maria and her younger sisters in the basement for days at a time. Because they were evil, had Mexican blood. She said that in court."

"Shit," Morganne said. "Sounds like Jim Jones."

"So after a while, the girls went down to DSHS after school and made a complaint," Lila said. "A caseworker investigated, took them back and turned the case over to a psychiatrist who decided that the girls were making it up. They had to stay with their aunt. All the neighbors knew what was going on, but no one asked them."

"Jim Jones," Morganne said. "He had the whole system wired. He had a big autographed picture of him and Governor Reagan in his office."

"Aaron rescued her," Lila said, "when she was sixteen. That's why she trusts him."

"How'd he rescue her," I asked.

"A dancer I knew used to baby sit the girls sometimes. She told me about them and I told Aaron. We knew this lawyer from when we both worked at the Firelight.

"I didn't know Aaron worked at the Firelight," Morganne said.

"He was the bouncer, Lila said, "when I first went to Seattle to dance. When you ran off to live in the hills with the hippies."

"It was fun," Morganne said.

"She lived in a tipi," Lila said to me. "With this mountain man with a dick like a buffalo."

"He did not," Morganne said. "He was very sensitive."

"Most dick heads are," Lila said.

"How'd he rescue her," I asked.

"All of them," Lila said. "Four sisters. All beautiful, but really screwed up. They weren't ready for the world at all. I picked them up after school, took them to a place called The Ark. Supposed to be a sanctuary for teenage girls in trouble. Mostly they were selling religion and setting up good publicity shots. Four little half Mexican girls were perfect."

"Didn't their aunt get in trouble?" Morganne asked.

"Get in trouble?" Lila laughed. "She almost got them back. Because of the evaluation where the psychiatrist said they made it up. The people at The Ark started apologizing and were ready to give them back. Especially when the girls told them they'd been helped to run away by a Topless Dancer.

We talked to the lawyer and he beat their aunt in court. It was a big deal."

"So they all lived happily ever after," Morganne said.

"No. So then The Ark would send the girls out as 'volunteers' to non-profit places. They sent Maria to some office and one of the men tried to hustle her, followed her to The Ark. It scared her to death, so she ran away again and hid out with Aaron and me. That's when they got together."

"She was sixteen?" Morganne asked.

"Almost seventeen," Lila said. "The age of consent was still eighteen, in Washington, so Maria's aunt wanted to prosecute Aaron for statutory rape.

"Where are her sisters?" Morganne asked.

"Scattered around," Lila said, "trying to survive."

"It seems like everyone is just scattered around," Morganne said.

"There is no direction," I said.

"Just one," Morganne said, "Down."

CHAPTER 19

We stopped just outside the security station on the concourse and Lila slipped Cree her full inhaler.

"You-all are bad," Cree said. She took a large hit on each side. She was dressed in a tight knit suit with nylons and heels and wore a coat with a deep hood. She winked and handed me a hatbox she carried. "You still Lucky?" she asked me.

"Near as I can tell," I said. "But I've been staying away from mirrors."

"You got it wrong," she said. "It's the shit on the mirrors. Speaking of bathrooms, I need to get out of this costume."

We waited in the bar while she changed. She quickly reappeared in boots, jeans and a sweater and the same hooded coat. "You can leave the hat box," she said to me. "It's empty. I just thought you looked cute carrying it."

Aaron was happy to see Cree, hugged her and pulled her inside. "Where's Lance?" he asked her.

"He's supposed to come tomorrow," she said. "There's some bullshit going on with him and the Poet."

"Maybe they'll kill each other," Morganne said.

"No, they're best buddies," Cree said, "but I don't trust them."

"Where's Linda?" Lila asked.

"She went to stay with her parents," Cree said. "Her mother came out to the island to get her. She took one look at me and freaked. She made Lee go in the house with her for protection. Lance told me she put her hands on Linda's head and prayed in German or something."

"Dutch," Aaron said. "Hollandisch."

"She yelled at the Poet," Cree said. "Called him the work of the devil. Blew his mind."

"So what are they up to?" Aaron asked.

"I'm not sure," Cree said. "I think they're trying to make some kind of buy, cut you out. Some guy named James."

"You know James," Aaron said. "Joanie's old man. Used to bring her to the club in the gold ride."

Cree laughed. "That James? He'll rip them off. He's a gambler, a bad jones for horses. He wouldn't know coke from baby powder."

"He's been buying a little," Aaron said. "From Gerard. He claims to know some Colombians."

"Colombians will cut his balls off," Cree said.

"They'll never get it together," Aaron said.

Lance called the next day, said he was in town and would stay with friends for now, lay low. He didn't know the phone number there and couldn't remember the street. He told Aaron he'd come down to Capitola the next day.

From Aaron's end of the conversation, I could tell Lance had dragged his boat all the way down the coast behind his Charger. Aaron told him to put it in the water in Monterey and get to know his way around down there.

After the call from Lance, Aaron took Maria into town for lunch. Lila and Morganne wanted to go into Santa Cruz, but Cree helped me convince them to just hang out with a bottle of wine and the remainder of the ounce at our place.

"I'm surprised this bed is big enough for both of you," Morganne said to me.

"It's bigger than my bunk on the Wigit," Cree said. "We slept in it for a while."

"Cozy," Morganne said. She took the mirror and straw from the table, took a hit. "We should just get a big bed, for all of us." She giggled.

"Too weird for me," Lila said.

Cree shrieked in laughter. "You got no business talkin' about weird, sister. The things you've told me! Mmmm-mmmm." Lila laughed with her.

"I'm having the dreams again," Morganne said.

"Whales?" Cree asked.

"Me, too," Lila said, "But I ignore them."

"They really bother Maria," Morganne said.

"Is that why she's so quiet?" Lila took the mirror from Morganne. "I talked right to her and she acted like she didn't hear me."

"She probably didn't," Morganne said. "She's not always here."

"Her spirit is low," Cree said.

"She's suffered a lot," Morganne said.

"She's so beautiful," Lila said. "She should be on top of the world."

"I think she's just not interested in any of this," I said. "It's like she's on an alien planet. Doing time."

"She needs a home," Cree said.

"Security," Morganne said. "What we all need. Maybe we should all just get straight jobs."

"That doesn't work anymore," Lila said. "All the good jobs go to these crew-cut bootlickers. The rest of us are supposed to be their servants. I don't know anyone working who isn't dying to quit whatever job they've got."

"The whole world is down on freaks," Morganne said.

"They're afraid of us," Cree said.

"And we're afraid of them," Lila said. "This used to be one country."

"Maybe if you're White," I said. "Let's go work in the orchards. We could make pretty good money and they don't hassle you. I could get us jobs as a crew, work together."

"The orchards are full of chemicals," Morganne said.

"I don't want to be a migrant," Lila said.

"You are, anyway," Morganne said. "We all are."

"We could work most of the year right around Chelan," I said.

"Draw unemployment when you don't work."

"It's a beautiful place," Morganne said. "Like Maxfield Parrish."

"I don't think I'd fit in," Cree said.

"You'd be surprised," I said. "It's more Charlie Russell than Maxwell what's-his-name."

Morganne elbowed me.

"I'm worried," Cree said. "I'm afraid Lance and the Poet will pull some shit on Aaron."

"Like what?" Lila asked. "Aaron's not stupid. I've been with him a long time."

"He doesn't pay attention anymore," Cree said.

"You never know if Aaron's paying attention," Lila said. "Sometimes it's a dumb act."

"He spends most of his time with Maria," Cree said. "I don't blame him. He's worried about her."

"We have to protect him," Lila said.

"Yes," Morganne said. "A pact. We'll swear an oath."

"I'm not too hot on oaths," I said. "Oaths can get you in trouble."

"Just an agreement," Lila said, "that we'll all look out for him and tell each other what's going on."

"We need a bond," Morganne said, "so no one can forget."

"I won't forget," I said.

"Look in each other's eyes," Morganne said. "Take turns and each look in each other's eyes." She locked her eyes on mine. "And remember that we will always take care of each other and Aaron and Maria."

"And Do," Cree said.

"Do most of all," I said.

"Never forget," Morganne said. She let go my eyes and looked at Lila. My eyes met Cree's, felt her power. Then it was Lila's blue eyes that promised, briefly suppressed a mocking smile.

We passed the mirror around.

The Poet looked at the ground and shuffled his feet. "I'm sorry, boss. I couldn't leave Linda up there. That woman, her mother, she's a maniac."

"Never mind," Aaron said. "The unit next to us is vacant. At least here she's with friends."

"We've already got a place to stay," the Poet said. He stretched and twisted his back.

"Where?" Aaron asked him.

"The Dream Inn," the Poet said.

"Too busy," Aaron said. "Move down here."

The Poet had trouble keeping his vocal chords open. "No," he said. "I-I want to stay there. They have a hot tub and a pool and room service."

"All the amenities," Aaron said.

"Last time you didn't want me here," the Poet reminded him. "I just think we should have more fun doing this," he said, "and make some real money."

"And live in style," Aaron said.

"Shit, boss, everyone is real nervous about this boat," the Poet said. "Even if it gets here, we won't make any real money."

"Depends on how much you invested," Aaron said. "No investment, no profit."

"I didn't have a chance," the Poet said.

"Then you wait until next time," Aaron said. He looked at the Poet in an intense way he rarely used. "Move Linda down here."

"Okay, boss," the Poet said. "But I'm staying at the Dream Inn for a couple of days. I need a vacation."

"Tell Lance I want to see him," Aaron said. "If he has time to drive you over here, he can come in and talk."

"Sure, boss," the Poet said.

Lance brought Linda the next day. She was tired and tense and relieved to see us all. The baby slept in her arms. She had named her Ruth. Lila and Morganne took the baby, examined her closely.

"She's beautiful," Morganne declared. "Look at all that black hair."

"Just like Lance's," Lila whispered to me. Her smile disappeared. "Lance went over to Aaron's," she said. "You better go over there."

"Yeah," I said. "Sure."

Maria answered my knock. She smiled, seemed to be in focus. She silently closed the door behind me and disappeared.

Aaron and Lance shared a line; Aaron offered me a rolled up hundred. I took a hit and sat on the floor.

"Uh, maybe we should talk later," Lance said.

"It's okay," Aaron said. "Lucky's a partner."

Lance was impressed with my sudden promotion. "Well," he said, "I guess the basic thing is, we want out."

"Who is we?" Aaron asked.

"One of Gerard's people," Lance said. "And a couple of others."

"Who others?" Aaron asked.

"Well, me." Lance gave me a look like a guilty dog. "And maybe Patrick and Pancho," he said quickly."

"You talk for Patrick?" Aaron asked. "Patrick can talk for himself."

"They were just afraid. Um, I guess they didn't want to upset Maria," Lance said.

"Right," Aaron said. "So you want your money back?"

"There's this Black dude in Seattle, knows some Colombians," Lance said. "They're sellin' nice kilos for thirty grand. Near pure. We need to move our money."

"If I buy all of you out, how am I supposed to operate?" Aaron asked him.

"That's the problem," Lance said. "We don't want to put you in a bind."

"I can see that," Aaron said. "So you want me to give you twenty-five thousand and you're out. How about unloading?"

"I'll still do it," Lance said. "And the sail north. For two percent. That's regular rate."

"So I buy you three out and sit on my hands until the boat gets in," Aaron said. "It costs money to sit down here."

"I'd take less," Lance said. "If we could get twenty thousand apiece, we could get two kilos and have a little to live on."

"You're sure that's what you want to do?" Aaron asked him.

"Yeah, I'm sure." Lance took a deep breath. "Coke is the business of the future."

Aaron went in his room and came out with the money in bundles bound with rubber bands. Lance took several minutes to break it out and count it. Finally he was satisfied.

"Okay," he said. "I'll go tell the others."

"Let them talk for themselves," Aaron said.

The Poet showed up with Patrick and Pancho in the Range Rover. Lila sent me to watch again. Patrick was still into the pirate thing and Pancho wore his usual dark shades of leather. The Poet had his serape on, with a brown beret pulled over his bright hair.

"Mornin', boss," he said.

"Hello," Aaron said.

"We wanted to talk to you," Patrick said to Aaron, looked at me.

"Here I am," Aaron said.

"When's the boat going to be in?" Patrick asked.

"Soon," Aaron said.

"I don't mean exactly, but within a week," Patrick said.

"I can't do that," Aaron said.

"You gave Lance his money back?" Patrick asked.

"Part of it." Aaron smiled. "He took a little discount."

"That won't seem very smart if the boat's here tomorrow." Patrick looked at Aaron closely. "It's here, isn't it? You're just sweating us down."

"No," Aaron said.

Linda came in and clung to the Poet with the baby in one arm. He pretended to be interested in Ruth, while he listened to Aaron. Pancho silently watched from the shadows on the far end of the couch.

"So what if we take our money back and the boat's here tomorrow?" Patrick asked.

"You're either in or you're out." Aaron said. "You want the same deal I gave Lance? Eighty percent."

"No," Patrick said. "I'll wait."

Pancho shook his head.

The Poet looked from one to the other of them. "How about Lance," he asked them. "He's waiting in Santa Cruz with his money. To go buy two kilos."

"He can wait," Patrick said.

"But you said I could buy in." The Poet looked at Aaron as if he hoped Aaron hadn't heard him.

"That's the breaks," Patrick said. "Try again next time."

Pancho got up and moved towards the door.

"We gotta go," Patrick said. "You know where to get me. It'll be good to be on the water again."

"I knew I could count on you," Aaron said.

The Poet got up and started to follow them.

"Stay here," Aaron said to him. "I want to talk to you."

"Okay, boss," he said and sat down heavily. Linda patted his arm.

"What are you up to?" Aaron asked him.

"Nothing," the Poet said. "Nada. I just rode with them. I didn't have anything to do with it."

"You said you had money to invest," Aaron said. "Last I knew you were broke."

"It's not mine," the Poet explained and patted Linda's leg. "Linda borrowed it from her father."

"Mom would kill my dad if she found out," Linda said. "I told him we needed to make a down payment on a house and I wanted to surprise her."

"That was my idea," the Poet said.

"I guessed," Aaron said. "So what is this bullshit about doing business with Colombians behind my back? With James."

The Poet's face whitened. "You knew all along," he said. I could hear his heartbeat in his voice. "Who told you? Lance? Patrick? What else do you know?"

"What else should I know?" Aaron waited, had all day.

The Poet stared at each of us in turn, then fixed on Linda. "You told them, didn't you." His anger grew. "I knew you would."

"She didn't tell me anything," Aaron said.

"What else do you know?" the Poet whined. "I never meant to hurt anybody. I just wanted to make a little money."

"By selling cut shit to my customers again and saying it came from me?" Aaron asked him. "Like you did a couple of months ago?"

"Shit, boss, it wasn't me." He was truly desperate now. "I just went along. I would have told you. It was Pancho's idea."

"I thought you were the idea man." Aaron laughed. "I should have let you do it. James would have ripped you off, or his Colombians would have killed you."

The Poet's hands shook. "You aren't going to shoot me, are you, boss?" he squeaked.

Aaron burst out laughing and the Poet's face turned red. "That's not how I do it," Aaron said. "I let people get even with themselves."

The chipped green double doors of the bar creaked faintly in the wind. The driftwood fire was dwarfed by the massive stone fireplace, a fragile spark on a foreign shore. The floor was rough, worn deck planks. It was too dim to see plainly but the table felt strong and heavy. Besides the fire, the only light was a soft glow from behind the bottles above the bar.

A strong surf slapped against the pilings beneath, sent small shivers through the timbers. My body soon anticipated each wave.

"You can feel every seventh," Aaron said as a strong wave passed. "See, the next one will be smaller."

I counted, and on the next seventh a strong shudder passed through the pier, the fire wavered, burned brighter.

"How about the seventh seventh?" I asked.

"We'd better be out of here before I have time to figure that out." Aaron surreptitiously took a hit on his inhaler, offered it to me.

I took a little, a pick-me-up.

The waiter stopped, pointed at our glasses. "You guys want another?"

"Not me," Aaron said. "I'm not waiting much longer. You got any coffee?"

"Coffee? You sure you want coffee?" The waiter looked at Aaron, stepped back. "I mean, you guys seem to be wired a little tight." He smiled. "On the other hand, there's an espresso place down the pier that will deliver up here if I call them."

Aaron ordered two double cappucinos. I had a hot chocolate.

Not long after the espresso came, the Poet sauntered in. He stopped at the bar for a bottle of Dos Equis that he sucked on noisily as he came over.

"Hey guys," he said. "Nice bar, huh?"

We both looked at him.

"I want to make it up to you, boss."

We waited. He choked the long neck on his beer.

"I've got that money from Linda's old man." He patted his jacket pocket. "I thought maybe I could buy Lance's share. Then you would have your money back."

"How much money do you have?" Aaron asked him.

"Fifteen grand," he said. He pulled the roll out of his pocket and fingered it.

"Put it away," Aaron said. "That's half what Lance's share was."

"Then I'll buy half."

"What are you going to live on?" Aaron asked him.

"It won't cost us much to live," he said. "I checked out of the Dream Inn. I'll move down to the Venetian with Linda and the baby." His shallow blue eyes were fierce. "I really want to do this, boss."

"I'll tell you what," Aaron said, "you keep five thousand to live on. That has to last until after we've sailed north and moved the load. That could be a couple of months. I'll sell you a third of Lance's share for ten."

The Poet was ecstatic. "Thanks, boss," he said. He grabbed Aaron's hand to shake it. "Partners." He reached for the money again.

"Bring it to me tomorrow," Aaron said. "When you move in. If you haven't lost it."

"I can't lose it," the Poet said. "I keep it right here with me."

CHAPTER 20

Aaron was on the balcony, shaded his eyes with his hand and looked out to sea. He beckoned and we stood beside him at the rail. He pointed towards the bay, into the clouded distance. "See it?" he asked.

"I don't see anything," Lila said.

"Me either." Morganne looked at Aaron. "What is it?"

"The Crystal Ship," he said. "The Argo, The Enterprise, The Endeavour."

"I still don't see anything," Lila said.

Aaron stepped inside and returned with a small set of binoculars, the kind that climbers carry. Lila took them and looked where he pointed, shook her head. Aaron reached around, aimed them for her.

Her mouth dropped. "Shit," she said, "It's here. It's the Quest."

"I never doubted it," I said.

"I want to see," Morganne said, grabbed Lila's arm.

"Easy," Lila said. "You'll jump over the rail." She gave Morganne the glasses, helped her find the boat.

"All right!" Morganne said. "Here, Lucky, look at it."

It took me a minute to search the broken mist. Then it emerged, first a tall mast, then another even taller and a long deck that seemed just above the water. It was much larger than the boat we'd practiced on.

The sails were furled and wrapped tight on the long booms, the gaffs swung empty. The distant hum of an engine followed the ship as it ghosted out of sight, back into the fog bank.

"Pete must be asleep," Aaron said. "They shouldn't show themselves yet. They'll ride out there until tonight. Smuggler's moon tonight."

"May?" Morganne asked.

"The new moon," Lila said.

"The dark of the moon," Aaron said.

"And there's been fog every night," I said.

"Beyond the veil," Morganne said. "They'll never see us."

"Let's hope," Lila said.

"Hey, Gus," Aaron called and waved at an older man in a plaid shirt who tied up a thirty foot cabin cruiser. The boat was from the fifties, all varnished wood and generous chrome. It looked like someone loved it.

"Aaron," Gus said, too loudly. "Took 'er out for a little trial." He pushed back a dilapidated skipper's cap, cupped his hand to his ear. "Just did some engine work," he shouted.

"This is Lucky," Aaron said, equally loud.

"Hello," I shouted and shook his hand.

"Well, I'm ready," Gus said, barely audible.

"Good," Aaron replied, seemed not to move his lips. "Get your first load at midnight. Pete will be glad to see you." They both appeared to examine the weather stripping around a hatch.

"I got the bunks and the galley stuff out this morning," Gus whispered. "Everybody knows I'm always workin' on this old tub."

"You're a good one, Gus," Aaron said. "Think you can get two tons on?"

"No sweat," Gus said. "The way I've stripped 'er out and with the fuel tanks nearly empty she won't even ride low in the water."

We walked along the dock towards Aaron's rental car.

"Nice meetin' you, Lucky," Gus shouted after us.

"Nice meetin' you," I shouted back.

Aaron crunched through the gravel in the Moss Landing parking lot then floored the accelerator in the yellow Caprice, headed north.

"What a fucking ugly car," he said. "It's perfect."

Lila had rented it in San Francisco two days before with fake ID. Aaron had his hair tied in a long ponytail which was out of sight under his leather coat. With the collar up, in his expensive jeans and Frye boots, he looked like any young businessman away from the office.

"Get some glasses and a pocket protector and you could pass for a computer programmer," I said.

Aaron laughed. "How in hell can I explain you?"

"Just tell them I'm some Mexican hitchhiker you picked up," I said.

"No radio," Aaron said to Lance. "None. Unless you're giving the alarm. If you get lost, get yourself found."

"No problem," Lance said. "You should see the fog on the Mekong. I never got lost there."

"Keep the clock tight," Aaron continued. "I don't want you and Patrick there at the same time. Drop the loaders first. You'll have two and Patrick two. Then keep some distance between you on each pass. It can't look like a convention. And don't give the alarm unless you see heat within five miles."

"I got it," Lance said.

"And don't take the Poet with you, no matter what," Aaron warned.

"I wouldn't want that asshole along," Lance said.

"I've been ready for a month," Patrick said. He gathered his hair, stuffed it in a backward Seattle Mariner's cap. His blond mustache drooped well down over his full lower lip. Morganne said women found him irresistible. I suppose his money didn't hurt.

"It happens when it happens," Aaron said.

"Yeah, I know," Patrick agreed. "It's just boring. We need to do something interesting."

"I'll think of something," Aaron said. "You've got the program then?"

"Drop the loaders and dance," Patrick said. "Make the radar monkeys hallucinate." He grinned. "Free acid."

"Don't let anyone see you with the reflector up," Aaron said.

"Pancho can drop it in about three seconds," Patrick said. "So I shadow the old man the first trip out, drop the loaders and pop up the reflector. Then run at the same speed towards Santa Cruz, let them think it's Gus going on out to fish."

"After ten minutes cut your power and drift for half an hour exactly. Lance will run the same trip towards Monterey ten minutes after you. Then you cross back and Gus will follow you in to Moss Landing. Stay close to him for ten minutes then drop the reflector and drift until you hear him on his way back out. Three times."

"Like I said, I'm ready," Patrick said.

Aaron dropped me at Moss Landing. Lila, Morganne and Cree got out of the Mustang and joined me. The fog damped the overhead lights, surrounded them with orange-pink halos.

Morganne smiled and walked beside me. "The radio said it was almost midnight," she said to me.

"Eleven-fifty-one," I said.

"Who made you scorekeeper?" Lila asked.

"Aaron," I said.

"I hear it," Cree said. "Ssssh."

"I don't hear anything," Morganne said.

"Which one?" I asked Cree.

"The deep pitch," Cree said. "The slower rhythm. I heard it run the other night when Aaron brought me out."

"What the hell are you two talking about?" Lila asked.

"The boat," I said. "Gus. They're close."

"Where's the truck?" Lila asked.

"Right there," I said, pointed to the motorhome, which had silently parked close to the end of the dock.

"Now I hear it," Morganne said.

The boat appeared so suddenly out of the fog that I was startled. Gus cut the engine and bumped softly against the row of tires nailed to the dock. I grabbed the bow line. Gus came out of the cabin and tossed the stern line to Cree.

"Not too tight," he said.

Three men came out of the motorhome, all dressed in dark clothes and tennis shoes as Aaron had directed us. One of them opened what appeared to be an equipment hatch, about three feet square, in the side of the LandCruiser. I could see a faint light from the interior through the hatch.

Gus stepped onto the dock, walked slowly towards the catwalk that led to the shore. He was dressed in a white jacket and his white skipper's cap. He did not acknowledge the three from the motorhome as he passed them.

Two figures appeared out of the boat's dark cabin and one of them handed me a burlap wrapped package that weighed about forty pounds. "Howdy," he whispered.

"Hi," I said.

"Next," said the second one and I moved out of the way.

I carried the package in my arms. It wasn't really heavy, just clumsy. I felt very conspicuous. I stopped at the side of the LandCruiser.

"Quick," said a voice from the inside.

I held the package in front of the hole and hands grabbed it. As it disappeared inside, I could see Spanish lettering on the burlap.

Cree was just behind me with a similar package on her shoulder and the others moved along the dock and catwalk. The last in line, a very large guy with unruly brown hair tied back with a bandanna, carried two of the burlap bundles in his arms.

They waited for me by the time I got back to Gus's boat. I took another package and headed back. It was almost an hour before the big guy carried the last two packages up from the dock.

"See you all later," he said and closed the hatch.

"It sure is riding low," Lila said.

He stood back and looked at the clearance, kicked one of the squashed back tires. "No sweat," he said.

"I don't ever want to see pot again," Morganne said after the second load. "The damned burlap has destroyed my nails. Look, they're bleeding."

"You'll live," Lila said. "And you'll never make an easier thousand dollars."

"I don't know," Morganne said, "I knew a call girl in San Francisco who made that much every night."

"Believe me," Lila said, "it wasn't easier."

"Do you hear it yet," Morganne asked Cree.

"No, not yet," Cree said. "Five more minutes."

"You don't even have a watch," Lila said.

"That doesn't mean I don't know what time it is," Cree said.

Lila took a hit from her inhaler. Morganne held out her hand for it.

"Want some?" she asked me when she finished. "It'll make this last load easier."

"Sure," I said. I took a strong pull and a clump burned my right nostril. I shook my head and took a smaller hit on the left. I hadn't realized how tired I was until the lift from the cocaine. I handed the inhaler to Cree but she passed it back to Lila.

"There," Cree said. We all listened. I soon picked out the sound and nodded.

"I think you guys are messin' with us," Lila said.

"No," Morganne said, "Listen. I can hear it."

"Oh, God, you too," Lila said.

"If you believe you can do something, then you can do it," Cree said.

"Anything?" Morganne asked her.

"Anything," Cree said. "If you believe strong enough."

"Well, I'm going to believe that we'll all stay together and make a lot of money and go somewhere beautiful," Morganne said.

"That's a lot of belief," Cree said.

"There's Gus," Lila said. "Where's that fucking truck?"

"It's almost daylight," Morganne said. "They'd better hurry."

Cree and I helped Gus tie up.

"Get away from the boat until they show up," he whispered as he sauntered past us.

We walked to the end of the transient dock and sat on the rough wooden bench kindly provided. The stiff dawn wind stirred the fog.

"Did you hear about the DC-10 crash?" Lila asked us.

"No," Morganne said.

"In Chicago," Lila said. "Yesterday. Two-hundred-seventy-some people dead. I told you they were a piece of shit."

"You don't have to convince me," I said.

"I'm not ever flying in one again," Morganne said.

"Where the hell are they," Lila asked herself.

"What if they got busted?" Morganne's voice was tired. "What if somebody talked?"

"Nobody talked," Lila said. "They're just fucking around somewhere. You know hippies." She took a hit from the inhaler, offered it.

"I'm too wired," I said.

The lights suddenly came on in the little cafe by the marina entrance.

"Shit," Lila said. "There'll be people all over the place now."

"I hear them," Morganne said. A vehicle pulled into the parking lot, headed towards us.

"That isn't them," Cree said. "Wrong sound."

"It had better be them," Lila said.

"Wonder Bread," said the sign on the truck as it passed by us to deliver at the cafe. The back door of the rickety building opened and we could hear voices.

"They open at six," Lila said.

"It's almost five-thirty," I said.

"There they are," Cree said. "The third set of lights."

Lila started to say something then stopped.

The first two sets of headlights passed and the third turned in. Gravel flew as it came towards us. We started for the boat as they backed in close to the top of the ramp.

"Where the fuck you been?" Lila asked the big one on our first round.

"Those assholes at the safe house took off for a drink between loads and didn't get back until we were almost unloaded," he said.

I knocked on the side of the boat and the cabin door opened. "About fucking time," the smaller of the two said as he handed me a bale.

"The cafe opens in fifteen minutes," growled the other from inside.

I hurried along the dock, across the catwalk and up the ramp. It seemed much further than it had before. "Good morning," I said as I handed in my load.

"No shit," was the response from inside the motorhome.

After about a dozen trips they handed me a package identical to the others except that it was several pounds lighter and smelled strongly of coffee. In the growing light I could see "Producto de Guatemala," and "Antigua" stenciled on the burlap. There wasn't any underlayer of plastic on these.

"All right," said the now familiar deep voice from within the motorhome. "The top of the load."

We all carried two of the lighter parcels at a time and we were finished in a couple more trips.

The motorhome moved almost before I could close the hatch. I looked up and saw that several cars were at the cafe and its sign blinked brightly. Gus talked to several people gathered outside. He pointed the other direction, away from us, and they all strained to see something. The fog was gone well out into the bay, and behind the low hills to the east, sunrise was imminent.

The low whine of the LandCruiser's tires faded. Gus walked slowly towards us. "So get the hell out of here," he said with a smile.

"What were you all looking at?" Morganne asked him.

His smile grew broader. "Whales," he said. "I was showing them the whales. They had a hell of a time seeing them."

As we walked towards the Mustang, Lance's Charger turned off the highway and slid to a stop in the gravel.

"Breakfast at The Ark," he said. "Aaron told me to tell you. I need to get Gus and Pete."

"Pete," Lila said. "Pete isn't here."

"Sure he is," Lance said. "He came in with the last load. Look."

We turned to see Gus and a short, stout blond man come across the catwalk and up the ramp. Pete's ponytail nearly reached his waist and his beard might never have been cut. Father and son were completely absorbed in each other.

"Pete and Gus," Lila said. "You'd think they got along."

Lila parked around the corner from The Ark. Capitola was quiet, seemed empty. Gulls swirled and squabbled behind the dockside restaurants. Early sun cast sharp shadows, reflected bright colors from painted storefronts. Windows seemed clean and clear, and for the first time in days, the water was blue not gray.

"They don't open until seven," Morganne said. She shivered and pulled the fur coat tightly around her. "I need a wake-up."

Lila handed her the inhaler.

"Better," Morganne said, passed it to me.

I hesitated, then took a large double hit. I needed sleep, but breakfast appeared to be mandatory. I could sleep in the afternoon.

Cree silently refused the inhaler, so I passed it back to Lila.

"Let's walk the beach," Morganne said. "We have almost half an hour."

"Cool with me," Cree said. She opened the door, stood outside and stretched.

"You don't even look tired," Morganne said to her and stretched her own frail body.

"Not the time to be tired," Cree said.

We walked past the commercial area. Beyond were scattered beach houses. No one stirred. I picked up bits of abalone shell and a few exceptional pebbles. Morganne made an arrangement of some slender driftwood twigs as we walked.

Lila sat down on a beached log and told us to get her on our way back. Cree said nothing, kept pace with us and stared out to sea.

Morganne took my hand and looked at Cree, but Cree didn't notice. When we'd walked for a while I checked my watch and it had been twenty minutes.

"Better turn around," I said.

"Why do we always have to turn around?" Morganne asked.

"Around is all there is," Cree said.

At a few minutes after seven The Ark was already busy. A waiter met us at the door and Lila winked at him. He took us up a steep flight of stairs to the balcony, which had only a couple of unoccupied tables. He left menus and brought water.

I heard a familiar deep voice from the next table. He was very large with kinky brown hair and a brushy beard. He sat with a slightly smaller, blonder version of himself. I recognized him as the guy who'd helped us unload.

"Good morning again," I said to the bigger one.

He gave an enormous chuckle. "Fancy meeting you here. I'm Dudley." He wrapped his hand around mine, shook it briefly.

"Lucky," I said.

"We needed all the luck we could get on that last one," Dudley said. "This is my brother, Will. They call him the Mule."

"Glad to meet you," I said.

I looked past him, and from a further table, Aaron gave me a small wave. Maria was beside him with Do. Pete and Gus sat across from them. Patrick and Pancho and Lance sat at another table. I realized that everyone on that balcony must be involved with the Quest.

The menu offered a Portuguese Scramble. In the margin a tiny red pepper burst into flame. It sounded about right. Lila and Morganne ordered omelets. Cree asked the waiter for a dozen raw oysters, a glass of tomato juice and some Tabasco Sauce. He looked at her strangely, but he wrote it down.

The Portuguese Scramble was good, but not hot enough. I borrowed some of Cree's Tabasco. Morganne shuddered every time Cree swallowed an oyster. I saw the waiter gag once when he came by just as she slid one down.

A waitress who seemed to know everyone helped clear the breakfast dishes, and then the waiter delivered glasses and a pitcher of Margaritas to each table. The waitress followed him and put a heavy white china plate beside each pitcher.

When they were gone, Aaron made the rounds and dumped a little pile of finely ground cocaine onto each plate. Pete passed around a bundle of crisp hundred dollar bills. I took one and rolled it into a tube. Morganne used her driver's license to scrape the coke into lines across the plate. Lila poured our glasses full.

Cree pushed her glass away. "I'll take a little line," she said, "In honor of Simbi."

"Who the hell is Simbi?" Lila asked her.

"The-snake-in-the-river," Cree said. "The helper of magicians. Our magic worked again."

I looked from Cree's exaggerated eyes around the boisterous balcony. Most of the men had braids or pony tails and wore leather jackets and boots. None of the women were what their mothers had wanted them to be. If you saw us in a bar as we looked that morning you would expect a row of Harley-Davidsons outside.

We inhabited a kind of shadow world that was parallel to the real world, but made the more invisible by it's bright colors and outrageous behavior. Nothing so bizarre could be real, so most people chose not to see us. They would stare now and then, but the stares were of defense, not perception.

There was a commotion at the foot of the stairs.

"I'm sorry sir," I heard the waitress say, "It's a private party."

"They can't hide from me," said the unmistakable voice of the Poet. "Get out of my way," he yelled.

Aaron walked over, looked down the open stairwell. "It's okay," he said to the waitress. "I think I know him."

"Think you know me," the Poet muttered as he came up the stairs. "Hi, boss," he said at the top. "Forget me?"

"Not likely," Aaron said.

"Why didn't you tell me?" the Poet demanded.

"I didn't know you were involved," Aaron said.

"What do you mean?" the Poet asked, hurt, "I'm a partner."

Pete stood up. "Who's this fucking jerk?" he asked Aaron.

"They call him the Poet," said the Mule. "He's the one I started to tell you about."

"So how'd you get to be a partner?" Pete asked the Poet.

"I bought a share," the Poet said. "Ten grand."

"Ten grand?" Pete laughed. "For that you can sweep up the shake when we're done."

"I'll handle it," Aaron said. "He takes a little getting used to."

"Well, he may be your partner," Pete said, "but he's no partner of mine. Come in here acting like an asshole."

"Sorr-ry," the Poet said.

"Time for me to go," Gus said and got up.

"I'll go with you," Pete said. "I'm not in a party mood."

"Let's get out of here," Lila said.

Morganne dumped the remainder of the coke from the plate into a bindle she folded out of a paper napkin.

We drove to Santa Cruz and wandered the streets downtown for a while. We got back in the Mustang and had a dip from Morganne's bindle.

"We should eat lunch," Morganne said.

"We'd all better get some sleep," Cree said. "Aaron will want us on the boat tomorrow. I'm surprised he didn't sail today."

"Me, too," Lila said. "What'd you buy?" She pointed to a paper tube Morganne had put on the dash.

"A print," Morganne answered.

"A print of what?"

"Just a print I like."

"Come on," Lila teased. "Let us see it. We're family."

"Maxfield Parrish," I guessed.

"Yes," Morganne said. "DAYBREAK." She pulled the rolled print from its plastic sleeve and spread it out. "It's like the other one," she said to me. "The one you said looked like home."

The virginal column didn't fit, but change the pseudo Roman portico to a wooden porch on a log cabin, give the characters a little color and put some clothes on them. I put my hand in front of the characters and the building, left only the natural scene. "It could work that way," I said.

"The people remind me of us," Morganne said.

"Too innocent," Lila said.

"Wrong color for some of us," Cree said.

"Yeah," I said. "Much too pale."

"You're not that dark," Morganne said to me.

"Not on the outside," I answered.

"I hope Aaron and Pete don't stay mad at each other," Morganne said. "I don't like it when people fight."

"They aren't fighting," Lila said. "They always growl at each other."

"I didn't know half the people at breakfast," Morganne said. "Too many strangers."

"I knew most of them," Lila said. "You just don't like to meet people."

"I already know enough people," Morganne said. "I can't keep track of all of them as it is."

"But if you'd felt that way a year ago, you wouldn't know Lucky or Cree," Lila said.

"And then I couldn't feel bad if something happened to one of them."

"You're impossible," Lila said. "What shall we do."

"I think we'd better get some sleep," I said.

CHAPTER 21

Surfers in wet suits worked the waves off Lighthouse Point. Several gave the familiar cabin cruiser a wave as we passed. Gus was at the wheel, Pete stood lookout in the bow and Aaron listened to the radio traffic. The Mule sat alone in the stern, leaned against the transom and silently smoked. He would make the trip north with us. We needed the extra hand but I think he was also there to watch Pete's interest.

It was midmorning, but we all clutched cups of coffee and shivered in the damp cold. My body had not yet adjusted to being afloat. Morganne leaned against me for support. She watched the surfers.

"I'd die," she said, "in that water."

"They think they're having fun," I said.

We saw a skinny guy in a yellow striped suit get up on a wave briefly, lose his balance and go under in a tangle of limbs and board. The other surfers cheered and clapped.

"Someone toss them a fish," I said.

"Looks crazy to me," Morganne shuddered.

"Me too," I said. "But I do things on a horse that some people think are crazy.

"Like what?" She asked.

"Like the Suicide Race," I answered. "At the Omak Stampede. Have you heard of it?"

"I think so," she said. "Isn't that where they all crash down the hill into a river and horses drown and stuff?"

"Not quite," I said. "We race down the hill and swim the river. A few horses and some riders get hurt."

"Did you ever win?" she asked me.

"No," I said. "But my cousin Nathan did."

"I always wanted to ride," she said. "But horses scare me."

"Horses like people," I said. "I train my own."

"So you live in this beautiful place that looks like a Maxfield Parrish print and train horses. No wonder they call you Lucky."

"I told you, it feels more like a Charlie Russell print up close," I said.

"I want to go there," she said. "And you can teach me to ride."

"When this is over," I said.

"What are you two whispering about?" Lila asked.

"Horses," Morganne said.

"Home," I said.

The Quest had followed the fog up the coast toward Pigeon Point as Monterey Bay cleared. It was another hour before Pete called out, "There she is, Dad."

Gus cut the engine as we came alongside. Patrick went up first; Aaron waited until last, shook hands with Pete. The four guys Pete had left in charge of the schooner nearly fell into the water as they scrambled onto the cabin cruiser. Aaron sent the Mule to take the helm. Pete gave a perfunctory wave. Gus turned from the wheel and gave us a thumb's up.

Everything was different on the Quest. The lines were heavy and coarse and my eye could make no sense of their tangle. The massive masts disappeared into the fog, were hung with heavy sails, streaked and frayed. The deck planks were worn and grooved, the iron fixtures ancient, utilitarian. Nowhere was there the sparkle of chrome.

We stowed our duffel bags in the cramped crew quarters below deck, forward of the main cabin. No ordinary-sized person could stand upright in the passageway or lie full length on the wooden shelves that were bunks. "There won't be any hanky-panky down here," Lila said. "I'll probably get splinters in my ass just sleeping on these boards."

"It's the smell that gets to me," Morganne said.

"Not much chance of smelling the cargo," I said.

"I heard Aaron talk to Pete about buying him out," Lila said.

"I think he should sell Pete his half," Morganne said. "Buy something that doesn't stink."

"Eddie wants Aaron to fix up the Quest, use it for whale cruises," Lila said.

"I know," Morganne said, "but I just can't see those people who came to the island to watch whales riding around in this old tuna can."

"It could be fixed up," Lila said.

"It would cost a fortune," Morganne said.

"Aaron will have the money after this trip," Lila said. "Prices are way up, and most of the load belongs to him."

"He should just take us all somewhere," Morganne said.

"He doesn't have to take us anywhere," Lila said.

"He wouldn't leave us," Morganne said.

"No," Lila said, "But he might go somewhere we don't want to go."

"I trust him," Morganne said.

Patrick stuck his head through the hatch. "Move your butts," he said, "We need to get out of here before summer. All hands up."

"I forgot what an asshole he is on the water," Lila said.

We all met aft of the cabin. Patrick was first mate, Lance second. "We're going to have to do it with two watches," Patrick said. "Six hours on and six hours off, two hours at the helm each watch."

"Oh, great," Lila said. "That way no one ever gets a night's sleep. This should be fun."

"You could swim to shore," Patrick said. "We're only fifteen miles out."

Lila glared at him.

"First and third will be mine," Patrick said. "Six 'til noon, six 'til midnight. I'll take Lucky, Lila and the Mule. You others with Lance on second and fourth. Any questions?"

"What if someone gets sick?" Morganne asked.

"We don't get sick," Patrick said.

"I'm already sick," Lila said.

"Captain Hook will throw you to the fishes," Cree said.

Everyone laughed except Patrick.

"Why is Aaron even here?" Morganne asked. "He hardly ever does anything. I don't think he came out of his cabin yesterday."

"He's here in case he needs to go down with the ship," Lila said. "Besides, his job is to plot the course, always have the next heading ready. And make sure it's all recorded in the log. And someone has to listen to the radios, figure out what's going on up ahead." She braced herself against the bunk as we heard and felt the schooner come about, take a large swell on the beam and roll precariously. "You better get up on deck or Lance will be in our faces."

"It's not my face he wants to get into," Morganne said. "He always reminds me that he has a cabin with a real bed."

"I wish Patrick would make me that offer," Lila said.

"Patrick spends all his time trying to get Supersonics games on the radio," Morganne said. "He thinks they'll win the championship."

"Who cares," Lila said. "Maybe I'll go sleep with Aaron."

"You wouldn't do that to Maria," Morganne said.

"I wouldn't be doing it to Maria," Lila said. "I'd be doing it to Aaron. It wouldn't be the first time."

"The first time since he's been with Maria," Morganne said.

"Maybe," Lila said.

The hatch opened and Lance called down. "Come on, sweetheart. Let's dance." He held the hatch open and spray swirled in on a cold gust. "We're tacking every twenty minutes,"

"Oh, God, my shoulders," Morganne wailed.

"Here, take one of mine," I said.

All we had seen in four days was a small patch of gray-green water that reflected an equal patch of green-gray sky. Occasionally a gull or tern would materialize out of the fog and scold us from high in the rigging.

"I keep waiting for the albatross," I said. "I forgot my crossbow."

"What the hell are you talking about?" Lila asked. She pulled the upwind side of her hood slightly open to hear me.

"Literary illusions," I screamed into the wind.

"I never know what the fuck you're talking about," she screamed back.

"Hang on," I yelled and grabbed her arm. She turned just as a huge roller loomed into our small circle of visibility. It towered above us then crashed heavily over the rail on the port bow. As the Quest rolled back, water that hadn't escaped through the scuppers sloshed over us.

Patrick forced the pilothouse door open. "Catch the boom," he shouted. We felt the helm ease, the edge of the mainsail fluttered. The boom moved towards us and we caught it before it had much momentum.

"All hands," Patrick shouted but the sound escaped downwind.

I held the boom while Lila tied it down. I crawled over to the crew hatch, pried it open with my fingertips. "All hands," I yelled.

Lance had joined Lila; they reefed in the mainsail. I went for the foresail and by then Morganne and Cree had struggled up the ladder onto the deck. They helped me drop the foresail and wrestle it into an awkward bundle that we lashed to the boom.

Patrick laughed as we crowded into the wheelhouse. "Not exactly Royal Navy material," he said.

"You bastard," Morganne said.

"I want all hands available until this blow is over," Patrick said.

"It never stops blowing," Morganne said.

We felt a shudder forwards. Another roller, not quite as large as the first, crashed over the rail and we heard a scream.

"Where is everybody?" The Poet's voice quavered, trailed off into the wind. "What's going on?" He opened the door, stuck in his head.

"Close the fucking door," Patrick said.

The Poet squeezed in. Morganne pressed against me to get away from him. "What's happening?" he asked, eyes wide.

"It's the big one," Lila said. "Cree says we need a human sacrifice. You know, like Jonah? You're it."

"You're fucking with me," he said suspiciously. No one smiled. "Fuck you," he said.

"You ignorant bastard," Lila said. "Grow up. You're useless. Aaron should have sent you North with the women and kids."

"I see you didn't make that group," he said.

"Get him out of here," Lila said.

"Go back below," Aaron said. "If I want you, I'll come and get you.

The Poet started to argue, then stopped. "Fine fucking friends," he said. "I try to do my part, but I never know what the fuck is going on."

"No shit," Lila said.

After our initiation, the sea gods smiled. The fog cleared not long after we passed Cape Mendocino and a steady southwest flow drove us towards home. A strong, smooth swell rolled in from the deep ocean. A low chop drummed against our port bow, like the beat of the ship's heart.

The Poet kept to his bunk except for meals and trips to the head. Patrick gave up trying to make him work. His beard grew and with the unkempt red hair and salty, soiled coveralls, we began to call him Davy Jones.

"How does he stay in that bunk?" Morganne asked. "I'd be a pretzel."

"He's just a blob," Lila said.

"He worries me," Cree said. "I think he has a bunch of coke with him. He might go over the edge."

"That's why I sleep on deck," Morganne said.

"That and something Lucky has between his legs," Lila said.

"Well at least it isn't Lance," Morganne said. "I have more pride than some people."

"Bitch," Lila said.

We saw several freighters and one huge tanker as we crossed the Seattle shipping lanes, but otherwise we had seen almost no other craft north of San Francisco. Then a Navy flotilla slipped past us just after sunset the evening before we rounded Cape Flattery.

In the straits, small craft traffic was thick and we had to keep two lookouts. Patrick was in a foul mood. A sleek white and chrome ocean racer bore down on us and flashed by our starboard bow. Patrick glared as the helmsman doffed his cap, mocked our pedestrian vessel.

"That's where I should be," he growled. "On my way to Maui. Not sailing this old tub with a bunch of cunts."

"They're spending money; we're making it," Aaron said softly.

"We haven't made any yet," Patrick said. "I don't like this unloading trip. We'll be sitting out there like a fat duck. We need a dock."

"We can't use Defoe," Aaron said.

"Thanks to Davy Jones," Morganne said.

"And a bunch of people," Aaron said. "But we can't use it."

"We at least need a dock for the boats," Patrick said. "This isn't Monterey Bay. Every retired pipefitter up here has a cabin cruiser and thinks he's Sherlock Holmes."

"Most of them are more like Inspector Clouseau," Lila said.

"The beach is the only way," Aaron said. "They can't watch all the beaches."

"Our people aren't the marines," Lance said.

"They will be after this," Aaron said.

"Or convicts," Lila said.

"Who's going to drive the third U-Haul," Patrick asked. "If Lance and I run it into the beach, that only leaves Pancho and Cree for drivers."

"I'll do it," Lila said.

"The Poet," Aaron said. "He needs to earn his money."

"He'll blow it," Lila said. "Let me do it."

"I need you here," Aaron said. "We have to get it into the boats fast. No one is going to believe we're coffee importers."

I started to volunteer, stopped myself. I noticed that the Mule watched them closely but said nothing.

"The Poet will fuck up," Lila said. "He hasn't been out of that hole in two days."

"I'll talk to him," Aaron said. "Get his head straight. He'll do better on land."

"You better send someone along to watch him," Lance said.

CHAPTER 22

In the end Lila went with them to rent the trucks with her fake ID. No one wanted their name associated with this amphibious landing. Patrick wanted to borrow a friend's boat, not use his own, but finally changed his mind. Lance was a good soldier and just did as he was told.

There was a lot of discussion of beaches and looking at charts. The final decision was to use a hard gravel beach we all knew, on the reservation about a mile and a half from the Club. The back-up would be a shallow bank on a channel deep in the Skagit Delta not far from the I-5 off-ramp at Conway.

Morganne stayed aboard and took the helm. That would leave Aaron and I and the Mule to drag the bales up from below and wrestle them over the rail so they dropped into the cockpit of a bobbing speedboat.

Aaron talked to Pancho on the radio every four hours as we mingled with the holiday traffic. Pancho had flown over Defoe and the reservation with Lee, everything was quiet. Aaron had Lila and Morganne put on swimsuits and lay around the deck. Cree stayed in the shadows.

Pancho came in Patrick's boat and the shore crew went to LaConner to split up. He had rented four storage garages at Smoky Point. It was almost an hour drive, but everyone agreed it was the last place you'd look.

Cree radioed from the Wigit when they were ready to leave Bellingham with the trucks. There was no sign of trouble.

Aaron took the helm while the Mule and Morganne and I reefed in the sails until we made slight headway, just enough for helm speed. Aaron showed Morganne how to rock the schooner gently off the wind and back to maintain a smooth course.

Patrick came alongside the Quest first, late in the evening. We had enough bags on deck under tarps to load him quickly. Lance came an hour later and the water was calm, the wind still.

On Patrick's third return he reported that Pancho was on the road with the first truck load and that Cree was in place. "No traffic at all," he said, "The beach is nice and hard. I don't think we're even leaving tracks."

About two hours after midnight Lance appeared to say that the Poet was a no-show. Cree had helped Lance stash the balance of his load under a little bluff along the beach so he could come back out. He took another load, said Pancho should be back from his trip by the time he got in.

"You'd better send someone to find the Poet," Lance said. "Everyone is really nervous."

"How about Lila?" Aaron asked.

"Haven't seen her, either," Lance said. "They're probably somewhere fucking."

"I'd worry more about that if it was you," Aaron said.

"Deception Pass is getting pretty rough," Lance said.

"Patrick will be okay," Aaron said. "But we should probably lighten your load a little next round. We won't finish until midmorning at this rate.

"So what's up?" The Mule asked as he came up on deck.

Aaron gave him a synopsis.

"I don't like that guy," the Mule said. "The Poet." He gave Aaron a very long look. "Pete doesn't think much of him either."

When Patrick finally showed up, daylight showed in the East and everyone was pretty shaky. His shouts were half lost on the stiff wind. The Poet had finally gotten there, he said, but by then Cree was back and she wanted to load first, let the Poet take the last load since he'd fucked up. Pancho was already gone with his second load.

"You'd better go in with' Patrick," Aaron said to the Mule. "See if you can get it under control."

"Yeah," the Mule said. "I need to get my piece."

When he came up, he put on his XXL leather bomber jacket that was rigged so that the long barrel of his .45 went down his left arm. He went over the side, clung to the railing, his feet slipping against planks. At the right moment, his massive arms propelled him through the air to land feet first in the speedboat cockpit. He gave us a thumbs-up as Patrick gunned away.

Lance wasn't far behind Patrick. He said they'd finished Cree's truck with his load and what he'd stashed before and got her on the road. Lila had gone with her. The Poet was waiting, but it was getting late.

We had to drag the bales through the low-ceilinged hold and each one was a little further than the last. By the time we got to the rail with them we had to rest before passing them over.

Aaron dropped his third bale too soon and missed the boat. Lance tried to grab it and missed. He got back into position but the floating bale got between his boat and the Quest and bumped him away just as I dropped my bale. It plopped into the water beside the first.

"We can't stop," Aaron yelled and started back below. I looked at the lost bales and decided he was right. We dragged the last several bales up and got them into the boat.

Lance tried to maneuver so that he could get hold of the bobbing bales, but he couldn't pull them over the rail without swamping his boat.

Aaron waved him off. "We'll get them," he yelled.

Lance saluted and moved away slowly.

The sun had broken through the overcast above the Cascades and early boats already scattered around the channel. I could just make out the San Juans to the north. The dark trees and jagged shorelines made me feel at home.

Aaron made a loop in a line, like a lasso, and tried to fish the two bales back aboard. Each time the bale slipped through the loop before it was high enough for me to reach. We had a long spare spar, but it was too heavy to handle with any dexterity. The chop was pretty bad and drenched us several times.

An old man with black-rimmed glasses and a stocking cap swung his shiny cruiser around and made a slow transit of our channel side, stared at us from his tall flying bridge. We stopped our salvage attempt until he'd passed.

"Fuck it," Aaron said, "With luck they'll float out to sea, make some fisherman happy."

"With our luck it will head straight for the Coast Guard," Morganne said when I told her. "Someone has to relieve me, my arms are dead."

Aaron took the helm. Morganne sat on the deck. "What do we do now?" she asked Aaron.

"Sit here," he said. "Until we get some more help."

"Then what?" she asked.

"Defoe," he said. "And get the business done."

"You're not worried?" she asked him. "About the Poet?"

"No," Aaron said. "He fucks up, but he's not dangerous."

"I think you're wrong," Morganne said.

"I'm going to cut him loose, anyway," Aaron said. "He just can't get along."

"He won't be easy to cut loose," Morganne said.

"I'm going to tell him I'm out of the business," Aaron said. "I may be."

"What do you mean?" Morganne asked. "You can't just go out of business."

"Go into a different business," Aaron said. "Something a little less dangerous. Maybe do some chartering. I'm going to buy Pete out. Fix up this old girl. She's been good to me."

"Why don't you sell it," Morganne said. "You could buy something really nice."

"The Quest will be nice when I'm finished," Aaron said. "The nicest boat you've ever seen. We could all live on her and charter wherever we wanted to."

"That would be a very different life," Morganne said. "I don't know if we could fake it."

"It wouldn't be that different," Aaron said. "We would only need to charter three or four months a year. The rest of the time the crew lives in the staterooms."

"What staterooms?" She asked. "Is that what you call the quarters. Have you ever been in there?"

Aaron laughed. "It will be staterooms soon. All that deck comes off, then we'll build staterooms with windows above the deck. And three more behind the main mast."

"I can't see it," Morganne said.

"You will," Aaron said. "She'll have a new name, too. The Orca."

"Isn't that bad luck?" Morganne asked. "To change a ship's name?"

"I don't think so," Aaron said. "This old lady's had a bunch of names. Pete and I named her the Quest. She was the Queen Jane when we bought her."

"I suppose it's like reincarnation," Morganne said.

"It will be," Aaron said. "A new life for us all."

Patrick never did come back. Lance didn't radio ahead, just suddenly showed up. The Poet stood like George Washington in the bow while Lila huddled in the stern.

"He blew it," the Poet yelled, "the Mule. He blew it bad."

I watched Lila as she struggled up the ladder. She looked like she'd just watched herself die. Lance was grim, signaled Aaron closer so he could tell him something.

The Poet continued to carry on, aimed now at Morganne.

Lila sat heavily on the deck at my feet. I squatted down.

"That asshole," she said. "He's the one who blew it. The Mule was just trying to get the job done."

The Poet turned back toward us. "I suppose you think it's my fault," he accused Lila.

"Of course it was," she said.

"That car was following me." He appealed to me for support.

"This dumb asshole drove around three counties half the night because he thought someone was following him," Lila said.

"Someone was," he said. "Aaron wouldn't have been happy if I showed up with the police behind me."

"It wasn't the police," Lila said. "It was a hundred different cars. Half the time there wasn't any car." She looked at me. "Then he would say they were following him with their lights off."

"So what happened?" I asked her.

"He got my truck stuck," the Poet said. "Out on the beach. He said I couldn't drive, then stuck the truck."

"We had to go way up the beach," Lila said. "Some asshole fisherman decided he had to fish right where we were working. So we had to back the truck way up the beach."

"It's buried up to the axles," the Poet said. "They'll never get it out. They can't call a tow truck."

"Why not," I asked him. "There's a station just a mile away."

"It's loaded" he wailed. "We had to leave it."

"On the beach?" I asked him.

"On the fucking beach," he said. "Loaded."

Aaron had obviously gotten the story. He was very pale when he stood up from the rail. "We need to move," he said. "Let's get some sail up."

"You'd better help" Lila snarled at the Poet.

"Check out Defoe," Aaron yelled to Lance. "We'll swing around Lopez and come down from the north."

Lance left. We got up enough sail to hold a steady course north northwest.

"Clean it up," Aaron said. "Any trace of a drug goes overboard. Lucky you do the main hold. Take a light."

As I found a flashlight he sent the Poet to do the crew quarters and Lila to search the cabins. Morganne had fallen asleep on the deck and Aaron carried her into his cabin.

The hold was not too bad; the load had been well wrapped. The Mule had broken one bale, dragged it across a nail head. I swept up the small spill with my hand, realized I didn't have anything to put it in so I used my pockets. I found a little still identifiable sludge from some earlier trip. Otherwise, there were some leaves and small stems on some cobwebs near the hatch.

I emptied my pockets over the rail, made sure none of it blew back on deck. The Poet came out of the crew quarters with a handful of assorted bags that showed coke residue. He'd also found a straw Lila had lost and several razor blades. Aaron had him stuff it all in a big zip bag with a chunk from a broken link of anchor chain to carry it down. He gave us some other chunks of the rusted iron to weight down our personal stash if it came to that.

Lila went through the crew quarters and found a gram vial and some more empty bags the Poet had missed. She wanted Aaron to flog him on the spot.

"Take it easy," Aaron said. "We're clean. Just out for a sail."

"They'll want to see the log," Lila said.

"All fixed," Aaron said. "We just came up from Portland. She was there all winter. Now we're taking her to Bellingham for refurbishing. I have a contract with a boatyard signed last winter."

"I'm impressed," Lila said."

"Just my job," Aaron said. "Seeing ahead helps."

"What do you see?" Morganne asked, came through the cabin door. "What do you see, Aaron? For all of us."

"You're not awake," Lila said. "Sit down."

"I'm okay," Morganne said. "I just want to know what Aaron sees. We all need to know."

"Riches and glory," Aaron joked. "What else is there?"

"Rock and roll," Lila said. "And there were a couple of other things."

"We've had enough sex and drugs," Morganne said.

No one accosted us as we sailed north. No one even came close. We relaxed and took one-hour turns on the helm and bow. Near evening, with the sun low and red on the horizon, we nearly ran down a little white day sailer that drifted with no sail or light. A gaunt faced man with a snarled beard cursed up at us as Aaron spun the wheel and we raced past him, nearly rolled him over.

Lila leaned over the rail and cursed back at the man. She seemed like the old Lila. Aaron stood like a dark shadow at the wheel and said nothing. I thought I saw a brief smile as he tossed the other Captain a salute.

"Poor drunk," Lila said, then giggled. "He'll think he saw a boatload of ghosts."

"It wouldn't be so funny if it was you," the Poet said.

CHAPTER 23

"What an incredible fuck-up," Gerard said. "It's all over the papers. Every cop north of Lynnwood had his picture taken with 'the haul.'"

"They think it's Colombian." Aaron laughed. "You heard that some fisherman saw Cree?"

"I saw him on TV," Gerard said, "telling a reporter, 'That big guy, the driver, was definitely a foreigner, not an American. And the other one was so dark I could just see his teeth.'"

Aaron grinned. "There wasn't anybody with her."

"I didn't think so," Gerard said. He offered Aaron half a line left on a pocket mirror. "It will take a few days to set a house up, a good one."

Aaron declined the mirror. "I need to turn some now," he said. "I need operating money."

Gerard offered the coke to me. I accepted.

"Have you seen the Mule," he asked Aaron.

"No," Aaron said. "Lila said he took off on foot, didn't say a word."

"Pete called me," Gerard said, "wanted to know if I'd seen him."

"He's laying up somewhere," Aaron said. "Watching the news and reading the papers. He'll know he's clear by now."

"Pete was wired," Gerard said.

"He was cool when I talked to him," Aaron said. "He'll relax when he gets his money. I'm buying his interest in the Quest."

"He told me," Gerard said. "You think it's a good buy? I'm not sure the whole boat is worth a hundred and fifty grand."

"She will be," Aaron said. "When I'm through."

"You're going to overhaul it?" Gerard lit a cigarette.

Aaron tried to wave the smoke away. "Top to bottom," he said. "She'll be worth two million or more."

"That'll take some money," Gerard said.

"I'll have some money if we get this business done," Aaron said.

"I've got a storefront," Gerard said. "It's in Wallingford. I'm going to open an occult bookstore. Next to Miller Richards' herb company."

"Is the lease in your name?" Aaron asked him.

"No," Gerard said. "My sister-in-law signed it. She's a nurse. She can say someone broke in and used it if anything goes down. You could work there until the middle or end of next week. Have everyone dress like construction workers. I'll have Angie tell them we're remodeling."

"Get a house," Aaron said. "As soon as you can. A quiet one. We'll go slow."

"Use U-Hauls," Gerard said. "People are used to seeing U-Hauls for a week or ten days after a place is rented."

"I'm a little leary of U-Hauls right now," Aaron said and Gerard chuckled with him.

"How much was in it?" Gerard asked. "The paper said it was more than eight hundred pounds."

"It should have been over twice that," Aaron said. "But I don't know if someone got there before the cops or the cops stole some."

"Probably both," Gerard said.

"I just want my half ton," Patrick said. "That was the deal, fifty thousand for a half ton. Shipping costs are yours. And all this other stuff."

"And you'll just take it out the door, accounts settled?" Aaron asked him.

"Out the door, one trip," Patrick said.

"That'll work," Aaron said.

"I wouldn't give the Poet a damned thing," Patrick said. "He's the one who fucked up. The Mule was just trying to bail us out."

"I know," Aaron said. "But I'm afraid he'll blow his mouth all over if he doesn't get something."

"He'll blow his mouth all over, anyway," Patrick said. "Tell him Lance will come put a bullet through his thick skull."

"He wouldn't believe it," Aaron said. "At least not all the time."

"I'd split his up with the crew," Patrick said. "They're the ones that had to pull his load."

Aaron cut a line on his small mirror and passed it around. Gerard was on it heavy, there wasn't much left for me.

"Can you move any weed for us?" Aaron asked Patrick.

"Probably not for a couple of weeks," Patrick said. "It will take us at least that long to get off mine. I've got one guy from Spokane that says he wants five hundred pounds, but they're always dreaming."

"Everyone has to have a dream," Aaron said.

"Hey, I gotta go," Patrick said. "There's a party for the Sonics. I missed the championship series thanks to this mess." He turned at the door and grinned. "It wouldn't have taken six games if I'd been around."

"I may have to take some smoke south," Aaron said to Gerard. "Pete says they're all out and the well is dry."

"They've got ten times our market," Gerard said. "You think Pete would move some for us? After that disaster on the beach?"

"He might," Aaron said. "The Mule doesn't blame that disaster on anyone but the Poet. And I'm through with him."

"Glad to hear it," Gerard said. "When are we going to talk to him? I agree with Patrick. Let him pay for his mistake."

"I just want him to go away quietly," Aaron said.

"There are ways to make sure of that," Gerard said.

"It's not intentional," Aaron said, "he just doesn't get it."

"That's worse," Gerard said. "Well, no more than a hundred pounds. Of that brown, crumbly shit that smells like tobacco. Tell him it's Nicaraguan Red or something."

"I'll finesse him," Aaron said.

"I don't know why you bother," Gerard said.

Gerard had a hammer. Every few minutes he would bang on the floor or the wall. In between he randomly buzzed a power saw and drill.

"You're driving me crazy," the Poet yelled.

"Don't blame me for that," Gerard yelled back.

"Ignore it," Aaron said. "Talk when it's quiet."

"He does it every time I start to talk," the Poet said. "I don't see why I have to pay...."

Gerard cut him off with the saw.

"You son-of-a-bitch...," the Poet started.

Gerard hammered on a pipe, rang it like a gong. "Talk quietly," he said. "Someone might hear you."

Someone knocked on the street door.

"Check it out, Lucky," Gerard said. "Tell them we don't open until next month."

I pulled back a torn piece of the butcher paper that covered the glass door. Some tall hippie with half a dozen rings in his ears and nose peered back at me. "I need some E-phed-rine," he mouthed at me.

I pointed next door. "The Herb Company," I said.

"Yes, The Herb Com-pa-ny," he mouthed. "E-phed-rine."

"Next door," I yelled at him.

"I've been here before," he said in a thin voice, I still had to read his lips. "I'm a friend of Miller's."

Gerard came over, turned the key, opened the door. He poked the hammer in the hippie's face, then pointed with it. "Next door," he said. "Comprende?"

"Sure, man," the hippy said as he disappeared. "Take it easy."

"So what's your complaint?" Gerard smacked the head of the hammer into his hand, looked narrowly at the Poet. "You caused a problem, it's your problem. Big problems cost big money. Front page problems sometimes cost more than that."

"That would leave me with nothing," the Poet said.

"Maybe that's what you're worth," Gerard said.

"It isn't fair, Aaron," the Poet said. He put his hand to his lips as if to hide their tremble.

"Maybe he's right, Gerard," Aaron said, thought about it. "He put in ten thousand. How about fifty pounds of that nice red? That'd make his cost two hundred a pound. That's half of wholesale." He looked at the Poet and waited.

"Lance said you gave him a ten percent bonus to take weed," The Poet said.

"He didn't get this red stuff either," Gerard said.

"Fifty pounds will barely get back the money we borrowed from Linda's father," The Poet said, dejected. "We're really broke." He couldn't look straight at Aaron. "The five thousand is gone."

"I thought you still had two left," Aaron said.

"I can't find it," the Poet said. "I had it in the pocket of my leather jacket, but it's not there."

Aaron and Gerard exchanged a look the Poet couldn't see. Aaron leaned over, whispered to Gerard.

"No fucking way," Gerard said out loud.

Aaron whispered again.

"Take it out of your share then," Gerard said. "I'm out of here." He banged on the floor with the hammer, just behind the Poet. "Don't be so jumpy," he said. "I'd use a gun." He handed me the hammer. "Keep it going," he said as he left.

The Poet started to talk and I buzzed the drill. He looked at me.

"Just testing," I said. I hammered on the concrete floor.

"I'll give you a hundred pounds," Aaron said. "Of that red. That's the best I can do."

The Poet smiled with relief. "Sorry, boss," he said. "I don't want to be a hassle. But I have to get Linda's old man's money back.

"A hundred pounds is worth more than twice that," Aaron said. "Take care of it."

"What do we do next, boss," the Poet asked, relieved.

"There is no next," Aaron said. "I'm out of the business."

"You can't do that," the Poet said. "What will everyone do."

"Whatever they do," Aaron dismissed him. "Lance will deliver yours, to LaConner or wherever. Where do you want it?"

"Cold," the Poet muttered. "Just quit on everyone."

"Where do you want it?" Aaron asked again.

"I don't know. How much room will it take? A hundred pounds! Can't I just get it a little at a time? You never did tell me where the storage was."

"I didn't intend to," Aaron said. "You need your own storage."

"Can't I leave it here?" He looked around. "I don't even see any."

"This is a place to talk," Aaron said. "Where do you want yours?"

The Poet pondered. "Would it fit in my old pickup? I have that old Dodge that doesn't run. It has a canopy."

"I wouldn't leave it there long," Aaron shook his head. "What are you driving?"

"Linda's mother's car," the Poet said. "The Buick."

"Where's the pickup?"

"At Linda's mother's," the Poet started.

"I could have answered that," Aaron said. "Where is that?"

"Camano Island," he said. "Sunset Shoals."

I grinned and Aaron chuckled.

"Of course," he said. "It is locked, right?"

"Yeah," the Poet said, "but her father uses it for storage. For his fishing stuff. We go fishing together."

"Tell him to get his shit out of it," Aaron said. "And get me the key. The sooner I have a key, the sooner I can deliver."

"Right, boss," the Poet said. "I'll get it to you tomorrow. No, day after tomorrow. Her mother has a hair appointment tomorrow."

"Where have you guys been?" Morganne reproached me. "I don't like being by myself."

"Where's Lila?" Aaron asked her.

"She went to get us something to eat," Morganne said. "At Daly's. There's nothing here."

"This is a good house," I said.

"Sure," Morganne said. "If you like the sound of trains bashing each other all night long down at the Interbay yard."

"I mean the garage," I said. "And the access."

"It's anonymous, anyway" Aaron said. "Does the phone work?"

"Since about ten this morning," Morganne said. "The Poet called. I think he wanted coke. Kept talking about powdered sugar."

"How did he get the number?" Aaron asked.

"He wouldn't tell me," Morganne said. "But you told me not to give it to him, so it wasn't me."

"It had to be Lance," Aaron said. "No one else has it yet. Just Gerard. And Lila."

"Lila hates him," Morganne said. "She says he's repulsive."

"Shit happens," Aaron said.

"No way. She's family, Aaron." Morganne was anxious. "She loves you."

"That's the problem," he said.

"Where's Maria?" Morganne asked him. "I haven't seen her since we got back."

"With her sister," Aaron said. "I didn't want her on the island, or here, while we do this business."

"You need a place," Morganne said. "A place to live. Away from all this. We all do."

"I know we do," Aaron said. "When the Orca is ready, she will be the place."

"That isn't a place," Morganne said. "Places don't move around, or sink. Besides, I can't get used to the 'Orca.' I remember sleeping in the crew quarters, curled up like a rat, with my arms so sore they were numb when I woke up. The only way I made it was to remember we were on a Quest, your quest. But we never got to the end of the quest."

"Maybe the Orca is the end of the Quest," he said and gently shook her shoulder. "I won't forget you," he said. "You can have some of your money any time you want it." He pulled out a roll of hundreds and gave her five.

She folded the money, slipped it in her jeans pocket. "It isn't the money," she said. "The money is fine. It's the future."

"I'm not in charge of that," Aaron said.

"I wish you were," Morganne said. "I trust you." She smiled and their look went back years.

"That must be Lila," Aaron said. The garage door opened, a car entered. Aaron looked out, hit a remote button that closed it.

"Hi, honey, I'm home," Lila called from the passageway. "I brought the bacon." She came in with several cheeseburgers and half a dozen orders of fries. She set it all on the coffee table. "Be right back," she said, "I got cokes."

"This is all for you?" Aaron asked in mock amazement.

"We haven't eaten since yesterday," Morganne protested. "And I just puked my way up the West Coast, remember?"

"They call that bulimia now," Aaron said and ducked as she pretended to slap him.

"We'll split this food," Lila said to us as she came in with two six-packs of cola. "Then I'll go get some pizza."

"You need to stay here," Aaron said. "Morganne's afraid of the bogey man."

"I am not," Morganne said, "It's Gerard's biker friends. They always try to hit on me. Real subtle. They get a merit badge for rape, you know."

"You're too skinny," Lila said. "Bikers like something with a little meat on it."

"You would know," Morganne said.

"We have to go," Aaron said. "We can't all sit in one place very long."

"What do we do if the cops come?" Morganne asked.

"You two came by to see your friend Gail who just rented the house," Aaron said. "She wasn't home, so you decided to wait for her. You have no idea what might be in the garage."

"Who's name is that rental car in?" she asked him.

"One of my many shadows," Lila said. "Don't worry. This is a good place."

"When you're down to a hundred pounds, call Gerard," Aaron said. "Just a friendly call, no talk. He or Lance or I will bring another load down."

"How about the money?" Lila asked him.

"I'll pick it up randomly," Aaron said. "Or Gerard."

"So if Gerard wants the money, I give it to him?" Lila asked.

"Unless I tell you different," Aaron said.

CHAPTER 24

"How much is left, really," Morganne asked. "Aaron just says 'there's plenty more.'"

"We're about halfway," I said.

"Half!" Morganne complained, "I thought Aaron had some buyers for big lots."

"There's too much Colombian around," I told her. "They're selling kilos for five hundred."

"It's shit," she said. "I smoked some that Lance had."

"Dealers can sell ounces for twenty-five and double their money," I said. "Nobody has seen an ounce for twenty-five since Woodstock. They've got hippies lined up around the block."

"We've been here six days," Morganne said. "I'm sick of it. Lila goes out all the time and leaves me. Aaron never comes by except for money. I haven't seen you for days."

"Aaron sent some money for you," I said. "And Lila. Five-thousand apiece."

"I have enough money," she said. "I need people. My people."

"We'll be back on the island soon," I said. "I was there yesterday. It's so quiet." I pulled her to me. "And the Poet was moving his shit out. Linda was crying."

"Too bad for her," Morganne said. "But I'm glad that asshole is gone."

"He was cutting lines clear across the dining room table," I said. "And passing out hundred-dollar bills."

"Was Aaron there?" she asked me.

"No, he went to get Maria. It wasn't working out at her sister's."

"I want to see Do," Morganne said. "She was everyone's baby in Santa Cruz."

"We'll be all together again," I said. "In just a few days. The Orca won't be finished until August or September. Aaron says we'll just hang out on Defoe and turn ourselves into a charter crew."

"Do we get uniforms?" Morganne laughed. "I want a very short skirt. And Lila's will have to be let out in front."

"You'll let my what out?" Lila growled and came out of the bedroom.

"Your teats," Morganne giggled. "Out to pasture."

Lila cupped her hands under her breasts, pushed the nipples against her soft nightgown. "These old girls aren't ready to retire yet," she said. She dropped her hands and shook her chest, the nightgown came alive. "I'll make a few bucks with them yet."

"You're going to dance again?" Morganne was unbelieving. "With all this money?"

"Not a chance," Lila said. "I'm going to buy a bar."

"You can't leave us. We couldn't do it without you." Morganne said.

"Do what?" Lila asked. "Brown-nose tourists and chase around after whales? You don't need me for that."

"Yes, we do. It would be fun." Morganne's eyes pleaded. "It's something we can all do that's legal and we can stay together. And still be freaks."

"Maybe I want a house," Lila said. "And babies. How do you do babies on a pirate ship?"

"It's not a pirate ship," Morganne said. "It will be elegant, like something out of an old painting. We'll be like visitors from the past."

"I want a future," Lila said. "And a man."

"You just have an ad-dick-tion," Morganne teased.

"You should talk, you little sleep around," Lila said.

"I haven't been sleeping around," Morganne said and glanced at me.

"How about Aaron the other night?" Lila shook her head. "I suppose you just gave him a back rub."

"Mostly," Morganne said. "He was lonely."

"Dicks are always lonely," Lila said. She counted her money. "Lucky, did you bring any coke?"

"No," I said. "We're all out. Aaron and Gerard don't want to mess with it until after the weed's all gone."

"Aaron had coke the other night," Morganne said, looked quickly at me.

"Well, I sure didn't get any," Lila said. "What do they have you doing?" she asked me.

"Mostly watching the storage," I said. "They like to have someone there all the time."

"And Lance won't do it," Lila said.

"Cree gives me breaks," I said, "but she's been out fishing."

"Is there a bathroom there?" Morganne asked.

"At the gas station," I said. "Across the freeway."

"I guess we don't have it so bad," Morganne said.

"I told you," Lila said.

"Aaron's in Bellingham most of the time," I said. "Watching them work on the boat."

"Why does he need to watch them?" Morganne asked. "I thought he had a contract."

"So now he has to enforce it," Lila said. "How is it going?"

"Okay, " I said. "Maybe a little slow. He said when they tore out the crew quarters there was some hull rot they didn't know about. It wasn't included."

"I knew I heard worms in there," Morganne said. "Every time I tried to sleep. I kept dreaming a whale would bash through there while I was asleep."

"How much extra does that cost?" Lila asked me.

"I heard them talking about a hundred thousand," I said, "for openers. But the whole job is almost a million anyway."

"Aaron has plenty of money, now," Morganne said.

"He doesn't need to waste it," Lila said.

"It's going to be beautiful," I said. "You saw the plans."

"Plans are always beautiful," Lila said.

"I think Lance is a lying bastard," Gerard said. "Colombians would have killed him. And mailed us his balls or something."

"He was pretty scared," Aaron said.

"Scared you'd catch him," Gerard said. "How's he happen to know they were Colombians? Check their passports?"

Aaron shrugged. "He said they spoke Spanish, but not Mexican Spanish. And carried those little silver automatics."

"He wouldn't know Mexican Spanish from Pig-Latin," Gerard said. "He can make up the loss."

"A hundred thousand is more than half his share. He's already picked up more than that in Product. He might go sideways on us."

"He already did," Gerard said.

"I think we should just cover it and not let him handle any more money," Aaron said.

"That means you'll have to do the collecting." Gerard said.

"I'll do it," Aaron said. "Except your people. I don't deal with heavies."

"They aren't heavies," Gerard said. "Just bikers. They're gentle as your Aunt Nellie."

"If my Aunt Nellie was a wolverine," Aaron said. "They're the Bad Angels, remember?"

"Just overgrown boy scouts," Gerard said. "I can handle them. They brought me some good coke."

"I thought we weren't doing coke," Aaron said.

"It's personal," Gerard said. "Just stash."

"I'm going south to pick up something nice when we're through," Aaron said. "I figure we can move enough to make stash. And a little for PR. With charter customers."

"Guests," Gerard said. "As long as they pay the bill."

"Mostly the universities and foundations will pay the bills," Aaron said. "We've booked a total of seven weeks already. Twelve in six staterooms, at two hundred and fifty bucks each a day. One week, Seventy-five hundred. Weekends extra. I might have two grand in overhead on a bad week."

"A bad week," Gerard said, "is when you have no customers and a whale rams the boat. Or a tanker from Indonesia."

"If we have no customers, we'll sail somewhere," Aaron said. "Suffer in Santa Cruz or Belize. We only need to charter twenty weeks to clear a hundred grand plus. That should take care of ship and crew nicely for a year."

"And then you bring a small cargo back from Belize," Gerard said. "Fine if it all works. It will take a good crew."

"I'll have a good crew," Aaron said.

I met Morganne and Lila at the dock. Lee gave me a friendly wave as he gunned the plane in a tight circle. They both hugged me like I guarded the gates of heaven.

"Where's Cree?" Morganne asked. "I don't see the Wigit."

"She's fishing again," I said. "For three days. Went out this morning."

"She must not have known we were coming," Morganne said.

"Yes, she did," Lila said. "I talked to her yesterday when I called."

"Is Aaron here?" Morganne asked. "I want to talk to him."

"He's here, but he's going down to get Maria in the morning," I said.

"Where's Maria now?" Lila asked. "With her sister again?"

"No," I said. "She's at an apartment, in Bellevue."

"By herself?" Morganne asked.

"I guess so," I said. "I didn't ask him."

"Someone should," Morganne said. "She needs her friends."

"She was doing too much coke," I said. "At her sister's. Aaron paid them to take care of her with an ounce so they sat down and tooted it up. In about a week."

"No wonder he moved her," Lila said.

"She needs her friends," Morganne said.

"She'll be here tomorrow," I said.

"How about the whale people?" Lila asked.

"You mean Mr. and Mrs. Macbeth? They aren't seeing eye to eye right now," I said. "They can't agree on how to steal the Orca."

"How would they steal it?" Morganne asked.

"Eddie wants Aaron to sign a contract with them," I said. "So they can book all the trips and package them with seminars and symposiums and really make some money. Suzette just wants a cut of every week's take without any risk."

"Are they here?" Lila asked.

"No," I said. "Another whale conference. In the Virgin Islands, this time. They're going to sign up a bunch of suckers."

They both went to their rooms to commune with possessions they hadn't seen since before we went to Santa Cruz. I put some reggae on the stereo. I almost missed the Poet's goofy antics. The big old house had gotten much too quiet without all of us. The sound of Lila and Morganne's voices upstairs reassured me.

Aaron came in from the study where he had laid out the drawings for the Orca.

"Lila and Morganne?" he asked me. "I heard Lee."

"Yeah," I said. "Morganne said she wanted to talk to you."

"Morganne," he called up the stairs.

She came down and gave him a daddy hug. He rubbed her butt and she pulled away, looked at me. I smiled, so she laughed and grabbed him again and kissed him.

"Whoa, Nellie," Lila said, came down the stairs.

"What did you want to talk to me about?" Aaron asked Morganne.

"When do we get the rest of our money?" She sat down on the steps. "We've been finished for days."

"You need money?" Aaron asked her. "I can advance some more."

"I don't want an advance," she said. "I just want my money. Just so I know how much I have."

"What are you going to do with it?" Lila asked.

"I still don't know," Morganne said. "Maybe put it in the bank?"

"You can't do that," Lila said. "IRS will get you."

"I'll just pay the taxes," Morganne said. "It can't be too much."

"Probably half," Lila said. "Then they'd want to know where you got it. And they'd have us all."

"So that's why you're doing the under-the-table deal on the tavern," Morganne mocked herself. "Someday I'll get it."

"I'd never get a liquor license anyway," Lila said. "Because they know I'm a dancer. Just one of the State's friendly gestures." Lila thrust out her hand. "You do it with your finger, like this."

"Aaron, you didn't answer me," Morganne said to him. "About our money."

"As soon as I settle with Gerard," Aaron said.

"What's the problem?" Lila asked. "Who didn't he collect from?"

"The bikers!" Morganne said. "I knew it."

Aaron nodded.

"How much?" Lila asked. "How much did they get away with?"

"Almost a ton," Aaron said.

"A ton?" Morganne stared at him. "That's like a million dollars!"

"Not quite," Aaron said.

"About half," Lila said. "How did they do it? We never let anyone have any unless you or Gerard told us to."

"This was the big guys," Aaron said. "Gerard let them get it straight from the storage. His storage, the one he didn't want Lucky to watch."

"So that's his problem," Lila said.

"He thinks it's two-thirds mine," Aaron said. "At least until he collects it."

"He won't ever collect it," Lila said. "I know bikers. They don't ever see that much money at once. It's long gone."

"It isn't fair," Morganne said. "Then it costs all of us."

"Net profit was the deal," Lila said. "We hang together. Probably from a rope."

"Can't we get our share, up until now," Morganne asked. "Everything but what the bikers stole? Before it's gone too."

Aaron laughed. "It won't be gone," he said. "It's perfectly safe. It's just that once we settle with Gerard, it will be harder to come back for the balance. I can't touch it until we settle."

"Let him carry the debt," Lila said, "they're his friends."

"It would be half of his share," Aaron said. "He'd only have half a million. He has big plans."

"We all have plans too," Lila said. "Even if they're just little bitty plans."

"It's not that," Aaron said. "It's just that he doesn't get his money until everyone does. Except for the advances we all got."

"How much was your advance?" Lila asked.

"Two hundred fifty," Aaron said. "But I had to pay Pete one-fifty and cover all your advances. The boatyard wanted fifty just to let us dock." Aaron sat beside Morganne, grinned down at her. "Then there are expenses, like airplanes and trucks and food and rent and crying towels and diapers."

She grinned up at him. "I'm just ragging," she said. "I'm happy to be here. I don't ever want to leave again."

CHAPTER 25

The solstice sun drove mist off Elliott Bay, made a distant ferry waver as though it would melt. The cool green cavern of the Pike Place Market swallowed us up. I turned away from the noisy fish vendors into the farmers' hall. Rows of wooden bins spilled over with tomatoes and carrots and lemons and artichokes. In one stall bright strings of peppers hung. A pineapple forest covered a table in another.

A man and a woman bought oranges from a perfectly stacked pyramid. The man spoke and the woman laughed. She turned and I knew her.

"Judith," I said. She stopped, looked hard before she recognized me.

"Cousin?" she said, wasn't sure.

"It's me," I said. "I know my way around over here, too."

"Of course," she said. "Harry, this is my cousin, actually second cousin, from Chelan."

I put out my hand. "Lucky," I said.

If Harry smiled it was hidden under his dark, curly beard. His handshake was strong, like a farmer's.

"This is my husband," Judith said, and touched his broad back. "We got married a year ago, in Electric City, at Mom's house. Joseph was there."

"Old Joseph?" I asked her.

"The elder," Judith said. "He comes to see us sometimes. We just built a house out in Redmond. Harry works for a contractor. You should come see us."

"I don't know," I said, "I've been busy."

"We'll meet you later," Lila said and poked me in the ribs, "downstairs in the bar."

"I'm sorry," Judith said and looked at the two of them. "I didn't realize...."

"Didn't realize Lucky had friends," Morganne said.

"I didn't mean that," Judith said.

"She's just bitchy," Lila said. "We're happy to meet you." They both smiled, then Lila led Morganne away.

"What are you doing here?" Judith asked me. "I thought you went to the Stehekin every summer to...uh...grow plants."

"Not this summer," I said.

"Where are your horses?" she asked me.

"I left them with a guy, up on the Skagit," I said. "An old farmer."

"I'd miss them too much," she said, "if they were mine."

"Yeah," I said. "I'll get them this fall."

"I'm going to have a baby," Judith said and poked out her stomach. "This winter." Harry looked vaguely uncomfortable.

"Congratulations," I said.

"Have you seen Nathan?" Judith asked, very serious. I watched Harry look away, control himself.

"No," I said. "Not since the Stampede last year. He was really drunk, I had to tell him who I was."

"He's always really drunk," she said. "Joseph tries to help him, but he doesn't want help."

"He's just waiting to die," I said. "Like the rest of us."

"Not me," she said and put her hand on my arm, "I'm happy, Cousin. I have a good job and a new house. And Harry. And the baby." She patted her stomach, still flat beneath her bright yellow blouse.

"Yeah," I said. "We should all be so lucky."

"What have you been doing?" she asked me.

"Sailing," I said. "I live on an island called Defoe."

"With those ladies?" Her eyes sparkled. "Ladies always like

you."

"Them and some other people," I said. "I'd better go find them."

"It was good to see you, Cousin," She said and smiled darkly into my eyes, "Tell your ladies goodbye for me."

I nodded, then looked at Harry. "Sure," he said. "Good to meet you." But his eyes didn't meet mine.

I looked into the deep shadows of the bar to find Lila and Morganne. I could tell by their bowed heads that they were doing a line. My timing was perfect. I slipped my straw from my bag as I slid into the booth. The familiar tingle caressed my sinuses. Even the shadows brightened. Who needed the sun?

"Who was that?" Morganne asked me, "Your cousin?"

"Some sort of cousin," I answered. "Her mother's Uncle Joseph was my grandfather's cousin."

"She's Colville?" Morganne asked.

"Half," I said. "Her father is a White engineer at Grand Coulee."

"She's beautiful," Lila said

"I guess so," I said.

"She's very dark for half," Morganne said.

"We're all dark on the inside," I said.

"Who's this Joseph?" Lila asked. "She talked like he was God or something."

"Whites call him Long Joe." I said. "He's a brush Indian. Some kind of a holy man. A Dreamer. Follows the old ways, some old prophet named Smohalla. I never could get into it."

"You always talk about your grandfather," Morganne said.

"He wasn't like Joseph," I said. "My Grandfather lived in town and had a job. Most of the time. Joseph just sort of drifts around, on a dream."

"Like us," Morganne said.

"No," Lila said. "We don't even have a dream."

"I do," Morganne said. "I want us to keep on living our lives."

"You sure are contented," Lila said. "I didn't know you liked money so much."

"I don't," Morganne said. "But we did the trip for money, so it didn't feel like we were finished until I got mine."

"We still aren't finished," I said.

"Gerard hasn't gotten a dime from the bikers," Lila said. "I knew he wouldn't."

"I don't really care," Morganne said, "It's enough for me. I just keep it in the bottom of my overnight case and take it out sometimes and count it."

"I hope no one else knows that," I said.

"Just you two," Morganne said.

"You've spent some," Lila said. "Like those two-hundred dollar boots."

"Not much," Morganne said. "I haven't even finished that five thousand advance."

"You're a wonder," Lila said.

"How much have you spent?" Morganne asked her.

"About ten grand," Lila said, "but twenty-five hundred was this ounce you've got your nose in."

"I'll pay for my share," Morganne said. "I like being able to pay."

"Never mind," Lila said. "You can buy the next one."

"How about you, Lucky," Morganne asked me with a grin, "do you have any left?"

"I spent all mine," I said, "on whiskey and cheap whores."

"You're worse than Morganne," Lila said. "I never see you spend any money."

"I don't need anything," I said.

"What are you going to do with your money?" Morganne asked. "I can't decide what to do with mine."

"I don't know," I said. "I never thought it would be a problem."

"I'm just afraid I'll lose it," Morganne said.

"You will if you keep it in your overnight case," Lila said. "You need to invest it."

"Like in a bar?" Morganne asked. "I don't want a bar. Or a flower shop or an art gallery. I like to go there, but I don't want to own one."

"Buy gold," Lila said. "Gerard has a lot of gold."

"Jewelry? That's more your style," Morganne said.

"Not jewelry," Lila said, "gold bars. It's up to three hundred dollars an ounce. Gerard says it will double. Or stones, you can make a lot of money on stones."

"If I liked them, I could never sell them," Morganne said.

"I'll buy land," I said. "Some day. I'm not ready yet."

"What kind of land?" Morganne asked.

"Real land," I said. "With everything there still."

"Stehekin?" Morganne asked. "I thought it was all National Forest."

"It's all inside the boundary," I said, "but there are some private pieces scattered around, old mining claims and Indian allotments, a few homesteads."

"I'll buy land there, too," Morganne said. "And some horses. You can teach me to ride."

"You better take a look at it first," I said. "It's a long way from nowhere."

"That sounds nice to me," she said. "I'll buy a whole library full of books."

"My Granny'd love you," I said.

The days crowded one upon another, with no chance to savor them as my Grandfather had taught me to do on the Stehekin. At dawn, when he always had mumbled his song to greet the sun, I would just get to sleep. Still sleepy at noon, it would take a nice, fat line and a joint or two before I felt normal. The others would stir as the day declined and evening became morning, and morning evening.

Except on rare moonlit nights, there was no landscape for our drama; just us, in the electric lights, and the swirl of colors. Between the lighted places, the darkness was without shape. On the sound, as we crossed from the island and back, the clouds and the whales passed us like unseen spirits.

At the end of one line, there always was another. Tied to my waist, a small leather bag, beaded with a Haida seabird, had become my constant companion. In it were a round chunk of mirror, my fine, framed screen and crystal pestle, the tiny filigree spoon Lila had given me and the engraved gold straw from Morganne.

At the heart of it all throbbed an opalescent vial, never more than half empty, of Northern Lights. Deep within those crystals glowed the faint embers of our communal fire. As we huddled there, we were transfixed and made to dream.

Aaron took Maria and Do to Santa Cruz for a week. When they got back, Maria was in much better shape. Her eyes were in contact again. I hadn't realized how beautiful she was. The Santa Cruz sun had cleared her face, enriched the dark coil of her hair. Her nursing breasts were almost too large for her wiry body.

Whenever we were out, she got a lot of attention which still seemed a strange surprise to her. She had begun to play a blue guitar, strum softly and sing so low you could not hear the words. Do was with her everywhere.

Aaron had gone to patch things up with Pete. I don't know if he got the job done. He did run into someone who imported container loads of bold Bolivian pottery and bright rugs and ceremonial weavings. He brought back several pots with almost pure coke still hidden in them. There was just the faintest yellow cast to the crumbled rocks.

Gerard said it wasn't worth his time to clean it up any further, but I paid him to do four ounces for me. I needed the rainbow sparkle of Northern Lights, like winter in the mountains.

Patrick made a high-speed run across the strait from Port Townsend occasionally, to buy some coke or show us some he'd found. He and Pancho were never without at least one young lady apiece.

Patrick's brother had helped him buy stock in the family furniture business without alarming IRS. He showed us pictures of the old Bentley he'd started to restore.

He and Pancho flew down to Colombia to ski for a week. Some of Patrick's ski-racer friends introduced him to some big-time connection. When they got back, he spent hours in the study with Aaron. I didn't hear much of it, but I do know Aaron did not want to deal with Colombians and Patrick said these were different, upper-class Colombians. It began to look to me like before long to do business, you would do it with Colombians.

Lance did not adjust easily to the fact that four Spanish-speaking gentlemen had put guns on him and one of them held him by the nuts while the others searched him and took his leather bag with Aaron's hundred thousand in it. He came and went without warning. He carried a .357 Magnum for a while, then switched to a .380 automatic. He kept a Smith and Wesson "Bodyguard" .38 in his boot for a hole gun. Whenever he did coke, he got very paranoid. We soon hid all the coke whenever he showed up.

No one had seen the Poet for a while. Morganne asked Lance and he said Linda's mother had paid the fee for some fancy drug-treatment program. Morganne said it was probably Esalen, that he'd fit right in there.

Eddie and Suzette came back from the Caribbean sleek and tanned. They got their per diem reimbursements and bought two ounces of Aaron's Bolivian. They spent a lot of time in their room on research. One afternoon they came down very shaken. Philippe Cousteau was dead, the radio said, killed in a helicopter crash or something.

The Cousteaus were all supposed to be at the International Whaling Commission meetings in London that summer to argue for a moratorium on whaling. Eddie condemned Philippe for a daredevil and muttered darkly about sabotage by the Japanese or the Norwegians, maybe even South Africa. We all did a line with them for consolation.

Cree went home to Bella Coola, had Lee fly her up. She took so much stuff to her mother and grandparents that Lee had to make another trip the next day. Before she left, she showed me a cashier's check for a hundred thousand dollars Canadian, payable to her mother.

"Now we're even," she said. "The next one is for me."

The reincarnated Orca struggled from her cocoon in Bellingham. When first I saw the old ship in the repair yard, I thought it was some hulk they'd kept for salvage. Her guts were laid open. Everything was torn off except the masts. The crew quarters, the entire cabin area and pilothouse, even the deck above half the hold, was gone. The hull had been sand blasted and patched and primed in spots. The rusted steel rail lay in a heap to be taken to a plate shop.

Aaron let me look at the drawings in the little job shack on the dock while he talked to the superintendent. There was a color rendering on the wall complete with an orca breaching in the distance.

The paper ship ran full-rigged with crisp white sails. She had been painted glossy black with a low, white half oval just above water near the bow and a larger one near the stern. White eye patches circled the anchor ports. A high, wide cabin ran from the foremast to well past the old pilothouse. Through the large windows of the new wheelhouse they'd drawn a young hunk at the helm with a jaunty sailor's cap, and below him a wooing couple strolled along the near rail.

I couldn't make much sense of the blueprints. They'd been scribbled over and worn away along creases. In a bare spot, someone had doodled a frightened little guy who peered out of a barrel. "Oh no, Massa, not the Orca again!" was printed beneath it.

"Well, they're all in line to get those pay envelopes full of tax-free cash every week," Aaron said when I told him about it. "It's all under the table, so it's a sweet job for everyone."

"Doesn't anyone notice?" I asked him.

"No one cares," he said. "No one can prove anything, anyway. I'll have paperwork that says this overhaul was done in Panama two years ago."

CHAPTER 26

Spring lingered past the first of July. Still the mornings broke cool and foggy. Last winter had been the coldest on record and there was talk again of the return of the ice age. Another group, including Eddie, insisted that the trend would be warmer, hot from the greenhouse effect, although not in our children's lifetimes. They measured in cycles of centuries and eras and aeons. I figured that particular year wouldn't stand out much from the others in the long run.

I hardly left the island unless Aaron wanted me with him. I fished a little with Cree, but I couldn't stand the endless hours waiting. She would put on music and make tea, maybe smoke a little. Always she worked at something, a net or line or lure. Even in bad weather she seemed at home.

"Everyone waits for something," she said. "At least I know what I wait for. Fish. Sooner or later they come."

Lila negotiated her bar deal, spent days on the mainland. Whenever she was gone, Morganne slept with me. As soon as Lila was back, Morganne would visit me, but never stay the night. She couldn't decide if she wanted to go with Lila when she took over her bar the first of September.

"Lynnwood," Morganne would say. "My grandmother told me I would end my days in hell."

Maria slipped silently about the house, endlessly smiled. Warm afternoons she would take Do out on a blanket on the lawn. She would work on one of her quilts or make something beautiful from sticks and shells and bits of string she found here and there.

Sometimes we all gathered around her as if she was our teacher, but even then she seldom spoke. She practiced the guitar for hours whenever Aaron was gone, hummed her soft songs and whispered the lyrics.

Aaron and Gerard set up an artifact and import business called Primal Power. They opened a showroom in an old stone house in Seattle's University District. They hired an archaeology graduate student to run it and got good press coverage. The Bolivian stuff quickly became a fad, especially the Andean Shaman's coca leaf bags with broad shoulder straps and multi-colored tassels. Each bag had wrapped a kilo on the way north, the concentrate from four hundred pounds of coca leaves. Gerard thought that was a great joke.

Aaron came out of his room when he heard the Poet's voice and asked, "How the fuck did he get here? I told Lee not to bring him over here."

"Some pilot from Bellingham," Lila said. "Damn near took out the dock turning around in the cove."

"Hi, boss," the Poet said, "I was just talking to Eddie about this whale concert thing. I think we should do it. We need to pay back for the bad we've done."

"What bad?" Lila asked.

"All the ways we've hurt those around us," he said, "because we didn't take responsibility."

"Speak for yourself," Lila said.

Embrace your disease," the Poet said. "I'm an addict, I'm an addict...."

"Isn't that kind of like sucking on a loaded shotgun?" Lila asked him.

"It's like running around saying, 'I'm a leper, I'm a leper," Morganne said.

"You have to let those around you know you need help," the Poet said. "Deep down, they all love you."

"Oh, God," Lila said. "I should have known."

"Known what?" He was hurt. "That I could take responsibility for my own life?"

"That you couldn't get to the toilet without help," Lila said and went upstairs.

"It's okay, Lila," he called after her. "I don't expect you to be perfect."

"You asshole," Morganne said.

"Stinkin' thinkin'," he said. "Don't blame your problems on those around you."

"We don't have problems when you aren't around," Morganne said.

"Well, I'm glad to see him get it together," Eddie said, looked at the Poet with approval.

"He wouldn't even recognize 'together,'" Morganne said and followed Lila.

"You need to get a handle on this," Eddie said to Aaron, "you can't have your people fighting all the time."

"The problem isn't my crew," Aaron said. "I thought you were going to call if you came over here," he said to the Poet.

"I tried, boss," he said, shrugged. "I guess the phone was out."

"You must have skipped the part of the program on truthfulness," Aaron said.

"Jesus Christ," the Poet said. "I can't do anything right."

"Sometimes I wonder," Aaron said.

"Well, Greener Pastures was good for me. I didn't want to go at first, when Linda and her family did the intervention, but they really understand me." The Poet straightened his back, ran his fingers through newly cropped red hair that stood almost straight up. "I think you should all go. They have a cut rate for groups. They said one whole Real Estate office came and stayed three weeks."

"Sounds like a good time," Aaron said. "Now Eddie and I have business to talk about."

"No wonder I have no sense of self worth," the Poet said.

"Let him stay," Eddie said. "I'll vouch for him."

"As long as we're clear about that," Aaron said.

"Well, how about Lucky?" the Poet asked. "You always let him stay."

"He's my shadow." Aaron laughed. "I don't even notice he's here." He shook me gently by the shoulder. "But I'd sure notice if he wasn't."

Morganne passed the joint to me and the coal fell off onto my sleeping bag, burned a tiny hole before I could brush it off.

"Sorry," she said. "I'll buy you a new one. I need to spend some of my money."

"No thanks," I said. "I've got too long a history with this one."

"Do you ever get anything new?" she asked me.

"Not if I can help it," I said.

"What were Aaron and Eddie talking about half the night?" she asked, took the joint back.

"A concert," I said, "at the Kingdome."

"What kind of concert?"

"Some big deal to raise money for whales," I said. "They call it 'Operation Crosstalk.'"

"Sounds like a military campaign," she said.

"They're going to build a research center on Skagit Bay," I said. "Where that old shake mill is."

"And Eddie's going to run it and make a lot of money and be a famous scientist," she said. "So much for the poor whales."

"They claim they can talk to them," I said. "Some guy named John C. Lilly is supposed to be able to talk to dolphins."

"I heard about that," Morganne said. "But it isn't like talking, it's more like guessing."

"I don't care," I said. "I don't think we need to talk to whales. They can talk to us whenever they want to."

"You mean the dreams?" She looked out across the sound. "I haven't had one for weeks. I miss them."

"They'll be back," I said. "They aren't through with us." I thought of my great black and white friend. "They are very persistent."

"Maria still has the dreams," Morganne said. "I'm always

jealous when she talks about it."

"Maria is different from the rest of us," I said.

"She says the Guardians are still here," Morganne said. "I don't know what to think. Aaron just humors her."

"I don't know if they're real," I said, "but sometimes I see lights, in the corner of my eye, but when I look they're gone."

"Gerard says it's just hallucinations," Morganne said.

"He thinks the whole world is just hallucinations," I said. "He seems to know a lot about the subject. Is Lila staying with him again?"

"Yeah," she said, "He's helping her negotiate on the bar. But he's tried to get in her pants for a long time."

"I remember him at the Club," I said, "with his tongue hanging out."

"She thinks he can get her a better deal," Morganne said, "but I don't trust him."

The tape on my little portable came to an end and I turned it over. "If it's problems that you're running from, there is no hiding place..." it began.

"Peter Tosh," Morganne said. "Why do you listen to that tape so much? I never hear you play anything else."

"It just got in my head and I can't get it out," I said.

"I think it's kind of morbid," she said, "all about dead prophets and wicked people. I like the Doobie Brothers."

"He has a lot to say," I said. "If you know how to listen."

"I'll have to listen, sometime," she said. "But I'd rather make love again right now." She kissed me, dropped the joint in my lap.

"Watch out," I said, saved my tender parts. "One thing at a time."

"Let me get rid of this in that case," she said, tossed the joint into an ashtray.

"No thanks," Eddie said, grandly waved off the mirror. "We don't use cocaine any more."

"More for me," Lila said, took another hit off the line.

"Why not?" Morganne asked him. "What's wrong with cocaine?"

"It's illegal," Suzette said. "He has his academic career to think about."

"It's not really that," Eddie said. "It messes up your head. I didn't realize it until I saw how much the Poet changed when he stopped. It was like a miracle."

"Will wonders never cease?" Lila said.

"None of you give him a chance," Eddie said. "He's very intelligent."

"He hides it well," Lila said.

"And sensitive," Suzette said. "Have you ever heard his poetry?" she asked me.

"I'm not into poetry that much," I said. "I like my own way of seeing things."

"He really understands people," Suzette said, "especially women."

"Right," Lila said, "I always confide in him."

"You're just prejudiced," Eddie said.

"Against moronic assholes?" Lila asked. "You bet."

"How's your deal on the bar, Lila," Suzette asked.

"Fine," Lila said. "I take over the end of September. Gerard got me a really good deal."

"Gerard?" Suzette was surprised. "I thought you and Gerard didn't get along."

"He's not that bad," Lila said. "When you get to know him."

"In the biblical sense, she means," Morganne said.

"Is that all any of you ever think about?" Eddie asked her. "There is more to life than drugs and sex and rock-and-roll."

"You mean money?" Lila asked him.

Eddie glared at her. "No, I mean important work."

"Like the 'research' you and Suzette do with a quarter ounce and those old Crosby, Stills and Nash eight-track tapes?"

"We don't do that anymore," Eddie said. "When you're involved in a crusade, your personal needs come second."

"And third and fourth and fifth," Lila said.

"Well, at least we don't own some funky bar where you charge men to look at teats," he said and Suzette nodded.

"You used to spend plenty of time looking at teats," Lila said, "when you hung around the Club."

"I didn't know you hung around the Club," Suzette said to him.

"I just went there a couple of times to meet Aaron," Eddie said, waved it off. "I didn't even like the place. I paid for a few table dances just to fit in."

"It didn't work," Lila said.

"Are we here to talk business or bullshit?" Aaron asked him. "Lee will be here in less than an hour to take me to Bellingham."

"The problem is," Eddie said, "is the producer Tim hired to do the concert isn't getting it done. Looks to me like we'll lose another year. By then, there may not be any whales to save."

"What do you think I can do?" Aaron asked him.

"You have connections in the music business," Eddie said. "I know the Brotherhood used to do festivals. I thought maybe you could get it moving again."

"I don't know what the Brotherhood did and I'm no producer," Aaron said, "I just know some people. Actually, Lila knows as many musicians as I do, maybe more."

"This producer, Wilkie Thomas, he's telling Tim he's just too busy to get it together this summer." Eddie said. "I thought maybe we could get something going ourselves, at least scare him into moving."

"I know that name," Lila said. "Wilkie Thomas. I just can't remember why."

"He's a big producer," Eddie said. "Does lots of benefits."

"How long has he been working on it?" Aaron asked.

"Two years," Eddie said. "The thing is, he's spent a bunch of money. He put together a book and a poster and a lot of other stuff. He says that everything has to be right if we're going to make a million dollars or more."

"A million dollars!" Lila said. "This whale business is as good as drugs."

"A little different moral plane," Eddie said. "And we need a lot of money to establish the Cetacean Link. With the whales' knowledge and our knowledge we may be able to save the planet."

"How did it ever survive until you got here?" Lila asked.

"It's no joke. The truth is," Eddie said. "Is the planet is in trouble. It may not survive another fifty years."

"Then what?" Lila asked him. "It just goes poof, vaporizes or something, like Star Trek?"

"The ecological systems," Eddie said. "As the planet warms, the weather will be very erratic, huge storms, floods and droughts."

"And cancer," Suzette said. "All the poison we're putting in the air will give us all cancer."

"And the whales are going to save us?" Lila asked. "Why should they? We just kill them. They'd be glad if we were gone."

"Not just the whales," Eddie said. "Us with the whales. Once we can talk to them, they will be able to give us great knowledge of the planet, from long before we were here."

"How do you know they have all this knowledge?" Lila asked.

"It stands to reason," Eddie said. "They have such large brains and we know they communicate with each other."

"Cows communicate with each other," Lila said.

"I'll give you an example," Eddie said. "Why don't orcas kill people? They could easily do it and they have lots of opportunity right here in the sound. Yet there has never been a report of an orca killing a human. Even if they or their young are being attacked, they just swim away."

"If someone was after me with a machine gun or a harpoon I'd run like hell too," Lila said. "Does that make me a genius? A cow would run away too."

"You don't understand," Eddie said.

"You got it," Lila said. "I don't think you're trying to help whales or people or anyone but yourself."

"All behavior is selfish," Eddie said. "Altruism is an illusion."

"So Mother Theresa is just a selfish old broad who gets her kicks watching poor people die?" Lila asked him.

"Self deception," Eddie said. "We deceive ourselves into believing we are unselfish because this helps us convince others that they can trust us."

"So who is she fooling?" Lila asked, "I mean other than herself?"

"Maybe she has a more enlightened sense of self interest," Eddie said.

"I think we just went in a circle," Lila said.

"Natural selection has favored the evolution of self deception," Eddie said in a slow, methodical manner. "We instinctively believe that we are unselfish because that serves our self interests."

"Now I am dizzy," Lila said. "So what we call morality, you call selfishness. If we redefine all the words, then nothing is what we thought it was. I see why you need whales to explain it to you."

"You need to get an education Lila," he said, "so you can understand things like this."

"You need to get some common sense," she retorted. "Then maybe you could understand me."

"This sounds like Biology 101," Morganne said. "How about the concert?"

"I don't know what we could do," Aaron said.

"Would you make some calls?" Eddie said. "See if the bands agreed to do it. Thomas doesn't have any contracts, says he's so big time they all trust him on a handshake, but I'd like to know for sure."

"So who's supposed to play the gig?" Lila asked him.

"Just about everyone," Eddie said. "Santana, the Youngbloods, Joan Baez, C-S-N-Y, Bachman-Turner, Heart, Taj Mahal."

"We could get hold of some of them," Lila said, "Or at least their managers. I know Taj's road manager."

"Just find out if they are going to play," Eddie said.

"You know I would only do this for selfish reasons," Lila said.

Eddie looked at her. "I can't pay you," he said. "All my money's in PREDATOR."

"So why should I do it?" Lila asked him. "I wouldn't want to violate your biological laws."

"You should do it," Eddie said, "because it could help make a better world for your great-grandchildren."

"So it's selfish to care about my great-grandchildren," Lila said. "I'm beginning to understand this stuff."

CHAPTER 27

"No one has ever heard of Operation Crosstalk," Lila said. "I think it's Operation Doubletalk."

"Who all have you talked to?" Aaron asked.

"Taj's road manager," she said, "and an old friend of mine works in Bill Graham's office. They manage Santana and a bunch of others. She never heard of it. And remember Josie, down in the Santa Cruz Mountains? She knows a guy from Palo Alto who just built some cabinets for Joan Baez. She had him call Joan, and she never heard of it."

"I talked to Heart's sound man," Aaron said. "They hadn't heard of it either. Did you ask them about Wilkie Thomas?"

"Oh yeah, everyone knows him," Lila said. "He's the guy who ripped-off all the money from the Concerts for Mozambique or whatever they called them. Remember? George Harrison and a bunch of people played them, but no money actually went to the people."

"I remember," Aaron said. "So Tim got ripped-off?"

"For two-hundred-thousand bucks. That's what Eddie said Tim gave this guy." Lila tapped her finger on the side of her head. "For publicity?"

"Yeah," Aaron said, "that poster Eddie showed us and a book about whales, and you saw the business cards and mugs. There's a T-shirt."

"Tim paid for all that shit?"

"Thomas told him it had to be done professionally. And he's the big Hollywood promoter, he should know."

Lila shrugged. "Par for the course in the business now, I hear."

"I wonder if Tim knows his history?" Aaron asked.

"I don't know," Lila said. "But I'm sure Eddie didn't, so probably not. They're just hicks from the sticks. You going to tell Eddie?"

"I guess I'll have to," Aaron said.

"Serves the arrogant bastard right," Lila said. "We'll see how this fits his biological laws. I guess he isn't the great predator after all."

"If we tell them," Aaron said, "it wouldn't hurt our position with Tim."

"What do we need him for? He's just some rich geek." Lila said.

"If he's in this whale thing," Aaron said, "it can't hurt us. We have to think like business people, now."

"Yuck," Lila said.

"Tim won't believe it," Eddie said. "I'm not sure I do."

"Check it out," Aaron said. "It makes no difference to me."

"Why would he do it?" Eddie asked. "He could make more money doing the concert."

"No one would play a concert for him, not with his reputation," Aaron said. "He's just living on the advance money. That crap he put out didn't cost two hundred grand."

"It's nice stuff," Eddie said. "Looks expensive to me."

"Just another illusion," Aaron said.

"Will you go with me to tell him?" Eddie asked. "I don't really know all the details. I'm sure he would appreciate the help."

"I don't know," Aaron said. "Half the time the messenger gets blamed for the bad news."

"Not Tim," Eddie said. "He's very fair. If you're straight with him."

"This isn't my deal," Aaron said. "I don't want to get in the middle of it."

"But if it happens," Eddie said, "and we get the Orca Center built, think of how many charter customers there'd be. And you'd have the inside track."

"I'll think about it," Aaron said.

"What if it falls on us?" Morganne asked, scanned the sky through the window.

"Then we won't have to worry about it," I said.

"If what falls on us?" Lila asked as she came in from the kitchen with tea for us.

"Skylab," Morganne said. "It's supposed to come down somewhere any minute the radio said."

"You mean, just fall out of the sky?" Lila asked.

"They got the orbit wrong," I said. "So now it's coming down. They just don't know when or where."

"Great! So how big is this thing?" Lila asked.

"The size of a bus," I said, "but going a few thousand miles an hour."

"Wonderful," Lila said.

"It might make some good fireworks," I said. "They think most of it will burn up on the way down."

"We should go sit on the lawn and watch for it," Morganne said. "If it's going to hit us, I'd rather see it coming."

"Maria's out there," Lila said, "Waiting for Aaron. He should have been back by now."

"Let's go out and have a toot and see if we can see it," Morganne said.

"I like the toot part," Lila said. "You got any for sale, Lucky?" she asked me.

"Does the bear shit in the woods?" I asked her.

"I never saw a bear shit." Lila said, "but I'll take your word for it."

Maria nursed Do, so Lila held the mirror for her while she took a hit. It was almost nine, but still there was a lot of daylight. The small waves off the sound slapped a staccato cipher against the dock pilings.

"I hear an airplane," Morganne said.

"I know," Maria said, "but it isn't him."

"How do you know?" Lila asked her.

"The Guardians," Maria said. "They're brighter. That's what happens when they don't like someone."

Lila rolled her eyes at me over Maria's head. "It is too him," she said. "Look, it's coming in here."

"It isn't Aaron," Maria said. She gathered Do's stuff and headed for the house.

It was Lee's plane. He made the usual tight circle to the end of the dock.

"I guess the Guardians blew it, this time," Lila said.

"Don't count on it," Morganne said.

The airplane door opened and it was the Poet. He yelled something at Lee, pulled a bag out of the back, fumbled the door shut and jumped to the dock. Lee gunned it and was gone.

"What are you doing here?" Lila asked him as he came across the lawn towards us.

"Where's Aaron?" he asked.

"Gone," Lila said.

"I'm supposed to meet him and Eddie here," he said. "They called me from the meeting with Tim. Aaron is going to produce the whale concert and I'm his assistant."

"I don't believe it," Lila said.

"Well, this time you're full of shit," the Poet said.

Morganne chopped a line on my mirror, took a hit, handed it to me. I did my share and passed it to Lila. She finished the line, wiped the mirror with her finger and licked it.

"You still use that garbage?" the Poet asked.

"It's not our fault you can't handle it," Lila said. "It's for adults only."

"There's nothing wrong with knowing your inner child," the Poet said. "It's a sign of maturity."

"Whatever it is, I don't want any," Lila said.

"Is that Northern Lights?" The Poet asked me.

"What else?" I said.

"I never did like that shit," he said.

"No one offered you any," Lila said.

"Would you cut me a little line," he asked me. "Just so I can prove to myself I can handle it."

"Cocaine costs money," I said.

"Here's a twenty," he said. "That should pay for a line."

"Just about," I said. I cut a small line, handed him the mirror.

"I don't have a straw," he said helplessly.

I handed back the twenty and he rolled it, snorted up the line, stuck the bill in his pocket.

"I thought you didn't do cocaine," Lila said.

"I'm just proving I can handle it," he said. "I'm much stronger now, I deserve a little celebration. But don't tell Eddie, he might not understand."

"So he's your mama now?" Lila said.

"You never give me any slack," the Poet said. "Who made you Mother Superior?"

"It comes naturally," Morganne said.

"Why are you all out here?" The Poet asked. "Waiting for Aaron?"

"No," Morganne said. "Waiting to die."

"You're fucking weird," he said.

"I'm serious," she said. "Skylab will fall on us."

"What the fuck are you talking about?" The Poet's voice quavered and he wiped his forehead.

"Skylab's coming down tonight," Morganne said. "May as well be on us."

"Fuck Skylab," the Poet said. He stood up and stretched, paced around with his hands behind his neck.

"You going to make it?" Lila asked him.

"I'm fine," he said. "Just thinking."

"Seems to be quite a strain," Lila said.

"Where the hell is Aaron?" he said, dropped heavily to the ground.

"He may not even come back tonight," Morganne said. "It's pretty late."

"He has to," the Poet said. "We were supposed to talk about the concert." He ran his hands through his hair, left it standing askew.

"If he does come tonight," Lila said, "He'll want to see Maria, not you."

"This is important business," the Poet said. "Eddie says we can do these concerts all over the country, maybe a hundred of them. We'd all be rich."

"I thought this was for the whales," Lila said.

"It is," he said, "but Eddie says we should all be paid well, that's how natural selection works."

Morganne searched the sky for the hundredth time. "I wonder when it will come down," she said. "The moon is so bright I can hardly see anything." She looked at Lila. "Let's all sleep out here. If I'm going to die, I'd rather be outside."

"We're not going to die," Lila said, "but it would be a nice night to sleep out. I haven't done that since I was a kid. Not intentionally."

"I'll go get some blankets and stuff," Morganne said. "You want your sleeping bag?" she asked me.

"Sure," I said.

"I want another line," the Poet said. "It always takes too much of this weak shit."

"You didn't pay for the last one," I answered. "But a line is a good idea." I poured a little onto my mirror, shaped a line.

"Here he said," handed me a fifty.

I let him do the line, wiped the mirror with my sleeve when he was finished.

"I'm not contagious," he said.

"Can't be too careful," I said, poured a line for Lila and me.

Morganne came into view, dragged a bundle on the grass behind her. She sat down beside me, patted her chest as she breathed rapidly.

"You should have told me you were bringing everything you own," I said. "I would have helped."

"Aaron won't be back tonight," she said when she caught her breath. "He called Maria."

"Maria's here?" the Poet asked. He squatted, rocked on his heels, poked at the grass with a small stick.

"No, they took her to the meeting," Lila said.

"I haven't seen her in a while," he said. "I'll go say hello."

"Leave her alone," Lila said. "She doesn't need any of your weird trips."

"I'll see if Aaron gave her a message for me," the Poet said.

"If he had, I'd know about it," Morganne said.

"Not anymore," he said. "I'm the Assistant Producer."

"Producer of bullshit," Lila said.

"I'm going up to the house," he said.

Morganne was all over me. "If I die," she said, "I don't want to die horny."

"I'm afraid you're stuck with that, dear," Lila said. "But if you two are going to get nasty, I'm going in." She wrapped her blanket around her shoulders. "Have fun."

"We can share," Morganne said. "Lucky's a big boy."

"No thanks," Lila said, started for the house.

"More for me," Morganne said.

The moon hung low in the west, it's light dimmed. A cool breeze penetrated the sleeping bag and we shivered.

"Let's do another line," Morganne said. "It will warm us up."

I held the mirror in my palm while she took her line, then I scattered another small pile onto it. The pure drug came alive, refracted starlight. As I took my share, I noticed the sky in the mirror, the stars like more distant crystals that I couldn't quite reach.

I saw the Great Bear, the constellation called the Big Dipper by the unimaginative English. My grandfather had told me that Natives along the coast called it The Whale and saw a powerful fluked tail where we imagined the head and neck of a bear.

"Both are there," he had told me. "The difference is the point of view."

Cree would say it was a Great Wigit.

"Are you asleep?" Morganne asked me.

"No," I said. "Just dreaming."

"I know what you mean," she said.

"Look in the mirror," I said. "You can see the sky."

She moved her head close. "It's beautiful," she said.

"How about Skylab?" I teased her.

"It missed us, this time," she said. "Maria said the Guardians would never let it fall here." She dropped her head into my lap, was still.

I held up the mirror, saw in it the orange flare of the refinery at Anacortes, and far to the northeast the faint lights of Bellingham. I moved it and saw light in the west, a glow above the trees at the top of the slope. Victoria I thought, but as I turned further, looked towards the south, the vegetation was lit as though some bright city lay in that direction, not the dark, empty strait I knew was there.

I turned to look directly, see better, and the light was gone. Again I held up the mirror and the glow was there, sparkled along the branches and dripped from the leaves.

I covered the mirror with my hand and looked closely at the trees along the south edge of the lawn. They looked as they always did, barely visible in the pale moonlight. But in the mirror, as I looked again, they had grown brighter, sharp golden flames against dark water.

I nudged Morganne and she sat up. I held the mirror at the right angle and pointed to it.

The glow lit her face as she stared into it. "Maria was right," she said. "We just didn't know how to see them."

"It wasn't your fucking business," the Poet said. "You're not her chaperone."

"Aaron said to keep an eye on her," Lila said. "So I did."

"She was hot for it," he said. "You're just jealous."

"Aaron will cut your balls off," Lila said.

"He's always fucking someone," the Poet said. "Why shouldn't Maria? He's just afraid she'll like someone else better."

"He doesn't have to worry about that," Lila said."

"What's going on?" Morganne asked, dropped her rolled up blankets on the floor."

"When I came in last night," Lila said, "this asshole was trying to put the big move on Maria. Had his clothes off, trying to talk her into giving him a back rub."

"Nudity is healthy," the Poet said. "Eddie says clothes are just part of our self-deception."

"No one wants to see your fat ass nude," Lila said.

"Maria seemed to like it," he said. "She couldn't keep her eyes off me."

"Probably couldn't believe what she saw," Lila said. "You need to go home to your wife, maybe she'll lay you."

"Lots of women like me," he said. "Poets are good lovers."

"Spare me," Lila said. "Especially the details."

"I lived with Logan Johnson," he said proudly, "the greatest love poet of the century. I didn't just study under him, I lived with him. He called me the 'heir apparent.'"

"So, I suppose you sucked his dick," Lila said.

"Just to see what it was all about. We all...." the Poet stopped.

Lila cackled. "Queers always follow men like Aaron around," she said.

What must have been fury glared from his pale eyes. "Bitch," he said. "Everybody knows you and Morganne do it. When you're not laying someone else."

"Girls get to do it," Lila said, "it's sweet. But guys, ugh, disgusting. Especially fat guys."

He sucked in his stomach. "I'm not fat," he said. "Linda likes my love handles."

"We all have fetishes," she said. "You should see Fat Fanny pack them in at the Club."

In the noon sun, the trees south of the lawn seemed perfectly normal. I surreptitiously looked at them in my mirror.

"What are you doing?" Lila asked.

"Just checking my rear view mirror," I said.

"We saw them," Morganne said. "The Guardians. In the mirror."

"You can see most anything in a mirror," Lila said, "if it has enough coke on it."

"It wasn't a hallucination," Morganne said. "Lucky saw it."

I shrugged.

"Well, did you?" Lila pressed me.

"I saw something," I said, "or the reflection of something."

"Of what?" She looked from me to Morganne and back.

"Some kind of light, on the trees," I said.

"It was probably sunrise," she said. "I'm sure you two screwed all night."

"It was not sunrise," Morganne said. "We could only see it in the mirror."

"Whatever it was, I want some," Lila said.

"How's Maria?" Morganne asked her.

"Okay," Lila said, "I guess. I never know. She acts normal, that's all I hope for."

"Where's the Poet?" I asked her.

"Passed out on the floor in the living room," Lila said. "I made sure he was out of circulation before I came out."

I could hear the Wigit from around the point at the mouth of the cove. Cree had been gone for several days and I missed her. I stood up and started towards the dock.

"Where are you off to?" Lila asked.

"To see Cree," I said.

"Cree isn't here," Lila said. "You are seeing things."

"I'll just go check," I said.

"I believe you," Morganne said, jumped up to join me.

"Well, I'll be here when you two are through hallucinating," Lila said. I could see the Wigit's dark nose poke around the point.

"Hey, look, Lila," Morganne said. "It's Cree. And Aaron's with her."

Cree flashed me that great smile and tossed me the bow line. I wrapped it double and tied it. She nudged into reverse, the boat swung towards the dock and Aaron jumped the gap with the stern line, fastened it.

"Lee's gone up north for three days," he said. "But I ran into Cree in LaConner. She has great timing."

Cree smiled again, stepped to the dock. "Believe it or not, I missed all of you," she said.

"Even the Poet," Lila asked her as she came along the dock.

"I thought he was gone," Cree said.

"He's asleep up at the house - right now," Lila said.

"Why?" Aaron asked her.

"He said you wanted him here for a meeting," Morganne said. "He says he's your assistant."

"Not mine," Aaron said.

"We could use him for bait," Lila said, "troll for orcas."

"When did he get here?" Aaron asked.

"Yesterday," Lila said, "about sunset."

"He did a bunch of coke last night," I said.

"So much for sobriety," Aaron said. "That'll finish him with Eddie."

"He begged us not to tell," Lila said. "Like Eddie was his mama or something."

"Pretty close," Aaron said.

Maria had slipped up behind us with Do in her arms. She leaned against Aaron and he silently put his arm around her.

"The Guardians knew you were gone," she said. "They were here all night long." No one had a clever comment or a disdainful look.

CHAPTER 28

Businesslike brick columns broke the floor in a square/diamond pattern that reminded me of an orchard. Whichever way you looked, they receded in rows into the far corners of the empty warehouse. Afternoon light fell through arched windows like those in the old schoolhouses built in all the small towns during the thirties. The floor was planked with old growth fir, it's dense grain hard as iron.

"It's great." The Poet hopped like a bird. "Perfect. And the Kingdome's just across the parking lot." He slid up the heavy window, leaned out, blinked at the bright sunshine.

"We could get by with one corner of this," I said.

"We'll need chairs, and desks and tables," Eddie said.

"Where's the bathroom?" Lila asked.

The lawyer pointed to a far door. "Down the back stairs," he said. "There's just one, no men's and women's."

"We always share," Lila said and he stared at her, fiddled with his tie.

"Lila's our joker," Eddie said.

"Tell Tim this will be fine," Aaron said. "Provided we can get a little furniture."

"We have a whole warehouse full of furniture downstairs," the lawyer said. "Out of the old buildings we've done. Tim won't let anyone throw it away, so we have it stacked to the ceiling down there. Use whatever you want, it's just a damned fire hazard. I'll get Eddie a key."

"I can get some people to move it," Aaron said. "They'll work cheap."

The lawyer looked closely at Aaron. "Tim wants to pay for everything," he said. "This is entirely his show."

"We're just here to help," Aaron said.

"Right, so what else do you need?" The lawyer asked Eddie.

"Food," Eddie said. "We'll need to eat."

The lawyer looked around at us. "What do they eat?" he asked Eddie.

"Mexican," I said. Eddie gave me a sharp look.

"No Mexican on this end of town," the lawyer said. "Chinese? Some of it's hot."

"I don't care for Chinese," Eddie said.

"There's a hippy place that Tim likes," the lawyer said. "Two blocks up, in the basement of the Pioneer Building. It's called Underground Picnic. I'll stop by and tell them to run you a tab."

"Does it have a bakery?" Eddie asked.

"I don't know," the lawyer said, "Check it out."

"How can we get this shit upstairs?" Lila asked, "without an elevator?"

"I'll make a couple of calls," Aaron said, "Get some hands up here."

"We can't waste Tim's money that way," Eddie said. "We have strong backs."

"Do you know how heavy this is?" Lila slumped on a gigantic burgundy striped overstuffed sofa that must have come from some ornate lobby.

I sat on a solid oak desk and waited for them to settle it. I tugged one of the brass pulls and a drawer rolled smoothly out, stopped silently. I gave a tiny push with a fingertip and it closed. I heard a faint snick as the catch engaged. The top of the desk was just two planks, joined so perfectly it took me a couple of minutes to find the discontinuity in the grain.

Eddie tried to lift a smaller desk. It didn't budge. He strained again and his face reddened. Aaron lifted the other end, waited.

"How about a little help?" Eddie snapped at me.

"Here, I'll help, boss," the Poet said, stopped admiring himself in a gold framed mirror that leaned against the wall.

He and Eddie each took a corner, got it off the floor, inched it forwards. Aaron set his end down and progress stopped. I moved over beside him, reached down with him and we lifted our end. Eddie and the Poet still couldn't find the handle. They looked up at us.

"You've got the easy end," the Poet said to me.

We set our end down.

"Come on," Eddie said. "On three."

He counted, nearly fell as we all lifted it until the top was shoulder height.

"Which way, boss," the Poet asked.

"Onward and upward," Aaron said. We moved forward, nearly tipped them over.

"Hey," the Poet said. "Take it easy."

"I thought we were going somewhere," I said.

"I can't walk backwards with this," Eddie said. Perspiration gathered on his forehead.

"Turn around," Aaron said.

"I can't," the Poet said. "Not unless we put it down."

Aaron held his corner with one hand and his knee, switched his grip and turned. I followed suit. We started again.

"Not so fast," the Poet said. Eddie grunted agreement.

We half-stepped to the stairs, Lila held the door and we struggled through, started to climb. The Poet fell to one knee against the steps and I saw him wince in pain. I ignored it.

We had to put it down on the first floor landing and let them breathe for a while. At the top, they both sat on the desk and gasped. Aaron winked at me. The desk looked like a matchbox in the cavernous space.

"I forgot," Eddie said when he'd caught his breath. "I'm supposed to meet with Tim. And some big contributors." His collar was wet and large patches under his arms dripped. He put on his suit jacket, looked in the pockets for his tie. "You think you could get some people to move that stuff?" he asked Aaron.

"No problem," Aaron said.

Eddie left and we decided to check out Underground Picnic, make the calls from there. As we walked along First Avenue the Poet suddenly remembered something he had to do.

"Go for it," Aaron said.

Underground Picnic was a flight and a half down from the street. Like the lawyer said, it was a hippy place, full of ferns and fresh food. When he heard that we were the group from the whale concert, the manager, a wiry little Jewish guy who looked at us out of a great bush of hair and beard, shook hands all around.

"I didn't expect freaks," he said. "Not many freaks doing concerts any more. Mostly suits, now."

Aaron made several calls from a pay phone hidden in an old wash tub that hung on the wall. He came back to the table. "Plenty of help," he said. "Tomorrow morning at ten."

I remembered several of them from the party on Defoe. Suras was there and Akbar, the filmmaker I'd talked to. They each brought several friends. Patrick and Pancho were in town and heard about it somehow, showed up in the Range Rover with a couple of hefty looking hippies. We'd stayed overnight with Gerard who swore a bunch of bikers would show up and carry the day but they never did. Lance did show up, the first time we'd seen him in a while. He didn't have much to say. At the last minute, Fuzzy Crook wandered in with a couple of his part-time roadies.

Altogether, more than a dozen semi-able bodies milled about or leaned against the brick columns. Marijuana smoke drifted in from a far corner and there was much sniffling and passing around of inhalers. Eddie had stayed away, another important meeting, but he sent Suzette to watch over us.

Aaron put Lila by a window for a lookout. "Anything with a

suit on," he told her, "or a uniform."

"I'll just give the old vice-squad whistle," she said. They both grinned at some memory.

Even with considerable avoidance of honest labor and time spent on the ingestion of a variety of substances, it took less than three hours to move up four times as much furniture as we were likely to use.

We set up extravagant artists' waiting areas and separated off the "executive suite" with painted silk screens. Aaron gave me a space next to his and I found one dusty old screen with five panels, like a comic book, about a man who meets and learns to ride a dragon. I held it out a window to shake off the dust and used it to fence my area.

When we were finished, Lila passed out half-gram bindles to all the workers. The Poet asked for his and she said, "I thought you were an executive. Executives provide their own."

Miller Richards showed up just before everyone left. He brought some skinny little friend in an old Nehru jacket who hung around Lila to see if she would give him a bindle. She didn't.

About half of us went to McRory's for Margaritas and it was late afternoon before Aaron and Lila and I piled into the old BMW and flew north on I-5. We stopped at the Arco station at Smoky Point to call the island. Morganne answered, said Maria was doing fine. Cree was there and offered to pick us up in LaConner.

Eddie and Suzette and the Poet caught up at the dock and rode across with us. It was a fine evening, a golden glow gathered in the west and a mild breeze skipped over the low waves towards the shore. The others hung around the fantail; I sat on the wooden seat across from Cree's place at the wheel.

"Hot time in the old town?" she asked me.

"Hot enough," I said. "Many strange and wonderful beasts prowl the streets of the city."

"Must be the Season of the Witch," she chuckled.

"How's Maria?" I asked her. "She still see angels with fiery swords?"

"Devas," Cree said softly. "In India they're called Devas. Like guardian angels. I've heard about them, but I saw them only once before. I was a little girl and I was lost."

"You think it's real?" I asked her. "The Guardians?"

"As real as anything," she said.

"I saw them," I said. "In my mirror."

"Anyone who needs to can see them," she said. "Without a mirror."

"Orcas," Eddie yelled. "Cree, cut the engine."

She idled back, let the Wigit drift. There was a splash but it was towards the sun and I could see nothing. Cree switched off the diesel and the silence leapt up around us. The boat turned broadside to the small waves. I stepped out from under the canvas to see better.

Just off the angle of the low sun, about fifty feet out, the water boiled, flecks of bright foam swirled. There was a noise like the air being blown out of a firehose as a great bulk curved out of the water. A very unpleasant and alien smell wafted over us. Just then I felt a bump on the other side of the boat. It bumped again, moved the Wigit.

"Oh, Jesus," the Poet said.

"Quiet," Eddie said. "They won't hurt us."

The bump came again followed by a long scrape. I looked off that side but the shadow of the boat obscured whatever was below. I turned to look at the orca already on the surface and for a moment the sun glared red from its eye. I looked for the familiar markings of my dream whale, but I could not be sure. The blowhole quivered and I heard the great inrush of air. It winked, closed and the orca sank two feet or more, tilted and it's great tail tore free of the water, hovered, then slipped, with almost no sound, beneath the black surface. Waves lapped the rim of the sun and it, too, sank from our sight.

"It was an omen," the Poet said. "A good omen."

"Or a warning," Lila said.

"Or a pod of orca's that got curious about us," Eddie said.

"The thing is, the world isn't symbolic."

"No," Lila said, "It's metaphorical and that's too subtle for you."

"The Guardians sent them," Maria said. "They work together."

Suzette exhaled in exasperation. "Can we agree not to talk about these Guardians?" she asked, then giggled. "They make me crazy."

Aaron took Do from Maria, pulled her to her feet, said, "We're going upstairs."

I slipped out the side door and down the narrow steps, sat at the bottom and took a strong pull on my inhaler. The moon was not yet up and there was no light. I felt my way around to the front of the house.

Cree spoke my name out of the darkness, guided me. I sat next to her. "Look at them," she said, swept her hand to indicate the circle of trees.

As I gazed at them the fire rose, flowed along the branches and flamed from their tips. Veins in the leaves stood in stark silhouette. We were ringed in a fiery palisade, flame within flame, row on row, pulsing like the aurora.

Lights on the distant mainland blinked through the golden apparition. The ferry to Lopez appeared, it's brightly lit deck half full of vehicles. It passed a couple of hundred yards off shore, every detail visible behind the ripples of light.

"I wonder if they can see it?" I asked Cree, "From the ferry?"

"No," she said. "They never see beyond their little circle of electric light."

The front door of the house opened softly, Morganne found her way down the steps.

"Over here," I whispered and it startled her.

"What are you guys doing?" she asked when she found us.

"Watching the light show," I said, pointed to the trees.

"What? The ferry?" She looked from one side to the other.

"Stay still," Cree said. "Just watch."

"I don't see anything," Morganne said. She seemed sincere. She laid her head on my shoulder, was silent for a few minutes.

"I see them," she said in surprise. "Whenever I'm not looking. I turn and they're gone." She moved her head back and forth quickly several times. "There." She stopped, stared hard.

It was so bright I was surprised the Coast Guard hadn't showed up. Morganne leaned forward intently and I could see the light from the trees reflected in gold rings in her eyes.

"I didn't really believe it," she said. "Not even when we saw them in the mirror. Even Lila could see this."

"Go get her," I said. "We'll make her see it."

Morganne crept across the lawn and up the steps as though she might scare them away. She was back with Lila in a few minutes.

"I was watching Johnny Carson," Lila said. "Jimmy Buffet was on. This better be good."

"Just watch the trees and don't think about anything," Morganne said.

"With as much coke as I've done tonight," Lila said, "that would be a trick."

"Try," Morganne said. "They are really beautiful."

"Probably UFOs," Lila said, "come to kidnap us."

"Ssshh," Morganne said, put her hand over Lila's mouth.

After a few minutes, Lila sat up. "No," she said. "It's just my imagination."

"What did you imagine?" Cree asked her.

"Light," Lila said. "Some kind of sparkly light on the trees. But it wasn't real."

"Did it go away?" Cree asked her.

"No," Lila said, "Not if I try to see it."

"Look hard," Morganne said. "But relax your eyes."

"It really is wonderful," Lila said in a while. "Do you suppose we just put it in each other's minds? Or maybe Maria puts it in all our minds like the Poet says she does with the dreams."

"Maria just sees more than we do," Cree said.

"It could get boring, after a while," Lila said. "Lucky, do you have a toot?"

I handed her my inhaler. "My Granny would say it was God,"

I said. "Speaking with fiery tongues."

"I don't hear anything," Lila said. "Is it music?"

"You have to learn how to listen, too," Cree said. "Everything is music."

My eye caught a movement, I turned to the house. The windows all blazed in reflection. On the second floor I could see Aaron's dark silhouette and in front of him, almost pressed against the glass, Maria's radiant face. Some trick of the reflection made it seem that lights danced like fireflies entangled in her hair. She smiled down on us and I felt her say, "I told you."

The moon had begun to rise across the sound, smudged at first by the smoke from the Anacortes refinery. Lila was right, after a while it was boring. Nothing really happened, they were just there. And there was no way to know what would happen if they weren't there.

"Past my bedtime," Cree said. She touched each of us on the head then walked towards the Wigit.

"Me, too," Lila said. "Maybe I can catch the end of Johnny."

Morganne clung to me as we went in the house. In the living room, we all turned to look out one last time. The lights were as bright as ever.

The Poet heard us and came in rubbing his eyes. "What are you all looking at?" he asked. "The Coast Guard again?"

"Nothing," Lila said.

"What's wrong with the trees?" He peered out, stepped over to get a different angle. "Some kind of light shining on them."

"You been dropping acid?" Lila asked him.

"You all see it," he said. "I know you do. It's getting brighter. Wo." He leaned against the glass.

"Someone playing tricks with a flashlight," Lila said, started up the stairs.

"You see it, don't you," he asked me.

"I didn't notice anything," I said. Morganne and I slipped away.

"They were there," I heard the Poet say. "I saw them. They were so bright it woke me up."

"Nothing woke us up," Suzette said. "We drank half a fifth of Cognac."

"You drank most of it," Eddie said.

"I saw them," the Poet insisted.

"Sight is just electrical stimulation of the visual cortex," Eddie said. "Anything could cause it."

"What do you mean, anything?" the Poet asked.

"A drug, too much alcohol, a blow on the head, a malfunction in the optic nerve. It could be a daytime memory superimposed on the darkness. The thing is," he caught his breath, "is you just never know."

"Well, I know what I saw," the Poet huffed.

"As long as we understand what seeing is," Eddie said.

"Everyone else saw them," the Poet said. "Ask them."

Eddie looked around at us. No one volunteered.

The Poet stared at us. "You were all looking out the window when I got up," he said.

"Watching the moon rise," I said.

"You're liars," the Poet said. "I know you saw them."

"I'd have to see proof," Eddie said.

"What good would that do," Lila asked him. "If you only saw it?"

"I mean seeing in a scientific sense," Eddie said. "With instruments. Then you can be sure."

CHAPTER 29

Morganne wanted to go to Seattle with us and Aaron didn't want to leave Maria and Do. Eddie and Suzette and the Poet flew out at six Monday morning with Lee, but there were too many of us left to fly together. Cree said she'd run us in to LaConner on the Wigit.

Lila had found an old lady with a spare garage just two blocks above the docks and rented it from her for twenty-five dollars a month. She hadn't driven the Mustang in several weeks and a layer of dust covered it. The woman stared at us through the window in her side door while Lila cranked the engine. We finally pushed the car into the street and it took a while to start it even with a jump from the BMW.

Despite our early start, it was nearly noon when we followed Aaron down the Dearborn Street off ramp. Thick diesel hung over the city and I took shallow breaths, starved for oxygen. From the tape deck Peter Tosh assured us "Dem haf a get a beatin'." I popped the tape out; it didn't seem relevant here.

Union Station stood as a red brick Georgian island against the tide of car and truck traffic. To the west, across endless railroad tracks and parking lots, the pedestrian gray rock of the Kingdome barely stood out in its concrete sea.

A red light stopped us, Aaron signaled left. Below us, where underground tracks broke from a tunnel into the open, I could see a transient wander along, pick up cans.

We moved again, into the maze of Pioneer Square. The horse-drawn-size streets squeezed and slowed the flow of cars, foot traffic flourished. We parked in a Diamond lot just past Underground Picnic and walked to the warehouse. Morganne loved the old furniture. Maria studied the screens while she nursed Do.

I noticed Akbar. He sat on a windowsill on the far end. He held a Bolex camera and wore dark glasses with the right lens removed. He raised the camera to that eye, looked through it at us, then lowered it and grinned.

Suras sat at Aaron's desk, talked importantly on the telephone. Miller Richards waved his arms in a far corner and harangued some well-dressed freaks I'd never seen before. I could hear Eddie pontificate from behind the screens. Fuzzy Crook sat dwarfed on one of the sofas and talked to Lance.

"Where you been, boss?" the Poet asked Aaron. "Eddie's going nuts."

"We aren't even supposed to be here today," Aaron said. "Not for business."

"We came in at nine," the Poet said. "All the phones were ringing."

"Tim must have some clout," Aaron said, "If he can get phones up that fast."

"We've got a copy machine and everything," the Poet said.

"Aaron!" Eddie said, "I need to talk to you. We need money." He turned to the Poet. "Get us some coffee, and brownies or cheesecake or something, from that Picnic place."

"I'm the Assistant Producer," the Poet said. "Have Lucky get the coffee."

Eddie glanced up at him. "I didn't say Assistant Producer, I said 'assistant to the producers,'"

"So what's Lucky?" the Poet whined.

"Just Lucky, I guess," Aaron said. I followed him into Eddie's office.

"We need money." Eddie said.

"For what?" Aaron asked.

"Everything." Eddie was exasperated. "People keep calling. One guy said he was going to file suit against us this afternoon."

"What did we do?" Aaron asked, nudged me with a look.

"Two hundred quilts," Eddie said. "Of totem poles and orcas. A hundred and fifty dollars apiece. They've already shipped half of them."

"Where?" Aaron asked.

"LA," Eddie sputtered, "To Wilkie Thomas. He ordered all this shit and hasn't paid for it. The printer who did the poster is really hot."

"Why is that our problem?" Aaron asked. "I thought Tim wanted to pay for everything."

"We're here to straighten things out," Eddie said.

"I didn't sign on as an accountant," Aaron said, "or a sugar daddy. Have you told Tim?"

"I can't get hold of him," Eddie complained. "The lawyer says it will just have to wait. The printer says he's going to call Bill Graham. Then none of the bands will play."

"Then we cancel it," Aaron said. "Before it gets out of hand. We can put another concert together. And we don't need that concrete bunker for the venue."

"Too many people expect this to happen," Eddie said. "It would ruin our reputations."

"As what?" Aaron said. "I told you, I'm no promoter."

"With the whale people," Eddie said. "Our followers."

Aaron turned around quickly as if to see who was behind him. "No one following me," he said, grinned at me.

Tim was a large, pink-faced man with an enormous office, the whole top floor of the Pioneer Building. The steel girders, ductwork and electrical conduits were exposed, painted in bright primary colors like a huge erector set. The lawyer led us through the zigzag of low walls, which divided the floor space into offices and work areas. Tim's space ran the length of the building against the west wall.

He looked at me briefly as we shook hands, then he talked to Eddie and Aaron.

"I hear we have some loose ends?" He smiled expansively. "These big projects have a way of getting a little frayed. How much do we need?"

Eddie calculated, muttered to himself. "Fifty thousand," he said. "That I know of."

I could see that Tim was surprised at the figure. "Just to set up?" he asked.

"Bills," Eddie said. "Stuff that Wilkie Thomas ordered."

"Like what?" Tim asked. "I can't believe he ran up another fifty thousand in bills. We paid him in advance for everything."

"He didn't have legal authorization to incur further obligations in your name," the lawyer said.

Tim had come to a decision. "I'll have my accountants look into this," he said. "Just refer anyone who calls to Braddock and Princeton."

"They won't like that," Eddie said. "They'll blame us. The bills are already past due."

"It has to be business," Tim said.

"If the bands spook," Eddie said, "we won't have a concert."

Tim patted his shoulder. "Don't worry," he said. "I know how business works." He turned to Aaron. "I think you and I need to talk about money," he said.

"We don't really need any yet," Aaron said, "I mean other than these bills. We've got the office and telephones and food."

The lawyer looked hard at Aaron. "How much in advance," he asked. "Tim would rather settle that now. What's your total fee?"

"I don't need anything," Aaron said. "Just expenses. You can pay the bands directly."

"You're planning to take part of the gate?" the lawyer asked. "How much?"

"I don't want any of the money," Aaron said. "I just came to help."

"Right on, man," the lawyer said.

I had to suppress a laugh.

The meeting seemed to be over, the lawyer brushed us towards a break in the wall. I saw Tim indicate that Eddie should wait. I lingered just beyond the divider to listen.

"Is he for real?" the lawyer asked Eddie. "What's his angle."

"That's Aaron," Eddie said.

"Very strange," I heard Tim say.

"Does he get a kickback from the bands or something?" the lawyer asked.

"We aren't paying the bands enough for that," Tim said. "Just expenses."

Eddie chuckled. "Aaron doesn't need the money."

"Is he some kind of hippy rich kid?" the lawyer suspected.

"Just an independent businessman," Eddie said. "He owns an import gallery in the U District."

"He isn't like any businessman I know," Tim said.

"Aaron is Aaron," Eddie said.

"But, if he isn't doing it for money," the lawyer asked. "How can we trust him?"

There was some discussion of where we all would stay. I kept out of it. No place I'd been lately felt much like home. The consensus favored The Edgewater for old times' sake. Morganne said she remembered when the Beatles stayed there. Suras overheard the discussion and called Aaron aside.

Aaron returned, said that Suras had offered a house that he owned in Bellevue. We could have it to ourselves. It might be better to stay low profile. No one would bother us in Bellevue.

Eddie and Suzette decided to stick with The Edgewater. The Poet stuck with them.

It was a very ordinary house just off 104th with a bright yellow "For Sale by John L. Scott" sign on a stake crookedly driven into the lawn. The street was crowded with cars and we barely found room for everyone to park. I saw several new office buildings nearby, so this house would soon face a D-8.

Suras let us in, showed Aaron and Maria around. There were four bedrooms, one with a toilet and shower in a rickety add-on.

"God," Lila said, "we'll each have a room. How long has it been?"

"Our room on Defoe is as big as this whole house," Morganne said.

"I know," Lila said, "but sometimes walls are a comfort."

"I'm hungry," Morganne said. "I don't remember the last time I ate."

Suras recommended a natural food place just up the street, said he'd see us tomorrow.

The food was decent, but not hot enough. The salad bar had a good selection of fruit and I ate as much of it as I thought I could get away with.

When we got back, Suras' car still was in the carport. He had made tea, served it to us in little china cups as soon as we came in the door.

"The Poet called while you were out," he said with a Ghandian smile. "He wanted to have a meeting. I told him to come on over."

Lila groaned.

Aaron gave her a look. "What kind of a meeting?" he asked Suras.

"He said you need to catch him up on everything that's going on." Suras flashed white teeth, his delicate gold rimmed glasses moved on his face with his broad smile. "This place should work well for you."

The Poet showed up in a cab, had some dispute with the driver. He came in without a knock.

"Hey, Boss," he said. "Long time, no see." No one laughed with him.

"What do you need?" Aaron asked him.

"Just trying to catch up," he said. "I didn't see you after that meeting. Eddie had me running all over the place."

"Nothing to catch up," Aaron said. "I'll let you know if I need you for something."

"Sorr-ry," the Poet said. "I just thought I should know what's going on."

"Fat chance," Lila said.

Suras put out his hand. He had changed into a shirt with wide sleeves that draped dramatically. "We all must work together," he said. He looked at Aaron. "This can't be a one-man thing. This is a great cooperative enterprise. The more we all know, the more we can help."

"What was the meeting with Tim about?" the Poet asked. "I know we needed money, then Eddie said it was handled."

"It's handled," Aaron said.

"How was it handled?" Suras asked. "Surely it can't hurt for us to know that. We're on your staff."

Aaron thought about it. "Wilkie Thomas," he said, "that producer from LA, ordered a lot of stuff and didn't pay the bills. Tim's accountants will handle it."

"You mean blow them off?" Lila asked.

"Probably," Aaron said. "It isn't my problem."

"It is our problem," Suras said. "We can't be part of cheating people."

"We aren't," Aaron said. "We don't need any of that shit."

"But what will we tell them?" Suras' reedy voice rose.

"We'll refer them to the accountants," Aaron said. "Braddock and Princeton."

"But what if they ask us for the truth?" Suras asked.

"Refer them to the accountants," Aaron said.

"Could I have a line?" the Poet whispered to me while they talked.

"What kind of line?" I responded. "Fishing line?"

Lila had heard us. "No, he means like 'haven't I met you somewhere?'" she giggled.

"What do you need?" Aaron asked him.

"A line," Lila said. "As if he didn't have any."

"Cocaine?" Suras asked. "I have some. Very good." He went to the coat closet, reached in a pocket and brought out a small bottle with maybe a quarter of a gram in it.

Lila snorted.

Suras set the bottle on the coffee table in front of us, then went to the kitchen and came back with a dinner plate. He laboriously chopped a crude line with a double-edged razor blade. I could see the dull yellow powder of ephedrine in his Product and scattered through it were fine, clear crystals I was sure were procaine. I estimated it overall at forty percent.

When Suras finished, the thin, clumpy line ran about three inches. "You first, sir," he mock-bowed to the Poet.

The Poet had rolled and unrolled a bill several times while he waited. It looked like a ten. He took the plate and quickly did the whole line, half in each side. He wiped the plate, licked his finger.

Suras watched with his mouth open. "That was a lot," he said. "Actually it was all I had."

"No problem," the Poet said. "Aaron always has some. Or you could buy some from Lucky."

I shook my head no.

Aaron hesitated, then pulled out his kit. It was a pouch Maria had made from a piece of wolfskin she'd taken off the collar of an old coat from Goodwill. He took out his bottle and round mirror and an etched glass straw. Suras asked to see the pouch, admired the leather flap embroidered with row on row of golden flames. He was very impressed when Lila told him Maria had made it.

"Where is Maria?" the Poet asked. "She should join us."

She's asleep," Aaron said.

"I heard her," Suras said, "A few minutes ago. She was singing to the baby."

The Poet started to get up.

"Leave her alone," Lila said.

"Peace," Suras said, commanded it so with his hands.

The mirror circulated several times. Suras took little pecks at it each time it passed. The rest of us cleaned out our straws and chased the dragon's tail around pretty good.

Past midnight Aaron put his pouch away and made signs that the party was over. The Poet and Suras didn't notice. After a few minutes Aaron reached across the table and tapped the Poet on the shoulder.

"You better call a cab," he said. "Closing time."

"I'll just crash here," the Poet said.

"No vacancies," Lila said. "Suras will give you a ride home."

"I can't drive like this," Suras said, held his head in his hands.

Aaron shrugged, got up and went down the hall to the furthest bedroom.

"I'm beat," I said, got up and stretched. "See you all tomorrow."

I hadn't been in my room five minutes when Morganne came in.

"I'm not sleeping in some room all by myself," she said. "Not with all the weirdos in this neighborhood."

"This is Bellevue," I said. "They have an anti-weirdo ordinance."

"I mean in the house," she said. "The Poet tried to grope me when I got up. Wanted to know if I would rub his back." She made a gagging face.

The doorknob turned, the door opened. "You guys doing it?" Lila asked.

"Come on in," I said, "you afraid of the bogey man too?"

"I thought you wanted your own room," Morganne said.

"It sounded like a good idea," Lila said, "But it's just an empty box."

When I awakened, light streamed through some awful orange and green polyester curtains. Lila was gone. Morganne stirred beside me, mumbled something.

"What did you say?" I asked, tickled her awake.

She looked at me.

"What did you say?" I repeated.

"What, was I talking?" She shook herself. "What did I say?"

"I don't know. Something about Maria." I stroked her back. "It doesn't matter."

"Yes. Maria. The dream." Her eyes cleared. "The Guardians," she said, "they aren't here. We're in danger."

"What sort of danger?"

"I don't know. The whales...I'm losing it." She leaned against me. "Too much coke, I guess," she said.

Aaron and I pushed through a small crowd at the top of the stairs. Eddie and the lawyer talked in Eddie's office. There were a bunch of telephone message slips on Aaron's desk. He sorted through them, gave me a stack.

"These are all mystery guests," he said. "Call them up and find out what they want."

It was half an hour before one of the lighted buttons on the phone went dark long enough for me to punch in on a line. I could only read part of the first message, "something...whale puzzle." I dialed, it was a seven-eight number - Ballard. A tiny female voice answered, "Peace."

"I'm Lucky," I said, "from Operation Crosstalk."

"You must have the wrong number," she said, "This is police harassment."

"It's about a whale puzzle," I said. "Or something."

"Oh, yeah, man, shit, you scared me. He's not here. But they're beautiful. The whale puzzles. Solid cedar."

"What's a whale puzzle?" I asked her.

"Cut out of wood. Alaskan Cedar. They only cost a hundred dollars. He'll be back about five-thirty if he scores... if he gets his business done."

"Like a jigsaw puzzle?" I asked her.

"Yes! No. More like an inlay but not glued together. You can put it together yourself."

"What are they for?" I asked. "What do you do with them?"

"They just put them together and leave them on the coffee table or somewhere," she said. "To impress people, I guess."

"Who buys them?" I asked her. "Why would we want them."

"I don't know," she said. "You'll have to talk to him."

"Okay," I said. "I'll call you back if we want any."

"Cool," she said.

The next message seemed clear. "Fuzzy Crook, wants to play gig." I wondered why Aaron had given that one to me. There was a Kirkland number with a question mark after it.

When I could catch a line again I dialed.

A very exasperated woman said, "No, I haven't seen him in two days. I don't know why he left this number. Try Gloria's." She continued to bitch as she got the number for me.

Gloria wasn't much happier to hear from me. "He finally got to sleep," she said, "Just now. I'm not going to wake him up."

"Will you give him a message," I asked in my professional voice, "Tell him to call Lucky at Operation Crosstalk."

"Who the hell are you?" she asked. "Operation what?"

"The Whale Concert," I said.

"Oh," she said, "It's about a gig. I'll tell him."

My third conversation was very short. It was a jeweler in Santa Cruz who claimed he'd made two hundred gold and enamel pendants of a totem pole with a superimposed orca. I gave him the news about Braddock and Princeton, explained that we had inherited all this crap. He was not happy.

The next one I hung up on. Some lady started hollering about whores and whoremongers and how Satan was Leviathan which was a Whale, so how come we were doing a benefit for the Devil and she knew all rock and roll was of the Devil anyway....

I took a break out back on the steel fire escape. Two hippies I'd never seen smoked a joint there. They offered it, but I passed, communed briefly with my inhaler, and went back inside.

I could see the Poet at my desk on the telephone. I waited, studied my dragon screen. I heard him say, "I'm telling you, I can get you on. I'll just add your name to the performers' list. They're letting anyone play." He paused, was not happy. "There's lots of coke here. And I thought maybe we could have a little fun again, you know, uh-uh-uh." I moved closer until he saw me. His face was red and his hair was damp. "Uh, I better go," he said, hung up.

I bumped into him as we passed and he gave me a quick look, backed off.

I could hear Aaron on the other side of the screen. "That's all I can tell you," he said. "The man wants everyone to deal through his accountants. Hey, I don't like it either. I'm just here to make it happen. What's past is past."

My next message was from Summer Rayne who promised "help with anything." The number was in the Fremont district.

Summer answered her telephone "Shalom."

"Peace," I said. "I'm Lucky, from uh...the Whale Concert."

"Groovy," she said. "Hey man, I thought like maybe you could use some help, you know, volunteers, like the old days."

"I think we're all volunteers," I said, "but I don't know if we need any more."

"I'd do anything," she said. "I just like the scene so much. It hasn't been the same since festivals got weird."

"No, I guess not," I said. "I'll ask the producer. I'll call you back. If we need help."

"Don't shine me on, man," she said. "I'm serious. I used to know Boyd Grafmyre."

"Who?" I asked her.

""You know, BG Productions." She paused. "This is freaking me out. You don't know who Boyd Grafmyre is? Everyone knows who he is."

"Sorry," I said.

"Well, John Chambless is a friend of mine," she said and waited.

"Who?" I asked.

"Man, you're just fucking with me," she said. "Where are you from."

"Just another illegal alien," I said, punched over to an open line.

Everyone wanted to sell us something. One guy from a fabric store was sure that we should drape the Kingdome in his Fourth of July overstock of red, white and blue bunting. If we didn't like that he had a great price on black crepe, to symbolize the death of the whales.

We could have had holographic totem pole medallions, tanning beds for the musicians to use backstage, or even a cheap truckload of dry ice to spread around the floor, for that mysterious foggy effect.

I referred them all to the accountants.

The few who didn't want to sell us something had causes of

their own. Most of these figured that when we were finished with this concert we could come do a benefit for them.

There were many fine causes - redwoods and rainforests, ozone and organic veggies, telephone deregulation and telepathic contact with aliens. They all sounded worthy, so I told them I had heard about a guy in LA named Wilkie Thomas.

I took another break, saw Akbar on his perch at the far end, his clear eye glued to his viewfinder. I stepped out of the frame and saw that he was filming Eddie.

Aaron was gone somewhere and Eddie frantically searched for him. "I hope he didn't go to lunch or something," he said to me. "He knows we have a meeting with the lawyer."

"I don't think Aaron's that driven by food," I said. I saw Aaron step through the window from the fire escape, pointed him out to Eddie.

Around one I decided I had to eat something, so I went to Underground Picnic and got in line. When I got to the cash register with my wooden tray covered with plates of lasagna and fruit salad and a bottle of Perrier, I told the cashier that I was from the Whale Concert.

She said I was supposed to have an ID card, so I had to stand aside while the manager called.

Aaron wasn't there so I said, "try Eddie, Doctor Randé."

He had to say my name three times before Eddie gave the okay.

"The Doctor says to get an ID card next time," the manager said as he wrote up my ticket.

I sat in a back corner and had just started to eat when Walt Gann sidled up to the table. I gave him a steady look, saw him flinch.

"Lucky, right?" he said.

"Can't complain," I answered.

"You're Aaron's... friend," he said.

"Aaron?" I said.

"I remember you," he said. "At the party. When Aaron and Robin Thomas got in the fight." He started to sit down. I discouraged that with a look.

"There was no fight," I said. "Just a bully doing his thing."

"You mean Aaron?" he asked.

"No," I said.

He tried to look in my eyes but I kept them in the shadow.

"I know there's a story here, somewhere," he said.

"No story I know of," I said. "Just people living their lives."

"I can feel it," he said. "Something is going on."

"No one tells me anything," I said. "I'm just the dancing bear in this circus."

He tried again to see my face, gave up. "See you later, man," he said and hurried away.

I hadn't seen Lila or Morganne all day. They showed up about three. Lila said they'd met Cree in LaConner.

"Why?" I asked them.

"It was a secret mission," Lila said as she went into Aaron's office.

"We picked up money," Morganne whispered to me. "A bunch of money."

We agreed we'd all done our share for the day. I stuck my head in Aaron's office and told him we were taking off. He came over by the screen and motioned Lila and Morganne over.

"Don't bring any coke out tonight," he said, "until Suras is gone. Do it in your bedrooms. If the Poet shows up, it's bedtime."

We all heartily agreed.

The Poet didn't show up and Suras seemed to get the hint fairly early, it still was daylight. When he was gone, Maria came out to the living room. We all sat on the floor around the low coffee table. Aaron's mirror was out, but no one seemed interested. Morganne rolled a joint of something she'd gotten from Cree and we passed it while Maria nursed Do.

"No telephones," I said. "I'd forgotten what it was like."

"It was nice today," Maria said. "With no one here." She smiled at us. "I mean no strangers." She smiled down at Do. "If it stays like this," she said, "maybe the Guardians will come here."

CHAPTER 30

"What day is it?" Lila asked as we raced across the Mercer Island Floating Bridge in her Mustang.

"Next Wednesday, I think." I said.

"It seems like we've been down here a month," Morganne said.

"I guess we know one business not to go into," Lila said. "I've never seen such a mess. Everyone fights with everyone. All Aaron does is listen to people yell at him or each other."

"There's a lot of money involved," I said.

"It's supposed to be for charity," Morganne said. "For the whales. I wonder if any of it will ever get to a whale."

"A whale would have a hard time spending it," I said.

"Eddie will help them with that," Lila said. She parked under the Alaskan Way viaduct, which left us several blocks to walk. The sun was bright. Despite the warm morning, Morganne had worn her old fur coat.

"Why are you wearing that rat fur again?" Lila asked. "It's July."

"I just felt like it," Morganne said.

"It's her security blanket," I said.

"Well I don't like being around all those weirdos," Morganne said.

"You mean on the street?" Lila asked her. "They won't hurt you. Drop a quarter and they'll be on the ground looking for it."

"I mean in the office," Morganne said. "There are a lot of

strange people in this business. I thought music was a freak business."

"Not anymore," I said. "Too much money."

"So how many bands are actually signed up?" Lila asked me.

"None," I said. "They all are interested at first, but someone has called around, told them about Wilkie Thomas. They start saying they'll agree as soon as the printer and the others get paid."

"What a bunch of shit," Lila said. "What's Aaron going to do?"

"Pay the bills," I said. "At least I think so. He told Eddie that he would advance the money so we could get contracts signed, as long as Tim agreed to pay him back."

"He shouldn't do that," Lila said.

"We should just go home," Morganne said.

I ignored the crowd in the office and went straight to my telephone. I'd started a tally of referrals on a back page in my notebook, one column for Wilkie Thomas, one for Braddock and Princeton. They had run neck and neck. But this morning I had to start a third column, which began to catch the other two. At least there were fewer sales calls.

About eleven Aaron looked over the screen that separated us and pointed to the telephone and held up three fingers. I punched line three and said, "Lucky."

"Oh, it is you," a vaguely familiar voice said.

"This is Lucky," I said in my best business voice.

"This is Summer," she said. "You didn't call me back."

"Who?" I asked.

"Summer... Rayne," she said patiently.

"I remember," I said, "Sort of. What did we talk about."

"Volunteers," she said. "Remember? I was going to work for you. You were supposed to call me."

"The producer says we don't need any volunteers," I said.

"They always need volunteers," she said. "I know what musicians like."

"This is a purely professional operation," I said.

"Hookers?" she said in disbelief. "What is this? Some Mafia deal? Rock stars don't want hookers. They want virgins."

"I guess I misunderstood you," I said, "Sorry."

"Listen, man, I don't know if you're some Greek pimp or what. But don't think you can cover Fuzzy's ass. I'll be there if I have to buy a ticket. He owes me eight months' child support and now you bastards get him hookers."

"Should I leave a message for Mr. Crook?" I asked politely.

"You will be sorry," she said. "I know Frank. He'll close your little popsicle stand. I'm not going to starve just because I fucked the wrong guy."

"I have a number you can call," I said. "They can help you out." I gave her the number I'd gotten for NASA Headquarters in Houston. "Now that's long distance," I said, "but it will be worth it." I put a check in my third column.

"Thanks, man," she said. "Sorry I got down on you so bad, but I'm a desperate woman."

"Glad I could help," I said.

"The thing is," Eddie stopped for breath, "is it's the end of the world, as we know it,"

Aaron and I slid two tables together to accommodate everyone.

"Isn't each moment the end of the world as we know it?" I asked Eddie.

He gave me a strange look. "The fact of the matter is," he said as everyone put down their trays, "is this is serious.

"Just born a clown," I said. "It was my unfortunate parentage."

Aaron suppressed a grin. "Nazis in the Burning Wasteland," he said to Eddie. "Pretty grim."

"I thought we were going to have an ice age," Morganne said.

"That was before the greenhouse effect," Eddie said. "The planetary temperature could trend upwards several degrees - Celsius. Combined with the ozone layer depletion we may only be able to go out at night."

"Like rabbits," Morganne said.

"Or owls," I said.

"This group can't take anything seriously," Eddie said. "This is our future, those of us who have a future."

"What's that supposed to mean?" Lila asked him. "Some kind of threat."

"Not from me," he said. "But those who can't adapt won't survive."

"Adapt to what?" Lila asked. "To this greenhouse effect?"

"That, yes," Eddie said, "And the political changes that are coming."

"Like what?" Lila asked.

"Like a big swing to the right," he said. He lowered his voice. "The word is out in academic circles, if you want a job in ten years join the Republicans now."

"I agree," Gerard said with satisfaction. "It's going to be a regular purge."

"After Nixon?" Lila said. "I don't think this country is ready for another Imperial President."

"You're wrong," Gerard said. "Americans would love to have a king, or a big daddy."

"Or a faithful gunslinger," I said. "Like Ronald Reagan."

"He'll be the next president," Gerard said.

"I don't know about that," Eddie said. "I think maybe Bob Dole or George Bush. Reagan's pretty extreme."

"That's what it takes to get the job done," Gerard said, "balls. I'd bet on Reagan."

"He looks like Howdy Doody with a makeover," Lila said. "You can see the wires if you look close. Watch how he moves. Buffalo Bob's up there somewhere."

"Not me," Morganne said. "He reminds me of Jim Jones. He has that same look in his eye, like he sees something different from everyone else. Like some of the old people in nursing homes."

"He'd be better than this peanut farmer," Gerard said. "With his 'Crisis of Confidence' bullshit."

"You must be crazy," Lila said. "Reagan wants to lead a holy crusade against drugs. That's you."

"I'll put all my money in straight businesses," Gerard said. "That's the point. He'll cut the hell out of taxes, so I'll make just as much."

"You bastard," Lila said. "You never did believe in anything."

"This is business," Gerard said. "Business doesn't believe."

"This is a country," Morganne said, "That used to stand for something."

"It would work a lot better if it was run like a business," Gerard said. "Reagan will be the chairman of the board."

"Right," Lila said, "The chairman of the bored and the lazy and the ignorant and the greedy."

"You're someone to talk about greedy," Gerard said. "Everyone runs on greed at one level or another. We just have to admit it and make it work."

"It's just as obvious as the sex drive or the territorial imperative," Eddie agreed.

"You said we're all predators," the Poet said. "Underneath."

"The only difference is," Eddie expounded, "is whether we admit it or not. If you understand it, you can prosper with it."

"It's time America quit sitting on its ass," Gerard said.

"The thing is," Eddie said, "is we need strong leadership. That's what everyone wants." He looked at Aaron.

"This last ten years has been an aberration," Gerard said, "A slight detour from the path of progress."

"The wheel turns," I said. "Have you read any of Arthur Schlesinger's articles? Or P.R. Sarkar?"

"You're always off on a tangent," Eddie said. "No wonder you don't understand it."

"Who's Schlesinger," the Poet asked.

"Nixon's Secretary of Defense," Eddie said. "I'm not sure it's relevant. So Aaron, have you decided to advance the money?"

"I'll do it," Aaron said, "as soon as Tim agrees to reimburse me."

"He will," Eddie said. "He's a straight guy. Some of his people might be a little shaky, but Tim is good as gold."

"A letter would do," Aaron said. "I need something."

"I'll get it," Eddie said, "this afternoon."

Eddie paced like a two-year-old trying not to wet his pants.

"He's going to drive me crazy," Lila said. "What's his problem?"

"Money," I said. "Aaron still hasn't advanced the money for Wilkie Thomas's bills."

"Because Tim still hasn't authorized it," Lila said. "I heard Aaron tell Gerard."

"I wish he would just forget this concert," Morganne said.

"He probably will," Lila said. "I don't think any of the bands will really do it. Too much bad Karma."

"So why are they still fighting with it?" Morganne asked. "We don't need to do this. We should be on the island, waiting for the boat."

"It's almost finished," Lila said. "They called Aaron for more money this morning."

"He should just take Maria and go home," Morganne said.

"Where did Suras take off to?" Lila asked. "He sneaked out of here like he'd just farted. I have a bad feeling about that guy."

"I have a bad feeling about all of this," Morganne said.

Aaron came out of his space, stuck his head into my area, smiled at us. Eddie came over expectantly.

"Still haven't heard from them," Aaron said to him. "The lawyer said that Tim won't be in at all today and he can't authorize it himself."

"He could call Tim," Eddie said. "Get authorization for the authorization."

"It's just a stall," Lila said.

Aaron nodded."

"I don't know what you know about big business, Lila," Eddie said.

"You'd be amazed," Lila said, "How well we get to know these guys in the clubs."

"This isn't the same," Eddie said. "I'll give you a security agreement, against PREDATOR," he said to Aaron.

"So in twenty years he might get some money back," Lila said.

"I wish you would stay out of this," Eddie said to her.

"I'll bet you do," Lila said.

"I have an idea," Aaron said. "Let me call Frank Lewis." He went back to his telephone. Eddie resumed his shuffle up and down the walkway.

In a few minutes Aaron called him in. "We can do it," he said. "Frank says I can file against the proceeds, the concert gate, if I have to. It isn't that much."

"Yes!" Eddie said. "We need to get an account open, start cutting checks."

"Just get me a list," Aaron said, "I'll wire it. Fewer tracks."

Aaron took me with him. I stood in the far corner of Western Union at a glass-topped table and counted stacks of hundred dollar bills. Aaron took each stack to the window and sent it off. The third time he saw Aaron in line, the clerk started to stare into my corner. I guess he figured I was the kingpin since I handled the money.

I stood with Aaron, watched him send the last few small amounts. The clerk tried hard to memorize my face. I don't think he had any more luck than most people did.

Aaron and I stopped by Underground Picnic for some espresso, stayed away from the office as long as we dared.

Morganne had watched out the window for us, met us at the head of the stairs. "Maria called," she said to Aaron, "she was really upset. Something about Suras."

"I have to talk to the bands," Aaron said, "this afternoon. Tell them it's a go." He looked at me. "Hey, man, could you run over to Bellevue and check on Maria?" He handed me his keys. "It's down in the Diamond lot," he said.

I had ridden in and out of the area a lot of times, but I had never driven it, felt like I had been thrown into the middle of a stock car race with no rules. I got mixed up and turned off on Mercer Island, spent twenty minutes finding my way across the East Channel to Bellevue.

Suras' car was in the carport. I parked half a block away and slipped silently through the side door. I could hear Maria crying. I moved quickly into the livingroom, stood above them. Suras started, caught himself.

"I was just talking to her," he said. "Something upset her."

"How did you happen to be here?" I asked him, stayed so close he couldn't stand up from where he sat cross-legged.

"I just came by," he said. "It is my house."

"I thought you had given Aaron possession of it," I said. I bent down, put my hand on Maria's shoulder. She did not look up. "Are you okay?" I asked her.

"I just want him to go away," she said, patted Do to keep her still.

"You heard the lady," I said, stepped back a little.

He kept his eye on me as he got up.

"I wouldn't harm her," he said. "I'm a doctor, I was just trying to help her."

"Help her with what?" I asked him, herded him towards the door.

"Her problems," he said. "She's very unhappy, with Aaron."

I pressed him forwards, almost into the door.

"She's very unhappy with the world," I said, "for good reason." I reached around him, bumped him as I opened the door for him, followed him outside.

"She's sexually frustrated," he said. "Can't you see it?"

"I hadn't noticed," I said.

"I'm a professional," he said, "I noticed right away. That's why I tried to help her. It's my duty to society."

"Just how were you going to help her?" I asked, moved him towards his car.

"She needs someone to court her," he said, "remind her how beautiful she is."

"I'm not sure she's forgotten that," I said.

"She says all she wants is for all of us to love each other," he said.

"So you thought she wanted to lay you?"

He stepped back a little. "I asked her if she wanted to love me and she said yes," he said. "I asked her if she wanted to love the Poet, and Eddie, and you. She said yes to all of us."

"I don't think you understand Maria," I said, opened the car door for him.

"If you aren't careful," he said after he got in and closed the door, "someone will call CPS. She isn't capable of taking care of that baby."

"I don't think you'd want to make that call," I said, banged on the fender for him to move.

He moved.

Maria smiled at me as I came in. "Sorry about the jerk," I said to her. "I don't think he'll bother you again."

"Don't tell Aaron," she said.

"He should know," I said.

"He'll just think I'm useless," she said, "just a problem. I try not to bother him."

"You don't bother him," I said. "Everyone else bothers him."

"Don't tell him," she pleaded. "It will just mess everything up."

"Okay," I promised her.

We sat for about an hour. She showed me all the tricks Do could do, gurgle and smile and stand with quite a little support. I remembered I had Aaron's car, but I didn't want to leave Maria. "Do you want to ride over to Seattle with me?" I asked her.

"No," she said and smiled in a way I hadn't seen in a while. "I have something I want to do."

Lila and Morganne were already gone when I got there. Aaron was ready to leave.

"I think we finally have this mess on track," he said. Most of the bands that haven't committed to something else are ready to sign. They want to verify that the bills are paid and get their expenses in advance."

"Is Tim going to do that?" I asked him. "He doesn't seem to want to spend any money."

"I may have to advance it," he said.

"Why would you do that?" I asked him.

"I like to make things go," he said. "I can afford to lose that much."

We caught up with Lila and Morganne on the 108th off-ramp, followed them the few blocks to the house.

Maria waited for us at the door. She wanted to know if we could see that she had cleaned the house.

"At least I can do that," she said.

"You should come with us tomorrow," Lila said. "There is plenty of room, couches where you could put Do and everything."

Maria agreed and Aaron was pleased.

We all went for dinner to a Mexican place in Kirkland that Morganne found in the phone book. The food was authentic, which means too greasy, but it was good and hot with a blistering salsa on the side.

When we got back to the house Eddie was there. His face was grim. He motioned Aaron into the kitchen, talked in a low voice.

"I really don't need this shit," Aaron said.

"I told you all along," Eddie said loud enough for us to hear, "this is a group effort. No one-man shows."

"You asked me to come down here and help you," Aaron said as he walked into the livingroom.

"But not to take over," Eddie said as he followed.

"I didn't take over," Aaron said. "The bands and their managers want to know who they're dealing with, who's responsible. There is still a lot of faith in the music business."

"Faith or no faith," Eddie said, "this has to be business. Tim might pull the plug if he knew you were going to sign the contracts yourself."

"Let him sign them," Aaron said, "but he'll have to talk to the managers personally – now - not sometime when he gets to it."

"He can't do that," Eddie said, "He's too busy. Besides, he doesn't know how to talk to music people."

"So how does Suras know all this?" Aaron asked him.

"He just got suspicious," Eddie said, "and called me. I gave him some phone numbers."

"So he called them?" Aaron asked, "That was probably a mistake."

"I'm the co-producer," Eddie said. "I can do whatever I need to - to keep an eye on things for Tim."

"Well, don't be surprised," Aaron said, "if we get a bunch of cancellations tomorrow."

"You wouldn't do that," Eddie said. "That's blackmail."

"I won't do it," Aaron said. "They just may not want to deal with a group of straight businessmen."

"This isn't the sixties," Eddie said. "It's all business, now."

Just after Eddie's car backed out of the carport, another car pulled in. There was a loud banging on the side door, then it opened. I stepped into the shadows of the hallway; Aaron stepped in front of Maria.

It was Fuzzy Crook and some wonderfully sexy woman in tight jeans and a very open blouse.

"Gloria," Lila said, waved her over to sit beside her.

"Hey, little lady," Fuzzy said to Maria. "Come give Uncle Fuzzy a hug."

She put Do in one arm, hugged him perfunctorily. He kissed her on the cheek, slid his hand down on her butt.

I came out of the hallway, surprised Fuzzy who started to freak. Aaron laughed.

"You met Lucky," he said. "On the island, and in the office."

"Never saw him before," Fuzzy said. "You do coke?" he asked me.

"He does a little," Aaron said. "Not as much as you."

I could see a white drift in the center of Fuzzy's long mustache. "You got any?" he asked Aaron.

"Just stash," Aaron said.

"I don't want to buy any," Fuzzy said. "Can't afford it. Just want to toot some."

Aaron laughed. He dug in his wolfskin bag, brought out his inhaler, handed it to Fuzzy.

"What's that?" Fuzzy asked.

"You know how it works," Aaron said.

"I can never get anything out of those," Fuzzy said. "I need a straw."

"Or a garden hose," Lila said.

"Hey, watch it," Fuzzy said. "I've seen that Shop-Vac of yours in action."

"You want to see it again?" Lila asked him.

"Sounds like a challenge," Fuzzy said. "Now, if we just had some."

"Just for old time's sake," Aaron said, pulled out his stash bottle and mirror.

"I knew you were holding out," Fuzzy said.

We all sat around the coffee table while Aaron chopped a line. Maria curled up beside Aaron with Do. Fuzzy was true to his word, vacuumed up vast quantities of coke.

Gloria wanted something to drink and we didn't have anything. She went out to the car and came back with a fifth of Bacardi rum. She sucked on it when she wasn't sucking on the coke straw.

After the mirror made it around for a third time, I brought out my portable tape player, put on Bush Doctor.

"I wish Cree was here," Morganne said. "We're never whole without her."

"Cree," Fuzzy said. "Now that's a weird chick." He looked at me. "No offense, man," he said.

"I don't know," I said, "I'll ask her."

Gloria ran out of rum. Lila and Morganne agreed to go to the liquor store with her.

"We'll have to go up to Crossroads," Gloria said. "That's the only one open."

Maria said she needed to change Do, went in the back.

When Aaron went to the bathroom, Fuzzy asked me, "Hey, man, don't you have something to do?"

"What did you have in mind?" I asked him.

"I want to talk to Aaron," he said.

When Aaron got back, I got up, headed for the front door. "I think I'll take a little walk," I said to him. "See what I can learn."

Outside, I waited a minute then slipped in the side door and sat in the dark kitchen to listen. I heard them working on the mirror, then the click of the razor blade as Aaron cut a new line.

"What do you think of Gloria," Fuzzy asked Aaron.

"She's always seemed nice," Aaron said. "I guess."

"I guess?" Fuzzy said, "I mean, isn't she a sex garden?"

"Looks fine to me," Aaron said.

"When she gets a little tanked up, she wants to fuck all night," Fuzzy said. "Or suck. She loves to suck."

"Sounds better than sleeping alone," Aaron said.

"Would you like to try her?" Fuzzy asked him.

"What?" Aaron said.

"Gloria," Fuzzy said. "Would you like to fuck her?"

"I don't know," Aaron said. "Hadn't thought about it."

"Think about it," Fuzzy said. "She's up for it."

"So what's the occasion?" Aaron asked him.

"I just thought we might do a little switch," Fuzzy said. "You know, trade for the night."

"Maria?" Aaron asked him. "I don't think so. She's not ready for that."

"They're all ready for it," Fuzzy said, "if you get a little coke in them and rub their pussy."

I quietly got a glass of water, walked nonchalantly into the living room as if I'd left a minute before.

Fuzzy stared up at me. "What the fuck," he said. "Is this guy your shadow or something?" he asked Aaron.

"My reflection," Aaron said. "Whenever I look in my mirror anymore, I see him."

Lila, Morganne and Gloria got back from the liquor store. They hadn't waited to get home to open the bottle. They held each other up and Gloria waved another fifth of Bacardi. They laughed like a bunch of housewives on ladies' night out. Even Morganne giggled and wiggled her hips at me.

I decided it was time for bed.

CHAPTER 31

I could see Tim's bald head bob behind the screens. It tacked one way, then the other, as he paced. It was several minutes before Aaron and Maria got there.

I caught Aaron's eye, pointed out the pink sail. He motioned Maria on and turned towards Tim. I took Maria to the furthest lounge area and held her diaper bag while she got Do comfortable on a broad sofa.

Maria took the bag from me and sat on the floor, stared at her baby with love. I heard a throat clear and turned.

"You can't have your women and children here," the lawyer said, gestured towards Maria. She smiled up at him.

"She's with Aaron," I said.

"I know you're with Aaron," the lawyer said. "But this isn't a nursery. I'm sure it violates an ordinance."

"You'll have to talk to Aaron," I said. "She's his wife."

The lawyer stared. "You mean Aaron?" He held his hand over his head to signify the tall one.

I nodded. Maria smiled again. Do gurgled.

The lawyer waited outside Aaron's office until Tim came out, led him to where he could see Maria on the floor with Do now at her breast. The lawyer said something I couldn't hear. I moved closer.

"I can't believe that," Tim said.

"That's what that Mexican said, Smoky or whatever they call him," the lawyer replied. "I think her name's Miranda. They all live together."

"All of them?" Tim asked.

"And a couple more. That blonde with the big teats, and the skinny one with the nice little ass," the lawyer said. "According to that Hindu chiropractor, Suras. He says they're staying in some house he owns in Bellevue."

"All of them live together?" Tim asked. "I was told just Aaron and his wife shared my house on Defoe with Doctor Randé, not some commune. Someone should have checked it out."

"This is the first I heard about it," the lawyer said.

"Maybe Wilkie Thomas is right," Tim said. "Maybe it's a double sting or whatever he said. They rip us all off."

"Well Thomas is a businessman," the lawyer said. "I got his Dun and Bradstreet. We should trust him."

"He sure has missed a lot of deadlines," Tim said.

Aaron came out to see what the commotion was.

Tim looked at him. "Who's the little girl?" he asked.

Aaron looked where he pointed. "Maria?" he asked. "That's my wife."

Tim paused, the lawyer looked away. Then Tim said, "Okay!" He put his large hand on the lawyer's shoulder. "Tell Eddie I want to see him. Right away."

"How does Wilkie Thomas know what's going on?" Aaron asked Eddie.

"Apparently a bunch of people called his office in LA, said someone here referred them." Eddie looked at me. "I don't know who would have done that."

"I don't know," Aaron said. "So when is this meeting?"

"Tomorrow," Eddie said, "right after lunch. He's flying up from LA with six assistants or something. We'd better have our shit together."

"It's not my project," Aaron said. "I'm just here to help."

"You have a lot of money into it now," Eddie said.

"I'll get my money," Aaron said. "Frank will file against the concert."

"If it ever happens," Eddie said. "How many cancellations are there."

"Five or six, so far," Aaron said. "But it will get worse. If Wilkie Thomas gets involved, that's the end of it."

"How can we stop him?" Eddie asked.

"We can't," Aaron said, "But maybe we can get him to stop himself. I need to make some phone calls."

I knew I couldn't accomplish anything until all the loose ends were gathered. I had a huge stack of messages, but I ignored them, sipped on my inhaler and waited. Lila and Morganne came back from some errand, wanted to go eat. Aaron heard us, pointed to Maria. I asked her if she wanted to go and she did. We went to Underground Picnics.

The Poet found us within five minutes. "I'm meeting Eddie here," he explained as he sat down at our table. "He says he has big news. He went to get the others."

A few minutes later Suras came through the line with tea and some plain, dark bread, sat next to the Poet. "Thanks for calling," he said to him. "They never tell me what's going on."

In a few minutes Eddie came in with Suzette. Aaron followed them. He came over to the table, sat next to Maria and held Do while Eddie and Suzette went through the line.

"What's up, boss," the Poet asked Aaron.

"I have no idea," Aaron said. "It's a big secret."

Eddie and Suzette sat at the next table so they'd have room for their heaped trays. Eddie started in on a large sandwich.

"So what's up?" the Poet asked.

Eddie finished chewing, wiped his mouth. "They did it," he said. "The International Whaling Commission. A complete moratorium on everything but Minkes. We won."

"Now what?" Lila asked him. "Won't you have to find something else to save?"

"The fact of the matter is," Eddie answered, "is there is still plenty to do. The moratorium is only for a year."

"I don't know," Aaron said. "Everyone will think the job is done."

"That's why communication is so important, the Cetacean Link," Eddie said with his mouth full of sandwich. "That could take years."

"And an incredible amount of money," Lila said.

"The truth is, Lila," Eddie said, "is everything costs money. Better spend it studying whales than killing them."

"From Captain Ahab to Captain Cousteau," I said. Aaron chuckled.

"Isn't Ahab in the Bible?" Suzette asked.

The lawyer waited in Aaron's office when we returned from lunch. I heard him ask Aaron, "What kind of people are we dealing with? I can't imagine who they could trust more than Tim."

"The problem isn't Tim," Aaron said. "It's Wilkie Thomas. There's a bad rap on him."

"We checked him out," the lawyer said. "Pulled his Dun and Bradstreet and everything. He's clean."

"That isn't what the music business thinks," Aaron said. "I didn't create his problems."

"Funny we didn't hear about any of this until you showed up," the lawyer said.

"I didn't call you," Aaron said.

"Sometimes I wish we hadn't called you," the lawyer said. "Things have gotten very complicated."

"There's a lot of that around," Aaron said.

"Well you have to understand," the lawyer said, "this is business. Tim sees it as a competitive situation. You can each make your presentations, and he'll choose a producer. You're the one who didn't want a contract."

"I won't fight over anything," Aaron said. "You asked for my help."

"That's what we thought," the lawyer said.

Aaron gave Lila a list of names and telephone numbers and sent her to make some calls. "Just tell them," he told her, "to be ready between one and three tomorrow."

I noticed that Eddie was back on the sofa where Maria had set up. I moved into earshot but where he could not see me and leaned against the wall. Akbar smiled in the distance and I felt the camera on me.

"You need to consider your options," Eddie said to Maria. "The thing is, is there are a lot of choices available to you. Don't let anyone restrict you."

"I don't," she said.

"You don't seem happy," he said.

"I am," she said, "for me."

"Well, I think you need to get out and have a little fun," he said. "You should go out with Suzette and me some time. We know lots of University students your age. You would enjoy it."

"Do any of them have babies?" she asked him.

"Not that I know of," he said after a pause. "You could get a baby sitter."

"I couldn't leave Do with anyone," Maria said. "No one understands her."

"Professional care wouldn't hurt her," Eddie said. "Have you thought about another man? Someone younger? Aaron doesn't seem to have time for you. I mean with all his other women."

"What other women?" She waited.

"Like Lila and Morganne," Eddie said. "Surely you see...."

"They're our friends," Maria said. "I don't worry about them."

"The truth is," Eddie said, "is that Aaron isn't faithful."

Maria laughed. "He's the most faithful friend I ever had," she said. "I don't care who he sleeps with."

I moved into their view and she smiled at me. Eddie looked at me, then at her and back.

"Some people are hard to understand," he said.

"I've noticed that," I said.

I asked Aaron if I should take Maria home. "Everyone bothers her," I said.

"Sure," he said. "I'll get a ride with Lila.

They got to Bellevue about six. We all piled into the Mustang and drove back to Seattle, went to a Greek cafe, one of Aaron and Maria's old University District haunts. They both seemed happy there. Do was seven months old that day. The Greek matron hugged Maria, brought Do a piece of sticky chocolate cake with a lit candle in it. Maria blew it out for her.

"I made a wish," she said, "for all of us."

We passed around Aaron's mirror in the car and Lila drove us on a pilgrimage of places they had known before. There was a dark old apartment building under the Fremont Bridge where Aaron and Maria had hidden for months while they waited for the court's permission to marry. Lila swung downtown past the Moore Hotel, pointed at a lounge that had been the Firelight Room in happier days.

She followed Madison deep into the heart of the Central Area, on a side street pointed to a featureless brown house. "Miss Anne," she said.

"Don't stop," Maria said. "She might come out."

"She can't hurt us," Aaron said.

"She already did," Maria said.

"She just stole our stuff," Aaron said. "That doesn't matter, it just makes her a thief."

"She stole my trust," Maria said.

"Miss Anne?" Morganne asked. "I don't remember her."

"It was when you were on the farm with Buffalo Dick," Lila said, "She was a prostitute we knew from the Firelight. When Maria first ran away and they had to hide out from her aunt, Miss Anne let them stay with her, move all their stuff in. Aaron had a nice television, stereo, furniture, everything. After they'd moved in, she threatened to turn them in if they didn't go and leave her all the stuff."

"So you did?" Morganne asked Aaron.

"Yes," he said. "Easy decision."

Lila toured several other apartments where they had lived, the sandwich shop where Maria had worked to demonstrate to the judge that she was worthy of emancipation.

"I don't want to see any more," Maria said. "It makes me sad."

"Sorry," Lila said. "I thought it might cheer you up. We used to have some fun. Anyway, I don't want to go back to Bellevue until all the weirdos are in bed."

"Some of them never sleep," I said.

I hadn't intended to be prophetic, but at 2:00 AM Suras pounded on the door. I pulled on my pants and answered it. "Where's Aaron?" he asked me as he tried to brush past.

"Asleep," I said, blocked him.

"I have to talk to him," he said.

"The office opens at nine," I said, crowded him back towards the door.

"This can't wait," he said.

I did not intend to let him in, but Aaron came up behind me, said, "I'll talk to him."

"What are you trying to pull?" Suras asked Aaron angrily.

"My eyes open, right now," Aaron said. "What's the problem?"

"I finally got through to Bill Graham's office this afternoon," Suras said. "They said you told them to be ready for a call between one and three tomorrow."

"Right," Aaron said. "I'm not going into a war with no weapons."

"Why didn't you tell us what you were doing?" Suras demanded.

"So that you couldn't do something stupid like call them and fuck things up," Aaron said.

"You're just trying to discredit Wilkie Thomas," Suras said.

"He discredited himself," Aaron said. "I'm just going to let him prove it."

"I don't know which side to be on," Suras said. "Whoever I talk to, it sounds like they're right."

"Maybe you don't understand what's going on," Aaron said. "Who have you been talking to."

"Eddie," Suras said, "and the Poet. They really seem to have a handle on things."

"They probably have their hands on something," I said, "or their heads somewhere they don't belong."

"This is not a dirty joke," Suras complained. "I wish I'd never got mixed up in this."

"Me, too," Aaron said.

We all were up early, so we took both cars to breakfast at the Dog House where we weren't likely to be found. I thought I saw Walt Gann in the parking lot, but if it was him, he never came inside.

After breakfast we took a drive along the Elliott Bay waterfront and got an espresso from a little shack on the docks below the Pike Place Market. Aaron was deep in thought, planned strategy or whatever he did in those times. The tourist piers were quiet at that hour, so we sat in the sun on some wooden chairs from a seafood stand that hadn't opened.

"What do you think will happen," Morganne asked me, "at the meeting?"

"Whatever happens," I said. "Life isn't a movie."

"Sometimes I wonder," Morganne said.

"I think Tim will have Wilkie Thomas produce the concert after all," Lila said.

"Not after they hear what they're going to hear," I said.

"Don't count on it," Lila said.

"I think they'll see how good Aaron is," Morganne said, "and let us do the concert."

"It won't be that easy," Lila said. "It will be a pain in the ass. I used to work on the festivals in the Bay Area. It's always some ridiculous scramble. Then someone takes off with the money."

"I want to go home," Maria said.

The lawyer waited in his now accustomed place. "Good morning," he said. "I thought maybe you'd all thrown in the towel."

"I'm not competing for anything," Aaron said.

"That negotiating stance won't work with us," the lawyer said, "now that there are alternatives."

"I came here to do a friend a favor," Aaron said.

"I'm telling you," the lawyer said, "that position is not tenable. If Wilkie Thomas convinces Tim, you're out."

"I just want the truth to be seen," Aaron said.

"Truth is what we make it," the lawyer said.

"That's why there are lawyers," I said in the background. The lawyer gave me one of his looks.

Morganne took Maria to Volunteer Park to pass the time until lunch. I wished I could go with them. I tried to keep people away from Aaron and Lila fended off the telephone calls he didn't want.

Akbar sat, as usual, clear eye looking at us through a long lens.

"He just sits there like a goddamned vulture," Lila said and gave him the finger. There was no response, just the soft whir of film through chrome guides.

"Aaron told him he could film it," I said.

"I know," Lila said, "But he still gives me the creeps."

About eleven thirty the lawyer came back, looked in on us with a smile. "Sorry about this morning," he said, "I'm just not used to how this business operates." His arms opened as if to give us all a long distance hug. "So I thought I would take you all to lunch at Picnics." He looked at me. "All of you," he said.

"We're pretty busy," Aaron said.

"Come on," the lawyer said, "I insist."

"We're supposed to meet my wife," Aaron said.

"Leave a message for her," the lawyer said, "to come and join us."

"I'll wait for them," Lila said. "It should just be a few minutes."

"The other girl," the lawyer said, "the...uh...slim one. Tell her to come too." Lila just looked at him.

I wasn't hungry, settled for a date bar and coffee. Aaron had a small sandwich. The lawyer loaded up with lasagna and a wedge of chocolate cake.

We tried to find something to talk about for ten minutes, then Lila, Morganne, Maria and Do came in. The baby was flushed with sun and Maria's eyes were bright and focused. They went through the serving line, sat at the table next to us.

The lawyer stared at Maria, changed subjects every minute or two. No one else said much.

He ran out of anything to say at about quarter to 1:00, looked at his watch, said, "Back to it," motioned us all up.

"We'll go back to the park," Morganne said.

"No, no," the lawyer said, "bring everyone. This won't take long." Aaron quietly assented and they all followed us.

I could see before we were halfway up the stairs to the office that something was different. Screens had been moved back and stacked along the wall. Several large conference tables had been jammed together to make one, and about a dozen people worked at stacks of papers along it.

At the far end a projection screen was flanked with several oversize easels displaying various renderings of the now-familiar totem pole and orca emblem. There was a giant painting of it in a heavy gold frame and a print of the painting reduced to poster size.

There was a quilt, shiny and machined-looking, and a macramé wall hanging. There was a large stained glass window, which required a beefed-up stand. There were leather jackets with the design appliquéd in color. On a table were buttons, embroidered baseball caps, wood inlays, stationery, business cards, balloons, and the book. Bouquets of tiny Operation Crosstalk flags festooned the corners of the head table.

Tim stood near the paraphernalia, talked to a small man with dark, greased hair who wore a tight shirt-and-pants matched ensemble in black. His thick shoes clicked on the floor as he moved back and forth, explained it all to Tim.

When they saw us, it became quiet. The assistants scurried around. Several of them took seats, the others withdrew into the shadows among the screens.

The lawyer led Aaron over towards Tim and the little man. No one stopped me, so I followed.

"Wilkie," the lawyer said before we were halfway there, "good to see you." He held out one hand, pulled Aaron forward with the other.

"This is Aaron...uh...I never was straight on your last name," he apologized.

"Just Aaron," Aaron said, "for now."

"Okay!" the lawyer said. "Your group can sit on this side," he indicated the empty side. There were eight chairs. Eddie sat in the furthest, had pulled it around towards the end. Aaron sat in the first chair and I sat next to him. He beckoned Lila to him, whispered in her ear.

She went into an office and brought back a telephone with a little speaker attached and plugged it in along the wall behind Aaron. The cord was short so he had her put the phone on the floor a few feet from him. She sat next to me.

"Ready?" the lawyer asked. Aaron nodded.

"Mr. Thomas will be back in a minute," said the blonde woman in a stylish pants suit who sat next to Wilkie Thomas's empty chair.

"We've sure had a nice summer," the lawyer said to no one in particular.

A long-haired guy with a paisley tie about halfway down Thomas's row said, "Seems cool to us up here. Feels good, but a little clammy." Several of his accomplices agreed.

Aaron looked at his notes. I could see that Morganne and Maria entertained Do on one of the ornate old sofas.

Wilkie Thomas appeared, wiped beneath his nose and sniffled. He sat and looked expectantly towards the lawyer, shuffled nervously.

The lawyer looked at Aaron. "Would there be a problem if they went first? They're all set up."

"I see that," Aaron said. "Sure, no problem."

One of Thomas's crew started a projector, began to flash slides onto the screen. Their side all leaned forward. We could barely see from our side because of the glare from the windows.

Mostly it seemed to be slides of the material that was displayed at the head of the table with a long series on Wilkie Thomas's creation of the great painting. The artist himself kept up a running narration for Tim and the lawyer but I'm sure no one else heard any of it. I saw Suras and the Poet come from the head of the stairs and stand away in the distance.

The slide show was over and Thomas took the podium. "So you see what we've accomplished with the indulgence and resources of our friends up here." He smiled graciously at Tim and the lawyer, let it fade as he turned towards Aaron.

"Now, I don't know what the motive would be for someone to cast doubt on us like this or why someone wouldn't want us to know his last name. I've been told that no one on that side of he table is paid, so I am at a loss to understand any of it."

He studied Aaron for a moment. "In any case," he said, "we are here to tell you that we are ready and able to do the Operation Crosstalk entertainment benefit. We have been involved in this from the beginning, and I'm sure I don't need to remind you that the trademark for the very name belongs to Thomas Productions."

I saw Tim and the lawyer exchange glances.

Thomas wiped a damp brow and took a deep breath. "I'm not here to muscle anyone, but we have promotional material nearly complete, artists committed and we are ready to roll. Now each of the assistant producers has a presentation."

He turned deferentially to Tim. "I assume you will allow us to complete our presentation all at once." Sweat dripped from his forehead and he had the galloping sniffles. "This humidity," he said as he mopped at his face.

"I can save us all some time," Aaron said.

Tim and the lawyer turned.

"I really would like to finish," Thomas said.

"This will just take a minute," Aaron said.

The lawyer smiled in anticipation of a concession speech.

"Go ahead, Aaron," Tim said.

"I'm not a producer," Aaron said. "I never claimed to be a producer. I came here because Eddie asked me to help him with a project that was in trouble. I want no money. I really have no interest in the concert at this point." He looked at the lawyer briefly, then at Wilkie Thomas. "Operation Crosstalk is considered to be just a scam by a lot of people in the music business."

Thomas blew. He jumped to his feet, nearly turned over the chair. "I hope you got that down, Jo Anne," he said to one of the assistants. "That's slander. If I lose this contract, you'll pay for it."

"I only came here today," Aaron said to Tim, "to demonstrate the truth. I would like to know which bands are committed to play, West Coast bands...."

"No problem," Thomas said. "Clarice?"

She stood up, looked through a stack of papers on a clipboard. "West Coast bands," she said, "Santana, the Youngbloods, Eagles, Starship, Doobie Brothers, Heart...."

"That's enough," Aaron said. "I need to make a phone call." He got up, squatted by the speakerphone, dialed a long number. "Mike," he said when they answered, "Mike Little please." He punched the button that turned on the speaker.

"Mike Little," a voice said.

"Mike," Aaron said, "this is Aaron. We spoke yesterday."

"Yes," Mike said.

"I have you on the speaker," Aaron told him. "Would you tell us who you are and where you are."

"This is Mike Little," he said, "at Bill Graham Productions."

"What do you do there?" Aaron asked him.

Thomas was on his feet again, handkerchief flying. "What is this bullshit?" he asked Tim. "You have my references, you've seen my work."

"Just go along for a minute," the lawyer said.

"I work in artist management with Santana and some other bands," Mike Little said. "I do schedules mostly."

"Have you heard of Operation Crosstalk?" I asked him.

"I hadn't until last week, when Lila first called my assistant," Mike said.

"What have you found out about it?" Aaron asked.

"It doesn't appear legitimate," Mike said.

"Will Santana play the date?" Aaron asked.

"We have no plans to play that date. In fact, we are committed in another city on the date you gave me. Have been for months."

"So you weren't contacted about playing Operation Crosstalk?"

"Not until you called," Mike said. "It's too late to schedule any of our major artists."

"Thanks," Aaron said.

"Anything else?" Mike asked.

Aaron looked at the lawyer, then Tim, then Thomas. Thomas was livid but silent.

"No," Aaron said, "I guess that's it." He turned off the speaker, hung up the phone.

"I can make five or six more calls like that," he said. "That's the story we get from everyone. We've just been trying to put it back together. But you heard Mike, it's too late. This isn't 1968 when you could call up and get a dozen good bands next week."

"Excuse us," the lawyer said, led Tim towards the back where they talked while we played stare-down with the row of assistants. They were back in a couple of minutes.

"We'll just leave things here, for now," Tim said. "We need to see how feasible the project is." He turned to Aaron. "We'll call you," he said, "if we need to."

"We'll cover the expenses," the lawyer said, "to this point."

Tim had turned to Wilkie Thomas, talked in low tones.

I headed for Maria and Morganne, had them follow me out.

Lila caught us on the stairs. "Weird," she said, "they acted like it was all Aaron's fault."

"It was," I said. "He told them the truth."

CHAPTER 32

We waited on the street for Aaron. When he came out, Suras was on one side, the Poet on the other.

"Way to go, boss," I heard the Poet say.

"What happened?" Suras asked. "Are we going to do the concert?"

"Not me," Aaron said, walked beside Maria towards the cars. "You saw what we're dealing with."

"They're just businessmen," Suras said.

"We can do it, boss," the Poet said. "You and Lila know all the bands. I could get poets to do readings."

"Not interested," Aaron said.

"You can't just drop it," Suras said, "a lot of people are counting on you."

"I'm out of that business," Aaron said.

"What business are you in?" Suras asked.

"The boat," the Poet said. "You know."

"You still have that sailboat?" Suras was surprised. "I thought you sold it. I thought that's where you got your money."

"They're rebuilding it!" the Poet said proudly. "You should see it. Up in Bellingham."

"I didn't know that," Suras said to Aaron. "Why didn't you tell me that?"

"Why should he have told you that?" Lila asked him.

"It's hard to work with people who keep secrets," Suras said.

"I agree," the Poet said.

"What work have you done?" Lila asked them, "except nose into other people's business and interfere."

Suras was instantly angry. "I don't have to take this," he said. "How about the house? You haven't paid me for that. And my time. I have a busy practice."

"You'd never know it," Lila said.

"I think you use too many drugs," Suras said.

"They need treatment," the Poet said.

"I've seen you both use whatever you could get next to," Lila said.

"Just my cover," Suras said.

"Cover for what?" she asked him.

"I'm a healer," he said, "and a counselor."

"And self-appointed busybody," Lila said.

"Stop, Lila," Aaron said.

"It just pisses me off," she said.

"That doesn't do any good," he said. He whistled, a soft, wavering siren tone.

Lila suddenly grinned. "Never mind me," she said to Suras. "I'm just mad at that little weasel from LA." There was a hard edge of control in her voice.

Suras studied her. "I'm not someone to dismiss," he said.

"Oh, I won't dismiss you," Lila said, "Friends?" She stepped next to him as we walked, stuck her hand towards him. He took it. She pressed hard, surprised him.

"What are we going to do?" Morganne asked Aaron.

"Get our stuff," he said. "Then we'll go home."

"Where's home?" she asked him.

"Where your heart is," he said to her.

"The Island," Maria said. "The Guardians."

Aaron took Do from her and carried the sleeping baby in one arm, held Maria's hand.

"We need to hurry," Morganne said.

"Here it is," Aaron said, turned into a parking lot.

"Hey," the Poet said, "we're clear down the other side of the

Kingdome. Could you give us a ride down?"

"Not going that way," Aaron said, unlocked the door for Maria. Lila's Mustang was a few spaces away. Suras and the Poet stared in disbelief as we drove away. On the next corner I saw Walt Gann standing at a pay phone. He looked up, didn't recognize us.

Aaron led us down Rainier to the I-90 on-ramp, accelerated hard as we hit the multiple lanes. Lila barely kept up with him through the tunnel and across the floating bridge. We raced across Mercer Island and the East Channel bridge, took 405 north to Bellevue then threaded the side streets to Suras' house.

Morganne nearly ran me down as she hurried into the house. As we came through the door she brought her overnight case into the living room. She sat down and opened it, checked under the tray for her money. She fingered the rubber banded bundles, then closed it.

"You ninny," Lila said. "I told you that wasn't safe." She handed Morganne her keys. "Put it in the trunk," she said.

We all gathered the few things we had with us and loaded the cars. Lila took one last look around. "Holy shit," she said when she opened the cabinet under the sink.

Morganne went over to look. "What is that," she asked Lila.

"Paper towels," Lila said. "Piles of wet, dirty paper towels." She poked at them with a finger. "They're fresh, at least some of them."

Aaron and I looked at the wadded, muddy towels. "I don't know," Aaron said. He looked at Maria who sat on the floor with Do. "Maria," he called to her.

She turned, smiled. "What?" she asked, dazed.

"Do you know how all these paper towels got here?"

"No," she said and smiled again. "Yes. I put them there."

"What's wrong with the garbage?" Lila asked her gently.

"They need to be burned," Maria said. "I was going to burn them in the fireplace before we left."

"Why burned?" Lila asked her.

"It's the filth from this house," Maria said. "While you were gone I cleaned, every day. But I couldn't keep up. I put basil leaves in the corners."

"What filth?" Lila asked.

"It's everywhere," Maria said. "Dripping from the walls, tracked all over the floor. Can't you see it? And the terrible smell."

"Nothing unusual," Lila said.

"Bad things were here," Maria said.

I heard brakes outside, saw a blue Mercedes park across the head of the driveway, block in our two cars. Aaron moved over behind me to see. Tim and Eddie came up the walk, knocked at the door. Aaron opened it.

"Aaron," Eddie said, "Glad we caught you. Tim wanted to talk to you, to explain...."

"Not necessary," Aaron said.

"Yes," Tim said. "I want everything to be clear. I have officially postponed Operation Crosstalk for now, until we can check all this out. I have attorneys and accountants to do that for me. I realize that Wilkie Thomas, or someone in his organization, may be culpable here. And some of my people may not have told me everything they knew. But we don't want any hard feelings. After all, we're all businessmen."

"Don't worry about it," Aaron said. "I won't think of it again."

"Now, I don't want any liability here," Tim said.

"No problem," Aaron said. "I want just what you owe me."

"You mean the expenses?" Tim said. "I'll cover those."

"I paid some of the outstanding bills," Aaron said. "Out of my pocket."

"You can turn the receipts in to the accountants," Tim said. "We'll handle it out of petty cash."

"It's about thirty-four thousand," Aaron said.

"What?" Tim asked no one. He looked belligerently at Eddie. "What is this? Did you authorize this?"

"The bands wouldn't play if these bills weren't paid," Eddie said.

"That's just a shake-down," Tim said. "I won't pay for that."

"They were legitimate bills," Eddie said. "You saw all the stuff at the meeting. Aaron paid the poster printer and the T-shirt guy...."

"We don't need that stuff," Tim said. "Not if we don't have a concert."

"Wilkie Thomas ordered it," Eddie said.

"Then he can pay for it," Tim said. "You deal with Thomas Productions," he said to Aaron. "My attorneys say he had no authorization."

"Forget it," Aaron said. "If the concert happens, I'll talk to you about it."

"What?" Tim asked. "You're just going to walk away from thirty-four thousand dollars? Is this some scam? Fake receipts or something? No one walks away from that much money."

"I'll have my accountant call yours," Aaron said.

"How much money do you have?" Tim asked. He looked at Eddie. "Are you in on something?"

"No, no, no," Eddie said. "It's all legitimate. Aaron inherited some money."

"Why didn't you tell me this before," Tim said. "I'm going to have to have someone check all of this out."

"Well, you've seen my credentials," Eddie said. "The University will vouch for me. I'm not responsible for anyone else."

Lila softly clucked like a chicken, Eddie glared at her.

"We need to go," Aaron said.

Maria took Do out to the car. I stood outside the door, but close enough. I gestured to Lila and she led Morganne out, started the Mustang.

"We need to catch a ferry," Aaron said to Tim. "If you could move your car."

"Sure," Tim said. "I want to see my lawyer before five." Eddie silently followed him to the Mercedes.

As we backed out, Suras pulled up in his Saab, the Poet with him. Lila backed towards him, gave him a scare. He pulled forwards, let us out. The Poet jumped out, ran towards Aaron. Aaron pulled away, so he turned at us, knocked on Lila's window.

"What did we miss?" he asked her.

"Creation," she said and drove away behind Aaron.

We went north through Lynnwood, left I-5 at Conway and cut across the delta on back roads. "I wonder if he'll go to Bayside, fly to the island," Morganne said.

"He'll go to LaConner," Lila said. "Find Cree."

Lila was right. We parked the Mustang in her rented garage. The old lady glared at us through the screen when Lila waved at her. Aaron parked around the corner.

The Wigit was at the dock. Lila found Cree in the Pisces. She asked no questions as she got under way, just smiled at us. Deception Pass ran strong with the tide; the current amplified the waves. Cree winked at me, took the waves head on and made good time. It felt good to be on the water again. I felt the balance come to my legs, clarity to my head. I touched the moneybelt under my shirt.

The sun was low; the dark line of Whidbey Island fell away behind us.

Defoe was quiet. Several storm-blown branches lay across the path from the dock to the house. The front door was locked and none of us had ever had a key. I went around the side, through a window, and let them in.

We all checked our stuff. Everything seemed normal. We gathered in Aaron and Maria's room around Aaron's mirror.

"Where can we go?" Morganne asked Aaron.

"Here," he said, "Until the boat's done. Then we'll sail away."

"How long will that be?" Lila asked him.

"They were close ten days ago," he said. "I need to get to Bellingham tomorrow. I'll call Lee." He tried the telephone, but it didn't work.

"I'll take you," Cree said. "I'll stay here tonight."

Morning came late. The days had been longer when last we'd been at the island. Morganne slept heavily beside me. I moved her arm to get up. I put on the moneybelt, then my clothes, carried my boots. The old house had a faintly familiar smell, like the shadow of some half remembered thing.

Maria sang to Do in the living room when I came down. She looked up at me where I sat on the steps to put on my boots. "The Guardians are still here," she said. "I watched them last night for hours. I was so happy to see them."

Aaron and Lila talked at the table in the kitchen, didn't notice me. I went out. The dampness of the night clung to everything. From the porch I could hear the soft knock of the Wigit against the dock. I smelled peppers and fried potatoes, dreamed of Cree's omelets. I drifted down to the boat and stepped over the rail.

At the rock of the boat Cree stuck her head through the open cabin door. "Hi, sailor," she said. "Hungry."

"Starved," I said.

"Five minutes," she said. Her totem-pole face studied mine. "How's a-Babylon?"

"Wicked," I said, "and faithless." I heard music. It seemed like a long time since I'd heard music. Bob Marley, something new to me.

"Exodus, movement of Jah people." The reggae rhythm steadied me, the burning food awakened my gut. I could feel my skin breathe.

We sat in the early sun and drank tea. Gulls called for our scraps. Cree lit a joint and passed it to me. I realized that it had been a while since I'd smoked anything. I also realized I'd forgotten my inhaler.

"Let your nose rest," Cree said.

The sun penetrated my clothes, warmed muscles I hadn't realized were stiff. I took off my shirt, squatted and stretched my lower back until I got a pop. I stood and pulled back against the rail, felt my muscles relax, let the sun warm my blood.

Aaron came down in about an hour, said he was ready to go. "Need anything before we go?" he asked me. I remembered my inhaler, ran to the house to get it.

Morganne woke up at my intrusion. I told her I was going

with Aaron. She went back to sleep. I filled the inhaler from a bottle, put the bottle in an empty pocket of the moneybelt.

The Wigit tugged gently against the stern line when I got to the dock. Cree let the line slack; I loosened it, jumped into the boat with it. The familiar deep throb of the fine old engine came up through my feet as Cree headed into the channel.

We ghosted north through Rosario Strait with the scattered pleasure boat traffic. Cree ducked around the end of Lummi Island and into the bay. She found a transient moorage open just down from the boatyard and we tied up.

I knew Aaron wanted me with him, so I silently followed him ashore and along the jetty. The Orca was again afloat, but it was draped with tarps on the dockside and we couldn't see much.

The dilapidated office was busy but went silent when we entered. The bookkeeper jigged nervously behind his counter while one of the shipwrights went for the superintendent. The super had always been friendly and he smiled as he came out of the back. He leaned over the counter, shook Aaron's hand, nodded at me.

"Damn near finished," he said, "Tomorrow or the next day." There was tension in his voice. "Let's go look at something," he said, led us out onto the pier and around to the Orca. He pulled back a corner of a heavy tarp to show the new paint. "Just a little trim left," he said, "and a couple of winches that need new mounts."

"How about sails?" Aaron asked.

"Haven't seen them," the super said. "You said delivery the end of July, but nothing yet."

"I'll call them," Aaron said.

"And the electric winches," he said, "If you want us to install the winches, we'll need a few days."

"We can do that if we have to," Aaron said. "But I would like to get finished up otherwise. I've got charter customers waiting."

"We'll need your final payment," the super said. "And time for it to clear the bank."

"Cashier's checks," Aaron said, "the second you're finished."

"Hey, man," the super said to Aaron, tried not to let me hear him, "someone called this morning. Some attorney's office from Seattle. They asked a lot of questions, ship's registry and ownership and all that. We didn't tell them much, but I don't think they're gonna drop it. Their client seemed to have enough money to press it. Whatever it is."

"He does," Aaron said. "I'm not surprised. Just get it finished."

"The yard doesn't want to get caught in a dispute over ownership or something," the super said. "Or anything illegal."

Aaron gave him a look. "I mean, other than the money," the super said. "Drugs or something. This attorney asked if we'd found anything illegal when we tore into her."

"It's nothing," Aaron said. "Somebody who owes me money and doesn't intend to pay it."

"We'll get her finished up for you," the super said, "But we don't want any trouble."

Cree ran us down to LaConner to get Aaron's car so we could chase down the sails. He told Cree to tell Maria and the others we'd be back the next morning.

"We'll fly over," he said.

I-5 southbound rolled well over the speed limit. Aaron played tag with a dark, pretty woman in a new BMW until she turned off at the Lake Stevens exit.

He cut over to Highway 99 in Lynnwood, made good time past the car lots and trailer parks. He took the back way into Ballard, wound down the hill past the park on Shilshole Bay. The sailmaker's shop was a converted old Victorian house across from the waterfront half a mile south of the marina.

The Norwegian sailmaker looked at Aaron. "Yah," he said, "I remember you. Big sails for the old schooner. Nearly done."

He led us into a long back room where a woman and two men worked at industrial sewing machines that stood like islands in a white sea of canvas. I wondered how they kept from sewing the wrong sail.

"You said delivery the end of July," Aaron said.

"I sent you notice," the sailmaker said. "In writing. The contract says if materials are not available the shipping date may be delayed. The wide footage, for the mains'l had to come from back east. You said, 'no extra seams.'"

"So what's the date now?" Aaron asked.

August 10th," he said. "Ten-day extension, like in the contract. But we be finished any day now - tomorrow or next day."

"I'll call you tomorrow," Aaron said.

We ate at a barbecue place down towards Fremont that Aaron knew. I ordered the hot-style ribs, adjusted it with liberal applications of ground red pepper from a shaker jar. Aaron drank a beer and stared off into the distance.

There was some raw reggae on the stereo. I asked the counter man what it was and he said, "Burning Spear, Kill the White Man." He shook blond dreadlocks to the rhythm.

Aaron didn't say much as we started north just before sunset. I asked him if he wanted me to drive, but he didn't.

It was too late to fly to the island, so Aaron drove into LaConner. We did a quick line before we got out of the car and I filled my inhaler. We walked the street several times in both directions. We spent some time in a record store and I bought a cassette of Exodus.

Dusk fell and the taverns along the fishing docks roared into life. Some of the artsy types furtively crept by, but most of them stayed in their Volvos until they got to the better part of town.

We went into a place called The Big Dipper, a kind of bridge between two worlds where intellectuals ate in the fern-ridden restaurant while some of the more genteel fishermen roistered at the bar. The food looked very European, so I drank a Tecate while Aaron tried to eat a salad. He gave up, ordered a coffee and rum drink, which seemed like a contradiction to me.

Before Aaron finished his drink, the Poet appeared. Linda was with him, the first time we'd seen her in weeks.

"Left the kid with her old lady," the Poet greeted us. "Hey, boss, I need to talk to you."

He pulled two more chairs to our table. They sat down. He leaned close, said, "They're after you, boss," waited for the effect.

Aaron just looked at him. "That lawyer," the Poet said, "He called everyone in, asked a lot of questions." He paused again. "About coke and everything." He laughed, "I didn't tell them anything. I didn't know nothin'." His face grew serious. "Suras spilled his guts."

"What does Suras know?" Aaron asked him, still showed no expression.

Linda watched him intently. "I'd be worried if I were you," she said.

"If you were me, you wouldn't be," Aaron said.

"What are you going to do, boss?" the Poet asked.

"Go on about my business," Aaron said.

A few minutes later Aaron excused us. We went back to the car, did a good line and tried to find some music on the radio, found only disco and redneck country. I remembered my tape, put it on. Marley explained it all.

We wandered the dark roads of the delta, could see nothing beyond the range of our headlights. Aaron parked in the low dunes above the beach along Skagit Bay and we got out of the car, walked towards the water.

Constellations glittered in tide pools and the salt grass rustled dryly in the seaward wind. I smelled the incense of the mountains, cedar and hemlock and resinous firs. I thought of the bears feeding themselves fat on berries and fish.

Aaron stared out across the black water towards Defoe. "How do you tell them?" he asked the wind, then looked at me. "How do you tell them there is no north? That a compass will follow any magnetic field, any electrical vortex that passes by."

"My Grandfather would say," I said, "that the only true compass is the heart."

"They don't want to hear that," he said. "They have no faith in hearts."

"My Grandfather had no faith in minds," I said.

We drove to a cafe on Chuckanut Drive just after dawn and managed to eat some breakfast. Aaron called Lee, woke him and got him to agree to meet us at Bayview in an hour. He was actually a little early.

Defoe sparkled green beneath us as we landed in the cove, taxied in across small waves. Aaron paid Lee while I steadied the plane. Aaron stepped back and I gave the pontoon a shove away from the dock. Lee grinned at us as he hit the throttle.

The Wigit wasn't in her usual place. Maria had come down to the dock, and as we all climbed the sloped lawn, Lila and Morganne appeared. "You guys look like shit," Lila said.

"Thanks. We were up all night," I said.

"Fighting Dragons?" Morganne asked.

"Chasing one," I answered.

"What's wrong?" Morganne asked me.

"Nothing," I said, "at least not yet."

"So, tell us," Lila said.

"Tim's lawyer," Aaron said, "or someone, is asking a lot of questions."

"That asshole! Asking who questions?" Lila asked. "The Poet!"

"He said he didn't tell them anything," I said.

"And you believed him?" Lila challenged.

"No," I said.

"Me either," Aaron said.

"He claimed Suras spilled his guts," I said.

"What does that little geek know?" Lila said.

Inside, Aaron tried the phone but it remained dead.

I put on the Exodus tape in my room and Lila and Morganne came in to listen. I was tired, cut myself a line and felt awake again. They were up for an all night run, but I knew I should sleep.

I heard the Wigit a while later and put on my boots, headed for the dock. Lila and Morganne followed. Cree had brought groceries and fillets from a ling cod she'd caught. She went back to her gas refrigerator, brought us a double handful of oysters.

"We eat tonight!" Lila said, loaded up with grocery bags and handed one to Morganne.

Aaron came down, told Cree he needed to get to a telephone before five.

"Anacortes?" she asked him.

"Sure," he said, untied the bow line.

I handed the fish and oysters to Morganne, untied the stern line and followed Aaron on board.

Cree filled her tanks with diesel at the service dock while Aaron made his calls. The air was thick with refinery smoke burnt orange by the low sun. A long, dark tanker marked with soot lay at anchor off the point. Cree circled well out then turned south. With a little help from a northerly flow, we made good time.

"So what's the deal?" Lila asked Aaron as soon as we were in the house.

"The Orca will be finished tomorrow," he said.

"How about Frank? Did you talk to him?" she asked.

"He doesn't want to answer my questions over the phone," Aaron said. "He wants me to come down for a conference."

"Sure," Lila said, "so he can run the clock on it, maybe get you to buy lunch."

"I called Gerard," Aaron said. "He said he hasn't heard anything funny. No one has been around Primal Power."

"I hope he pays attention," Lila said. "He's supposed to have my bar deal done next week. He put my money in escrow already. I just have to sign the papers."

While we were in Anacortes, they had cooked the fish and a big pot of steamed vegetables and we all stuffed ourselves. Cree brought some very hot salsa, which I poured over everything. There were a couple of oysters apiece. Cree and Aaron ate their share raw. The rest of us steamed ours and added some butter.

After dinner, Morganne tried to lure me off to bed but I was restless. I paced the shadowed porch, gazed now and then out across the sound at distant lights.

Full dark came late to the cloudless sky, but as it did I saw the familiar glow spring up around the trees and larger bushes that encircled the house. The flames steadied, row on row, a fractal phalanx defended us against the night.

CHAPTER 33

The telephone rang early, woke us all. It was the super from the boatyard. He told Aaron the Orca was ready to go. Aaron said he'd have the money for them the next morning. He hung up, lifted the receiver again and listened for the dial tone. It worked.

He called Lee, said we had four to fly to Seattle. Lee didn't want to land at Boeing Field or Issaquah, so they settled on Snohomish. Aaron told Lila and me to be ready.

Morganne was disappointed, but smiled at Maria. "We'll have fun," she said.

When Lee came, Aaron got a small footlocker from the Wigit and put it in the luggage area behind the seats on the plane.

Cree came out in a tight black pants suit with wide bells on legs and sleeves. She peeked at us through dark glasses from under a wide, flimsy straw hat as she climbed over the rail. Lee looked confused but gave her a hand as she stepped onto the pontoon.

Whidbey Island slid beneath us. I could see two rows of Navy fighter jets dwarfed beside the long gray runways. Then Camano, hardly an island at all, with busy traffic both ways on the bridge to the mainland. Morning updrafts gave us unexpected elevator rides and I saw Lila dig her fingers into the armrest. She hadn't liked to fly since that last trip on a DC-10.

I watched the miniature morning traffic on I-5 as Lee banked right over Lake Stevens and followed Highway 9 south. We circled Snohomish while a couple of takeoffs cleared, then landed smoothly on the little asphalt strip. Lee agreed to meet us again at four-thirty.

Lila and Cree stayed in the airport coffee shop with the footlocker while Aaron and I walked across the bridge into town to get a rental car.

The guy in the little office shack looked at us suspiciously, asked Aaron for a credit card. Aaron said he didn't have one but would put down a good deposit. He held out five hundred-dollar bills. The guy took them, filled out the papers.

It was a green Chevrolet, tinny and uncomfortable, with such a puny engine that it could barely haul the four of us and the footlocker up the Highway 9 grade.

Aaron drove into Bothell, stopped at the first bank he saw. He handed Lila several stacks of hundreds, which she stuffed into her shoulder bag. At a second bank he handed Cree a stack of cash. It disappeared into her gaudy handbag that looked like it was made of drapery fabric and curtain rings. She pulled the hat low and strode into the lobby.

At the next bank, Aaron reached into the footlocker, counted out eight thousand-dollar bundles to me, then four twenties for the fee.

"Cashier's check," he said. "Payable to Bellingham Marine Contractors. You're running an errand for your boss." He handed me a business card that said Orca, Inc. and had his name on it. "Show this to them if you have to, but don't let them have it. If it doesn't feel right, change your mind and split. Walk along Bothell Way and I'll be by in about twenty minutes."

No one in the bank batted an eye at my story. The teller smiled prettily as she typed up the check. Her supervisor barely looked at me, counted the money twice and signed.

Cree and Lila were with Aaron when I got in the car. They both had succeeded and Aaron had gone into the first bank after Lila came out and got a check from a different teller.

We hit four separate banks in Lake City and three in the University District. We took a break for lunch at the Greek place.

"How many more?" Lila asked Aaron.

"We have to do about twenty apiece," he said, "to keep the checks under ten thousand each."

"This could take all day," Lila said.

We bought checks in Wallingford and Greenwood and a string of drive-in banks on Aurora, then through Ballard and along Eliot Way. We skipped downtown and continued down Rainier Valley and along Martin Luther King Way back through the Central Area. Lila got asked for ID twice there and Aaron once. Cree and I must have looked trustworthy.

Aaron had to drive fast to get back to Snohomish on time. The three of us waited in the coffee shop with Lee while Aaron returned the rental car and walked back.

When we left for the plane I reminded Aaron about the footlocker.

"Leave it," he said. "It's empty."

"You aren't out, are you?" Lila asked him. "You can't be."

"No," he said, "one foot locker to go. And it isn't full."

As Lee opened the throttle for take-off, I ran my thumb along my moneybelt, slipped my inhaler out of my bag. A pod of Orcas surfaced just south of Defoe. Three breached, one after the other. Several more made shadows upon the water. I wondered if my friend was among them.

Morganne and Maria sat in a far corner of the lawn. Do slept on a blanket near them. Maria was very withdrawn.

"Eddie was here," Morganne said. "With Lance and some other people. Until just a little while ago. We came out here to get away from them."

"What's Eddie's problem?" Aaron asked her.

"I'm not sure, he was very mysterious," Morganne said. "But I think those people he brought want to rent the house." She took Aaron's arm, led him away a little and said, "I heard him talking to Maria. He told her she needed professional help. She's been like this ever since."

Aaron went to Maria, knelt beside her, stroked her back. She hardly responded.

"You shouldn't have left her alone," Lila said to Morganne.

"Eddie tricked me," Morganne said. "I didn't leave her for a second all day, then he said he'd found a print for me, a Maxfield Parrish I'd been looking for - to go with my others, called 'Ecstasy.' He said it was in the boat if I wanted to get it. When I came back with it he was talking to her. So was Suzette, and Lance."

Aaron picked up Do, led Maria into the house.

"Those bastards," Lila said. "Why won't they leave her alone."

"They think they can help her," Morganne said, "but they don't know her."

"No one needs that kind of help," Cree said.

"Maria is terrified of psychiatrists," Lila said. "All they've ever done with her is lock her up, give her drugs that made her crazy and give her back to her aunt."

"They gave her drugs?" Morganne said.

"You bet," Lila said, "the whole pharmacy. Stuff you can't give children unless they're psych cases."

"Like tranquilizers?" Morganne asked.

Lila nodded. "And tranquilizers and speed together so she didn't get so sleepy in school. But mostly it was Ritalin."

"I thought they just gave Ritalin to boys," I said, "Hyperactives like my cousin Antonio."

"And a few lucky girls," Lila said. "It made her feel really weird and sick so she started faking it and spitting them out. Her aunt caught her. After that, before Maria woke up in the morning her aunt would come in and stick the pill down her throat with her finger and make her swallow it. For a long time after she ran away, she couldn't sleep at night. She was afraid to wake up. I've seen Aaron sit up and hold her in his arms all night so she could sleep."

Lee came for us early. The air was chill and scattered wisps of fog blinded us an instant at a time as he raced for take-off. By air, Bellingham was just minutes away and Lee knew where to land close by the shipyard.

Aaron carried the stack of checks in a zippered leather folder.

The super saw us, came to shake hands and lead the way to the office. The shriveled bookkeeper did his dance while an assistant brought the file. They went over change orders and extras and holdbacks. The eventual number staggered me, but Aaron quietly nodded and opened his folder. He wrote down the number and amount from each check as he passed it over.

After several checks, the bookkeeper sputtered, "This is very irregular. How many checks do you have?"

"It will take fifty-eight," Aaron said. "My partners and I use several banks. Is that a problem?"

The bookkeeper turned, muttered, "How many partners do you have?"

The super came back to the counter. "What is it Jake?"

"All these checks," Jake said. "I'll have to break someone loose just to process them."

"I cleared it with Magnusson," the super said.

"You didn't want cash again," Aaron said.

"I'm short-handed today," Jake said. "Can we do this tomorrow?"

"No," Aaron said.

Jake frowned.

"I'll give you a hand," the super said.

We drank nasty coffee and paced the plank floor while Jake and the super totaled the checks twice and wrote down the complete number of each one.

They gave Aaron a stack of papers and he signed a completion document. "We need to get her out," he said.

"She'll be down on the slip this afternoon," the super said. "We just have to get some of our tools off and strip some masking."

The plane was tethered to the dock and Lee was gone. The sun grew hot as we waited, so we took off our coats, carried them. We cleared our sinuses in the shadow of a steel shed. In about fifteen minutes Lee walked down the steep street to the dock chewing a toothpick.

We stepped out of the shadows, startled him. "Ready to go?" he asked. "I was about to give up on you."

"They count money real slow," Aaron said.

We landed at Defoe just after ten. The midmorning sun drove steam off the dock and the graveled walks. A raven called from high in the trees then flapped away inland. Cree sat in the sun in the stern of the Wigit, repaired a net to a reggae rhythm. She smiled and nodded, did not miss a beat.

No one was downstairs, but we could hear Maria play her guitar and faintly sing. Morganne was still in my sleeping bag, tried to get me to rejoin her. I wanted to get outside. I hung my coat on a closet hook, made sure my bottle was full.

Downstairs Aaron was on the telephone, motioned to me to wait. When he hung up he said, "The sails are finished. We'll rent a U-Haul, see if we can get underway tomorrow."

"Right now?" I asked him.

"I was just going to call Lee," he said.

"How about if I meet you in Bellingham to unload," I said. "I'll pay for the flight."

"Bring any help you can," he said. "The two big ones are heavy."

"What time?" I asked him.

He thought. "It will be evening before I get there."

"We'll get stuck on that side," I said. "I'll see if Cree will go."

I walked down to the dock while he called for the airplane.

Cree grinned wide, "Sure, man," she said, "the Wigit and I, we need the exercise." She put down the net, slipped a joint out of her shirt pocket, offered it to me.

I took it, lit it with her lighter, handed both back.

"You need more ganja," she said. "Leave your nose alone."

"Too much to do," I said.

"Bullshit," she said. "You'd get more done without it."

"Not anymore," I said.

She grinned, handed me the joint. Aaron came down, carried his leather folder. He shared the joint with us while he waited.

"I'll bring everyone," Cree said to him. "We'll have dinner in Bellingham to celebrate."

"Watch Maria," he said.

Lee was there in about fifteen minutes. He barely paused as Aaron stepped onto the float and opened the door.

I've got time for a hike," I said to Cree. "I need to get into the woods."

"I'll go with you," she said. I waited while she put on a red and black banded serape over her jeans and sweatshirt.

I remembered the raven, found a path leading inland in the direction it had flown. Cree silently followed. The path entered a tall stand of firs where constellations of white trillium shone in the shadows. Glossy banks of sharp-spined Oregon grape filled the damp depressions. The path followed an inclined contour, made an easy climb of the broad, steep slope. In bright glades, salal sparkled and dew dripped from the leaves.

A raven started up just before us, squawked away through the trees on some air path parallel to ours. Near the top of the climb my legs began to tire and my breath came hard. Cree floated along behind me, her teeth flashed white when I turned. She tapped the side of her nose.

The rocky hilltop was flat, scattered with trees. It made me think of the glacier-cut landscape of the Columbia Basin. Here, in the dryness of the Olympic rain-shadow, there were patches of sagebrush, and someone had told me that one of the large islands, Lopez or Orcas, was plagued with an overpopulation of rabbits. I took off my boots and carried them.

The path widened and we walked side by side. Cree took my hand. I could feel the rhythmic surge of her blood, smelled the faint musk of her hair and skin. A breeze stirred, from the northwest, and we walked into it, followed the scent of cedar and sea.

The flatness ended in a rock bluff. We stared out across the near islands to the tall white peaks on Vancouver Island. Wherever mountains towered above water, I thought of Stehekin.

"It reminds me of home," Cree said, "the Rainbow Mountains above Bella Coola." She led me to a sunny depression near the bluff, took off the serape and laid it out for us. "I am in need of a man," she said.

"And I'm it," I teased her.

"You could be," she said.

"I'm easy," I said.

The others were ready to go when we got back to the house. Morganne and Maria looked forward to the outing. Lila was resigned to it.

A strong deep-ocean swell rolled in from the northwest, so Cree cut inside of Cypress Island to catch smooth water. Maria clutched Do on Cree's bunk. Outside, Morganne clung to the rail just in case.

"Where's your sea legs?" I asked her.

"Very funny," she said. "We're not all amphibians like you and Cree."

Lila wore a plaid scarf, huddled in the stern for the fresh air. I sat beside her, offered her my inhaler but she waved it off.

"I'll need it later," she yelled above the wind, "to keep going." I reached out and pulled her to me, held her for a moment until she relaxed. I looked down at her and she looked away.

"Damned wind," she said, wiped away tears. I sat with her until I had to help Cree tie up next to the Orca.

Aaron already waited in a large U-Haul van. When he saw us, he backed onto the dock and parked near the Orca's rail about halfway down. He rolled up the truck's rear door as we walked up.

"All of that?" Morganne asked as she looked into the van.

Aaron nodded. "We loaded them with a forklift," he said.

"The boatyard should have a forklift," Lila said.

"I don't want them to know when we're leaving," Aaron said. "It has a ramp. We can do it."

He had to back closer for the ramp to reach over the rail. The surge of each swell raised the rail well above the level of the truck's floor, then with the trough it sank a little below.

The canvas bags were huge, wider by far than the skinny ramp. We started with one of the smallest. "JIB" was stenciled on it in black in several places. Cree and I climbed onto the Orca.

Aaron, Lila and Morganne wrestled the bag to the back of the truck and slid it onto the ramp. The ramp lifted with the swell, nearly threw the sail back on them. They got the bag back onto the ramp as it started down and it slid to where Cree and I could just reach the corners before it started back up. We hung onto the rough canvas as it got steadily heavier with the increased angle. We sank again and at a critical point the bag slid along the aluminum ramp, faster and faster to land on our feet and against our legs.

Aaron came across the precarious ramp, showed us the new sail lockers which would double as broad benches for the whale watchers. One locker, beside the forward cabin had the identical JIB stencil. Aaron showed us how to open it and we slid the sail up the deck and into place.

There were several bags about the same size and smaller, marked F STAYSAIL and M GAFF TS and F GAFF TS, and a larger one marked F JIB that nearly put us all in the water. M T SS wasn't bad because the ramp lowered at the right time to slide it in one motion onto the deck. We decided to take a break before we moved the two big ones. Aaron coaxed Lila and Morganne to walk the ramp and take a look at the boat.

"It's beautiful," Morganne said when Aaron opened the door of a cabin.

"Too bad it wasn't like this when we sailed up from Santa Cruz," Lila said. "I'd be ten years younger."

Cree and I followed them across the ramp onto the truck. We helped slide the FORESAIL bag to the back, perch it as far out onto the ramp as we dared. Then the two of us climbed over it and onto the boat. It began to sink before we turned and I jumped just as I heard Aaron yell. The sail slid, one side hung over, caught on the rail. The momentum swung it around to land in a heap where I had just stood. Aaron and Lila came over and helped us drag it the few feet to its locker.

The light had faded and the orange vapor lights along the dock cast ruddy multiple shadows. We all looked at the MAINSAIL.

"We've got to do it," Aaron said.

"What if it goes in the water?" Lila asked.

"We'd probably lose it," Aaron said.

"We could unload it on the dock," Morganne said. "Then get a forklift."

"I want to be out of here tomorrow, early," Aaron said.

"We can do it," Cree said. "Concentrate."

We got it to the start of the ramp and stopped.

Aaron told us to wait, got a spare length of halyard and tied it through large grommets on two corners of the bag. He ran the double end through a slot at the top of the ramp then crawled underneath to wrap it around the truck frame and lay the free end where he could reach it.

We helped them start the sail on the ramp then crossed over to the boat. They inched it forward so it could start to slide then Aaron jumped to the ground, took the end of the rope and pulled the slack out. As the sail slid, he pulled against it to slow it. The water rose and the sail stopped in the middle of the ramp, started to slide back. Then the ramp bowed beneath the weight, looked like it would fold in half. The Orca sank, the sail started. Aaron let it go and it slid onto the deck in front of us.

"Just leave it there," Aaron said. "We'll need it tomorrow."

The ramp wouldn't slide back underneath the truck because of the bow. We put it part way in and pulled on the end with the rope to try to bend it back, but we couldn't budge it.

"That'll have to do," Aaron said. "I can drop it uptown and get a cab back."

Lila started to giggle as the truck pulled away. She pointed to the ramp curved up into the air. "It looks like a big hard-on," she said.

Aaron was back in only a few minutes, said he had paid the rental attendant an extra two hundred dollars.

"He'll put it in his pocket," Lila said, "swear he has no idea how that ramp got bent."

"It got me out of there," Aaron said. He went into the cabin to be with Maria and Do.

As Cree headed into the main channel, it was full dark. The wind grew stronger, pushed up four-foot waves that overran the ponderous swells, broke here and there into whitecaps.

I sat across from Cree, studied her face in the binnacle light. Whenever she was on the water the tattoos seemed bolder, her teeth whiter. She smiled and winked. "We'll all follow the whales yet," she said.

"We follow them every night," I answered.

CHAPTER 34

Defoe was quiet. I helped Cree tie up while the others went up to the house.

"Aaron should just sail away," Cree said. "He could charter from Bella Coola or Belize. Get away from all this bullshit. Exit-us.

"A king doesn't leave his country," I said, "no matter how sweet the exile."

"His kingdom floats, like mine," she said. "He can take it anywhere."

"Not Aaron," I said. "He's a land creature. He has to have a lair, like a bear or a pirate. Then it's safe to roam around."

"I don't get it," Cree said. "He could always come back."

"But it would be different then. I can go back to Granny's. You can go back to your mother's house. It will always be there, never change. Aaron has to make his own home, carry it around with him like a turtle. He can never go back."

"How do you know so much?" Cree asked me.

"I see it," I said. "They're all like that. Animals without tracks. With no past there is no future. That's what my Grandfather said."

"He was right," Cree said. "Marley says, 'We know where we're going. We know where we're from. I don't know what I would do without the old stories. They have so many answers."

"Aaron has to have all the answers, for all of them," I said.

"Then they argue with him," Cree said. "Strange species."

We cast off before dawn. Cree ran without lights, felt her way through Rosario Strait. As she swung the Wigit around the north end of Lummi Island the sky in the east lightened enough for me to see the massive silhouette of the North Cascades. I wondered about my horses.

Against the mute colors of sunrise, the crisp black and white Orca stood like a real ship against a painted background. Aaron went below. A few minutes later, I felt the new auxiliary engine start.

Cree messed with the wheel, said she did not like the feel of the new gear. I turned on the radio, squelched the static, and stared at the blank radar and sonar screens.

Aaron came up, checked the action of the throttle and watched the gauges while the engine warmed. He engaged the prop at low idle and went to the stern to watch the bubbles churn up as the Orca tugged against the mooring lines. He slacked it, and on the dock Cree cast off the bow line, signaled me to haul it in while she let go the stern.

If I hadn't watched the dock, I would not have known when we moved. The dark hull slipped soundlessly into Bellingham Bay.

"I can't wait to get the sails up," Aaron said when I got up to the pilothouse. It was hard to believe we were on the same ship that we'd sailed north from California.

The Wigit shadowed us as we ran on auxiliary power in the early sun. Lila and Morganne huddled on one of the wide upholstered benches provided for customers who wanted to watch the helm at work.

Aaron looked at them. "We'll skip the sails, this morning," he said to me. "I don't have the heart to make them do it."

The tall madrona trees along the eastern headland still shadowed half the cove when we dropped the new anchor about a hundred yards out. Cree came alongside and Lila and Morganne and I got into the Wigit.

Aaron broke out the skiff from under a canvas cover and lowered it. He climbed into the skiff, started the outboard and followed us in. He hurried upstairs to check on Maria and Do, carried the sleepy baby down with him. Maria came a few minutes later.

"Sure is quiet," Morganne said.

"I like it this way," Maria said. "No one to bother us."

"There'll be enough people bothering us soon," Aaron said.

"It's beautiful, boss," The Poet said. "When can we go out and see it?"

"Later," Aaron said.

"When they said you had a boat and lived on an island, this isn't what I pictured," Suras said.

"I told you," the Poet said proudly. "Has Eddie seen it?"

"Haven't seen Eddie," Aaron said.

"He's hiding out," Lila said. "I'm surprised you two aren't."

"What did we do?" the Poet asked.

"Nothing but be yourselves," Lila said.

"We didn't tell anyone anything," the Poet said, "not really. Nothing everyone doesn't know. It wasn't the police or anything."

"So what does everyone know?" Lila asked him.

"About the coke and everything," the Poet said. "But it's okay. No one cares anymore. Everyone does coke."

"They can still put you in jail for it," Lila said.

"Can I buy some?" Suras asked Aaron.

"Buy some what?" Aaron asked.

"Some coke," Suras said.

"I don't know where to buy coke," Aaron said with a laugh. "You must be confused."

"Don't treat me that way," Suras said. I've seen what I've seen."

"What have you seen?" Lila asked him.

"Lots of cocaine," Suras said. "An ounce at least."

"Well, that ought to bring out the FBI," Lila said.

"I've heard about a lot more than that," he said, "and some people seem to be interested."

"What people?" Lila asked him. "Who've you been talking to?"

"I mean," he squirmed, "it seems like a lot to me. I haven't told anyone."

"Right," Lila said. "Just your grandma's bridge club. Well, the only cocaine I've seen lately was in your house and you brought it out first. That's my testimony."

Suras started to say something, stopped.

"We're busy," Lila said. "We'll call you if we need you."

"I want to help," Suras said. "I really want to be part of what you're doing."

"I have a full crew," Aaron said.

"We'd do anything," the Poet said. "To, like, make up."

"Make up for what?" Lila asked him.

"Just whatever," he said. "Got any decks to scrub, boss?" he asked Aaron.

"We have Teflon decks, now," Lila said. "And they burned that bunk you died on."

"Give me a break, Lila," the Poet said, "I'm really trying."

"Some day you should get past trying," Lila said.

Lance ran Suras and the Poet to LaConner and came back. He was Aaron's dutiful servant as before, but I knew Aaron no longer trusted him. Aaron told us not to use coke around any outsiders. Lila and I already had talked about it.

A couple of days later Patrick and Pancho came to see the boat. Even Patrick couldn't find much wrong with it. He was all smiles but I could smell the envy. Pancho, as always, seemed to be from, or bound for, another planet. Aaron tried to get Patrick to sign on as First Mate, but Patrick said he was going skiing in Columbia again and winked at Aaron.

"You should sail down," Patrick said, "give me a ride back."

"Too many commitments," Aaron said.

It was almost a week before Eddie and Suzette showed up. They had been at another symposium, brought back a briefcase full of reservations and deposits. Eddie had several conspiratorial meetings with Aaron, made sure I wasn't there. He conducted a formal inspection of the ship and pronounced it acceptable, then hurried down to Seattle to line up more whale watchers.

Lila, Morganne and I spent several hours a day on the Orca. Cree brought the heavy winches from Seattle and we wrestled them on board, bolted them onto thick steel plates the yard had installed. Aaron showed us how to wrap a line around the drum and run it either direction with ease. There was even a little fold-down seat by each winch for more genteel sailing and a cargo boom that could lift a ton.

"We needed that when we were loading the sails." Morganne stroked the chromed steel of one of the winches. "My shoulders love you," she said to Aaron.

"Don't worry," he said, "there are cranks for when the power goes out."

"How often is that?" Lila asked.

"Never," Aaron said, "as long as the batteries are full."

"I want lots of spares," Lila said.

"We have a diesel generator," he said, "and the auxiliary engine will charge one at a time."

Aaron bought a bunch of tools and we screwed the furniture to the decks and secured everything that could move. There were some heavy crates of china and silver and five-star galley equipment to stow away. We ran heat ducts and electrical conduit and gas lines for the range and grill. Aaron offered to pay us, but it seemed unnecessary since we all had more money than we needed and nothing else to do.

Aaron had me help him with one special project that only he and I knew about. We pulled up several deck planks next to the hull in one of the holds and built a cabinet, which protruded into the bilge several inches but was hidden from above.

Aaron bought a shallow floor safe which just fit the cabinet and we bolted it in. Then we cleated the planks together and used cut-off screws except for the ends so that the whole section could be pulled up in a few minutes to get to the safe.

The day we finished it he put a stack of money in it and said, "Now all my money's in this tub."

I was surprised at how little was left.

He said I could put mine in the safe, but I decided to keep it in my moneybelt. He told Lila and Morganne he had a safe place for their money if they wanted one. Lila said hers was all safe in escrow except for what she had in her pocket. Morganne got her overnight case, gave Aaron a loose pile of cash, then took back a hundred.

"How much is it," Aaron asked her.

"I don't know," she said. "I haven't counted it in a while. About eighty thousand, I think."

"You need to count it," Lila said. "How can you keep track of it?"

"I'm sick of counting it," Morganne said. "You count it."

Aaron put the whole mess in a paper bag and taped it shut. "Just tell me when you want it," Aaron said. "Give me twenty-four hours notice."

I was glad no one else was around. Aaron had noticed the sheriff's boat near the Orca and had me go out with him in the skiff. The deputies drew their guns as we approached, but the IRS man called them off.

The two Federal Marshals with them had a fancy brass chain and a heavy padlock, but they weren't sure where to put it. Obviously they hadn't seized many sailing ships.

It wasn't a warrant he handed Aaron, just an order by the IRS commissioner. No one got read their rights or put in handcuffs. It was strictly business.

All they wanted was money. Quite a lot of money. Bellingham Marine Contractors had admitted to taking in large sums of cash in a very irregular manner, the IRS agent told Aaron while the marshals tried to find something to put their chain around. The government's share of that would have been over four hundred thousand. Then there was the original value of the craft. And, of course, this would trigger a close audit of any corporations or partnerships.

He was friendly, even magnanimous. "We won't impound the property," he indicated the Orca, "for ten days. We will have to put a guard aboard," he smiled sheepishly, "Rules, you know, and this close to international waters."

Aaron asked if we could get our personal property, but the friendly agent declined.

"A judge might have to decide what's personal and what isn't," he said.

The skiff, too, belonged to them for now. I think he would have let us swim to the island, but one of the deputies who'd brought them out offered us a ride in and there wasn't much he could say. I think the deputies just wanted a closer look at the island.

One of the marshals stayed on board the Orca and talked on the radio to the marshal with us.

"This is quite a rowboat," we heard him say. "When the time comes, I want to take this down to Frisco."

"There'll be a lot of competition for that job," the marshal with us replied.

It was a good thing we had gotten more careful with our drugs. Aaron said he didn't have anything stashed on board. The rest of us had begun to watch each other, make sure no one spaced-out.

They made us wait until they had tied up bow and stern and shut down the engine before we could step to the dock. They sat and watched us walk across the lawn and into the house.

Maria was upstairs. Aaron checked on her and came back down to use the telephone.

Lila had paid Lance to run her to Seattle to check on the bar deal. Morganne had gone with Lila to see the bar again and decide if she could survive there. Cree was out fishing.

Eddie and Suzette had been showing up at several-day intervals, grabbing a bunch of clothes, snorting all the coke in sight then flying back to Seattle. They had been around yesterday so we had at least a couple of days before they appeared again.

Aaron called Frank Lewis, who wanted him to come down for a conference. IRS cases were easy, he said, just expensive. Aaron didn't want to leave Maria alone, so he left me on the island and had Lee fly him to Snohomish.

It was a bright, still August day and I was happy to stay. I realized that it was as close to alone as I had been in months. I sat on the lawn and watched waves sparkle against the point at the mouth of the cove. Next summer I wanted to be in the mountains.

Lance brought Lila and Morganne home, but took off again immediately. "He has a hot date in Mount Vernon," Lila said.

"What's Aaron doing on the boat?" Morganne asked.

"He's not on the boat," I said. "He had to fly to Seattle."

"I saw the skiff out there," Morganne insisted.

"There's a Federal Marshal on the Orca," I said.

The color drained from Morganne's face. "I knew something was wrong," she said. "I told Lila."

"You were right, for a change," Lila said.

"It's the IRS," I told them. "Aaron went to see Frank Lewis."

"Frank will handle it," Lila said. "I've seen him handle worse than this."

"They just want money," I said.

"How much money?" Morganne asked.

"I heard him say four hundred thousand," I said.

"I don't think he has that much," Lila said. "He can probably borrow the rest of it from Gerard - or Pete."

"It's a lot of money," I said.

"Never count Aaron out," Lila said.

I heard the Wigit at the dock and went down to tell Cree.

She didn't seem surprised or worried. "Aaron will handle them," she said. "For now."

Lila went up and talked Maria into coming down for a decent meal. Cree had caught a fat King Salmon and sliced off thick steaks. She also provided potatoes to bake. Aaron had brought home two dozen ears of sweet corn the day before, so I went outside to shuck half of them. While I was there, it occurred to me that it would only be fair to share with the agent on the Orca. I knew there was no food on board yet.

I told Cree and she agreed. We set up a charcoal grill on the dock and carried down one of the picnic tables from the lawn. We set both so that they were in full view of the boat. We could feel his binoculars on us already.

Everyone got into the spirit and rummaged around for whatever enticing food could be found. I found a bowl of wax fruit on the fireplace mantel and washed and shined it up for a centerpiece.

"God, that looks real," Lila said. "I could eat it."

She had found some leftover salad and arranged it attractively. Morganne brought out a loaf of bread and spread it fan-wise on a plate with a block of cheddar cheese in the middle. Cree brought out several large pots and serving bowls and put them on the table as if they held food.

When the grill was hot we wrapped the potatoes in foil and put them on. Morganne brought half a dozen wine bottles, three of them empty and set them around. We made a great show of drinking while we waited for the potatoes.

When they were nearly ready, Cree grilled the salmon, made sure there was lots of smoke which to our amusement drifted out with the land breeze towards our food voyeur. Lila stripped to her shorts and halter-top and slowly smoked a cigarette on the end of the dock.

We had just started to eat when he started waving and hollering. We ignored him. Cree served more wine with a flourish and I pretended to eat a wax pear. Morganne started to laugh and couldn't stop. Finally she walked up to the house and came back under better control.

The agent jumped around and screamed as though the Orca was about to sink. I walked to the end of the dock and held my hand to my ear to listen.

"Hungry!" he bellowed. "Food!"

I made a motion to indicate I couldn't hear him.

He tried again. "Hungry! food!"

I shrugged, shook my head and walked away.

"I'm starving, you spick bastard!" he shouted across the water at my back. "I have money!"

I sat down and Cree served another round of wine. The agent was frantic, ran along the rail this way and that, like a horse in a pen for the first time. Then he disappeared.

A few minutes later he shouted at us again. I looked and he held a sign, skinny letters scrawled with a marker on the back of a nautical chart. "I NEED FOOD - $," it said.

I showed the others.

"Fuck him," Lila said. "It's just part of his nasty job."

"Doesn't look like he'll starve right away," Morganne said.

"We might plant a seed we can harvest later," Cree said.

"What do we need from him?" Lila asked. "He's just a foot soldier, he'll be in Pittsburgh or Phoenix next week."

"We should feed him," Maria said and startled us all. "He's a person."

Cree started the Wigit and I put together a plate: a chunk of salmon, a potato, two ears of corn and some of the limp salad. I was sure it was more than he deserved. While Cree ran out, I threw some fenders over on the port side so we could come alongside the Orca.

He waited anxiously at the rail. I showed him the plate. "Twenty bucks," I said.

"Twenty bucks?" he started, then caught himself. "Okay," he said. "Hand it up."

"Twenty bucks," I said.

He glared at me, pulled out a twenty and threw it. I handed up the plate. He stuffed in a mouthful of salmon, swallowed like a wolf.

"This is quite a boat," he said, then gulped another mouthful.

"I guess," I said.

"You were out here when we came," he said.

"Just visiting," I said.

"Who is this guy, Aaron?" he asked, picked up the potato and bit off about a third of it.

"I have no idea," I said. "I just met him."

"Pretty big operator, I guess," he said.

"I wouldn't know," I said.

"Who's the blonde?" he asked me, pointed with the stub of the potato.

"My wife," I said.

He stared. "I thought the little dark one with the baby was yours," he said.

"That's Aaron's wife," I said.

He stared again, choked down the end of the potato and held the ears of corn while he dumped the salad in the water. "Tell your wife, he said, "I would pay for three meals a day until my relief gets here."

"I'll tell her," I said, signaled Cree to pull off.

When we were out of earshot, Cree grinned. "I guess we know where his buttons are," she said.

We went back inside after Lila took one more slow stroll to the end of the dock and back. She had to stop and adjust the halter-top a couple of times.

Aaron got back just before sunset. Frank Lewis had taken all the information, would contact IRS the next morning. Maria had enjoyed the picnic, was in better spirits than usual. We all sat around in the living room and played with Do while we told Aaron about our encounter with the agent. It made him laugh hard, and soon he felt better too.

The next morning we ate breakfast together, sat in the sun and wondered how hungry it was out on the Orca. About ten, Cree and I decided to take him out our leftovers. He got half an omelet, two pieces of cold toast, some orange juice and a cup of coffee for another twenty. This time he did complain about the price but I told him the food was only two bucks, the rest was delivery.

"If you send your wife out, it might be worth it," he said.

We didn't take him any lunch.

Lila talked Morganne into posing with her on the dock. They carried lawn chairs down and put on two of Lila's skimpiest dancing costumes. They rubbed sun cream on each other and took down their straps to tan underneath. Lila did some yoga stretches on a blanket.

Frank Lewis called Aaron, said they had an appointment with the friendly IRS agent the next afternoon.

We took dinner out to our prisoner. He had an attitude. He was going to be relieved the next morning, so he wouldn't need us much longer. And when he came back in three days he'd bring his own god-damned food.

"Yes, sir," I said.

Aaron didn't get back from the meeting until the following morning. He was very quiet. Lila finally asked him.

"They want half a million," he said. "Cash, no installments."

"Can you get that much?" Morganne asked him.

"I don't know," he said. "I'll try."

"You can do it," Lila said. "I know you can."

"I don't know how I'll even get to the money on the Orca," Aaron said. "As long as the guard is there."

"So that's where your stash place is," Morganne said.

"Not a good plan," he said.

We saw the sheriff's boat bring the new guard, but they didn't come near the island. Maria said they were afraid of the Guardians. Lila said they didn't have a warrant, so we could throw them off if they did come.

Aaron spent a lot of time dialing for dollars. Pete claimed to be broke, or had all his money out. JJ said he had a little, but he couldn't afford to invest it in a sailboat, had to keep it turning. I could tell from Aaron's end of the conversation that Gerard was evasive, never did give him an answer. Aaron offered to sell his half of Primal Power, said Gerard would be better off, they could maybe avoid the audit.

"I'll talk to him," Lila said, "he'll listen to me."

"He'll pay for it," Morganne said, "but not that much."

No one had a good plan for getting to the money on the Orca. We hadn't seen the new guard since the sheriff brought him out. It looked like they would rotate every three days, but that didn't really help.

"We could get Lance and Patrick and some people and do a commando raid," Morganne said.

Lila laughed. "You'd make a great commando," she said. "Well, at least there wouldn't be much of you to shoot at."

"It would only be more trouble," Cree said.

"If you come up with the money," Lila asked Aaron, "what's to stop them from taking half of that too. Unless you can prove it was a loan."

"Frank says if they agree to take a certain amount, they don't ask where it comes from."

"Sounds like our government," Lila said. "You could sell an interest in the boat."

"No one has that much cash," Aaron said.

Aaron and Frank Lewis came up with a counter offer, which Lewis presented. It was three hundred thousand, half now, half in six months. The friendly agent said no to the terms, but indicated they might take the three-hundred-grand. Lewis was as surprised as Aaron was.

Lila chortled, "I knew you could do it."

"I don't have even that much," Aaron said.

"You should be close, and we can raise it. I'll get my money out of escrow, or sell the bar if it's too late."

"You can have my money," Morganne said. "I'd be glad to be rid of it. You could sell me part of the Orca." She looked at me but I said nothing.

"How do we get to the money on the Orca?" Lila asked.

"We need to think very hard," Morganne said. "I know we'll

come up with something."

Eddie and Suzette came on Lance's boat the next day before noon. Clearly they knew something was up. Suzette wouldn't look straight at anyone and Lance talked non-stop nonsense. Eddie called Aaron aside for a conference. I couldn't get within range.

"So, how much do you know?" Lila asked Lance when they were gone.

"Know what?" he asked innocently.

"Don't jerk me off," Lila said.

"Eddie heard IRS impounded the boat," Lance said. "That's all I know."

"So what's he in such a panic about?" Lila asked.

"The money," Lance said. "If they have to cancel cruises, they'll have to refund the deposits."

"So?" Lila said, "Shit happens."

"I don't think Eddie has it all," Lance said.

"That's his problem," Lila said.

"He knows a lot," Lance said.

"So do I," Lila replied. "Well, don't worry, Aaron has it handled."

"Right," Lance said.

"We'll see," Lila said.

Eddie was settled down when he and Aaron came back and he made calming motions and noises at Suzette. Lance seemed puzzled. They hung around for a while, finally Eddie asked for a line.

"I'm out," Aaron told him. "Doesn't seem to be much around."

I could see that Suzette didn't believe it, but Eddie seemed to. They left a few minutes later.

We shared a line to celebrate after they'd gone.

CHAPTER 35

Aaron had to go to Seattle to sign the papers. Either he came up with three hundred thousand dollars in thirty days or they took the Orca with no appeal.

Lila walked him to the dock to wait for Lee. When she came back in the house, she said to me and Morganne, "That fat marshal is back on the boat. The son-of-a-bitch was yelling at me, 'Take it off. Show me your teats, honey.'"

"You should report him," Morganne said.

"Right," Lila said to her, turned to me, "But it did give me an idea. I could go give him what he wants while you and Aaron get the money. I won't let him up for air for an hour."

"You wouldn't," Morganne said.

"I've done it for a lot less than that," Lila said.

"You never turned tricks," Morganne said.

"That's not what they called it," Lila said. "But I'd do it for Aaron in a second."

Aaron thought it was a pretty good idea, but we couldn't figure out how to get to the Orca while Lila did her deed. Even if she got him in a stateroom, anything with a motor would surely alarm him. And how would Lila get there, since they still had the skiff.

When Cree showed up, she had the answers. She carried a two-man inflatable for emergencies. This was definitely an emergency. And she would take Lila out to her rezendevous on the Wigit, help create a diversion.

"We have to do it tomorrow or the next day," Aaron said. When he leaves again, he might never be back."

Lila knew just how to entice him. She hung out on the dock much of the afternoon. Sometimes Cree was with her. There was lots of stretching and rubbing and adjusting of clothes.

Before evening he held up the "I NEED FOOD - $" sign.

They took him out a plate of scraps and got twenty dollars. He got his eyes full of Lila. They were laughing hard when they got back.

"God, I'd love to get him in a bar," Lila said, "He'd sign over his pension."

When they took him lunch the next day, he begged Lila to come back that evening, maybe they could share some dessert. Lila told him she'd think about it.

"I know he'll think about it," she said.

"It was too easy," Morganne said. "Be careful."

The inflatable wasn't my favorite part, but otherwise I was up for the raid. I wanted to beat the smug bastards whether they ever knew it or not.

Aaron and I wore the darkest clothes we had and Morganne and Maria painted our faces in camouflage with eye shadow and fireplace soot mixed with butter. Morganne added a few fierce flourishes with lipstick and Maria turned Aaron into a fearsome apparition.

We looked into the mirror and laughed.

"A regular war party," Lila said.

Aaron had some driving gloves and Cree loaned me some work gloves that fit. We had to lug the collapsed inflatable through the woods quite a ways so that we couldn't be seen from the Orca when we went in the water.

Aaron yanked the cord on the gas canister and the raft popped into existence. It wasn't bad, a lot better than my homemade one. There were even plastic locks for the paddle-shaped oars and a storm cover. Unfortunately, it was all bright orange.

We dirtied it as much as possible and broke some brush to lay across it. Still it glowed in the twilight. We left it and walked along the steep beach until we could just see the Orca past the point. We sat on a rock and Aaron offered me his bottle and spoon, but I had my inhaler.

The sky slowly darkened and we barely could see the Wigit when they went out. I took off my boots, set them beneath the overhang of a nose shaped rock above the beach. If I wound up in the water, I could swim better barefoot. And walk a lot quieter, too.

We had a little trouble at first with the balance of the raft, but soon we skimmed right along. I could hear voices across the water but could not make out the words. We circled well out to come in directly opposite the Wigit. It was only a few minutes until we felt the star shadow of the Orca and Aaron reached out to break our soft collision.

I could hear Lila tease and taunt and her victim plead. Aaron had told her to get him into one of the forward staterooms. We waited until they moved in that direction.

"A hundred bucks, tops," I heard him say.

"That's good for fifteen minutes," Lila retorted.

"An hour," he said. "I know prices."

"Depends on the product," Lila said.

We heard the door open and close, then we slipped across the deck and along the passageway. The galley was open and it was a mess. "I guess they don't do housekeeping," I whispered to Aaron.

We crept down the steep stairway to the pantry below. There was a small door for loading food stores from the main holds. We squeezed through that and Aaron switched on his flashlight. Everything below was as we'd left it, tools lying around, work in progress. We'd brought heavy screwdrivers and it took only a few minutes to loosen the planks and slide them aside.

We heard a creak, froze and listened. "I'll check it out," I said. "Get the money."

I felt my way back through the dark, remembered where I'd seen a heavy framing hammer and picked it up. At the foot of the ladder I stopped, listened carefully, heard nothing but the soft slap of waves on the hull. In just a few minutes Aaron came. When he was just behind me I went up the stairs, hammer ready.

We stopped in the galley, got the feel of things. There was not the slightest ripple of scent or sound or silence that seemed unusual. Before we went out on the deck, I laid the hammer across an open newspaper the guard must have been reading when Lila arrived.

The raft hovered on the water like an orange UFO. Aaron went down first. I untied the small lanyard from the rail and stepped as far into the raft as I could. A wave bumped us back into the Orca, nearly dumped me. I squatted down, got my balance. Aaron handed me one oar and we pushed away as far as we could, then paddled sideways until we were clear.

I put the oars in the locks and rowed while Aaron sat quietly in the bow and stared ahead for landmarks. We could still see the Orca plainly when we heard the voices of Lila and the guard out on deck. I rested the oars and laid low. Aaron took off his jacket and had me drape it over the stern to cut down the glare.

They argued for a while, then Lila went down the ladder and the Wigit pulled off.

"She's out of there," I said. When the silhouette of the Orca was out of sight, I turned us in towards the beach. With no moon, we couldn't distinguish one part of the shore from another.
Aaron made a guess and I caught a wave, drove up the beach as far as possible.

Aaron jumped out on the sand, I stepped into the water and we dragged the raft clear. I pulled the release valve as soon as we were on dry land. The sooner that Day-Glo bubble shrank, the better. I walked on it to force the last of the gas out, then rolled it as well as possible and dragged it into the brush.

I looked around for the nose rock and my boots, but I never found them. We decided to leave the raft there until the next day. I led the way back since I knew the paths better. Aaron carried a small backpack with the money wrapped in a couple of garbage bags.

Lila and Cree waited on the porch when we got there. When she saw us Lila gave a little cheer and Cree clapped her hand over

Lila's mouth.

"I'm sorry," Lila said. "I'm just wired."

Morganne and Maria heard us, came out on the porch. "You did it," Morganne said. Then she looked at Lila. "How was it."

Lila laughed. "It was a dry hustle," she said. "At least just a little damp. That fat bastard just wanted to look at my teats while he jacked-off." She shook her head. "It was weird. He told me not to touch him. Said he was afraid of some disease. An immune syndrome or something. He said the government knows about it, but they aren't telling anyone. He gave me the creeps. He said just queers and whores and niggers carry it. He's crazy, his eyes go two different directions."

Everyone got quiet.

"You're barefoot," Morganne said to me.

"Lost my boots," I said.

"Again?" she asked. "We're going to have to put them on a rope around your neck."

Aaron and I went to wash our faces. It wasn't easy to get the war paint off, but with my beard there wasn't a lot of skin covered. My forehead was the worst. I nearly rubbed it raw and I could still see the shadows of the paint. It reminded me of Cree's tattoos.

We had some tea and a line. Lila urged Aaron and Cree to take off immediately, head for Seattle with the money before something could happen. "I'm telling you, that fucker is crazy," she said.

Aaron thought it would be safer to fly down in the morning. It would be more in the normal pattern. If the Wigit headed out in the middle of the night it would be more suspicious. Cree and I agreed with that.

Lila went over to the window. "There's something going on out there," she said.

We all looked. All the Orca's lights were blazing. Aaron got his small binoculars. "He's looking for something," he said.

We watched for a few minutes. The fat guard came out to the rail, fired a flare. The angry red flame hung above him then drifted towards open water before it sputtered out. He fired again a few minutes later, then again.

A few minutes later a helicopter roared low overhead, searchlight slashing this way and that. Do was frightened and Maria nursed her. The guard was at the rail talking on the radio.

I went outside the back door so I could breathe. The light covered the house, held, but they did not have the angle to penetrate the deep shadows where I was.

The chopper made several passes, then searched up the beach. I didn't see how they could miss the raft. After a few minutes, it reappeared suddenly over the ridge behind the house and circled the cove then disappeared towards the northeast.

The Orca still was brightly lit, but otherwise everything was as quiet as usual. I looked at the near trees, relaxed my eyes, and the glow was there, dancing, shimmering. I almost could feel the heat from it through the chill night air.

I went inside and Lila chopped us a line. We watched out the windows but the helicopter never returned. Just after dawn the Sheriff's boat appeared and the two deputies went on board the Orca for a while. When they climbed back over the rail, one of them carried the framing hammer.

Aaron called Frank Lewis, told him he had the money. Lewis didn't believe him at first, questioned him about where it came from. He also told Lewis about the helicopter. They decided it would be better to wait a couple of days before they took the money in.

We needed a safe place for the money until then. They might search the house or the whole island. The Wigit seemed to be the only choice, although they might even search Cree on her way out.

Finally, I said, "I'll pack it over to the sweat, Cree can meet me there."

"Where's the sweat?" Morganne asked. "What's a sweat."

"It's on the other side of the island," I said.

"It's a healing place," Cree said.

I went first in case Cree's going out set them off. I found a spot on the ridge where I could see the Orca and watched from there until the Wigit was well out. Nobody stirred. I followed the sweeping ridge as usual, made good time. Walking was like being home, comfortable and familiar. The cool path felt good to my bare feet. The money hardly weighed anything although it was all of Aaron's and Morganne's as well as my moneybelt. A flock of ravens gave me a noisy escort, a dead giveaway if anyone was paying attention.

Cree was a quarter mile out with a salmon line set when I got to the sweat. I showed myself for just a minute, then sat back in the trees. A while later, she pulled in her line and slowly headed in.

She had said she could get in close enough to the beach for me to wade out and throw the backpack to her. We had timed it for high tide which was good for the Wigit but not that great for me. It got deep fast and I was glad I was barefoot. I gave up on wading and swam out to meet her. I hung onto the rail while she wrestled the wet backpack off me. Then she helped me clamber up. "Seems like we've been here before." She grinned. "But last time you were a dead weight and didn't have any money."

I rested a few minutes and she held the Wigit against the slacking tide as close to the beach as she dared. I slipped back into the water and swam only a few yards before I felt the bottom and waded in.

I took my time on the way back, stopped here and there, explored some side paths. Without the moneybelt, my body felt light and free. I free-climbed a little rock face, just for the sensation and talked back to a scolding raven. I stuffed myself on blackberries and fell asleep with my back against a tree. It was late afternoon before I got back to the house.

Morganne studied me. "Another short cut?" she asked me.

"No," I said, "I know my way home now."

We lay around for two days. I was hungry all the time, and with Cree not around to mother me, I spent a lot of time in the kitchen.

"You trying to eat everything in the house?" Lila asked me the second morning. "Make me some, too."

Cree had stocked us up on groceries so I had lots to work with. I fried potatoes and onions, whipped up some buckwheat pancakes and attempted omelets a la Cree. Lila called Aaron and Maria and we made it a family breakfast.

I didn't think they were hot enough, but Lila choked on her first bite and had to bury it in sour cream to get it down. Cree and I had just about trained Morganne to eat it as hot as we did. Aaron and Maria seemed comfortable with any kind of food.

Aaron called Frank Lewis and he called back with an appointment for the following day. Aaron wanted Frank with him in case IRS pulled a double-cross and tried to arrest him or something. Lewis assured him there was nothing to worry about. "They might doublecross you," he told Aaron, "but they won't doublecross me. That's what I get paid for."

Cree came in just at dusk. I heard the familiar rhythm well out. She idled past the Orca, shifted softly to reverse and nudged the dock. I was there to catch the line.

She had the money in a duffel bag she often carried and threw it to me with a grin. "All quiet on the western front?" she asked me.

"Quiet as you could expect. Everyone leaves us alone right now."

"Wait until Aaron has the boat back," she said. "They'll be on us like flies."

She had brought me some new boots, plain black, without any cavalry straps or zippers. They fit perfectly. She wouldn't take any money for them.

Aaron counted his money, was forty thousand short. "Take it from mine," Morganne said. Aaron offered her a share of the boat, but she wasn't interested. I put on my moneybelt without looking inside.

Everything went without a hitch. IRS counted money a lot faster than the boatyard had, and no one was going to ask them where it came from.

Aaron brought me along and Frank Lewis stared at me as if he'd never seen me before. I began to keep myself on the far side of Aaron from him and he ignored me as if I were a shadow.

The friendly agent gave Aaron some release documents, shook hands and smiled. Lewis checked everything, approved. I stood in the dark foyer and watched them. The parting was cordial. Lewis patted everyone's back, even smiled at me, although it was a stranger smile.

The fat guard was happy to see us. He unlocked the chain they'd put around the handle of one door to the wheelhouse. It was symbolic, I guess. The guard waddled back and forth along the rail with his radio on his ear while he waited for the sheriff's boat. He had Aaron sign a statement that the property had been returned in the same condition as when it was impounded.

"Tell her," he said to me and held his hands as though they supported large breasts. He dropped his hands. "Tell what's-her-name thanks."

As soon as he was gone, we went in and looked around. Everything was a mess, but there was no real damage. He'd thrown his candy wrappers and pop cans everywhere and used a china service platter for an ashtray. There were a bunch of dirty towels on the floor, one of them with spots of blood.

It didn't look like they'd ever been below, even when they were searching for the intruder. There could have been a team of Soviet agents down there, for all they knew.

Aaron called Eddie at the University and told him the Orca would be ready on time. He had to repeat it several times. He called Gerard who was obviously relieved, but they still expected an audit of Primal Power. Gerard's friend who was an accountant agreed to dummy up a set of books that would take care of most of it. Then they would plead stupid to the rest of it, get off with a fine.

CHAPTER 36

We had to get the Orca under sail, make sure everything actually worked, before the first load of tourists was due the middle of August. Aaron talked Cree into going on a shakedown but we were still short several hands. Patrick and Pancho finally agreed to do it for an ounce apiece. Suras and the Poet got wind of the cruise, flew out to volunteer. Aaron assured them we had a full crew.

While he cast about for more hands, Lila, Morganne and I cleaned up the boat and finished the trim work that had been interrupted. We had it very shipshape in just a few days.

Aaron called Santa Cruz. Pete said he didn't know anyone who'd be interested in "chasing whales around the bay." Aaron finally decided to go out short-handed, anchor at night and get some practice in the daytime.

He installed Maria and Do in a stateroom next to the wheelhouse. Maria seemed happy, talked a little and smiled at everyone. We all passed Do around and remarked on how big she'd grown.

When he came on board, Patrick looked at my new boots and shook his head. "I don't know how you can stand up in those things," he said.

We sailed through the San Juans, tacked a lot and beat into the wind whenever possible. Patrick understood that the job was to make something break, if possible. Nothing broke.

He spent a lot of time moving spreaders, tightening and

loosening stays and plucking at them like they were strings on some great instrument. He told us he was tuning the rig, and explained how it all must be in balance, ship and masts and sails, like a suspension bridge. With the new sails and new superstructure he had to do it all again.

The helm was so smooth and easy that I couldn't relax. It felt like something in a speedboat or motor cruiser. You had to watch the wind instruments and the compass to be sure the ship actually turned. Two hours of it at a time was plenty.

We anchored down from Roche Harbor and Cree and I made omelets for everyone. No one was as tired as the easiest day we'd spent on the Quest. Maria and Aaron ate with us and after dinner we all gathered in the deck lounge and watched the stars appear. The Great Bear was directly above us, pointed north.

The crew quarters beneath the forward cabin had full headroom. There were ten soft bunks in little cubicles with small portholes, and each had a built-in desk and a chair. My duffel bag fit easily in the locker under the bunk. There were small, deluxe cabins for Master and First Mate next to the crew.

It all seemed spacious, until you looked in a stateroom and saw that each pair of whale watchers had as much area as half the crew, with wide windows and queen sized beds and their own toilets. Who paid whom definitely made a difference.

The space was perfect for me, a snug sea-going cave with room to read and think and dream. I wrote in my notebook for a while, then put Exodus on my portable, laid back with my new lightweight headphones. Just after dark, Morganne came into my cabinette and announced she would spend the night.

"The boat looks nice - now," she said, "but I liked the Quest better. There are too many walls between us now."

"After all your bitching," I said. "You'd better not tell Aaron that."

"It's beautiful," she said, "but it doesn't feel like ours anymore."

We zigzagged around the sound for two more days. Patrick confused us as often as possible, but by the third day, we knew what we were doing. We took turns at all the positions, and I could tell that Patrick was impressed in spite of himself. He had fewer insults and even an occasional compliment. Wherever we went, everyone stared at the Orca.

It was only a week until the first three-day cruise and we all were apprehensive. Walt Gann wheedled Aaron into letting him do an article on the boat. He hung around for a couple of days, took rolls of pictures and scribbled on his pad. He tried to talk to Maria a couple of times and went away shaking his head.

The way he watched us, I was sure he wanted a drug exposé, but we were careful and he didn't even see anyone smoke a joint. He asked me if he could buy some Northern Lights, but I went Native on him.

"You've all changed so much since that party," he said. "What's going on?"

"We haven't changed," I told him, "It's the rest of the world."

Aaron finally had to tell him to finish up and be ready for a ride to the mainland. He reminded Aaron that a favorable article could generate more customers.

•

That first cruise was okay. We avoided the three couples who came on board. They mostly stayed inside or sat on the plush seats in the covered lounge amidships. The two times we did sight orcas, they acted like it was an unwelcome intrusion.

Cree was chef with Morganne and me for KPs. We turned out some decent food. Maria loved to help us cook.

The crew ate in the galley and, off watch, stayed in our quarters until nightfall when the paying customers all retreated to the main cabin and broke out the liquor. They bothered us some on watch or when we had to adjust the sails, but we learned to treat them with professional disdain. Morganne served meals. She thought we needed Love Boat uniforms.

Aaron kept the sailing easy and Patrick didn't holler at anyone. I think Patrick made it with one of the women, because she and her man had a screaming fight in which his name appeared several times. None of them knew what to make of Cree.

When we got back to Defoe, Patrick told Aaron to find another First Mate, that he wasn't a limo driver. Aaron said he was working on it.

Patrick did go out once more, but his heart wasn't in it. He left the sailing to the crew led by Cree. He sat around the lounge with the passengers or barricaded himself in his cabin with Pancho and they did lots of sniffling and nose blowing.

Except for the mandatory dinners with the guests, you wouldn't have known Aaron was aboard. Maria stayed in the spare stateroom and avoided everyone, even at mealtime.

Eddie and Suzette came along on the second cruise, a four-day run to the mouth of the straits where there had been early sightings of migrating grays. We never saw any whales at all that trip and Eddie took most of the blame. He tried to shift responsibility to the captain, but after all, he was the Great Biologist. It didn't take him long to learn that it was hard to blame him if he wasn't there. And it paid the same.

The crew problem became acute. Patrick refused to go out again even for two ounces. Aaron finally asked Cree to do it and she agreed to sail as First Mate one trip at a time. Eddie found three graduate students gullible enough to volunteer as deck monkeys in return for some whale watching. We had learned enough to be able to coach them or carry their load and get the job done, but there was something lacking in the spirit of it.

We became even more secretive about our drug use with so many strangers aboard. Several of them were seen smoking a joint or snorting, but no one shared. The only common denominator was alcohol, but Cree and I didn't participate in that.

It was always a great relief to get back to the island. Cree would go out in the Wigit, but usually I would just wander around the woods barefoot.

Lila was nearly due to take over her bar and Morganne was depressed. She didn't want to go with Lila, but she hated the thought of the Orca when only she and I and maybe Cree remained of the original crew. She talked often of going with me to the mountains, but I told her I had to follow this particular trail to its end.

"I know," she said to me one day, "I feel the same way, but I try not to. I don't want there to be an end."

She did go with Lila to look at the bar again but came back more down than ever. "It's awful," she told me. "It's full of these greasy, sloppy men with hard-ons who buy beer and stare at nipples."

"They pay well for it," I said. "I guess that's all that matters."

"I hate it," Morganne said. "It's what I thought hell would be. She's going to live there, too, upstairs in an apartment across the hall from four rental rooms -fron with hourly rates. It's disgusting."

"Most ways of making money get ugly somewhere," I said. "It's just a little closer to the surface there."

Lila was nervous. She'd asked Gerard when the deal would close and he was evasive. She had a very bad feeling and called the escrow agent who said he was ready to close on the first as soon as her money was deposited.

She managed to control herself until she was off the phone, then called Gerard. "Where's my money, motherfucker?" she asked him.

She listened to his lie. "I called the escrow agent," she said. "Where's my fucking money?"

She listened again. "Well you have three days. If you blow it, I'll come down there and cut your balls off."

"He used it on a deal, then fronted the Product and hasn't been paid yet," she said when she hung up. "Probably his god-damned biker friends. That asshole. I will cut his balls off."

I thought Morganne looked relieved.

We had a group to take out the next day. Lila didn't want to go until her money problem was settled. Aaron got hold of Lance, who wanted to be First Mate if he went. Cree didn't care. She was happier as cook and deck hand. I don't think much of her self-identity depended on her rank on the Orca.

We had four new graduate-student volunteers. One of them was worthless, reminded me of the Poet. There were two women and they were very good hands, got into the teamwork of the thing. Lance figured out by the second day that the less he said, the better things worked.

The "johns," as Lila called our paying guests, filled every cabin. They were a diverse group, which made for a better time. They couldn't keep playing the same old games, like the organized groups we'd started with. And somehow, with all the cabins full, it seemed less crowded. Aaron and Maria and Do jammed into the Master's cabin and Maria hung out with us in the galley, helped cook and sometimes helped Morganne serve.

We saw lots of orcas and even a small pod of grays that had wandered into the sound on their way south. The passengers insisted that the crew eat with them on the last night out, and all of us were sorry to see it end.

Gerard had managed to get Lila a thirty-day extension on her closing, but she needed more money.

She shrugged. "Interest rates are up," she said. The Fed or whatever is supposed to raise the discount to twelve-percent next week. What a bunch of shit."

Gerard had promised her he would cover the extra as interest on the loan.

We had another full load. Lance stayed and Lila was back. The two volunteers we'd liked came back and the worthless one disappeared. It was a good enough cruise, except for the weather. The routine had become easy for the crew, so the storms were a welcome challenge for us. And the passengers stayed out of our way when it was rough.

At the end of this cruise, Aaron had several stacks of hundreds to put in the safe with what remained of Morganne's money. While we had it open, I decided to put in my moneybelt as well. It had begun to annoy me.

Gerard called, claimed he had Lila's money and she went down to Seattle to take care of it. She came back elated. She had physically carried the cash to the escrow agent and watched him count it.

"The way he stared at my teats," she laughed, "I could have paid him with monopoly money."

"That's all this is anyway," Morganne said.

The upcoming cruise looked interesting. There was to be a full eclipse of the full moon on the 6th of September. There is no better view of such an event than from the water.

Miller Richards booked three staterooms.

"That will be snaky," Lila promised. "And Aaron said Patrick and Pancho are coming as passengers."

"They're more cut out to be passengers," I said.

"Akbar is going to make a movie of it," Morganne said. "And Walt Gann is writing an article."

"Why don't they invite 60 Minutes?" Lila asked.

"It will be nice to have music," Morganne said.

"What music?" I asked.

"Fuzzy," Morganne said, "and his band. Gloria is into astrology really bad and she talked him into it. Aaron offered Fuzzy a discount if they'd play a couple of sets every night."

"Party," Lila said. "Hope you're stocked up on Northern Lights, Lucky."

"Gerard's bringing some with him," I said.

"Gerard's coming, too?" Lila asked. "He didn't tell me that."

"He's bringing some bimbo," Morganne said. "He didn't want you to be jealous."

"Jealous!" Lila said. "He should hope."

Eddie got wind of the eclipse cruise and insisted on going. Aaron finally agreed but no one was happy about it.

"Some party," Lila said. "Ozzie and Harriet for chaperones."

"They're okay when none of Eddie's university friends are around," Morganne said. "That's when they always get weird. Like when you were a kid and people from your church came over and you had to pretend to be saved."

"Except that Eddie thinks he's the savior," Lila said. "And we're all sinners."

We were due out on Tuesday, two days before the eclipse. We were more likely to have clear weather out of the sound, so the consensus was to get out into the Pacific past Cape Flattery and cruise off the south coast of Vancouver Island.

It was a major pain in the ass, getting all the stuff on board without a suitable dock. The band's equipment was the worst, but everyone had brought enough for an ocean voyage. We used the Wigit as well as Lance's boat. When Patrick and Pancho got there, they unloaded their stuff out of Patrick's boat and helped us with what was left. Many times, we blessed the new cargo boom.

While we'd been chartering, Eddie and Suzette had taken over the house and turned it into a kind of hotel for passengers. They had hired a Filipina cook, who lived in my old room, and found two Native women from Anacortes, who came over three days a week to clean and do laundry.

Everyone from the eclipse cruise stayed overnight at the house except, Miller Richards and his entourage of six, who would come up on a charter boat the next morning. Walt Gann called, didn't have a ride. Aaron connected him with Richards so he could come up with them.

Cree picked up Akbar in LaConner, helped him get his equipment on the Orca then brought him to the house. He had a Bolex with him and shot film now and then when no one paid attention.

The party started early. The crew had agreed with Aaron that there would be no more open drug use. The passengers obviously felt no such restriction. Patrick and Pancho had brought matching teen-aged blondes, promised them all the drugs they could do. Two of the three band members were similarly obligated, while the third sought chemical consolation for his solitary state. Fuzzy and Gloria were old pros and Gerard was there to show his shy little hippy girl how it was done. Eddie and Suzette mingled wherever they saw a bottle or mirror come out.

As for the crewmembers, we would step unobtrusively out onto the porch for a hit on an inhaler or a quick dip with a spoon. Our graduate students had long ago figured out why we disappeared into our cubicles occasionally and returned with the sniffles. More and more often they joined us.

Everyone began to run out of Product about ten. I was prepared.

Eddie was first, sidled up to me as though we were on First Avenue and said, "Hey, man, you got a gram?"

"No," I said.

"What do you mean?" He looked at me. "Morganne said you'd have some."

"Some?" I asked.

"Coke," he said. "Northern Lights."

"I do," I said. "You asked for a gram. I don't have any grams."

"I can't afford an ounce," he said.

"How about a quarter?"

"How much is that?" he asked me.

"A thousand," I said.

"A thousand?" he said. "It used to be seven-fifty."

"Supply and demand," I said.

He grumbled, tried to give me a check, finally talked to Suzette and came back with the cash.

When Patrick saw it, he wanted some, bought an ounce for thirty-five hundred with no complaint. Fuzzy and the boys took up a collection, managed a half ounce when I agreed to take a hand-made

Morseth sheath knife some groupie had given him for a hundred of it. It was a fine, balanced blade and had never been used. He offered me a date with Gloria, but I liked the knife better.

Gerard, of course had his own drugs, and Aaron kept his business private. I did sell Akbar a gram, made it overweight. Anyone who appreciated it the way he did deserved a better deal.

About midnight it began to get a little ragged. Eddie had launched into his "we're all just helpless, selfish bastards" lecture and had about half the newcomers in his class. Fuzzy tried to trade Gloria for either or both of the blondes from Port Townsend. Gerard's flower child was deep into Patrick's eyes and Patrick prepared his date for a three-way. Gerard desperately pursued Lila. She wasn't buying it. Morganne went upstairs with Maria and Do.

I asked Cree if she would run me out to the Orca, and she agreed. As we left, I saw that the dark-faced cook watched it all from the shadows of the kitchen. As Cree and I passed, she shook her head at me.

"White people!" she said.

CHAPTER 37

Half of the partygoers still were awake the next morning; the other half couldn't wake up. We finally got them all aboard by about ten. Miller Richards showed up on a Seattle harbor cruiser. Two of his group turned out to be Suras and the Poet.

Lila was livid. "I thought we were rid of that bastard," she said to Aaron. "Send him back."

"I can't do that," Aaron said. "I don't like it either, but they paid their fare. Just be careful."

Walt Gann ducked and grinned and scribbled. Occasionally, he would take a shot with his camera, usually of one of the crew at work. Lila gave him the finger every time and he quit taking her picture.

Nothing she could do affected Akbar. Unless you were close enough to hear the Bolex whir, you never knew if he was filming or not, because he looked through the camera most of the time. His other, dark-lensed, eye seemed blind to this world.

"He just sits there on the rail like a vulture," Lila said.

"Or a raven," I said.

When we finally got sail up, it was after noon. The light wind wouldn't settle down in any particular quarter, so we made slight headway and less progress. Aaron decided to run on the auxiliary until we were in the straits.

With Patrick around to watch, Lance had almost nothing to say. You never would have known that he was First Mate. Cree took the lead, as usual.

I could see that the Poet was off on something new. He had greased his hair down and wore a red cap embroidered with a mandala. He had on a loose tunic that came down over his jeans, belted with a tasseled tie. I had seen him and Suras greet each other with some kind of hand sign.

"What the hell is a Pawo?" Lila asked Morganne and me on a break in the galley.

"An extinct bird," I said. "Like a Dodo."

"It's some kind of warrior bullshit," Morganne said. "He and Suras went to some seminar in Colorado."

"So now they're warriors?" Lila asked.

"Warriors of Shambhala," Morganne said. "The guy they went to see is some Tibetan monk."

"Warriors of Shangri-La," I said. "Isn't that a motel in Tacoma?"

"Don't worry," Morganne said. "You'll hear all about it."

They had cornered Lila in the dining room.

"The first principle is not to be afraid of who you are," the Poet said. Suras nodded.

"That must be pretty scary for you," Lila said.

He looked at her gravely. "Another principle," he said, "is, 'you must never give up on anyone or anything.'"

"I try not to," Lila said, "but sometimes, in your case, I wonder."

He glared at her, regained his warriorly composure. "When you feel the Drala energy flow and the Great Eastern Sun shines over your shoulder, then you will understand," he said.

"You better watch that sun," Lila said. "You burn easily."

He ignored her. "You need to synchronize your mind and body," he said.

"You mean like coordination?" Lila asked him. "I'm not the one who trips over shadows."

"At least I'm not a whore," he said.

"No," Lila said, "you're the only thing lower than a whore. You're a john."

"I don't pay for it," he said. "Never."

"Oh, yes, you do," Lila said. "You pay every day. Whether you get any or not."

"Shambhala, bitch," he said and stalked away.

By evening most of the guests were well wired. Miller Richards also had been to the seminar in Boulder. He held forth in a corner of the lounge on the subject of "The Magic Path to Warriorhood" with Suras and the Poet as an 'Amen corner.'

Richards had seen already that much of what the Master had said was a corruption of the original. All of that business about an obligation to change the world and the essential goodness of all humanity must have been added later.

The great principle, of course, is to not be afraid of who you are, which obviously is the same as "'Do as thou wilt' shall be the whole of the law." He could see that it fit right in with Magic. Probably came from the same source in Egypt.

"Yesss!" Suras said.

Gerard's competing symposium should have been entitled, "How to Profit from the Coming Worldwide Depression." He had his notebook full of charts and graphs and articles, proof beyond doubt of the shape of the future. His disciples included Pancho and Fuzzy and the lone-wolf band member, as well as Patrick's blonde. Suzette joined them whenever Eddie wasn't watching. Lila said she'd heard it all.

Patrick held his all-female circle without much effort. All he did was gaze into their eyes and occasionally straighten his hat or re-curl his mustache. If he said anything at all, you could see several sets of lips follow his. Everyone knew that soon he would make his choice.

The two deserted band members had moved an amp onto the fore deck and played some blues riffs on a guitar and bass while they watched to see if Patrick released their companions. Maria held Do and watched them play, traced the chords with her left hand on Do's back.

Walt Gann tried to ask Akbar questions, see if he knew what the story was, but Akbar looked through him until he went away. I heard the Bolex whir now and then. Cree and I were technically on watch, but on auxiliary power, there wasn't much to do. Lance had the helm until nine o'clock and I was the bow lookout. Akbar started to film from near where I stood and Cree came over to join us.

We could hear loud voices from somewhere, Aaron's and Eddie's, ".... all these drugs," Eddie said.

"Not my drugs," Aaron responded. "You don't see my crew doing drugs."

"No, I don't see them," Eddie said. "You're the Captain, you're responsible for the safety of passengers. I don't think this is safe."

"I see you do your share of coke," Aaron said.

"The thing is, is I have to fit in," Eddie said. "But this is out of hand."

"What's out of hand?" Aaron asked.

"They keep on giving Suzette coke," Eddie said. "And God knows what else. She's so loaded I can't even talk to her. If she isn't hanging around Patrick, she's listening to Gerard's bullshit."

"And I'm responsible for this?" Aaron asked.

"Well, the safety part of it," Eddie said. "What if she gets confused and jumps overboard."

"An orca will save her," Aaron said. We didn't hear any more.

The swell was stronger in the mouth of the straits. The wind, too, flowed from the open sea, smelled of wildness and freedom. And another smell - alien, familiar, orca. I saw them, saw that Cree already watched them. I pointed and Akbar swung his camera and it whirred.

They formed a wedge escort, flickered in the refractions of the waves. Akbar tried to shield his lens from the low sun with his hand, finally had me grab a flotation cushion from a bench and hold it as far out as I could. He took off his one-lensed glasses, put them in a pocket.

"I have to see this with both eyes," he said. He tried to find an angle, to penetrate the reflection, finally gave up. "All I'll get," he said, "is a blinding light.

We heard the rush of water as several of them broke the surface, joined our world. Akbar ran the camera again and I shaded it. Maria walked towards us with Do in her arms and looked where we looked. A medium sized-orca breached high and splashed. After a pause two more followed. A minute later three breached in succession. Cree studied them silently.

"Now four," I said. On command, a salvo of four leaps and splashes.

Cree grinned at my surprise. "They got so much things to say." she said.

The music stopped and the two musicians looked into the water. Morganne came out and up the deck.

The pod left us behind, made a great circle and came at us head on, split around the Orca just beneath the surface, then turned and caught us again from behind. Akbar's camera hung silent. The orcas went down, out of sight.

We all watched the water for several minutes. They were gone. The music resumed, conversations continued. Then Maria sang out, startled us all. "There! And there! Look!"

Far ahead, but directly on our course, orcas popped to the surface, one after the other, like bubbles from a submerged spring. It was the largest pod I had ever seen, too many to look at all at once. Groups breached and blew and slapped their flukes. I remembered I was lookout.

"Orcas dead ahead," I said to Lance on the intercom. "Cut power." It was our standard procedure.

"I'll ask Aaron," the tinny voice said back to me.

Aaron came out on deck, walked towards us. I pointed and he looked. "Cut power!" he yelled back to Lance.

"Cut power," I said again into the grille beside me. The engine throttled back, prop disengaged. The boat's momentum ebbed and we lay dead in the water just short of one group of orcas.

They showed no inclination to move. Several of them spy-hopped - stood on their tails, a quarter of their length out of the water and watched us. They were like black and white buoys, bobbing there to warn of some hidden danger.

Everyone aboard soon crowded the bow rails. Eddie pushed his way to the front.

"Let me through," he said. "I'll need to determine our course of action."

Akbar kept his perch on the rail; the Bolex softly whirred.

"What do we do, boss?" the Poet asked Aaron.

Aaron ignored him.

"What's the problem," Gerard asked from the back.

"Killer whales," Gloria said.

"Orcas," Suzette corrected her.

"Orca means whale-killer, not killer whale," Eddie explained from the rail.

"What's the difference," Lila asked him.

"None, except to pompous asses," Morganne muttered.

"What?" the Poet asked.

Gerard found a place where he could see the water. "Okay, I've seen them," he said. "A bunch of black and white dog food. One more natural resource."

"You asshole," Lila said.

"Just a realist," Gerard said.

"You don't understand their true value," Eddie said. "They have much to teach us."

"They can talk to them," Patrick's girl friend said.

"Not talk, exactly," Eddie said. "Communicate."

"I can communicate with a cow," Gerard said, "with a two-by-four, but I don't think it would teach me much."

"You might be surprised," I said.

Eddie shook his head. "The smart-ass section," he said.

A group surfaced suddenly all around us. One bumped the boat as it came up, pushed off with a fluke. One of the band members' girl friends gave a little shriek.

"They won't hurt us," Eddie said.

"How do you know?" Pancho's bunkmate asked Eddie.

"He's an expert," Suzette said.

Eddie waited. "The fact is," he said, "is they could sink boats every day - if they wanted to. But they don't."

"I don't like knowing that they could," Gloria said. "What if they change their minds?"

"They don't have minds to change," Gerard said. "Cows could turn over cars, too, but they don't."

"It's a sign," the Poet said.

"A sign," Suras echoed.

"A band of warriors," Miller Richards said, forced his way to the rail, "come to pay their respects." He spread his arms in blessing.

Several of the closest orcas arched their backs as though to dive, but froze motionless, dorsal fins high in the air like semaphore pennants.

"It's a warning," Maria said, "Of a great storm."

"How do you know?" the Poet asked her.

"I just see it," she said.

"You see a lot of things other people don't," he said.

"They just got in the way, like a herd of cows," Gerard said.

Those right around us submerged together and slid away. Almost immediately there was a new group. They performed the same maneuver as the others, like an interrupted dive, held as an invitation to join them. A large orca breached fifty yards off and we all ducked as though the splash could reach us.

"Now that's a performance," Patrick said. "Can you imagine that power and speed. That's an athlete."

"...athlete," several female voices finished with him.

Fuzzy put his arm around Gloria, pulled her close to him and laughed. "Somebody throw them some toot," he said, "We'll get a real performance."

"Depends on what they need to perform," Gloria said.

There was a soft bump against the hull, then another, distinct from the rhythmic idle of the diesel. Everyone held their breath. The knocking came again and all my senses fastened on it. I knew it was my friend.

"What nonsense," Gerard said. "It's like a tribe of cave men with a herd of woolly mammoths, seeing God in a dumb beast."

"Or seeing the beast in God," I said.

Fog arose in the distance, paled the sun. The insistent bumping on the hull continued, distracted me until I couldn't follow the conversation. It was though she worked at something, or tapped out a signal. I looked over the side, tried to see down, but the soft light died at the surface. There seemed to be no pattern, just a live, electric feeling as when a fish nibbles your bait.

Morganne was beside me. "What are you staring at?" she asked me.

"I don't know," I said. "Nothing, I guess."

"It's them, isn't it?" Morganne asked me. "The ones from the dreams."

"Maybe," I said. "How would we know?"

"I know," she said. "So does Maria. Look at her."

Maria, too, stared down. She was so entranced that I had a momentary fear she would drop Do into the water.

Lila saw us whisper, came over. "Is something funny going on?" she asked us.

"No funnier than usual," I said.

"It's our orcas," Morganne said. "From the dreams."

"Bullshit," Lila said.

"What do you feel," Morganne asked her. "Not think, feel."

"Kind of weird, I guess," Lila said. "Like I should know something, but I don't."

"You do know," Morganne said. "You just pretend you don't, even to yourself."

"I don't know nothin'," Lila said as she stared into the sea with us.

The bumping came closer, seemed just beneath my feet. Still, I saw nothing. A towering wave of fog rolled in from thc west, broke across us, left us submerged in an opaque fluid where vision was useless. I felt my eyes stare, wide open, unfocused, blind.

I closed my eyes and felt her presence. I knew she was just below the surface. I could feel her heat. I wished for a pole or rod I could touch her with to read her shape and texture and size as with a blindman's cane.

There was a stirring among the people around us.

"It's cold," Patrick's girl complained.

"This is weird," another one said. "I can't see anything."

"They're gone," Eddie said. "We never see them in the fog."

"Let's get this tub underway, Captain," Gerard said to Aaron. "We've got places to go and things to do."

"It's a sign," the Poet said, "for us to change our ways."

"What way is that?" Aaron asked him.

"Well," the Poet paused. "Your way."

It grew silent. The fog held. Everyone left me except Lila, Morganne, Maria and Cree. Even Akbar went inside for one of his blistering rum drinks.

Walt Gann came out, tried to look through the fog. "What's happening?" he asked us. "Somebody said there were whales. I was in my cabin working on my notes. I guess I missed it."

"It was nothing," I said. "Just a bunch of fish going nowhere."

He went away and we relaxed, felt the great presence around us. Maria had that smile I knew made some people nervous, but we grouped around her and the baby, let no one see it but us.

Aaron decided to anchor where we were, lay over until dawn. He had some portable strobe lights to be used for emergency signals and he had us hang them fore and aft, port and starboard. We also turned on our working lights so that they shone up onto the masts. That lit us up pretty good, although it must have been a ghostly effect if anyone was out there in the fog to see.

No one wanted to cook, so we set out a buffet. There was plenty and no one complained. After we ate, everyone was subdued and soon retired to their various cabins.

Morganne and Lila were on the late watch, so I sat with them on the foredeck. "A lot of good a look-out is," Lila grumbled, "when you can't see anything until after it hits you."

"Someone has to yell 'abandon ship,'" I said. "It's a tradition."

"No one would hear us," Morganne said.

"That doesn't matter," I said. "We still have to yell."

"But if no one can hear us and it's already too late, what's the point?" Morganne asked.

"I don't know," I said. "Sometimes traditions are like that."

Morganne woke me at a quarter to four. I'd had only a couple of hours sleep, so I quickly chopped a line and woke myself up.

The fog was gone. Stars shone, and far in the west the cutout white ghost of the moon dipped towards the sea. They'd turned off the lights and already had the anchor up. In the east, the pre-dawn shadow of the day rose above the horizon and a slight breeze began to move across the water.

Aaron was with Cree at the wheel. "There's a low off the island," he said to me. "Should get some wind today."

"They're still here," Morganne whispered to me as she went below. "We could hear them all night."

The auxiliary drove us forward. The black hull cut the waves cleanly, rode lightly on the ponderous swell, poised like a great bird. As the breeze stiffened, we spread her wings. It was a restive, land-born wind, but dead astern. it caught us up and carried us along. Wing and wing, with a spinnaker ballooned full out, we flew westward.

The channel widened until we could see only the dim outline of land in either direction. Unbroken seas from the coasts of Asia met us and passed beneath with almost no sound. Only the creak of the gear and the rush of the wind accompanied our westward flight.

The sun rose warm and followed us; our wake was flecked with gold. The passengers slept in their queen-sized beds and the helmsman was sleepy and bored. I shook myself awake at the wheel, searched in my bag for my inhaler. It was empty. I had some in my bottle, but I needed to screen it. Lately, chunks burned and made my nose bleed.

I corrected two degrees back to my heading. Akbar, as usual, was at the bow rail, looked dead ahead, one eye in each world. Off the starboard beam, the outline of the coast loomed, resolved into the high peaks of Vancouver Island. To port, the shadow of land faded away, left open ocean.

Morganne came in with coffee. I gulped it down and asked her to go screen my stash. A little while later, she came back and I got myself normal.

We saw orcas in the distance several times, but we had no way to know if they were the same as our visitors. Most of the passengers used the opportunity to rest up for the eclipse, so we didn't see many of them until noon, which seemed to be breakfast time for most of them.

At ten, I yielded the wheel to Lila and went to the bow with Morganne.

"I couldn't sleep," she said. "I just listened to that 'knock, knock, knock,' like they wanted to come in."

"Or wanted us to come out," I said.

"They want us to go north with them," Morganne said. "Like the dreams." She stared at nothing in the distance. "I think we should. There's nothing to go back to. Not really. We have only what's ahead."

"What's ahead is what's behind," I said. "It's all the same."

"How about this trail we have to follow to the end?" she asked.

"I'm beginning to think it's a circle," I said. "And there's no short cut."

"This eclipse scares me," she said. "We should have watched it from land. Anything could happen out here."

"Anything can happen anywhere," I said.

Aaron decided to cruise back and forth on one-hour legs. He didn't want to anchor in Canadian waters, and on the US side of the imaginary line, the water was too deep. We would run on the auxiliary and keep the sails down for the best view. We were several miles offshore, but I could feel the presence of the mountains that ranged down the island.

Most of the passengers spent the afternoon tuning their heads. Each one wanted to have just the right combination of up, down and sideways for the event. My business was brisk. None of the crew got carried away, but our First Mate began to hang out with Eddie and Suzette after Eddie broke out what was left of his Northern Lights.

Maria and Do stayed out of sight and Morganne and Lila took turns hanging out with them. Cree took lunch to Maria and brought Do out for some air. Aaron was with them on and off all day.

"How is she?" I asked Morganne.

"She seems normal," Morganne said. "For her. She talks a lot about orcas and Guardians."

"Sounds normal to me," I said. "At least compared to our cargo."

"I don't think there is any normal," Morganne said. "Everyone just makes it up as they go."

CHAPTER 38

There was a dark line on the western horizon, but the evening remained clear with only a fitful wind. Occasional riffs of white caps cut this way and that across a lazy swell. The energy on the Orca was very high, everyone's senses taut. There was much coming and going and seeking just the right vantage point.

Several people had brought music for the occasion. The Poet and Suras brought out a cassette player with a tape of Tibetan Temple Music. They had some painted sticks and finger bells so they could play along.

Son of a Son of a Sailor blared from Patrick's stateroom.

Eddie set up on the foredeck with a fancy reel-to-reel machine, a power amp and some serious speakers. He had a synthesizer version of Gustav Holst's "The Planets" that he thought might call orcas or gray whales if he played it loud enough.

Gerard got as far away from that as he could, hung his Nakamichi portable from the aft rail and played a succession of Alice Cooper and Kiss tapes, which from a distance, sounded like hordes of devils shrieking in hot pursuit.

Lance put his old eight-track on top of the main cabin and tried to play Dire Straits' Communique, but it jumped from track to track and scrambled the message.

Miller Richards' three women made a rare appearance, carried a large portable stereo to the spot he'd chosen on deck not far back of Eddie. They sat in a circle around the machine and he put on a record. It was Pink Floyd's The Wall. I was surprised at how well it played on the rolling deck.

"It's the best self-balancing turntable made," Richards told me. I watched it swing in gimbals like a compass to maintain it's level.

I traded with one of the graduate students, took the wheel at six-thirty so she could watch the eclipse. I was not sleepy this time. Lila and Morganne came into the wheelhouse holding their ears. The door closed, pinched off the wave of bedlam from the deck. I had my little earphones on, listened to Exodus

"That's not fair," Morganne said. "You're off in your own world.

"You can join me," I said, pulled out the earphone plug, let the speaker blare.

"Marley," Lila said, "I should have known."

"I like it," Morganne said. "When I can understand it."

"It's very plain," I said.

"I have a tape I want to hear," Morganne said. "Dog and Butterfly."

"Yuck," Lila said, "the broads from Bellevue. I'll go get Darkness on the Edge of Town."

"Springsteen's too down," Morganne said.

"Too real, you mean," Lila said.

"My tape player," I said. "I vote for reggae."

There already was a shadow, like a smudge on the face of the moon as it rose. We had come about just at sunset and sailed eastward towards a rosy glow, like a second sunrise. I forgot the compass and steered straight for the glow. It grew quiet except for the cacophony of music. The brightness of the twilight behind made it hard to see.

"This is it, this is it," the Poet hollered and Suras beat his sticks together. The swollen moon floated free of the horizon. Miller Richards faced it, spread his arms and froze, struggled to maintain his balance against the motion of the deck.

Eddie had a Hasselblad camera someone had funded and he madly snapped pictures and ordered people out of his way. He cranked up the synthesizer music and commanded a watch for orcas.

"There are reports that they surface during eclipses," he said. He had several boxes with wires and tubes and dials, and something dangling in the water. He moved from machine to machine, hardly looked up.

"Is that it?" Gloria asked as she and Fuzzy walked by below. "I can barely see it. I think that's just smog from Seattle."

"Looks like a celebration to me," Fuzzy said. "Who's got a toot?" No one responded.

Maria crept softly into the wheelhouse to join us. Do slept in her arms. Cree came in and closed the door behind her. I turned down the reggae and we stared ahead.

As it grew dark, the eclipse was more apparent, but in about another half-hour, one edge glowed brightly and a sliver of unshadowed moon appeared. It was not long before the brightness made it impossible to see the dark area, although the color was not normal, but reddish and dim. I held the wheel steady, followed the ruddy wake.

The eclipse nearly was over when the chime rang for eight-o'clock. Morganne offered to take the wheel, but I had nothing better to do.

The eastward hour was up, so I had Morganne ask Aaron if he wanted to come about, but he sent her back with a compass heading just south of the moon's track, back into the straits. No one paid further attention to the still-shadowed moon.

Eddie's instruments glowed and needles jumped, but there was no one there to read them. He and Suzette celebrated with the Poet and Miller Richards and a fresh quarter ounce of Northern Lights they'd bought from me. Akbar regained his bow-starboard-rail position, looked through his camera, the other eye darkened.

Walt Gann wandered by on the deck below us and into the main cabin, rubbed his eyes as though just awake.

"I thought it was later," I heard him say.

The celebration in the main cabin grew. Fuzzy fired up the band and they played all the moon songs anyone could remember. The deck beneath us pulsed with bass; the guitar vibrated the windows.

Voices grew louder, laughter more shrill. I heard Gerard yell; the Poet, wounded, yelled back. The desperate giggles of pursued women escaped now and then as doors opened and closed. Drafts of air stank of cocaine and adrenaline and testosterone. Patrick's chuckle, Gloria's whine, Miller Richards' pronouncements, Eddie's lecture, all tangled together into an unknown language.

"Where have you been?" Morganne asked Aaron as he came in, secured the door behind him.

"The Feast of Fools," he said. "Don't sell them any more coke, Lucky. I don't think they can handle Northern Lights."

"People never can handle getting what they want," I said. "Okay, I'll cut them off."

I saw a light ahead on the water, couldn't make it out. I pressed the bow lookout call button to see if Lance had a better view, but he didn't answer. The light moved on and was soon out of sight. Lila went to take the bow lookout. Morganne, Aaron, Maria and Do stayed with me.

About nine-thirty the moon broke out of the faint penumbral shadow and sailed westward, clean and white. The passengers took no notice. Aaron advanced the throttle and the diesel sped us into the straits and towards home.

Several surreptitious visitors found out the store was closed. The Poet was sure it was just him I wouldn't sell to, so he sent his money with Eddie.

Eddie told me he was beginning to understand how a dope pusher worked, and if I thought cutting him off would just make him want it more, I was wrong.

Suras reminded me that when he'd had some, he offered it to me. I couldn't remember that.

Miller Richards offered to teach me his brand of magic as a bonus if I'd sell him a quarter ounce, but I declined.

I thought Fuzzy would cry. He actually had money, although Gloria was not far away so I suspected it was hers.

"Toot brothers have to stick together," he said. "I'd let you have some. If I had any." I told him I was out so he would give up.

I did slip Akbar a gram towards morning.

The sunrise began as the moonrise had, with a fine scarlet glow off the port bow. Behind us, a Gulf of Alaska storm hung a gray curtain across the mouth of the straits. Aaron changed course to almost due east and we skirted the US-Canada boundary.

Morganne was at the wheel and I spelled Lila on the bow. Dawn stirred a northerly breeze that woke me. Sun spread across the soft September swell. Gangs of small whitecaps chased us into Puget Sound.

Passengers began to appear on deck at midmorning. They stumbled in and out of the main cabin, none of them awake. I went in the galley for a cup of coffee and several of them glared at me across the serving line.

"You sure are bright eyed this morning," Eddie said. "For just coffee."

"It's a beautiful day," I said.

"Right," Eddie said. "The fact is, is most days are alike."

"Another day, another dollar," Gerard said.

Breakfast was long over, but several of them wanted to eat. Someone went to look for Cree. I offered to make oatmeal, or even pancakes, but they wanted more sophisticated fare.

Cree came in. "What's up?" She asked me.

"They want food," I said. "And drugs."

"They should have been here at breakfast time," Cree said.

The Poet heard her. "We're paying customers," he said. "The customer is always right."

"Wrong," Cree said. "The Captain is in charge of the ship."

"I really think we should get breakfast whenever we want it," Patrick's girl friend said. "Like a restaurant."

"I'm starving," Gloria said.

"We want food, we want food...." the Poet started to chant.

Suras joined him, tapped on the table. Patrick's girl friend and two of the others chimed in, but it only lasted a few repetitions then faded.

It was enough commotion to bring the others out of their staterooms and soon the dining room was full. Everyone asked everyone what was going on. No one knew. They did all agree they were hungry.

"It isn't like land," Gloria said, "where you can run out to McDonalds or something."

"We're like captives," Pancho's girl friend said.

"What if we're going the wrong way?" one of Miller Richards' witches asked. "We wouldn't know until it was too late."

"You can see the sun," Lila said. "And you do know what direction is up, right?"

"Well, we want some food," Gloria said.

"Get it yourself," Lila said in a low voice.

All hell broke loose. Fuzzy jumped to Gloria's defense, called Lila a bitch. Lila threatened to kick his ass. At that point, several of the women urged their men to get involved. The Poet and Suras stepped forward to back Fuzzy against Lila. Patrick grinned and pushed his girl friend into the fray. Cree silently stepped up beside Lila. Eddie yelled at me to get Aaron. As I turned, I nearly ran into Akbar who filmed the melee from the shadows of the passageway.

Aaron was not in his cabin. Maria nursed Do on the bunk. She grimaced at the noise as I opened the door. She said Aaron had heard the noise and was on his way. I opened the door to leave and the shouts echoed louder, woke the baby who began to cry.

Maria frowned and stood up, followed me through the door. I let her go ahead of me into the galley. Aaron was in the dining room, surrounded by a dozen different accounts of recent events. Clearly he couldn't hear any of them.

Maria carried the crying baby, stepped into the dining room and glared at them. No one noticed.

"Quiet!" she said, louder than I ever had heard her speak.

Everyone stared. Do cried more softly, searched for the breast.

"Be quiet, you fools," Maria said, nearly as loudly as before. It was as though a tree had spoken; they were struck dumb with amazement.

"You must let the children sleep," she continued.

"This isn't a nursery," Eddie said. Several others agreed.

"The whole world is a nursery," Maria said. She looked at me and I wasn't sure what she saw. Then her wide eyes swept the room.

"You will be punished," she said to them, "this Sodom and Gomorrah pipeline will break. Soon they will come for you and the Guardians will turn their backs. Whales cannot save you. Only the babies can save you and you will not let them sleep."

"The world is overpopulated as it is," Eddie said. "The fewer babies, the better."

She whirled on him. "You, Science Preacher," she said to him, "you will also suffer. And your whores."

"The only whore here is Lila," the Poet said.

Suras snickered, but no one else moved.

Lila stepped as if to go for him, but Maria looked at her and Lila demurred. Everyone was silent again, but behind us I heard Akbar's Bolex.

Maria's voice took on an echo, like Granny's when she spoke in tongues. "I have watched you," she said, "and I have seen your golden idols made of snow. You think they will come for me, but they will come for you - they are here already, you just do not see them. I am only a leaf in a stream, but they will come for the trees, to hack you down and burn you like firewood."

She laughed at them and they squirmed in shock and embarrassment but no one argued. Do settled down and whimpered softly.

Aaron started towards her, but her look stopped even him.

"No one follows the true leader," Maria said more softly. "Like dogs in a pack you fight over scraps while the thief steals away with your souls." She patted Do and smiled secretively. "It's the babies," she said softly, "It's the babies."

The smile did not fade as she slowly carried the sleeping baby back to its bed.

Everyone forgot their hunger and the gathering broke up. Lila continued to mutter about hurting someone, but Morganne joked her out of it. The day continued fair and the forecast was favorable, but far out in the straits, the gray line of the first storm of fall came nearer.

CHAPTER 39

Rain began some time that night. Wind off the straits drove the Orca to the end of her anchor chain to strain and heave with the chop. The decks were slippery and everyone clung to a lubber line as they moved about.

The passengers couldn't leave fast enough. I thought some of them would swim for it before Cree and Lance and Patrick got them ashore. Everyone who had a way off the island took it.

Miller Richards offered Cree five hundred dollars to run his group to Seattle on the Wigit, but she refused, said her engine needed work. Miller and his women crowded onto Lance's boat, left behind most of their luggage as well as the Poet and Suras. Lance tried to buy a quarter ounce from me when Miller paid him, but I had decided not to sell any more.

Lee made two flights, one for Fuzzy and Gloria, another for Gerard and his hippy girl who were no longer speaking. Walt Gann bummed a ride with them.

The Poet and Suras wanted to stay aboard until they could fly out the next day, but Aaron told them they could stay at the house. Eddie didn't like that.

Akbar filmed until they all were off the Orca, then he went aboard the Wigit, waited for Cree to run him to LaConner.

"Let's get out of here," Lila said as soon as he went down the ladder.

"We have a charter next week," Aaron said.

"Cancel it," Lila said. "Let's go south, or north or something."

"We need the money," Aaron said. "Besides, we have a contract."

"You only have a couple of weeks until you leave anyway," Morganne said to Lila. "What do you care?"

"I care about my ass," Lila said. "I don't like the feeling I have. You feel it, too," she said to Aaron.

He was noncommittal, went to his cabin.

"I feel it," Morganne said. "I wish it was ten years ago and we were in Santa Cruz."

"Santa Cruz was just a dream," Lila said.

"I like dreams," Morganne said. "No one has dreams anymore."

"Sure they do," I said. "Dreams of riches and power and vaults full of cocaine."

"Those aren't dreams," Morganne said. "Those are nightmares."

"Even the cocaine?" Lila teased her. "I've heard you say you wanted enough to make snow angels in."

"I'd give it up in a second," Morganne said, "if we could have our world back."

"It's a brave new world," I said.

"It's an ugly, cowardly world," Morganne said, "without the guts to dream.

We went into the galley and Morganne poured us coffee. We sat down and I offered my inhaler.

"We need to stop," Morganne said.

"Stop what?" Lila asked her.

"Coke," Morganne said.

"Speak for yourself," Lila said.

"No, that's the problem," Morganne said. "I've tried to stop a dozen times, but then someone comes around with a line, and I don't know how to say no."

"Just say 'I don't use that shit,'" Lila said.

"I can't do that," Morganne said. "I love all of you. I wouldn't hurt your feelings."

"You have to watch out for yourself," Lila said.

"No," Morganne insisted. "We have to watch out for each other. No one can do it alone."

"You sound like AA or something," Lila said.

"It's just common sense," Morganne said. "How can each person be completely in control of a separate world? Even animals have the sense to work together."

"Well, you stop if you want to," Lila said. "I'll decide each time for myself. I believe in free will."

"That way we all lose," Morganne said.

"I'll do it," I said.

"What?" Morganne asked me.

"Stop," I said.

"Are you serious?" Lila asked me.

"No problem," I said.

"I'll bet you won't," Lila challenged.

"I started," I said, "I can stop."

"I never knew anyone who could," Lila said. "Not really, for good."

"I'm going to stop," Morganne said, "even if no one else does." She looked at me.

"I will," I said.

"I'm going to see if Aaron will," Morganne said, "and Maria."

"Maria hardly does any because of the baby," Lila said. "That's why she's always by herself, away from temptation."

"That's not the only reason," Morganne said.

"If you're going to quit," Lila said, "you need to get away from it, so you won't see it and think about it."

"You should sell all you have, Lucky," Morganne said to me.

"I don't want to sell it," I said, "I already decided that."

"What are you going to do for money?" Lila asked me.

"I don't know," I said. "I'll think of something."

"You're going back to the mountains," Morganne accused me.

"Not until this is over," I said.

"Maybe it's over and we just don't know it," Lila said.

"What are you going to do with your coke?" Morganne asked me.

I opened my bag, took out the half full bottle. "I don't know," I said. "Give it to Aaron, I guess."

"He needs to stop too," she said.

"Give it to me," Lila said. "I'll sell it for you."

Morganne grabbed the bottle from my hand, ran outside to the rail. We followed her out.

She held the bottle over the water. "A sacrifice to the orcas," she said.

"The water will destroy it as soon as it hits," Lila said. "Then it's no good to anyone."

"That's the point of a sacrifice," Morganne said.

"Do it," I said.

She dumped the bottle and a shower of finely screened crystals dissolved into the air.

"So how much more do you have?" Lila asked me.

"An ounce," I said.

"You going to throw that away too?"

"I don't know," I said. "I didn't know I was going to throw any away."

"I'll do it," Morganne said.

"That's like throwing away three thousand dollars," Lila said.

"I'll pay for it," Morganne said.

"I don't need the money," I said.

"I do," Lila said. "My money is all in escrow."

"You can have it," I said.

"Don't do it," Morganne said. "Get rid of it."

"Relax," Lila said, "I've been messing with drugs since I was a kid."

"Maybe it's time to stop," Morganne said.

"What is this?" Lila asked her. "You're the one who never wants anything to change."

"It's all changed anyway," Morganne said. "I don't even recognize the world anymore."

"Well, we can't go back," Lila said.

"I don't want to go anywhere," Morganne said. "I'm tired of going all the time. When do we get to rest?"

"No rest for the wicked," I said.

"If we didn't go all the time," Lila said, "you'd bitch there was nothing to do."

"We need a home," Morganne said. "I've never had a home. In my whole life, I've never lived anywhere more than two years. In my whole life!"

"No one lives anywhere anymore," Lila said. "Even people who own houses always try to trade up. My bar will be my home. I'm going to call it 'LILA'S DEN.' You two should come live there with me."

"We could be the three bears," Morganne said. "I always wanted to be baby bear."

"I always wanted to be Goldilocks," Lila said. She giggled, "Goldilocks with big teats."

"I'll be Papa Bear," I said, "and eat you all up."

"I won't leave Aaron," Morganne said. "He needs us. And Maria - and Do. Wouldn't you worry about them if you didn't see them every day?"

"I can't watch everyone," Lila said. "I have to just watch myself."

"That's so lonely," Morganne said.

"Welcome to the world, sweetheart," Lila said.

"I'll be right back," I said.

I went to my cubicle, pulled the ounce out of my locker. I unrolled the bag, stuck my finger in and touched it to my tongue. I hadn't really tasted it in a while, it was too familiar, like the way you don't taste water - or winos don't taste alcohol. I let the acrid bite of the hydrochloric acid sweep across my tongue. Then the other flavor, the delicate essence of the coca plant, like bubblegum or sarsaparilla. It had seemed so alien when I'd first blasted it into my sinuses that night in the Club. Now it posed as an old friend.

I went back into the galley, tossed the bag to Lila at the crew table.

"Really?" she asked me.

"I don't need it," I said.

"You may be surprised," Lila said.

The next day was not bad. I drank lots of coffee in the morning, then asked Aaron if I could borrow the skiff for a couple of hours. He said he wasn't going anywhere. I offered to take Morganne, but she sat on her bunk cross-legged, head down.

"I have a terrible headache," she said. I rubbed her neck for a while before I went and she relaxed some.

The Wigit was not at the dock. I beached the skiff out of sight of the house and circled around to intercept the path to the interior, walked fast and silently. I had no particular destination in mind, but I needed to walk. The path felt cool through my boots and I longed to take them off, but given my recent record with boots, I decided to leave them on.

I had gotten familiar with the island's topography and had explored many side paths, but never again had found the short cut I'd taken back from the sweat. As far as I could see, there was no place left for it, but my memories of it were too clear to doubt that it existed.

When I'd mentioned it to Lila and Morganne, Lila laughed and said she wanted some of whatever it was I smoked that day. But there weren't many places I'd been in my life that I couldn't get back to. I wasn't very comfortable with the idea.

I followed the broad, high ridge to about where I thought I'd left it that first time and again went down the slope on a direct line towards the cove and the house. I tried to measure the time that had elapsed that day before I noticed something wasn't right. By the time I thought I had gone the right distance, I was nearly at the house and could hear Eddie yelling about something. There just was no such place as I remembered.

I walked westward from the cove, along the less familiar part of the beach. I tired much sooner than I expected and turned back. By the time I circled behind the house to the skiff, I wondered if I'd have the energy to row back. The unsteadiness of the little boat made me queasy. I had to sit and catch my breath before I struggled up the ladder and stumbled to my bunk.

A few minutes later, Morganne came in. "Do you feel as bad as I do?" she asked me.

"Just tired," I said. "Really tired."

"Me too," she said, and we were asleep.

I awoke from a hollow, bloody dream some time that night. The sleeping bag was soaked and cold, and sweat ran from my body. Morganne huddled in the fetal position, shivered and said something I couldn't understand, over and over. My mouth was stuck closed, my eyes streamed and I shook, could not stop. I knew that if I did not get cocaine soon, I would die. I fumbled in my locker, found my inhaler.

A week ago I would have called it empty. Right now, the sprinkle of flakes that fell into a corner of the glass cylinder when I shook it seemed like the promise of renewed life. I turned the arrow towards the cylinder and tipped the remnants into the chamber, then opened the valve and drained it into my nose. I felt the sharp caress deep in my mind and within a minute, I felt better. But that was not nearly enough. I realized Morganne watched me. I shrugged at her.

"Me too," she said. "I don't care if it kills me. I would rather die than feel like this."

"I don't have any more," I said.

She looked at me in despair. "Find some," she said, "buy some. I have the money."

"Lila," I said.

"She'll laugh at us," Morganne said. Her teeth chattered and she held her mouth with her hand.

"Well, she was right," I said.

"I don't care," Morganne said.

Lila did laugh, offered to sell it back to me. Morganne got angry. Lila relented and chopped us a big line although she took her time about it.

I let Morganne go first. She sighed and smiled and yawned. The little rush from the remnants in my bottle had faded fast and I was eager to feel normal. I took a good hit in each side and felt the tension in my back relax. I sat back, breathed easier and felt warm for the first time in a while. It seemed foolish to give up such a feeling. I could afford it.

Lila handed me the bag. "I figured you would be around for this," she said. "You would have felt like a fool if you'd thrown it to the fishes."

"Well, I guess I learned my lesson," I said and we all laughed. We stayed together until morning.

Cree tied up alongside, came aboard to cook us a decent breakfast. I didn't eat much, but Morganne and I visited the ounce a couple of times. My nose had begun to bleed off and on. It didn't seem like much of a price to pay.

CHAPTER 40

I needed to score again before the next cruise or we would run out.

"Can you imagine running out in the middle of the sound?" Morganne asked me.

"I don't imagine things like that," I said.

The next day I called Gerard from the house, but he was evasive and Eddie was around the corner in the hall trying to eavesdrop on me. I knew Aaron depended on Gerard too, so I mentioned it to him.

He called and got the same response. "We'd better go down there," he said.

Cree dropped us off in La Conner. The BMW battery was dead, so we walked downtown and bought a new one at the Gull station, waited for them to quick-charge it and carried it back up the hill. All we had for wrenches was a pair of pliers, so it took us a while to get going.

Gerard was not at his apartment, but his sister-in-law had moved in with him and she said he had a new lab. She gave us an address.

"Across from University City," she said. "Go around behind."

Where the address should have been, there was a dog and cat hospital so Aaron drove on, had me check the number. He turned back and we saw the right number on the veterinarian's mailbox. He turned in, stopped in the driveway. A tearful lady in a fur coat walked in front of us, carried a small dog smothered in bandages.

Aaron worked his way to the back of the parking lot, found a small drive that led behind the building. Gerard's van was backed up to a stairwell that led down into a basement apartment below the clinic.

The apartment was stacked full of boxes and cardboard barrels, many with designations written in scientific jargon. There were several long folding tables scattered with tall brown glass bottles of chemicals. Among the bottles were some burners with long tubes and an electronic chemist's balance with fluorescent dot matrix numbers that ticked up and down as the door opened and closed.

"It's perfect," Gerard said. "Traffic coming and going at all hours, cats yowling and dogs yapping. And it stinks. No one will notice me."

I tapped on one of the barrels marked "Ephedrine" and watched the yellowish grains dance on the metal lid.

"That will make you go faster than cocaine," Gerard said to me. "Especially after a little chemical alteration. Ever hear of methamphetamine? That's its natural mother. Try a little."

"No thanks," I said, "cocaine is faster than I need to go."

He said he couldn't cook up any Northern Lights for at least several days, when he was through with this batch of speed, and even then, he had no raw material to work with.

There was nothing in town but some shitty Colombian, and they wouldn't sell it to you unless you agreed not to buy from anyone else.

"You better go south," he said to Aaron, "if you're in a hurry.

"We are," I said.

No one wanted to make the trip, but no one wanted to run out. Aaron made several calls to San Francisco and Santa Cruz, but couldn't get a definite yes. Finally he decided to go check it out, take Lila. I was glad he didn't want me to go.

They couldn't call us on the Orca and we didn't want to run any messages through Eddie, so Cree called down to the Venetian each day from La Conner, then radioed the news out to us. She couldn't say anything private, so all we knew for three days was that they were okay but hadn't been successful.

The fourth day, Cree said only, "We'll see you tomorrow."

They were in terrible shape. Lila looked like she hadn't seen a shower or a hairbrush in days. Aaron had little to say, but his face was tight and gray. They had eight ounces of ugly brown Colombian Product that someone had walked all over. I immediately saw Ephedrine and Procaine.

"It's full of Inositol too," Lila said. "Cuts your nose like a buzz saw. And it's too hot by at least a point."

"Gerard can fix it," I said.

But Gerard didn't get his speed done in time and we went out on a charter before he could process our coke. My ounce of Northern Lights was gone and we had no choice but to use the new Product as it was.

They had gotten it, Lila said, in San Jose, in a rickety motel full of bikers and prostitutes. The Mexican who delivered it gave them five minutes to make up their minds and left with his hand on his gun. Lila said it was the worst trip she had ever made. The Product bore her out.

Every time I used it, I got too wired because of the Ephedrine. I tried to do just enough to keep the cravings under control, but not too much. I seemed never to get it right.

Lila said they had run into some fake coke in Santa Cruz that was nothing but Ephedrine and Procaine.

"People buying it now," she said, "don't know the difference. They don't even care. It's just the cool thing to do. They'd snort strychnine."

Our graduate students were back in class and Eddie told us that there were no volunteers this term. Unless Aaron wanted to go hire some people out of the Union Hall or off skid row, we would have to go out very short-handed. The only answer, Aaron said, was to forget sails for now and just go on motor cruises until we could get some compatible crewmembers.

This next group didn't seem to mind. I don't think any of them realized there should have been sails. I don't know what they thought the masts were for. It was another random collection, which was fine with me after the eclipse cruise.

Eddie came aboard, escorted a small band of academics who had spent the night at his whale motel. As soon as they were settled he disappeared.

There was a gay couple who loved to hold hands in the wind near the bow rail and just look at each other.

There were two old ladies who couldn't get their eyes off Cree.

"They're terrified of her," Lila said.

"No, they aren't," I said. "They think she's Super Woman." After dinner the first night I saw them discussing recipes with her.

Akbar was aboard again. "I can't quite see the ending to this thing," he said to me. "One more trip will do it." He put down the camera, looked at me through the clear-lensed eye. "Hey, man, you got any of that Northern Lights?"

"No," I said. "Just some shit and it's not for sale." As I walked away I could hear the Bolex.

Walt Gann was back, as well. "There's a story here," he said, "if I can just get the right focus."

This time he had brought a photographer, a short, husky Jewish guy who smiled a lot and made you forget he had the camera.

It was a full load, but I don't remember all of the faces or names. I spent a lot of time trying to fly my head right, somewhere between wired and depressed.

If I waited too long, I got sleepy, even with my eyes wide open, and strange noises and shadows passed through my mind as though real. If I slept, it was a strange and empty time, and I struggled to consciousness as though dragged from the depths.

Morganne just stayed wired, but it began to wear her out. She talked incessantly when we were alone, but became silent and withdrawn around strangers. Once or twice I know she talked to someone who wasn't there, but I didn't mention it, just paid closer attention to my own conversations.

Lila didn't seem to use any more or any less than usual, the soft iron of her face didn't change. But there was something too slow about her movements and something muted in her eye.

You could never tell about Aaron, he spent so much time alone or with Maria and Do. He might have used far more or far less than we did. As much as he was in the center of things, there was something very private about him, and I don't know if anyone ever knew what he was about.

His inexorable shipboard routine continued. Though he didn't do a lot himself, there was not much that happened that he was not aware of, but he never mentioned most of what he knew. And inevitably he had the next compass heading when it was time.

We saw orcas the first evening out. Several of them arched their backs as before. Everyone got lots of pictures of them against a spectacular sunset.

Walt Gann was ecstatic. "I've got the story," he said to whoever would listen. "It's about luck. That's what the orcas represent. It's all luck. I was out here eight days the first time and I didn't see them at all. Then the next time it was the third day. This time we've barely gotten here. No one can predict it. It's just luck. Everything is!"

"Well, that was profound," Lila said after he told her. "Nothing we can do matters, it's all just luck."

"Doesn't surprise me," I said.

I noticed that Akbar had stopped filming even though there still was plenty of light. The capped Bolex hung at his side. The glasses were off and I saw both eyes together for a change. "I see, now," he said as I walked up.

"See?" I said.

"Why I couldn't find the end. There is no end." An orca breached, splashed and swam away from us. He pointed to the receding wake. "Cree told me her mother's people and tribes of orcas used to follow the gray whales from Koona in B.C. to Kona in Hawaii and back. For them there was no end. People invented endings. There are only beginnings."

That made sense to me too. But Eddie would say that it was just the random interactions of billions of selfish acts with billions of other selfish acts and none of us really cared who else lived or died. I wondered why I had begun to make his nasty arguments for him.

As luck would have it, we saw no more orcas. The cruise became four days of circling the San Juans on auxiliary power until even the passengers noticed we'd been there before. By the third day, I was sure we were being followed.

At first I thought it was the Ephedrine or some other contaminant in the coke making me paranoid. But there it was, off and on all day, just on the horizon, a white smudge with the suggestion of black and steel. I felt absolutely sure it was a cutter. I didn't mention it to anyone, but I began to watch everyone aboard.

I soon realized that Aaron had seen it, too, and surreptitiously scanned it with his small binoculars. He made an unexpected turn between Lopez and Orcas Islands and I saw him watch to see if they made the turn. The white smudge threaded through the narrow passage behind us.

No one else seemed to notice. Now and then, someone would look in that direction, but I never saw anyone focus on it. At night, I could just make out distant running lights, like stars that never quite broke the horizon. Cree noticed it then, and when she saw me look where she looked, knew that I knew.

By morning; the cutter was closer. It was hard to believe that everyone didn't see it, but no one gave the alarm. It was the last day and we headed in; the passengers slept late.

I asked Aaron if I could put a couple of things in his safe.

"Let's be quick," he said. "I have some money to put in it."

Akbar came to the door of the wheelhouse. "I was looking through my long lens and... I see you know," he said. "I wondered if there was a safe place for my film. They will take it, you know. As evidence."

"How much is there?" Aaron asked him.

Akbar made a shape in the air. "Ten rolls or so," he said. "Just this cruise and the last."

"Bring it to the galley," Aaron said. "Right now. I'll try."

Walt Gann sat at the crew table with a cup of coffee and his notebook. The photographer was outside on the deck. I went over to Gann.

"You got anything that you don't want the Coast Guard to see?" I pointed at the notebook.

He started, stared at me. "What do you mean?" He closed the notebook, held it tight.

"We might get a visit," I said. "I could put that away for you. In a safe place. And your buddy's film."

"No way," Gann said. "You just want to see my notes, or expose the film or something."

"Why would I do that?" I asked him.

"Only to cover criminal activity," he said.

"Your choice," I said.

Akbar brought his film and Gann watched us, scribbled on his pad. The photographer looked in, but I frowned at him and he found something else to do. The loose cans of film were hard to carry but we split them and got them down into the hold.

We had found only one screwdriver so it took a while to loosen the planks. Aaron had me watch the passageway while he opened the safe and put in our remaining Product and a stack of cash from the last cruise along with my notebook and moneybelt. I could hear him fighting with the film cans. Then I heard the planks sliding into place.

He came out. "I better go up," he said. "If you hear me gun the engine, get out of here fast." He handed me the screwdriver. The screws went in more easily each time, but I was afraid some of them would pop out. I tightened them carefully and found a rag to wipe off any traces of our entry. There were some empty pallets and I dragged two of them over to that side to cover the area.

Back on top everything was normal. I had to tell Morganne

and Lila. They were in the wheelhouse taking half-hour turns on Morganne's helm shift.

"The Coast Guard is following us," I said. "We put everything away."

"Can't scare me," Lila said. "I've been doing this shit too long."

"I'm serious," I said.

"He's serious," Morganne said. Her face grew pale; her hands froze to the wheel. "What can we do?"

"Get a lawyer," Lila said.

"They might put us in jail," Morganne said.

"No shit," Lila said.

"I'll jump in the water," Morganne said. "If they come. I'll drown myself. I'm not going to jail."

"That's why you get a good lawyer," Lila said. She removed Morganne's stiff hands from the wheel and moved her out of the way. "My turn," she said.

I put my arm across Morganne's shoulders but I couldn't think of anything to say. I'd kept out just enough of the Colombian to get us through until morning. I figured I could get that over the side before they could sneak up on me. We had to dry it under a light bulb each time before it would chop decently. No one enjoyed it. But then there was the alternative.

CHAPTER 41

The Coast Guard made their move just before we reached our anchorage off Defoe. They came up on us fast and ranged alongside. An officer with a bullhorn ordered us to cut power and come about for boarding pursuant to warrant number so-and-so, U.S. District court.

They maneuvered next to us, didn't have long enough fenders over and scraped a large patch of black paint from theOrca's hull. Three of them came across, the officer and two goons with guns. They asked for Aaron, took him aside and read the warrant to him. I saw him shrug and nod his head.

The passengers began to appear, formed an audience on the foredeck. The officer sent the goons to knock on all doors and get everyone on top. Some of the passengers still wore nightclothes and seemed very confused.

"Get Maria," I said to Lila. She went into the crowd and came back with them, the baby in only a diaper and a thin blanket. Do started to cry and Maria nursed her.

When everyone was accounted for, the officer took Aaron and one goon and went below. The other remained to watch the prisoners.

Morganne shook so that I had to hold her up. Lila glared at the guard. The passengers began to grumble and ask questions, but the guard only looked at us and fingered his gun. I moved Morganne as far out of his way as I could and sat with her on a sail locker. Lila followed with Maria and the baby.

In about half an hour, they came back on deck. The officer walked up beside our guard, looked at us for a minute until there was silence. He held up a paper and read, "This vessel is being seized by the United States Government under Title..."

I tuned out the rest of it, tried to make a plan. The cutter bumped against us with each wave like some sea-going bulldozer. Crewmen lined the rail and stared at us. I saw that they had the tarps off a large machine gun on the bow and several of them stood around it. Swimming wasn't an option.

Morganne clung to me and cried. Lila hovered over Maria and the baby, made them invisible. The passengers were in an uproar, crowded around the officer. I moved close enough to hear him.

"Everyone will be searched," he said. "If your name isn't on the warrant, you will then be free to go, provided we find nothing illegal."

I went back to the others. "If you're carrying anything," I said, "get rid of it." I turned my back to the commotion on deck and took two large hits on my inhaler then tossed it overboard.

One of the Coast Guardsmen looked over at the "plink." I stared back at him and he turned away.

By now, some of the passengers were yelling and the officer nodded to his men, who put their hands on their guns and faced the crowd.

One of the two old ladies started in, "Young man, if you think I'm going to stand by and watch you treat people this way, you are mistaken...."

More shouts drowned out the rest of it.

"Okay," the officer said. "This is how we'll do it. I will read a list of names. Those called will step over here behind me. Everyone else will form a line along the rail to be searched."

The old lady's voice called out from the back. "If you search me or any of these people you don't have on your warrant, my attorney will take care of you."

"This is a suspect vessel in US waters," the officer said. "I am allowed to take whatever measures necessary."

"Don't do anything you don't want to explain in court," the old lady said.

He pretended not to hear her, started to read his list: "Aaron Adams or Adamson."

Aaron moved slowly to the designated area. One of the guards made a point of watching him.

"Brad Bennett..."

No one moved. We all looked at each other. Lila shrugged.

The officer frowned. "Fred Carter."

Again, no one moved.

"We will be checking identification," the officer said. "Don't try to play games. It will just be harder on everyone. Now, then, Frederick Crook, also known as 'Fuzzy.'" He paused, then repeated, "Frederick Crook."

"I think you better check your list," someone in the crowd said. There was a general murmur.

He tried again. "Robert 'Bob' Danielson."

He wasn't there either. There was a giggle from among the passengers.

The officer was not happy. He whispered to one of the men who climbed over to the cutter and disappeared. We all waited. In a while he was back with a large Black petty officer who conferred with the man in charge. The Black man took the list.

"Now don't you-all go playin' games with us," he said. "If you hear your name, you move over here smartly." He squinted at the list.

"Lila Jean Eskinazi," he said and waited. She didn't move. I forced myself not to look at her and hoped no one else betrayed her.

"All-righty," he said, finally. "Next. Lance Ferguson."

Lance took his place beside Aaron.

"That's more like it," the petty officer said. "Now, let's see, Jaime Garcia." He looked at me. I looked back. "Ohhkay," he said. "However you want it." He drew a line under the name. "Gerard Jackson," he continued.

It was clearly alphabetical, so I was not on the list. I would have been just after Aaron. "You're not on it," I whispered to Morganne.

"What?"

"It's alphabetical," I said.

"Oh," she said, and started to calm down. "Maria isn't on it either."

"Right," I said.

"Me either," Lila said with a grin. "I don't ever carry my own ID."

"Keep it down," the officer said to us. "No one is in the clear, yet."

I tossed him a salute and one of the guards smiled briefly.

"No Gerard Jackson either," the petty officer said, shook his head sadly. "Let's see if Kimball Kramer recognizes his own name... no. Let's do it this way. I'll read through the list and anyone who recognizes their name join these gentlemen behind me. The rest of us will just do it the hard way."

He read quickly. There were several more names I didn't recognize, but Patrick was on it - and Pancho. They had a picture of Pancho, said his name was Robbie Lerner. Miller Richards had made the cut and so had the Poet. Suras wasn't on the list, which didn't surprise me.

He finished and looked at us. "You-all don't look like that kind of people," he said. "Okay, make me a line along the rail."

We stayed where we were, became part of the ragged line. The old lady kept lipping off, made us all laugh.

Our captors seemed a little tense. The officer went back aboard the cutter and sent two more enlisted types to help sort us out. Everyone who demonstrated they were not on the list was allowed their choice of the cutter or the main cabin on the Orca.

By the time they got to us, it was clear something was wrong.

"Now, we're just doing our jobs, folks," the petty officer said. "We're sorry for any inconvenience."

So far, no one else was on the list.

The petty officer checked my ID personally. I handed him my Library Card. He looked at it carefully then motioned for me to hand him my wallet. I did and he looked through it, found nothing but a few dollars. He studied the card again for a minute.

"What are you doing on this side of the mountains?" he asked me.

"Made a wrong turn," I said.

"I can dig it," he said. "I went to high school in Moses Lake. Even played a little basketball. Sometimes I think I should have stayed there." He handed me the wallet. "I'd get back home if I was you."

"I've been thinking about it," I said.

He glanced quickly at Maria's ID card, patted the baby and asked her name.

"Dolores," he said. "That was my grandmother's name."

He patted Morganne's trembling hand. "Not on my list," he said. "Don't worry."

We stayed on the Orca, made coffee for the others who were there. About two-thirds of the passengers had gone over to the cutter and the deck was crowded. Twice more, the officer went over, then back to confer with the petty officer.

The two old ladies had stayed with us and one of them played with Do, got Maria to smile and even talk a little. The other old lady asked Cree if it would be okay to cook something for anyone who was hungry and Cree said sure. Soon she had scrambled eggs and toast to order.

The Coast Guard didn't seem to know what to do. The officer brought a new list which they compared to the old one, then shook their heads again.

The passengers on the cutter were irritated and grew louder as the afternoon wore on. They were taken inside in groups for food, but they didn't stay long. The chop was a little higher and the cutter repeatedly scraped against us.

The officer crossed to the cutter once more, went inside, then came back out and called across to the petty officer, "We'll take this group to the island, Chief. Stand by."

"Yes, sir," the petty officer replied.

They banged us a couple of times casting loose. Apparently no one remembered that the Orca had no anchor out and no power. As soon as we were free we began to drift. The petty officer tried to yell to the cutter, but it was gone. He looked this way and that, went over to Aaron.

Aaron got up and came down the deck, then climbed to the wheelhouse. I heard the diesel start, felt the Orca steady, then slowly come about.

One of the guards poked his head into the main cabin. "They want you," he said to me.

He followed me to the wheelhouse.

"Take the wheel," the petty officer said. "Keep her steady." He turned to the guard who'd come with me. "You stay here."

"No," I said. "I'm not under arrest. I might help you out, but not with a guard. Take him with you."

The petty officer looked at me. "Okay," he said. "Just don't pull anything. I know where you live." He grinned.

Aaron gave me an almost imperceptible wink, then he looked through the glass, down towards the deck. I followed the look. The skiff. I noticed Cree in the shadows near it; the tarp was partly off.

"It will be dark soon," Aaron said, as if to the petty officer.

"What?" he responded.

"We'll need to get some lights on," Aaron said. "They might never find us again."

The petty officer gave Aaron a narrow look. They all left.

I maintained the heading, just off the wind and directly into the swell. We made so little headway the rudder felt even mushier than usual.

I saw Lance move along the deck towards the upside-down skiff. He bent as if to tie his shoe and loosened the stern tie. The line on the bow was already undone. He moved on and soon Cree was back, slid the skiff near the port rail. She looked up at me and was gone.

Through the twilight I could see the cutter near the end of the dock on Defoe, but it looked like they couldn't get in close enough. Soon they had a dinghy in the water, ferried groups of four or five to the dock.

It appeared that the plan was for Cree, Lance and Aaron to

drop the skiff into the water, then one or more of them jump into it. I wasn't sure how I could help.

Cree came with a cup of coffee. I winked at her.

"We need a diversion," she whispered.

"I could lay her over pretty hard if I had a little more speed," I said.

"Ease it up slow," she said, "and see if you can run in near the northeast point."

The guard poked his head in and Cree left.

I began to work the throttle open in tiny, unnoticeable increments. I changed the heading half a degree at a time until we were on course to just miss the shallows off the point. I soon had pretty fair speed and no one had noticed. I boldly stepped it up more.

"Hey," I called, then again. A few minutes later, a guard came in. "I've gotta go," I said.

"Go where?" he asked.

"The head," I said.

"Oh," he said. "What do you want me to do?"

"Someone probably ought to take the wheel," I said.

"Oh, yeah," he said. "Not me. I'm not rated."

"Get Cree," I said. "Or Lance."

"The black chick?" He asked. "No way! Who's Lance? The tall one?"

"Not Aaron," I said. "The other tall one."

He came back in a few minutes with Lance, watched us as he took the wheel.

I went to the crew head. Cree was there.

"Get it in the water," I said, "and get ready. Who's going?"

"Aaron and Lance," she said. "They can't hold the rest of us."

"Tell them I'll lay over easy to port, so they'll know to go over. Then I'll lay hard over to starboard and anyone still on their feet won't be watching anything."

I went back to the wheel, said nothing to Lance or the guard. They went out.

In about ten minutes, I saw Aaron, Lance and Cree appear at the skiff, wrestle it over the rail and drop it with a splash. Aaron quickly tied a thin line to the rail and I saw it tighten and strain as it pulled the skiff alongside us.

A guard came around the side of the cabin, looked at them. They continued as if in casual conversation until the guard went away. I eased the throttle a little higher.

I spun the wheel to the left, felt the deck tip, held it, spun back before there was too much momentum. As the port rail dipped I could see Aaron and Lance slip over. The line towing the skiff went slack.

I waited until I was sure they would be clear of the stern, then spun the wheel hard right, felt the Orca swing like a pendulum, lay over further and further. My heart pounded as I spun the wheel back. We hung suspended on our side for a moment. Slowly the down rail rose, then faster and we came upright, rocked past center, then back. I corrected as much as I could each way.

The petty officer stormed into the wheelhouse followed by two guards.

"What the hell are you trying to do?" he demanded.

I made a show of watching the compass, held the boat dead level.

"That heading you had me on," I said. "We would have hit the bar back there. It's a good thing I know my way around here."

"I didn't give you the heading," he said. "I assumed it was right. I thought you knew what you were doing."

"I do," I said. "I steer to whatever course someone gives me. I'm not the navigator."

"Where the hell are we?" He tried to see through the glass. "We've moved quite a ways."

"I just steer it," I reminded him.

"I don't even have a god damned radio," he said.

"We could come about," I said.

"Do it," he said.

I cut back the power, let her slow, then made a slow wide turn that carried us well away from the island.

"There they are," the petty officer said, pointed to the

floodlights of the cutter which lit up the house and cove on Defoe.

There was a crowd there, distorted shadows moved against the trees. Without thinking I did the trick with my eyes, looked for the Guardians, saw nothing but the glare from the lights.

I steered in towards them, cut back to minimum power. The spotlights switched off and the cutter moved out towards us. When they got close, they turned the big lights on us.

The dinghy was alongside them. It came up to our rail. A young officer stood in the bow.

"Okay," he said. "Those not listed on the warrant are free to go. Someone may want to talk to you again later. We have your names. There is room for six at a time. You will be shuttled to the dock. Transportation from that point is your own responsibility."

Two seamen came on board and started trying to figure out the anchor. The guard asked me, but I played dumb. One of the seamen took the wheel and I went down to the deck.

The two old ladies insisted that the younger women go before them. They were particularly concerned for Maria and Do. Lila and Morganne went next. The trip took about half an hour. Cree and I waited until last, got into the boat with the two old ladies.

"Bring the prisoners," the young officer said.

Two of the guards went into the main cabin. They came back and whispered to the officer. He called the petty officer. The petty officer went into the main cabin and came out with the other two guards. They all talked furiously, but in low tones. The petty officer pointed at me.

The young officer came over. "Chief Thomas says you may know something about the prisoners' disappearance?"

"Me?" I asked. "I was in the wheel house all the time. Except I went to the toilet."

"Chief says you nearly hit the island," he said.

"They gave me a bad heading," I said, shrugged.

"Well don't leave the island," the officer said. "We will want to talk to you."

"Sure," I said. "No problem. What can I tell you?"

"I don't know," he said.

CHAPTER 42

Lila, Morganne and Maria were huddled around the sleeping baby on a corner of the lawn. The boat headed out to the cutter. We watched for a while, but they were too far out for us to see much.

When we felt they weren't watching us, we all went onto the Wigit and Do slept on Cree's bunk. Cree made some tea in the dark and we warmed up in the small cabin.

Sometime after midnight the bright lights on the cutter went off and they seemed to settle in for the night. Cree started the engine and let it warm.

I cast loose the lines and she nudged away from the dock, half-drifted out into the cove. She turned as close to the point as she dared, cut power as we bumped across the bar.

About halfway along the north shore we saw a light flash three times from the beach, then twice more. Cree flashed back and let the Wigit drift.

We heard the noise of oars and a few minutes later the skiff came alongside. Cree handed Aaron a small line which he tied to the bow of the skiff and brought the other end on board with him. I took the line from him and worked back to the stern, let the skiff trail behind.

Cree got underway and headed south, ducked behind Cypress Island and around the lower end of Lopez. She cut power, idled the diesel. We couldn't see or hear anything except a distant airplane headed towards Bellingham.

We crossed the channel to the point on the long neck of San

Juan where the American Camp was during the famous Pig War. That seemed like a good place for them to find the skiff.

"We need to give them some tracks," I said. "Can you get in close enough for someone to swim out?"

"Maybe," Cree said, "if they swim pretty good."

Lance said he didn't swim that well. Aaron said, "If I have to." I decided to impersonate Lance.

I pulled the skiff close and we climbed in. Cree tossed me the line. Aaron rowed for a while, then I took over. We didn't want to be obvious and leave the boat on the end of the point, so we rowed past for maybe a half mile, then ran in on a nice little beach. We dragged the skiff up above high water and threw some brush and driftwood over it as though we had tried to hide it.

We left a clear trail through the sand wherever there was any. We bore to the right just off the road that leads to Friday Harbor. A couple of dogs barked at us, but no one came out to investigate. After a mile, we made nice tracks up to the pavement and walked on it another stretch in case they used tracking dogs. We doubled back down the hard surface.

When we left the pavement, we took off our boots and carried them, walked in the double heavy socks we'd worn. We waded a shallow pond and walked in a ditch for a ways. Aaron began to limp, but my feet were accustomed to the ground.

It seemed much further than it could have been before we came to a rocky stretch of shoreline on the west side of San Juan Island. I could hear the idle of the Wigit's engine somewhere.

We found a clear spot and Aaron flashed the signal out over the water. In just a few seconds it came back.

As we looked for a decent approach to the water, we could hear Cree come in closer. I buckled my belt through the straps of my boots and put the belt over my neck. I took off the double socks and stuffed them in one of the boots.

The water was very cold and I hoped we didn't have to swim far. I could hear the sound of the diesel, but reflected off the water it was impossible to tell how close or in what direction. I thought of that night on the Skagit.

My boots filled and began to weigh me down. The more I struggled, the more they pulled my head under. I felt a little thrill of relief or irony, as I let them go.

I swam forward more strongly, felt Aaron close behind. The engine definitely was louder.

"Here," Cree said, close to us. I relaxed, drifted until I got my bearings and took the few strokes towards her voice. I felt the rough skin of the Wigit and it comforted me like a mother's touch. I let myself bump against it gently, then felt Cree's hands drag me over the rail.

I tried to help her with Aaron, but I was too weak to stand. Lila helped while Lance watched. We stripped off our clothes in the cabin and Cree gave us blankets. As soon as we were settled, she headed north in the shadow of San Juan Island as dawn lightened the eastern sky.

I crouched on the bunk and shivered. As I warmed and the adrenaline wore off, I craved cocaine. It had been hours, and I was not feeling good. I saw that Morganne, too, was in trouble. She was curled up in a corner and the skin on her forehead was taut as a drum. I knew she had a screaming headache. I soon would as well.

Lila looked at me, shook my shoulder. "You're pretty sick, aren't you?" she asked me.

I nodded.

She went outside to talk to Cree.

Cree cut power and came into the cabin. She looked at me, then Morganne.

"I was going north," she said. "I thought we would hang out at Saltspring or somewhere, be just one more Canadian fishing boat. But I need to get you two where we can take care of this."

"Where?" Aaron asked her.

She thought for a minute. "I hate to say this," she said. "The best place would be on Defoe. I have a sweat set up there." She looked closely at Aaron. "You could use it, too," she said. He didn't argue.

I think she went around the north end of San Juan and down

the channel between Orcas and Shaw, but I didn't see any of it. A fair storm kicked up and in my weakened state I got tossed about. I was thrown out of the bunk twice, so I stayed on the floor, huddled with Morganne. We rolled around some, but it was better there.

I knew it was daytime, but the gray light of dawn never brightened, and by what must have been midafternoon it darkened again and the wind rose higher. I heard Do cry a couple of times, but mostly no one said anything.

Lila came in, grew pale and started back out. "Seasick," she said. I wondered if that was all.

I'm sure we doubled back and criss-crossed and all the things Cree usually did to confuse anyone who might follow. She let us drift a couple of times while she came in and made tea for us. I tried to get some down, but my throat wanted only one thing. The same thing every cell in my body had begun to demand.

I thought of asking Cree if she had any but decided I couldn't do it. I thought of all the cocaine I'd wasted and spilled and given away. I remembered dimly a time when I hadn't cared about it at all and could have walked away from a mountain of it.

I had to find a way to get just enough to feel good. Permanently. I couldn't imagine a worthwhile life without it.

Cree waited until just before high tide, then ran the Wigit in close in a little steep-banked creek inlet down the shore from the sweat. Morganne and Cree and I waded through the freezing water. Morganne collapsed on the bank. Aaron threw a long line to Cree and she carried it up the steep slope.

Morganne and I sat while Cree found a strong tree and fastened the line. Aaron coiled the extra line on the Wigit's deck so they could let it out with the dropping tide.

Cree led us along the shore to the sweat. It was much as the last time I'd seen it. The cover was tightly closed and there were four blankets neatly folded inside. Morganne and I wrapped them around us and held each other in the dark, while Cree built the fire.

She had good dry firewood stashed under a dense cedar and soon the flames made shadows on the sailcloth cover. It seemed like a long time before the smoke died down and she opened the flaps, extended them like a funnel to catch the radiant heat. Still we both shivered.

Cree stacked rocks in an openwork structure over the flames. As the fire found it's way through, much of the heat was absorbed by the stones. When a few were warm, she put them in the sandpit in the center of the sweat and we held our hands over them and let go the blankets a little.

She handed in cans of tea and I got some of mine down.

Morganne gave up, said, "I can't swallow."

Cree urged us to drink all we could.

The next rocks she put in were hot. We dropped the blankets and tried to feel warm. She put in a few that glowed dull red and tossed some water on them and lowered the flap. Finally, I was warm. Now, if I could just stay this way.

But soon she opened it again, fanned a flap to let the cool air circulate, then added hotter rocks. This time she threw on a whole large juice can of water and quickly dropped the flaps. The humid heat exploded on my body. The flaps stayed down and the heat went around, seemed to come back hotter. I wondered if Cree would open it if one of us screamed.

By the third wave of steam, I had to lie flat. Sweat poured from my body and my head felt tight and raw. Morganne lay across from me, her face splotches of flushed red and ashen gray. I assumed my own must look the same. I was glad for the beard to hide me.

By this time there was a good-sized mound of rocks in the pit and Cree brought several cans of water.

"Whenever it's cool enough to sit up," she said, "pour on more water. And drink all the tea you can. I'm going to get the other two."

I continued to pour on water whenever I thought of it. Morganne sat up a couple of times and even smiled once. I tried to smile back.

The rocks began to cool and the water wouldn't steam. I thought about getting more rocks from the fire, but I was tired. Too tired to move, like a lizard on a cold day, I thought of things to do but could not do them.

Eventually there were voices and Cree's face appeared. "Better," she said.

Aaron and Lila squeezed in. They didn't look much better than Morganne. Cree raked out most of the rocks and replaced them with some that had gotten very hot while she was gone. She closed the flaps and let it warm up thoroughly before she put on more water.

Lila groaned at the first wave of heat. It felt good to me. I sat with my head down and thought of the great effort required to raise it, or move a leg. To stand seemed a supreme exertion, a distant memory.

I began to sleep, almost, to float on the clouds of vapor that rose from the stones.

CHAPTER 43

When I awakened, I moved only my eyes, had no strength to do more. The faint light through sailcloth told me it was morning or evening. I had no idea which. I lay in a larger shelter than the sweat, newly made, the saplings still green.

I recognized the cover as part of the old sails from the Quest, which Aaron had given Cree. My mattress was made of the same material and felt like it was stuffed with grass or leaves.

Morganne slept beside me, and across from us I could just see Aaron and Lila.

Cree opened the flap, looked in as though she had felt me awaken, smiled at me. "Once again, you will live," she said.

"You say that to all the guys," I whispered.

"Seems like I'm always saying it to you." She grinned. "If you really are determined to go to the Lower World, I can't stop you."

I sat up slowly, tried not to move my head more than necessary. "I've seen as much as I need to," I said. "I want to go home."

"Sometimes it isn't so easy to go back," she said.

"I'll walk there barefoot in the winter if I have to," I said.

"You sound a little more like Lucky," Cree said. "Drink this." She handed me a can of steaming tea. "Now I have to get back to the Wigit, and Maria."

The can burned my fingers and I nearly dropped it, set it on the blanket and held my head in my hands.

"I wish I had a home," Morganne said softly.

I looked at her and she gave me a weak smile. Her face was a more natural color, but she dripped with sweat. She struggled as if to sit and I helped her.

"I feel like my brain is dried out," she said. "I wish I could pour water in my head."

"It isn't water I need," I said. The better I felt, the more I craved it.

"Me, too," Morganne said. "But we can't get any."

"Maybe Cree would take one of us somewhere, just to score," I said.

"We don't have money," Morganne said.

"We have money on the Orca," I said.

"If we can't get to it, we don't have it," she said. "At least not soon enough."

"We could borrow money," I said. "From Patrick, or Gerard. Everyone knows we're good for it."

"Even if they would," Morganne said, "they were on the warrant, too. They're either in jail or hiding. Everything is changed."

"I wonder why we weren't on the warrant," I said.

"Because you have Guardian Angels," I heard Lila say. "I pissed mine off a few years back."

Morganne giggled and it started her shivering. "You're tough as an old shoe," she said. "You don't need a Guardian Angel."

"I heard you talk about getting some," Lila said. "I could get my money out of escrow. We could go south and score, sell enough to pay for some."

"I don't want to do that anymore," Morganne said.

"Would you rather do without?" Lila asked her.

"God, no," Morganne said. "There must be something else we can do."

"I think we've already done all of them," Lila said.

"We have to quit," I said.

"Don't say that," Morganne said. "I don't want to quit."

"I think it quit us," I said. "I don't see strong prospects of finding any."

"Well, I've been able to find some pretty much every day for more than ten years," Lila said. "I don't think it will go away now. I've been dry before, but I just tell myself it's not forever, and it never is."

"Nothing is forever," I said. "Including the way we feel. People get over it."

"I don't know if they ever do," Lila said. "I've seen people go back a hundred times."

"What's the point?" Morganne asked. "Why make yourself sick then go back and do it again?"

"Not me," I said. "I'm finished with it."

"I've heard that before," Lila said.

"Not from me," I said and slept.

The next thing I remember is the smell of food, clams and potatoes and peppers. I sat up more easily.

Cree heard me move, opened the flap. "Soup's on," she said.

I crawled outside and hunched by the fire. It was dark, no stars, and bursts of wind sent the flames this way and that. Cree ladled soup into a large can with a small one, handed it to me with a spoon.

My throat did not want to swallow at first, but the soup tasted wonderful. I couldn't remember tasting food in a while although I had eaten my share. The chowder was thick with bits of smoked salmon; the clams were tender and clean. I soon needed more.

Morganne and Lila crawled out to join us. Cree handed them cans of soup. Neither of them seemed hungry.

Lila picked at hers and asked, "What stinks?"

"Probably octopus or something," Morganne said. She held it away from her face.

Cree grinned at them. "It's Mother's Soup," she said.

"Your mother?" Lila asked.

"Everyone's Mother," Cree said. "Her soup is made from what you find around you. Very strong medicine. It will ground you again, give you real energy. Cocaine is for an emergency, or a party, but not for living every day. It makes you a Zombie and you call it life."

"I'll take my life any day," Lila said.

"You have no choice about that," Cree said.

"How's Aaron?" Morganne asked. "Has he been awake?"

"No," Cree said. "He is very tired - but he will be okay."

"How long has he been asleep?" Lila asked.

"Just two days," Cree said.

"Just two days," Lila mimicked, "maybe he's dead."

"He's breathing," Cree said. "He's okay."

"Maybe he's in a coma," Morganne said.

"His body will sleep as long as it needs to," Cree said. "His spirit knows it is safe here."

"Two days is a long time to sleep," Lila said.

"Only if you think there is a law that says you must sleep every day," Cree said, "so you can get up and go to work in the factory in the morning. In the old days, hunters, or mothers with sick children, or warriors on a raid might stay awake for many days then sleep for as long as eight days when it was over. Many people in the world sleep only two or three times a week."

"Aaron hasn't slept much for a long time," Morganne said. "When he wasn't working on something, he was with Maria. I used to hear them talk all night."

"I can't believe anyone has that much to say," Lila said.

"He has to get her ready for the next day," I said. "He has to think of anything that might happen and give her a plan for it."

"He does a lot of that for all of us," Morganne said. "I hope he's okay."

"He's okay," Cree said.

"How about Maria?" Morganne asked.

"I think she will come back to us," Cree said. "Right now she is very lost."

"How about Do?" I asked her.

"Maria does all right with the baby," Cree said. "That's her anchor, her way to hold onto the world."

I went back inside to sleep and I dreamt of orcas, jumping, splashing, blowing, boisterous, exuberant life. They breached and breathed as though delivered from bondage. The great one was there, quietly watched. They seemed as happy to see me as I was to see them. I had missed them and not known what it was I missed.

My point of view made several sudden shifts, on and under the water. I was not sure where I was. I wondered if Maria and the others were there. We never had been able to see each other within the dreams, or know for sure what form we took. I felt that they felt as I did.

We went north, I think. I didn't care. The pleasure of their company was enough.

When next I awoke, Aaron sat alone by the fire and it was evening. Bright colors of sunset bathed the shelter. The flaps were open and a breeze flowed over us. Morganne's face was relaxed. I watched her take deep, regular breaths. Lila's face sagged into a round moon shape, and her lips twitched as if she had a smart remark.

I crouched out of the shelter, stood near the fire.

"Cree will be back in the morning," Aaron said. His back was to the western light, his face dark except for an occasional flicker of flame. A stranger might have mistaken him for a much older man, his worn back hunched against the sea wind. He said nothing more.

In the firelight, his face reminded me of Cree's, skeletal from the exaggerated shadows; his eyes were red and burnt. There was something hollow and husk-like about him, as though some flame had scorched his soul.

I sat across from him, watched the colors fade behind his head and a planet appear over his shoulder, hold steady against the night. On the beach, the low surf murmured, made me think of Maria's voice.

We sat long into the night, said nothing, but much was told. Waves of light from the faded fire moved upon his face, cast shadows of time. I saw him young and younger, but not much older. I saw sorrows and losses, a few fleeting joys, and a hunger for something that could not be his.

My face, too, must have spoken, for he watched me and softened and finally said, "I guess I'm out of miracles."

"Rabbits multiply fast," I said. "Just reach in the hat again."

"Lost the hat too, I think," he said. "Or threw it away."

"Magic wears on you," I said. "It just goes on and on."

"I guess that's the opposite of luck," he said.

"My Grandfather said luck was the Great Spirit's way to make everything come out even in the end," I said. "Bad luck means good luck has to be on its way. Just maybe not in this generation."

"People now have a little trouble with that time frame," Aaron said. "If it doesn't pay off within thirty days it isn't worth doing."

"I'm responsible for seven generations," I said. "One lifetime doesn't mean a lot by itself. Except for what you pass on to the next generation."

"That's a lot of responsibility," he said.

"It's something a person can actually do," I said. "What you can't do is be responsible for a bunch of other people."

"Like me," he said. "I didn't do a very good job of it."

"No one could," I said. "People have to be responsible for themselves."

"They don't want to be," he said. "They have to have a leader. Sometimes I hate being a leader."

"My Grandfather said, 'If there is no chief, the people will make one.' He said we have all lost our way and have to pretend that someone must know where we are going."

"He was a wise man," Aaron said.

"He believed in doing things," I said. "To him that was an expression of faith. To do something you must believe in the future."

"So what do we do?" Aaron asked me.

"Oh, no," I said. "I'll tell you what I'm going to do, but I don't boss anyone else."

"So what are you going to do?" he asked with a dry smile.

"I'm going to build a house," I said. "Winter's coming. I can predict that."

I slept and dreamed again. Morganne came to me in the night and our lovemaking was part of the dream. We held each other and she whispered, "Take me home with you." I couldn't answer.

We woke to a glad, glorious, golden sun. Cree sang by the fire. Aaron and Lila stirred as we did and sat. I went through the flap on all fours, stood near the fire, warmed my bare feet on the heated soil.

"Lazarus walks among us," Cree said.

"Amen," I said. "What's breakfast."

Cree laughed. "You are back to normal. If you feel like a walk, we could have omelets on the Wigit."

"Show me the way," I said.

We gave everyone a few minutes to wake up, then Cree led us along the crumbled beach between the sweat and the boat.

The Wigit was well hidden now, at high tide, pulled in close under the arch of some tall Madronas.

"At low tide, we have to let out quite a ways," Cree said. "They could see us then, but it's the best I could do."

"Has anyone been around?" Aaron asked her.

"Not here," she said, "but I heard a bunch of talk on the radio about helicopters searching San Juan. Looking for an escaped drug kingpin."

"Congratulations, Aaron," Lila said. "You've been promoted."

Maria smiled shyly from the bunk when we looked in the cabin and Do played with some hand-made stuffed animals on the floor.

Aaron said nothing, just held Maria and pulled the baby to them. We left them alone.

"Where's Lance?" Lila asked Cree.

"He took off, day before yesterday," Cree said. "He was pretty sick. I think he would have killed someone for cocaine."

"Why didn't he come to the sweat?" Lila asked.

"He wouldn't," Cree said. "I tried to talk him into it, but he said he was fine, didn't feel anything. But you could see it. And he slept all the time or just stared into the water. He wouldn't eat."

"Where'd he go?" Lila asked.

"Wherever there might be cocaine," Cree said. "The house, I'm sure."

"So everyone will soon know where we are," Lila said. "They'll catch him and he'll turn. Aaron needs to know."

"Give him a few minutes," I said.

Cree went to make the omelets. Lila, Morganne and I sat on the deck, let our bodies soak in the sun. I heard a noise high above, searched until I found them. A great tribe of geese strung out in a wedge of staggered, intersecting lines like a many-barbed arrow, pointed south; family joined to family, youngsters followed elders, all urged on by the distant calls of the vanguard.

"It's time to go south," Morganne said.

"Or underground," I said.

"What do you mean?" Morganne asked.

"We need a house," I said. "It's almost October."

"So where do we get a house?" Lila asked.

"Build one," I said.

"Right," Lila said. "And no one will notice."

"Not a regular house," I said. "Underground."

"I'm not a troll," Lila said. "Or a cave woman."

"It sounds interesting," Morganne said.

"Yeah," Lila said, "you thought living in a bus with Mr. Bigwrench was interesting, too."

"It was," Morganne said. "Besides, we only lived in the bus until we got the tipi poles cut and peeled."

"Well, I'm going to get off this rock and close the deal on my bar," Lila said. "What day is this?"

"You can't do that," Morganne said, "you were on the warrant."

"I've got my other ID," Lila said.

"But the bar will be in your name," Morganne said. "They'll find you."

"I'll find a way," Lila said. "Or Gerard will."

"Gerard was on the list, too," Morganne reminded her.

"I'm going to build a house," I said.

"I'll help," Morganne said.

"I'll watch," Lila said.

CHAPTER 44

The next morning, we brought Maria and Do onshore and Cree made a run to LaConner for supplies. She wanted me to go along, but I couldn't leave the others. Lila decided to go, see what she could find out about her bar.

We sat around the fire, ate sandwiches Cree had left for us and watched a storm roll in from the west. There was rain towards evening and we all crowded into the little shelter. The roof dripped here and there and the floor soon was mud.

"I'm beginning to like this house idea," Morganne said.

"We could do it," I said. "If we work together. If we're going to be here we may as well be comfortable."

Everyone could see it was a good idea.

I knew where Cree had put a piece of the sailcloth, so I had Morganne help me stretch it over the top and weight down the corners against the wind with rocks. Most of the leaks dried up, but the fire was out. We heard the Wigit sometime that night, but it was raining so hard no one wanted to try for it. I was sure Cree wouldn't come in close in that weather.

It still rained the next morning, so we didn't even look out. We had another round of sandwiches and a jug of water. Do nursed constantly. She and Maria seemed to be in some sort of suspended animation. Around midmorning, Lila scratched at the flap and I untied it. She was soaked. She shivered next to me and kept her head down.

Morganne stroked her back and asked, "What's wrong."

"Oh, nothing," Lila said. "I just lost everything."

"What's everything?" Morganne asked.

"My money, the bar. It's October! When I wasn't there on the first to sign the closing papers, they took my money. It was a non-refundable deposit."

"Can't you do something?" Morganne asked her.

"Cry a lot," Lila said. "Gerard laughed at me. Said he lost twice as much just on Primal Power." She looked at Aaron. "They closed it," she said. "Seized everything. Gerard is going to the Grand Jury."

Aaron nodded.

"He'll talk," Morganne said.

"Not Gerard," Lila said. "He may be an asshole, but he hates them."

"You mean he loves himself," Morganne said.

"Don't we all?" Lila asked. "Psychiatrists say that's healthy."

"For them," I said.

"How about the Orca?" Aaron asked.

"They have guards on it again," Cree said. "Two this time it looked like. We didn't get too close but I think they tore things up when they searched."

"They always do," Aaron said.

"Now do you want to build a house?" Morganne asked Lila.

"We can't stay here," Lila said. "They'll find us."

"As long as we are here," I said, "we might as well have some place dry and warm." No one could argue.

I had picked a little knoll buried in cedars, off to the side of the natural route across the slope above the sweat. The outlook was to the west, but it was nearly obscured by tall alders and Madronas. When the storm passed, I paced a thirty-foot circle and cleared the dense growth of saplings with a bow saw Cree carried on the Wigit. I didn't have a decent tool to peel them, so I set them aside to use with the bark on.

Cree had a good shovel and I used some of the smaller pieces of sail to make a sling on poles like the movie Egyptians used in The Ten Commandments. Morganne and I could carry about half a wheelbarrow load of dirt at a time and move a lot faster. Maria helped when she could and Aaron seemed to enjoy the physical work.

Lila laughed when she saw the tangle of stumps and roots where I told her I was going to dig a four-foot deep hole. But it went faster than even I expected. Cree pitched in and Lila couldn't restrain herself from helping us yank out the long, fibrous roots.

My feet soon toughened and I could use the shovel barefoot as well as the others could with boots or shoes. They laughed at my broad, splay-toed tracks. It didn't bother me as much as it once had.

We left the larger rocks in the hole and rolled them to the edge to become part of our wall. We didn't have enough rocks to reach the top, so we carried in smaller ones to finish off. I was not entirely confident in my roofing materials so I decided to put in a floor drain just in case. We filled a foot-deep trench with fist-sized rocks that would allow water to trickle out the opening on the west.

I was glad the hole was finished before rain began, but a floor was imperative. There wasn't enough flat rock close by for pavers and gravel would have to be washed free of the sticky clay or be packed from the beach.

The omnipresent clay which seemed to be the problem at first, turned out to be the solution. I tried some in the fire and it baked nice and hard.

We packed in enough of the mottled, fishy clay from a nearby spring to spread a couple of inches over the thirty-foot hole. We carried up some driftwood from the beach and found as much deadfall wood as possible. The afternoon was dry enough and we stacked our wood inside and fired it off about two hours before sunset.

The heat drove us back and scorched the low branches of the surrounding cedars. We had a good firebreak and as wet as it was I didn't think it could get away. I hoped it wasn't seen. I'd lit it late in the day so that the flame would not be seen in the late sun, but later as the smoke rose, it would do so at night. We needed to have the fire out by morning.

The wood burned hot and fast and was a heap of embers a couple of hours after sunset. I used a long, green pole to rake the coals evenly around the floor. Now and then a rock would crack from the heat with a sharp groan. The smoke and smell from the clay lessened and the embers collapsed in powdery white puffs.

The others went to sleep in the shelter, but I stayed by the fire and continued to stir and rake the hot ashes. In the gray morning as the clay cooled, cracks ran through it, cut it into an unknown mosaic.

I nearly blistered my feet as I used the shovel to throw the last solid coals into a pile in the center where they could burn out quickly. I hoped there was no rain for a day or two.

By mid morning there was not a trace of smoke. The others came to see our handiwork. The floor still was too hot to walk on for more than a couple of steps. It was blackened and splotched and riddled with cracks.

"Beautiful piece of work," Lila said. "I can't wait to move in."

"You'll see," I said.

I left the house to cool for that day. Aaron wanted to cross over to the cove, see what we could of the Orca. He borrowed Cree's binoculars and we headed out before noon. I knew the way well, followed the path without thinking. Aaron was slow, distracted.

I clicked my tongue at some ravens that challenged our passage. They called and circled and kept up a fine din in our wake. We cut through the woods out of sight of the house to the point of the cove and looked for the boat. It was about where it had been before, quietly at anchor.

Aaron studied it. "Bastards," he said. He looked longer. "See for yourself," he said, handed me the glasses.

Through the windows of the main cabin I could see overturned tables piled upon each other and a jumble of chair legs and other furniture. The deck looked normal, but there was the great scar on the side scraped by the cutter. I couldn't see much more, but doors and hatches were open, sails dragged out of lockers and left on the deck. I handed the binoculars back.

"It's not over yet," he said.

The day grew warm and we took our time walking back. The ravens continued their escort. We found several places we could climb on a rock or a stump and see the water north and east of the island.

Nothing stirred but a few lazy gulls. I told Aaron about the strange place I'd been on my short cut.

"Most of the places I've been you can't get back to," he said.

The floor had mostly cooled by evening. I used the shovel to scoop out all the unburned material. I swept the ashes evenly across it all with a branch end.

"Now what?" Lila asked me.

"Pray for rain," I said.

"You don't have to pray long here," Lila said.

The fine drizzle I'd hoped for came the next morning. It was dark and chilly and no one wanted to go with me to check on the house. I stirred some of the ashes and they still were dry underneath, so I smoothed out some humps and left it.

Back at the shelter, it took me a while to get a fire going. The drizzle drifted in under the cedars. Our dry wood supply was low and we had to carry it further each day. We would need a good store for winter. Maybe Cree could find a woodstove for us.

When Lila and Morganne came out, I told them some of my plans.

"It sounds like you're planning to stay," Lila said. "The only problem is they'll find us and we'll have to leave."

"I still have to live, wherever I am," I said. "I can't just do nothing with winter coming."

"Even if you're going to lose it all?" Lila asked me.

"It wouldn't be the first time," I said.

"How can you just keep on working?" Morganne asked me.

"That's what I do best," I said. "So I do it."

A couple of hours later I checked the floor again. It had become a sticky morass. I hoped that the clay was fired enough. A trickle of ash-laden water came out of the drain trench. I used my cedar broom to brush excess ash towards the opening. At least for now the cracks were filled with my rustic plaster. I had to get a roof on before a hard rain came and washed it all away.

The rain eased in the late afternoon and I took the others to see the result. The ash was sticky, yet, but the floor had the appearance almost of finished concrete. It was much better than anyone expected, even me.

The next day they helped me lay the cedar saplings I'd cut in a tipi style cone. The floor was dry except for a few spots, and our movements soon loosened any of the ash that hadn't gone down into the cracks and we swept it out.

First we tied together two of the saplings' tips with a couple of feet overlap, then lashed on a third across those two and used it to raise the union until it was over the center of our basement. The result was a very steep pitch, more than we needed.

I was going to cut off the butt ends, then decided to dig them in a foot or so instead. The result was so solid that I think we could have made the roof with just that structure. But it was easy to lay more saplings across the angles formed by the first three. We put on a total of ten more. I left them long so that the tips formed a large inverted cone.

Cree brought several large pieces of the sailcloth from her storage in Anacortes, and we ended up with three full layers and part of a fourth. We sewed the loose edges and weighted the bottom all around with rocks.

The result pleased every one. When you walked in, the roof was high above, almost a cathedral effect. Sunlight glowed softly through the layered canvas.

We made a large, heavy flap from more sailcloth and hung it over the opening for a door. Then we built a stone hearth in the center and lit our first fire. There was a strong draft through the smoke hole that drew in fresh air as it carried away the smoke.

"Let's move in," Morganne said.

There wasn't much to move - we carried it all in two trips. Cree promised to bring a stock of food. I asked for more sailcloth to make a wood shelter. Lila wanted a radio. Morganne said she would go for a walk and pick some flowers.

"In October?" Lila asked her.

"Everything else is upside-down," Morganne said.

CHAPTER 45

Cree brought news. She had a Sunday Seattle Times and we took turns reading the story. Gerard had been indicted, was out on bond. The Poet, Suras, Patrick and Fuzzy Crook were on the "probable Grand Jury witnesses, possible indictments later" list. Akbar was sought as a material witness along with several others. The Canadian Government had been contacted to apprehend and extradite Cree although they didn't have her name, just a description. There were Federal Fugitive warrants for Aaron and Lance and Lila.

But the BIG story was Pancho, who they suspected was the real kingpin. His sour, newly-shaven face glared at us from the front page above the fold. He had been arrested with Patrick in Port Townsend, carrying forged Mexican papers.

His real name was Robbie Lerner and he had been on the lam from the Feds for nine years over a bombing at San Diego State. He even had made the ten-most-wanted for a couple of years and they had followed his trail as far as Mexico. He was considered an assistant saint in the New Left hierarchy.

Walt Gann had been liberal with interviews, said he had been that close to breaking the Lerner story when the Feds moved in. He'd had a tip from an old SDS contact, he claimed, and had pretended to work on other stories to get close to the fugitive. He planned a book and had friends in Hollywood who might produce the movie.

Walt's photographer friend had established his career with his shots of that last cruise. We studied the pictures closely. I only appeared in one of them, from the back and in the shadow of the mainmast.

Ex-governor Reagan had called from San Diego to congratulate the Coast Guard. There was a picture of Reagan smiling into the telephone and a transcript of the conversation.

He called for more use of the military in drug interdiction and reminded everyone that the violent politics of the left and drugs went hand in hand and probably this gang supported some rebel group in El Salvador or Guatemala or even in Watts. He said he wouldn't be surprised if this Lerner was a major narco-terrorist.

A small story on page three said theOrca was to be seized and sold at auction. They estimated it was worth at least three million. They would move it to San Francisco in the spring. Meanwhile it would be anchored locally.

"They don't even mention us," Morganne said to me. "I think I'm insulted. Everyone else is in it."

"Aren't we lucky?" Lila said. "They didn't mention Eddie, either. I wonder why?"

"What do you mean?" Morganne asked her.

"Well," Lila said, "they had to know Eddie was involved with the Orca, but there's no report that they even talked to him."

"You mean he's the one who told them?" Morganne said. "Of course!"

"Then the others bail themselves out as cooperative witnesses," Lila said. "I've seen it before. They'll hang crimes on Aaron that we never dreamed of. They can clear the books of a lot of shit this way."

"But if they don't catch him?" Morganne asked, "What's the point?"

"That's better," Lila said, "Then there's no chance the truth will come out. People can imagine anything they want. And fugitive hunts are great press."

"Look at this," I said, showed them a small article in the education section about the grant of over a million dollars a group of local businessmen had given to the soon-to-be-built whale research station on Skagit Bay. There was a rendering of a magnificent scholarly edifice to be called The Orca Center.

Nothing less than interspecies communication was the goal,

as important as contact with extra-terrestrials, the article assured us. The effort was to be headed by internationally acclaimed whale expert, Doctor Edward Randé, who said he expected Operation Crosstalk to mark a major turning point in human history.

"The fact of the matter is," they quoted him, "is this has never been done before. It will undoubtedly help answer the riddle of human origins."

Part of the grant was to be used to refurbish a retired car ferry as a whale-watch platform.

"Accommodations will be available to the general public," Doctor Randé told them, "on a limited basis."

"I told you," Lila said.

"That doesn't prove anything," Morganne said.

"Maybe not to you," Lila said, "but I vote guilty."

"It doesn't matter," Aaron said.

"I smell Lance," Lila said. "He told me about this friend of his who had an old ferry he was trying to peddle as a houseboat."

"It doesn't matter," Aaron said.

We took the newspaper with us to the house. Maria wanted the comic section. Aaron and I passed the news and editorials back and forth but he didn't read much. Morganne wanted style and culture. Lila took the classifieds.

It was increasingly apparent that our current situation was probably temporary. By now, Lance must have told someone where we were, so even if he didn't testify to the Grand Jury, still the information was loose out there somewhere. And if they mounted a serious search, Defoe was just not that big.

With the Canadians looking for Cree and the Wigit, fleeing north was out. We could get to the mainland any time, but with no money, we'd be easy prey.

I began to think about taking us all to Chelan. Lila suggested another raid on the Orca, for the money, but it didn't sound survivable. Besides, they might already have found the safe. Everyone's depression was obvious.

I couldn't stop working on the house even though it seemed that we might have to flee any time. After the hearth had heated for several days and the perimeter stones gradually warmed, it became a very comfortable place. Maria pitched in and helped me a lot. She enjoyed the work, and Do always settled down as if she knew she had to wait until her mother was finished.

Maria loved the routine daily tasks. She kept everything picked up and made sure the floor was swept and sprinkled with water. Cree brought us a cheap set of dishes and silverware, which Maria washed at the spring.

At first, we ate canned stuff and sandwiches, but after Cree brought groceries and a few utensils, I did eggs and pancakes and other camp fare. Cree also had fish for us whenever we wanted any. There were lots of clams and mussels and with a little effort, crabs. We kept a large pot of water hot most of the time to cook the seafood.

The potatoes Cree planted the winter before had spread and we easily dug up handfuls of the knobby, branched fingerlings. They were great boiled or roasted on the coals. Cree said there was another good crop at the old campsite where she'd gotten her starts if we needed it. I spent some time planting cull potatoes in wet spots close to the house.

Aaron and I crossed the island twice to look at the Orca. We picked times when Cree was away, then had Maria, Lila and Morganne stay close to the house in case we stirred up anything.

On the second trip we saw that the Orca had been moved into the cove and anchored just a hundred feet off the dock in water Aaron had considered too shallow in case of an extreme tide or a heavy storm. The anchor chain struck the water at a steep angle, kept short so she didn't swing into the shallows.

We found a good spot where we could get a look. The mess had been straightened around and the sails stowed. There didn't seem to be a lot of outright damage, which made sense if they wanted to sell her. All the working gear we could see was in decent order.

The house was quiet both times. There was a speedboat at the dock, so Eddie and Suzette may have been there, but we saw or heard no one. I suggested to Aaron that we go in and use the phone, make some calls and see where it was all at, but he didn't want to do it.

Cree brought Lila the radio she wanted, a little AM/FM portable. She also brought a dozen extra batteries. Lila kept it on all the time, even at night as we slept. It wasn't loud enough to be annoying, just a distant murmur to remind us that they still were out there. Lila seemed to take comfort in that.

I talked her into listening to the Reggae show every night for an hour on a jazz station. She didn't like it, but humored me. It sounded good to me. The preaching didn't annoy me as it had for a while. Live clean, let your works be seen, seemed like sound advice again. Whenever I was on the Wigit, I got Cree to play her tapes.

Cree brought more blankets and tarps and sailcloth and liked to inspect the little improvements I made in the house. She particularly liked my gutter system which was a shallow ditch lined with sailcloth around the roof perimeter which drained on each side of the door opening into buckets so that most of the time we had fresh water just outside the door.

She found a nylon cargo parachute in an Army surplus store in Bellingham. It was just larger around than the house and even had a hole in the middle. Best of all it was dyed in a green camouflage pattern. It stopped the few remaining leaks.

October wore on and I completed more projects. Lila's favorite was the latrine, two small logs laid across two stumps to make a seat over a pit I dug. I put it in the middle of a blackberry thicket for privacy with a sailcloth awning over it.

The sweat was in almost daily use. Cree insisted that the most efficacious process was to alternate blistering sessions under the tarp with total immersions in the icy sea.

At first she had to make us do it. Before long we all competed to see who could spend the longest time under the surface. The trick was to get as hot as possible. The hotter you were, the longer before you even felt the cold. And it seemed like I could hold my breath forever.

Out of the water, the brisk autumn breeze was a warm caress; muscles, taut as springs, felt twice their normal strength. Lungs stripped oxygen from the air and flooded body and brain with it. If you wanted you could walk across the water or fly off a cliff.

Morganne ate constantly. She began to gain weight and her face grew more round and happy.

Lila lost weight. She wouldn't admit it at first.

"You really look good," Morganne said to her after one trip to the sweat. "But if your butt gets any smaller your pants will fall off."

"I'll hand them down to you," Lila said. "Along with my bras. You've grown teats and mine are melting away." She pulled her sweatshirt tight and stood sideways to show us."

Maria didn't talk much more than she ever had, but she smiled a lot and sang to the baby. She made dry arrangements and wall hangings from driftwood and weeds and feathers and shells.

One day I found two glass Japanese fishing floats washed up on the beach and gave them to her. She made a hanger from some old net of Cree's and asked me to suspend them over the fire, one above the other. At night, the effect was remarkable as the flames were reflected and refracted by the slowly turning balls.

Cree brought Maria several dozen diapers and an old canning kettle to boil them in. I ran a length of line across the house that could be hung with laundry then pulled up above our heads to dry. Most things dried in a couple of hours that way.

Do seemed to thrive. We all spent time with her. I couldn't remember acting as silly as I sometimes did with her. She brought out something in the others too, even Aaron, who would carry her around for hours or let her hold his finger while she tried to walk.

We tore down the shelter by the sweat where Cree had treated us and rebuilt it next to the house as a storage shed for the stuff we began to accumulate. Cree brought lots of warm clothes from the thrift stores and good boots for everyone.

I wasn't sure I wanted to use mine, set them aside in case it got really cold.

Cree brought salmon and cod and showed me how to make a quick smoker with more sailcloth. We set it up in a clump of Madronas near the edge of the cliff upshore from the sweat and only a hundred yards from our house. Wisps of sweet smoke from the green alder wood dispersed among the mists of the high tree canopy.

A flock of ravens hung around the camp, watched for scraps and screamed their displeasure at any alterations we made to their environment. They bothered Lila some; I think she took it personally. The rest of us enjoyed them and encouraged their rowdiness, threw them tidbits to fight over.

Cree brought the newspaper a couple of times a week, but there wasn't a whole lot more about Aaron and the Orca. We did find fragments here and there: Gerard awaited trial, had hired an expensive lawyer; Akbar was long gone; the Canadians had found no trace of Cree although there was an unconfirmed report that the Wigit had been sighted in Dutch Harbor, Alaska. The Poet, Suras and Fuzzy Crook were to be charged with a minor trafficking count in return for their cooperation. Patrick had been indicted for giving aid and comfort to a known federal fugitive and was being sought.

But in general, the news had moved on. Panama had taken over the canal under Carter's treaty. Reagan and the conservatives were bitching and moaning about that and about the discount rate going up to 12%. They also reminded everyone that the Soviets had just set a record of 175 days in space while America sat on its hands. A State Department report said there were at least three thousand Soviet combat troops in Cuba. None of it had much effect on our daily routines.

CHAPTER 46

"I can't believe it's almost Halloween," Lila said. "It's so warm."

"We should dress up and trick-or-treat the house." Morganne giggled.

"They won't be there on Halloween," Lila said. "Too many parties."

"We should go soap the windows and string it with toilet paper," Morganne said.

Very funny," Lila said.

"What are we going to do?" Morganne asked. "I love it here, but if we just stay, they'll find us. Aaron must have a plan."

"I'm not sure he does," Lila said, "this time."

"Aaron isn't responsible for all of us," I said.

"He always takes care of us," Morganne said.

"He has a family now," Lila said.

"We're family too," Morganne said. "He won't let us down."

"There isn't always an answer," Lila said. "It's not Aaron's fault."

"He's our leader," Morganne said. "Why can't he be Moses or Jesus or someone?"

"Why don't we decide what to do?" I asked them. "Give Aaron a break. He needs friends, not followers."

"Everyone is someone's follower," Morganne said.

"What's your suggestion?" Lila asked me.

"Working in the orchards," I said. "Until the heat blows off."

"What kind of work?" Lila asked.

"Pruning," I said, "in the winter. And thinning, picking."

"Like migrants?" Lila asked. "I don't think so."

"The work isn't bad," I said, "and no one messes with you. If you don't like the boss, get your check on Saturday and go somewhere else next week. We could work together; Maria could bring Do. That many of us could make good money."

"Good by migrant standards, maybe," Lila said. "I don't see too many of them traveling in Mercedes."

"It wouldn't be forever," Morganne said. "We could try it."

"I don't want to wind up in jail in some podunk town," Lila said. "And get my face sunburnt and be all stooped over, like some old farm woman."

"It isn't like that," I said. "We could rent some farm ground and grow a bunch of produce for ourselves and sell the extra. No one checks on that kind of stuff. In a year or two, they'll forget about us."

"You're clear, anyway," Lila said. "Why don't you just go. Take Morganne. No one is looking for you."

"I can't leave," I said, "until I know how this comes out."

"I'd leave - if I could," Lila said.

"I don't think you would," Morganne said.

When the two of us were alone, Morganne said, "She'll come around. If we all do it. And I think by now Aaron would like the idea."

"Maria would fit in," I said, "make us seem more normal."

"What a funny idea," she said.

I began to think about it a lot. In the orchards, there were plenty of young to middle-aged white men with haunted looks whose past no one asked about. And white women of the sixties who just couldn't settle down. As for Maria and me, no one would even see us. If anything bothered us, we could all be in Yakima or Fresno overnight.

I decided to call and see how things were with Granny. I didn't want the others to know. I spent a couple of days watching the house. There was some traffic in and out in the daytime, but at night it appeared that only Eddie and Suzette remained. I knew they were sound sleepers.

I saw the guard change on the Orca one morning. There were two fresh marshals to replace the two on board. They came in the sheriff's launch as before, but none of the four was Lila's fat friend.

I also noticed that two of Eddie's long-awaited Zodiacs were dragged up on the beach near the dock. They were supposed to be fast and stable in any weather. Greenpeace used them to run down whalers. So if we needed to make a run for it, this might be the way.

I remembered what Lila had said about the probability of Eddie and Suzette going somewhere on Halloween. That morning I took the new notebook Cree had brought me and went into the woods to scribble in it as I often did. Sometimes I designed new projects for the house... the homestead, as I started calling it. Other times, I just wrote whatever came into my head.

This time, I wasn't interested in writing at all. I walked to a vantage point I'd found a good half-mile from the house but with a good view of the front, the grounds and the cove. I sat and doodled, listened to the ravens tell everyone in hearing exactly where I was. I knew Eddie didn't listen to ravens.

Before noon, I heard the airplane. It was Lee. He landed and taxied to the dock. A few minutes later, Eddie and Suzette appeared with a bunch of luggage that Lee helped them with. Suzette had to run back into the house for some last-minute thing. I watched her try the lock on the front door as she left.

Lee had to change his normal take-off run to avoid the Orca in her new position. One of the guards came out on deck and watched the plane disappear. When it was out of sight, he yawned and pissed over the rail. Gulls dived at the stream, scolded him. I didn't see any means they had to make a quick trip to shore if they saw me. They didn't seem like swimmers.

When the guard had been inside for several minutes and there was no human sound, I quietly approached the house from the back. Despite Suzette's concern for the front door, nothing in the back was locked. I went in through the kitchen and quickly checked the downstairs, found no one.

I used the phone in the hallway. I took a minute to remember the number, dialed the first time without the area code and got some chiropractor's receptionist in Seattle who asked me where I hurt.

"Pretty much all over," I said and hung up on her.

I dialed again and on the fourth ring, Granny answered. When I heard her clear, steady voice I froze.

"Hello," she said, then again, "Hello, is anyone there."

I pushed the button down, raised it, and the dial tone echoed in the hallway. I hung up.

I decided to look around a little. Downstairs was pretty much as we'd left it. The second floor had been turned into offices and a conference room with a long gray table. There were three computer terminals with dark screens in one room marked "PREDATOR" on a placard thumbtacked to the doorjamb. Other placards said, "WHALE WATCH," and "OPERATION CROSSTALK" and "DR. RANDÉ." Papers were strewn about and stacks of books slumped in corners.

I thought about leaving a message on one of the computers, but didn't. I was about to head up to the third floor when I heard footsteps. I flattened against the wall and waited. A door opened and someone started down the stairs. I ducked into Eddie's office and closed the door.

Whoever it was opened several other doors. Footsteps continued. There was no place to hide and the window was too high to jump unless it was life or death, so I waited.

After a little more searching, I heard the Poet's voice.

"Come on, who is it? I know someone is here. I'll find you."

He opened another door, closed it. The door where I was started to open. I pulled it, dragged him into the room.

"Hi," I said. "I'm looking for Eddie. I have a message for him."

The Poet was pale and speechless for a moment, then asked, "How did you get here?"

"I have a boat down the beach," I said, waved vaguely to the south.

"Why do you want Eddie?" he asked, ran his hand through his new-cropped hair.

"Why are you here?" I asked him.

"I'm out on bail," he said, "in Eddie's custody. I have to call in every day. Why are you here?"

"Just came to say hello," I said. "I'm not in trouble for anything."

"We wondered about that," he said. "Maybe you're an agent. Sent to find Pancho. Makes sense they would send someone who looks like a Mexican."

"Why is that?" I asked him."

"I don't know," he said. "That's what Eddie said. Lance said he knew how to take care of you."

"Tell Eddie," I said, "that the bureau is getting tired of his interference."

"Is that why you came here?" the Poet asked me. He looked at me closely. "Maybe you came to kill someone, keep them quiet? Everyone knows you carry a gun."

"Well, you know it isn't you I'm after," I said, "or you'd be dead."

He laughed, waited for me to join him. I didn't.

"They told us that if Aaron or any of his people threatened us to just let them know and they would take care of it." He nodded his head in self-affirmation.

"Who's they?" I asked him.

"The Assistant US Attorney," he said, with a touch of pride. "They'll find Aaron. They promised that. I'll bet you know where he is. There's a reward. Unofficially."

"I thought they had him," I said. "I haven't seen him since that last cruise."

"Cree helped him get away. They figured that out easy," he said.

"I heard he drowned up by San Juan Island," I said.

"You know he didn't," the Poet said. "We saw Lance in Mount Vernon. When Eddie brought me here. Lance wouldn't tell us much, but he obviously didn't drown. He said Aaron went to Canada, but that's a lie."

"I'm sure you know," I said, "but I've got to go. Catch you later."

"I'll tell the cops about you," he said. "We were all in this together. It isn't fair that some of us got caught and some didn't."

"Just lucky," I said, pushed past him and down the stairs. I could feel him stare at me as I went out the back.

I headed southwest along the beach, in plain sight, so he wouldn't have to wonder. Once I was hidden by the curve of the shoreline, I walked in the low breakers for a stretch in case he followed. I climbed out and circled inland before I headed north to the trail home. The ravens chattered along as usual, but I hardly noticed them.

The weather was erratic. A line of squalls passed over and onto the mainland. Between storms, it was sunny and still for a while, then another dark wave swept in from the west, broke into ragged cumulus clouds as it hit the shore. A brief shower pounded the islands and gathered into steady rain along the base of the Cascades.

I was on the high ridge just about to the main path when I realized someone had followed me. The ravens grew still, then flapped raucously away to circle something a hundred yards or so back the way I'd come. I found a side path, stepped behind some tall salal and waited.

The Poet stumbled along the path, followed clues only he could read. I couldn't believe he could follow me even this far. He stopped on the path where I'd left it and looked around as though he sensed something. He took a couple of steps onto the side path and somehow saw me. He ran towards me and I moved away through the brush, quickly left him behind.

"I'll follow you wherever you go," he shouted after me.

I didn't want to take our usual route in case he did manage to get my trail again. The going was much slower off the path, but there was lots of hard surface and deep brush where I could hide my tracks. Still in half an hour, I heard him crashing along behind me.

I decided the most important thing I could do was to warn the others, so I went down the slope quickly, headed for the short cut to make the best time. I went through the worst obstacles I could find, berry patches and skunk cabbage ponds, but still I heard an occasional curse or splash behind me.

I moved quickly and quietly, set my mind to out-distance him. The next time I stopped, I couldn't hear him at all. I had been moving according to my sense of direction without much thought to my route, so I tried to get a mental fix on our homestead and headed straight that direction.

I knew that from where I was I would need to climb the shoulder of the large slope and head directly across it to get home. But whenever I turned upslope at all, I obviously headed back the way I came. It only happened twice before I knew what it was. I started down.

I was noisy and made sure I could be seen in the clearings. As the stream began to drop more steeply, I almost ran. A raven started up ahead of me, squawked and landed on a branch. It watched me for a minute then flew away up the slope. A few minutes later it squawked again and circled. I stood on one of the boulders and looked back, could not see him, so I waited.

In a few minutes I heard him, far back up the slope, then saw his red hair bob along behind a screen of brush. The raven circled over me.

I waved my arms to get his attention, and when I was sure he watched, I jumped from the boulder and moved on downstream. The raven followed, kept up its indignant narration. I broke brush and low branches as I went, scuffed the earth in bare spots.

The little stream surprised me even though I had expected it. It didn't seem to be exactly where it had been before, but it made the long curve to the east that I remembered. At the point where the path joined the stream, I planted each step firmly in the mud to show the way.

I skimmed along the edge of the stream that reminded me of a loggers' sluice in its directed, downward rush. The valley narrowed and the last two boulders nearly squeezed off the stream. I stood again, on one of them, and waited for him to see. I climbed down and squatted at the pool to drink, left some clear tracks for him then plunged downward.

As the slope lessened, I began to watch closely for the little bluff on the left-hand side and the clear spring at its base. It was further than I remembered, but looked exactly the same.

I knelt to drink again, more from ritual than thirst, then looked for the path that switched back to the lookout point. It too seemed a little further than before.

There were no visible tracks and I would bet no human foot had touched it since mine last had. The intersecting path was there as I remembered and so were my boots. The dense brush had protected them from the rain, and other than a little dust, they looked as good as the day I set them there. I carried them with me to the lookout point. The raven landed on a crooked branch stump a few feet away, looked back and forth from me to the path below.

As I sat and waited for him, I tried the boots. My feet really didn't want to squeeze into them, but I worked at it for a while and got them both on.

A few minutes later I saw him. I thought he would stumble on past the spring, but the raven flapped and called and got his attention. I didn't let him see me, but stared at him from behind a low-hung cedar branch. I didn't know if he would be able to feel my look, but I did my best.

Something seemed to bother him. He looked around, picked up a rock and tossed it at the raven that flew screaming at his head. He ducked, held his arms up for protection. It flapped on and lectured from a safe perch. He stared in my direction, then continued along the path.

I wasn't sure at first if he'd taken the bait, but soon I heard him snuffling along the side path behind me. I froze, looked steadily at the spring below. I could feel him see me. He got very quiet, then I sensed him crouch forward towards me.

I ignored him until the last instant, then leapt forward, dropped about ten feet, rolled into heavy brush at the foot of the bluff. The raven flapped away into the treetops.

"They'll get you, you bastard," the Poet shouted. "You can't get away now. They'll bring dogs."

I stayed out of his sight, went back the way we'd come as quickly as I could with no noise. I didn't hear him again.

It took about half an hour to get back to the path I hadn't taken that first time, the path which appeared to climb the high ridge towards home. It was a broad path on a steady incline and I was back at the new house in less than an hour.

My feet hurt some from the boots, but it was comforting to touch something from that long ago, on the other side of some great divide in my life.

CHAPTER 47

"Aaron, Aaron," the Poet called from the beach. "Aaron, we know you're here."

I could see the three of them from my hiding place just above the sweat. I faded back into the trees. Everything was ready for them. I was sure they could follow the trail I'd spent a couple of hours stamping out for them.

Lance led them directly to the sweat and they poked around there for a while, then Patrick pointed to the path worn by my boot heels. I slipped along ahead of them, just out of sight. I noticed that Lance had a chrome automatic in a clip holster on his belt.

I stood behind a large cedar trunk and watched them approach the house. Lance poked at the flap, stood back, called, "Aaron," then opened it and looked inside.

The other two watched while he went in. A minute later they ducked inside and the flap dropped. I crossed to the door, closed my eyes to let my pupils dilate so I wouldn't be blinded by the dark. I slid through the flap and stood inside.

They were busy going through things, didn't notice me until from just behind Lance I said, "Put the gun on the floor, Lance." He slipped it out, hesitated. "Now," I growled in my strongest voice. He stooped, laid it on the floor.

I picked it up quickly, slipped it in my waistband.

Lance looked around at me. "You bastard," he said.

"Guns make me nervous," I said. "What can I do for you gentlemen?"

The Poet glared at me. "We want to see Aaron."

"No can do," I said. "I don't know anyone by that name."

"Did he go with Cree?" he demanded. "We know she went to Alaska."

"Cree who?" I asked him.

Patrick tried. "Hey, man," he said soothingly, "we just want to see Aaron, get his advice."

"Right," I said. "What kind of advice?"

"We're in real trouble," the Poet said. "We need Aaron's help. We're all in this together."

"I don't know," I said, "I keep my nose clean."

They all glared at me.

"We want to make peace," Lance said. "We realize Aaron's been right all along."

"Right about what?" I asked.

"What we should have done," Lance said. "If we'd listened to him, we'd be better off."

"Great," I said. "If I ever see him again, I'll make your excuses for you."

"If we all stick together," Patrick said, "we can still get out of this. I've seen worse. Everyone has to tell the same story."

"That will be quite a strain," I said. "Besides, I'm not in any trouble."

"Trespassing," the Poet said. "Tim will have you thrown off the island."

"It's my land," I said. "I homesteaded it. Isn't that how White people get land? No one was using it."

"We don't want a hassle," Patrick said. "We just want to talk to Aaron. To work together."

"So what brought on this spirit of cooperation?" I asked him.

"They're trying to hang us," the Poet said. "They revoked my bail, and Suras'."

"And me," Patrick said. "They told me that someone is going to take the fall. If they can't find Aaron, then someone else is it."

"So you came to find Aaron for them," I said, "maybe pick up a little reward money."

"No way," Lance said. "We're all on the same side."

"Which side is that?" I asked him.

"There's a Federal warrant for me," Lance said. "I'm in the same boat as Aaron."

"We have a plan," the Poet said.

I waited. Neither of the others wanted to talk.

"To take the Orca," the Poet said.

"What do you mean, 'take it?'" I asked.

"Commandeer it," he said. "Or whatever you call it."

"And?" I prompted him.

"And get out of here," Patrick said. "Go to Belize or Costa Rica."

"You have some sort of Star Trek cloaking device?" I asked him.

"We'll lay up somewhere for a while," Patrick said. "Repaint her and change to a Marconi rig. Go south as the White Dove or something. Aaron can get papers."

"It might work," I said, "except for the marshals. Guns make me nervous."

"We'll get the drop on them," Lance said, glanced at his gun in my belt.

"I know!" I said. "Then we put them adrift in a small boat once we're safely away."

"Right," Lance said.

"Well, I don't know where Aaron is," I said. "If you find him, I'm up for it."

"You know where he is," the Poet said. "Arrange a meeting."

"Where?" I asked him.

"Here," Patrick said. "We have nowhere else to go."

We hid Lance's boat next to a large rock with driftwood and seaweed for cover. I doubted it would fool anyone in the air. When they thought I wasn't watching, they passed around Patrick's stash bottle.

I heard the Wigit idling offshore an hour after dark. I had a large, dry fire laid at the sweat and I set it off to warn them as we had agreed. The flames lit the undersides of the trees and reflected on the steep, cobbled beach below.

The Poet ran clumsily down the path towards me. "What the hell are you doing?" he shouted at me. "The cops will see it."

I waited until he was close. "Full moon ritual," I said. "My Grandfather taught me. To celebrate."

"I thought bonfires were for the new moon," he said. "Out of fear that the moon would never come back."

"Somebody's been pulling your leg," I said.

I heard Cree engage power and move quietly away. I knocked the fire apart, rolled some of the larger pieces to put them out. Coals sputtered in the mud. A column of steam and sweet smoke rose into the night, reflected the white light of the moon, merged into the Milky Way.

"I didn't tell anyone," the Poet said. "That I saw you the other day. Lance came by the house and told us where Aaron was, then Patrick came. But I didn't tell them."

"When did you see me?" I asked him. "I haven't seen you around here before."

He hesitated. "At the house," he said. "When you came to see Eddie."

"You must have the wrong guy," I said. "I've been right here all the time."

"I followed you," he said. "Into that place...." He stopped, considered whether to go on.

"What place?" I asked him.

"I don't know," he said. "There's a creek, then it gets real dry and dead. I couldn't find my way out for a long time."

"That's what happens when you use drugs," I said.

"I saw your tracks," he said. "Barefoot."

I held out my boot to show him. "I don't run around in the winter barefoot," I said. "Probably a bear track."

"You can't fool me," he said. "I know what I saw. I went back and looked at the tracks." He laughed and wiped sweat from his forehead.

"Does Eddie know you jumped bail?" I asked him.

"Patrick said they were going to revoke it anyway," he said. "He saw the papers." He scuffed the ground. "Hey, man, I can't go to jail again. I've got a little baby."

I just looked at him and started for the house. He followed me.

"What was it?" Patrick asked the Poet when we got there.

"Lucky had a big-ass fire on the beach," he said. "But it's out now."

"What kind of fire?" Lance asked, looked at me.

I shrugged.

"It was a signal," Patrick said. "Aaron is out there somewhere." His eyes accused me. "Probably on Cree's boat."

"Beats me," I said. "How long are you guys planning to stay here? This place is a little small."

"It's pretty slick," the Poet said. "Where did you learn how to do all this?"

"In the other world," I said.

He looked at me, started to say something.

"I don't believe you did this all by yourself," Patrick said.

"The bears help me at night," I said.

"We have to talk to Aaron," Lance said.

"What do you want? Money?" Patrick asked me.

"I could use some," I said, "but I don't sell friends."

"So how are you Aaron's great friend?" the Poet asked. "We've all known him longer than you. You only met him a year ago."

"That you know of," I said. "Anyway, with friends, time doesn't necessarily count."

"Shit," Patrick said, "Aaron and I backpacked a hundred pounds of Oaxacan across the border west of Nogales in sixty-nine. We ran into a patch of peyote and I got so fucked-up I had to find shade and lay up in the desert for three days. I talked to God and everything. Aaron wouldn't leave me and we missed our meet with Lila. But there she was, in that fucking Mustang, when we showed up."

"You could always count on them, back then," Lance said.

"I'm not sure they're the ones who changed," I said.

"Well, Aaron and I go way back, too," Lance said. "Before he got hooked up with Maria, we did runs to Santa Cruz in his BMW. Before he bought in to the Quest. Pete and some friends had this old trimaran that they took all the way to Thailand twice. We would drive down, pick up some Thai stick and some acid, whatever else good was around. Then we would drive it to Seattle.

"One time, on our way back - I was driving - the Highway Patrol stopped us up in the Siskiyous. The airplane had clocked me at ninety-five and they were pissed. The trooper stayed in his car until a second car showed up with two more and I was ready to go to jail.

"We got out and Aaron turned on that voice, when he wants something and no one can resist him. He apologized, told them he'd had a message that his wife in Seattle was about to go into labor. He offered them a phone number to call to verify it, said he'd sign a ticket if they'd just let him get on home to his wife and baby.

"They completely forgot that I was driving. One of them kept looking at the trunk like he had some kind of radar, but the one in charge bought the whole story, didn't even give us a ticket."

"I wish I'd known him then," the Poet said. "I missed all the good times."

"Aaron's treated you pretty well," I said.

"But he won't ever treat me like an equal," the Poet said. "He never treats anyone like an equal."

"Maybe you aren't," I said.

"He runs you around," the Poet said, "makes you do errands and stuff."

"I'm a volunteer," I said.

"We all volunteered," Patrick said. "Aaron didn't make anyone do anything."

"Not like that," the Poet said. "It's just that you can't get away from him."

I looked at him. "You can't get away from him?" I said.

"I mean in my head," he said.

"Maybe you need therapy," I said.

"You sound like Lila," he said, "nothing is serious."

"This is serious?" I said.

"I just need to figure it all out," he said. "To understand it."

"It's simple," I said. "You're in trouble, you want his help."

"He owes us," the Poet said. "We did things for him."

"Aaron does what he does," I said. "If you want to follow him around, that's your choice. I've heard you beg him to let you in on something."

"But once he lets me in," the Poet said, "then we're in it together."

"He didn't marry you," I said.

"That's his main problem - his wife," Lance said. "He spends too much time with her instead of taking care of business."

"It was fine when you were the family," I said.

"We need someone new," the Poet said. "Someone who has time for us."

"Try the want ads," I said. "While you're at it, get a job."

"I'm a poet," he said. "Poet's don't get jobs."

"There must be some bull poet you can follow," I said.

"We can all split up when we get out of this," Patrick said. "For now, we'd better work together."

"If I could find Aaron," I said, "what's the plan?"

"If Cree would help," Lance said, "we could come up on both sides at once, at night."

"Then they would each have their own flock for the turkey shoot," I said.

"How would you do it?" Patrick asked.

"Quietly," I said. "Get their guns before they know you're there."

Lance looked at his gun in my waistband. "When do I get that back?"

"This?" I said. "I found this abandoned on my property."

"Forget it," Patrick said to him. "How do we talk to Aaron?"

"The best I can do is tomorrow night," I said. "I'll take Lance's boat out and talk to them. Alone."

"Then you take off with them," Lance said, "leave us stranded."

"Okay," I said, "What's your plan?"

The water was a little choppy and I wasn't used to Lance's patched-together control system, so I kept it slow. I went out just after dusk, drifted with the lights off and listened mostly, started the engine when I needed to move back upwind.

The Wigit came in as if under a blanket, her engine so muffled in the fog I might have missed the sound. I flashed the running lights three times, then twice, waited, then did it again. Cree flashed the signal once, then cut power.

I started the smooth little Volvo engine and steered towards the after-image of the lights' flash. When I was close, she flashed them again. I made out the silhouette just in time to partly stop my momentum as I bumped against the Wigit. A spotlight blinded me and I covered my eyes so the irises didn't shrink. The light switched off.

"Just making sure," Cree said.

"We have visitors," I said.

"I see that," Cree said. "I'll tell Aaron it's all right."

I kept the power engaged, tried to throttle down to match the drift of the Wigit. Aaron came to the rail.

"Greetings," I said. "We have visitors at the castle. The Poet, the Knave and the Fool."

He grinned. "You seem to have gotten the better of them."

"They want to talk to you," I said. "They have a plan. It's not a trap."

"It can't hurt to talk," he said. "I'll get my coat."

Cree agreed to meet us again in two hours, and I ran Aaron in to the shore, beached the boat without running the prop in the sand.

The three of them met us, came into the water to pull us onto dry land. Everyone looked at everyone for a minute.

"Who else knows where I am?" Aaron asked Lance.

"No one," Lance said. "Just us. And Gerard. He made me tell him."

"I hear you have a plan," Aaron said.

No one admitted it.

"So why are you here?" he asked them. He turned. "I thought you skated," he said to the Poet.

"I didn't tell them anything, boss," the Poet said. "My lawyer said they didn't think I was important. Until now."

"What's now?" Aaron asked him.

"They revoked our bail," the Poet said, "all of us. And Gerard. They said if they couldn't catch you, someone else would have to pay."

"Well," Aaron said. "I'm not going to turn myself in."

"No," Patrick said, "not that. We want to take the Orca."

"Take it?" Aaron said.

"Hijack it," Patrick said.

"And do what?" Aaron asked.

"Lay up somewhere up north," Patrick said. "Repaint and re-rig, make a run south in the spring."

"We could go to Costa Rica," the Poet said, "or Belize. Get away from all this and get a new start. I'll bring Linda and the baby."

"There's a new pro-US government in El Salvador," Lance said.

"We could get away until the heat is off," Patrick said. "They really want to take you down."

"Why would you do it?" Aaron asked.

"We don't have a choice," the Poet said.

"It's our best chance," Patrick said. "If we don't make it, the worst we can do is go to jail anyway."

"With an extra rap," Aaron said.

"We owe you, boss," the Poet said. "We can't just leave you stranded here."

"We're kind of in it together - now," Lance said. "Like the old days."

"We'll need guns," Aaron said. "This will be for real."

"No problem," Lance said.

"I have mine," I said, showed the handle of the automatic.

I ran Aaron back to the Wigit when it was time. He pointed at the automatic. "Where'd you get that?" he asked me.

"Lance brought it for me," I said.

Cree came in just at daylight while the tide was high. Morganne hugged me. Lila obviously was happy to see land, even if she did have to wade to get to it. Aaron carried Do in on his shoulders. Maria smiled at everyone when she got to the beach, then wandered off towards the house.

We barely had gotten there when we heard an airplane come low across the island. The Poet and Lance stumbled out, looked like they would run for it. Before we had a chance to duck, I saw the plane.

"It's Lee," I said.

"What the fuck is he doing here?" Patrick asked.

"I don't know," Aaron said. "But Lee's okay."

The plane made one circle overhead as if searching, then set down offshore and taxied towards the beach. Well out still, he reversed the prop, then turned.

Just as he turned, someone jumped from the right-hand door and splashed into the water. When the plane was clear, he stood, and we could see that it was Gerard. We watched him struggle through the waves, go down once and come up sputtering.

Lila started to giggle.

"It wouldn't be funny if it was you," the Poet said.

"It would be funnier if it was you," Lila retorted.

"I'll go talk to him," I said. "Lay low."

He didn't see me until I was a few feet away. He started, caught himself. "I didn't know you were here," he said.

"Here I am," I said. "What can I do for you?"

"Where's Aaron?" he asked, started to go around me.

I blocked him, he glanced at the gun butt and stopped.

"If you have business here, tell me about it," I said.

"I want to talk to Aaron," he said, "not you."

"Aaron isn't available," I said.

"He'd better be available to me," Gerard said. "We're old friends, he can't bail out on me now."

"He hasn't done any bailing out," I said.

"Maybe not on you," Gerard said, "but a lot of people think he ran out."

"I'll give him the message," I said.

"Hey, man, he owes me. I lost my investment in Primal Power and they have a warrant for me," he said. "Thanks to Aaron."

"I thought we were all in this together," I said.

"I didn't come up here to play head games," he said. "I want to talk to Aaron. We can help each other."

"How is that?" I asked him.

"We have to work together, now," he said, "or we'll all be in jail."

"I'm not in any trouble," I said.

"People are wondering about that," he said.

"What people?" I asked him.

"A lot of people," he said. "Listen, I just want to get us all out of this. Aaron can do it. I've seen him do things you wouldn't believe. Shit, man, years ago when Aaron used to bring weed and acid up from Santa Cruz for the festivals, Pete had a line on the Quest, offered Aaron a partnership. He needed to raise a hundred thousand fast, three weeks or something.

"I had been playing around in the lab, learning to make crank because the acid market was flooded with cheap shit. I knew all these bikers who needed ephedrine and had a hard time getting it.

"Aaron was collecting herbs, selling them to Miller Richards - Oregon grape and Pipsissewa and stuff. They used to do a lot of business with this Mormon company in Utah. Aaron had heard that an herb called Mormon Tea was raw ephedra. He called the company in Utah for a sample of the tea and they airmailed it to him.

"I checked it out and he was right, it had very good ephedrine, a lot. Aaron ordered ten barrels of it through the herb company, had them express it. Altogether, it cost us almost three thousand dollars, which was everything we could raise at the time.

"In about a week, it was delivered. He used the hammermill at the herb company to grind it fine and I set up to extract the ephedrine. He had his hundred thousand early, flew it down to Pete. When we were through, we each made a hundred twenty grand. It's still the slickest deal I ever saw."

"That's great," I said, "but money won't necessarily fix this."

"Money will fix anything," he said. "That's why it's the first thing they take."

"So you think Aaron has money?" I asked him.

"I know he does," he said. "He told me just before that cruise that he had over a hundred grand. And if the cops had found it, they'd be crowing about it. We could all get a long ways on that much."

"I thought you were the one with all the money," I said.

"They confiscated everything," he said. "The store, my bank accounts, my lab."

"You wouldn't have had everything in your name," I said.

He paused and looked at me. I looked back.

"I have a commodities account," he said, "in my Dad's name. But he won't let me have it. Says I'll just blow it."

"So you want a loan?" I asked him.

"Well, yeah, a loan would work. But we need to do this together." He looked in my eyes for the first time. "I need Aaron's help," he said.

"Come up here," I said, led him along the beach to the sweat. "You stay here, I'll go give Aaron a message. If you poke your head above that bank, it's off."

"How long will it take?" he asked me.

"It could take all day," I said.

Lila wanted me to go back and shoot him. Morganne said we should have Lance take him somewhere and drop him in the ocean. Patrick was his only defender.

"He's a smart little weasel," Patrick said. "And the more, the better when we go for the Orca."

Aaron went down to the sweat and talked to him for a while, then they came back to the house. Gerard wanted to grab the Orca now.

"The sooner, the better," he said.

"It won't be dark enough," I said. "It was full moon last night."

"We can't wait two weeks," Gerard said. "They might move the boat. They want to take it to San Francisco."

"Not this time of year," I said. "The worst they could do is move it somewhere on the sound. It might be better if they did move it, make it easier. We just need to watch." Everyone agreed that it made sense to wait. Besides, we needed guns.

Lance wanted me to go with him, but I didn't like being gone at night with so much to watch. I suggested Morganne, because if they got caught she could say she was just a hitchhiker or something. Lance didn't like the idea at first, but I think the more he looked at her new body, the better it sounded.

They left after sunset and moved as quietly as they could. Lance said he had friends in Marysville, some fishermen who kept a good arsenal and did enough business with him to trust him.

They weren't back by daylight, so I was concerned, wished I hadn't sent Morganne. But they showed up a little before noon, came in from the west fast and hit the beach hard. They both scrambled out in the shallows, Lance with three long-barreled guns. Morganne struggled with a heavy duffel bag.

I had been watching from the sweat, ran down the beach to help them.

"They followed us," Morganne said.

"Who?" I asked her, took one end of the duffel bag.

"The sheriff's boat," she said. "That's why we circled around. I was going to shoot them if they came too close."

I looked at her. "You know how to shoot?"

"Sure, I'm a farm girl," she said. "I never shot a person, but I would. To help us."

"We're not going to shoot anybody," I said.

Patrick and the Poet and Aaron helped drag the boat up and this time we hid it a little better. I watched from above the sweat for a couple of hours, but never did see the sheriff's cruiser.

Lance had brought two rifles, an M-14 and an old Winchester 30-30. The other long gun was a twelve-gauge double-barreled shotgun. The duffel bag contained four handguns - two .380 automatics similar to the one I'd taken from Lance, a long-barreled .357 Magnum, and a .38 snub-nose. They had managed to get about twenty boxes of assorted ammunition. I put it all in my little storage shed wrapped in a couple of old sleeping bags we'd discarded.

"Did you hear the news?" Morganne asked me when everything settled down.

"What news?" I asked her. "About the DC-10 crash in Mexico City?"

"That was days ago," she said. "From Iran. A bunch of students or something. They burned the American Embassy and took everyone hostage. Some holy man is running the country now."

"Khomeini," I said.

"How did you know that?" she asked.

"I pay attention," I said.

CHAPTER 48

We spent hours going over the plan. We couldn't have any mistakes. Even in the dark, I didn't think we could depend on getting the Wigit right up to the Orca without being noticed. Aaron and Patrick agreed with me.

We finally decided that the best bet would be to have Cree approach from the sound, lights on, very obvious, with some nonsense story. While the guards dealt with her, Aaron and I, Patrick, Lance and Gerard would come from the cove side in Lance's boat and surprise them.

Then, if all went well, Cree would shadow us north in the Wigit, warn us of pursuit and pick us up in case of trouble.

We considered all jamming into the Wigit, just making a run for it, but nobody really liked that idea. Especially Aaron. I think he was thinking about the money. I gave that some thought myself. We spent some time planning routes for once we were on board and deciding who would carry which gun.

The Poet didn't like any of it. "I don't want to carry that old thirty-eight," he said. "I shot a Magnum before."

"We aren't going to do any shooting," I said. "It's just for show."

Other than meals and meetings, I stayed away from camp. Cree invited me to spend the night out on the Wigit, come back in with her on the morning tide. I used the chance to take a good look at the island. From a little distance, it was hard to believe everything that went on there.

Just before dark, Cree ran the route we would take on our assault. She turned just short of the point and headed out to deeper water for the night.

We drifted and smoked and talked.

"Crazy days," Cree said.

"Do you think we'll make it?" I asked her.

"I don't know," she said.

"You don't have to do it," I said.

"You don't either," she said.

"Yes, I do," I said. "But I'm not sure why."

"They need us," she said.

"They need something," I said.

"It's Maria," she said. "I can't leave her. And the baby."

"I want to take them away from here," I said.

"You should do it," she said.

"She can't leave Aaron," I said. "None of us can."

I thought about Aaron. I'd known him only a year, yet in some ways we seemed like the oldest of friends. We all knew it was dangerous to follow him, but it didn't matter.

It was an old story. Take a tall, brooding man with a faraway look in his eyes. Don't let him talk too much. Put a dark coat and boots on him, hang a sword or gun from his belt, put him on a horse or a ship, and most of us will follow him into the eye of the hurricane or the jaws of hell.

It is no secret that these folks always lead to trouble. If they're lucky they escape, but their trail is littered with the corpses of the people who followed them. Sometimes they go down with the ship and someone escapes to tell the story. In any case, the odds didn't seem that good.

The question became not if I would make that final passage with Aaron, but whether I would survive it.

"I have to get out of here for a while," Morganne said to me as soon as she saw me.

"What's up?" I asked her.

"This place is just too small," she said.

"I didn't know I was building an apartment building," I said. "Or a barracks."

She laughed. "Let's go for a walk," she said. "You know your way around. I'm afraid I'd get lost."

I could hear Maria's guitar from the house as she softly fingerpicked chords and sang to herself. Aaron and Patrick talked in low voices and I could hear the Poet snore. Lance was outside, smoked a cigarette and stared at us.

A fine rain had begun to fall and little beads of it sparkled in Morganne's hair. I wore a knit fisherman's cap and Morganne went inside to borrow a scarf from Lila. The mud built up on our boots as we walked and I considered taking mine off but decided against it.

Morganne had developed a strong stride and we moved quickly. I led her down to the beach below the sweat and we wandered southwards towards the old campsite where Cree had found the potatoes.

With the rough weather of late, the bottom was well stirred, and new bits of flotsam and jetsam littered the shore. There were plastic six-pack holders and pull-tabs from aluminum cans. Offshore I could see an orange flotation cushion bob just beneath the surface and other unidentifiable shapes made shadows in the water.

A half-submerged barrel gonged against the rocky bottom and trailed a rainbow slick.

"Let's get that out of there," I said and Morganne helped me roll and drag the dented drum above the tideline. There was a black trail where we'd moved it. "We didn't gain much," I said, "the rain will just wash it in anyway."

"In the future, they'll call this the Garb-Age," Morganne said. "Everything is so filthy."

"There have been people here for a very long time," I said "and they never messed things up like White people have in only a hundred years."

"You sure don't like White people," she said. "But you aren't that dark, really, just kind of a golden color."

"It's a state of mind," I said, "not the color of your skin."

"Sometimes I'm embarrassed to be White," she said.

"I always am," I said.

"When we leave here," she said, "I want to go some place warm where the people are dark and happy and the beach is clean.

"I don't think there is any such place," I said. "White people are everywhere."

Morganne poked into a shallow pool with a driftwood stick, brought up something jagged and rust colored.

"I wonder what this is," she said. "It looks old."

I flaked away some of the rust, got to a harder surface. It was some sort of steel or iron bar about eight inches long and two wide. There was a projection to the side that had a hole through it.

"Maybe it's the head of an old harpoon from a Nantucket whale ship," I said, "that a whale carried until it died. Or part of a Spanish sword. Cree says the Spanish were all over here long before the history books admit. There were private little renegade ventures out of Peru or Mexico with a ship or two looking for gold and slaves. They would make the natives dig their mines and overhaul their ships. The natives eventually killed most of them."

"Conquistadors," she said, "right here. That isn't what they taught me in school."

"They also don't teach you how many native people there were," I said, "and how long they'd been here. Much longer than Englishmen or Spaniards or whoever had been where they came from. But that doesn't fit with the Virgin Country theory of history. 'Virgin Country' means country they didn't screw yet."

"They always talk like there were only a few wandering tribes who didn't know what to do with the land anyway," Morganne said.

I handed her the chunk of metal. "A souvenir," I said.

"I don't want it," she said, threw it into deeper water. "Let it sleep."

"There were pirates here, too," I said. "Francis Drake came by the mouth of the straits, anchored here for a while hiding from the Dons, and many others followed him. Unofficially."

"There might be hidden treasure here," Morganne said. "Plundered from a Spanish Galleon. The pirates could have buried it and then got killed before they could come back and get it."

"All we need is a map," I said.

"Who came after the pirates?" she asked me.

"The Hudson's Bay Company," I said. "They had a Trading Post over on San Juan Island. They might have traded with Natives right on this beach. Cree showed me where there was an old village above where she ties the Wigit."

"Show me," Morganne said.

I almost couldn't find it myself. With the overcast, there was so little light under the towering cedars that I groped around like a blind man. I finally went back to the beach and looked at the grove from a distance and could see a spot with tops twenty or more feet lower than those surrounding and the trunks not as large. It once had been cleared.

We went back into the tree shadows and I found the little open knoll where Cree had dug potatoes. We scratched around with our hands and came up with a few. Morganne washed hers in the little stream and took a bite of it.

"I love these potatoes, they're so sweet," she said. "Not like our potatoes. I didn't know potatoes could taste so good until we came here." She sat on a large, moldering stump and ate it.

I absently pulled away some of the leaves and other debris around the base of the stump and noticed an odd protuberance. I cleared some more. It was like a large gall, but too smooth. As I exposed more, it was obvious that the shape was carved. I showed Morganne.

"What is it?" she asked excitedly.

"I don't know," I said. "Let's find out."

We cleared all the way around, but the carving was all on one side. We dug deeper there but just under the surface it all had rotted away.

"A totem pole," I said.

"It must have been huge," she said. "This stump has to be

four feet across. I wonder what it meant."

"Someone's history," I said, "or a burial pole. Either way, the owner is long gone."

"I wonder who they were," Morganne said, "and what happened. Maybe the Spanish burned the village because they wouldn't be slaves."

"Or a Haida raid," I said. "They used to swoop down out of the Queen Charlottes like Vikings and take slaves and booty."

"Maybe it was the pirates," Morganne said, "when they buried their treasure. They killed everyone so no one would know where they hid it."

"Or the English Navy," I said, "Or the Russians - they were here too."

"I guess a lot of dreams have come to an end here," she said as she looked through the trees and across the water at the dark line of the islands to the west.

"A lot have begun here too," I said.

"I have this terrible haunted feeling," Morganne said. "I think there was a dream we almost had. All of us, I mean, with Aaron. He took care of us all so long and loved us. He had so much going. We wasted him."

"He's still here," I said.

"I keep feeling that it's too late," she said. "In this world."

I heard a speedboat. The sound grew louder, came from the south.

"I want to see who that is," I said, helped Morganne to her feet. We stayed within the tree line on the rise to the south of the creek and searched for it. Finally I saw it, in close, going very fast.

As it came closer, Morganne said, "That's Patrick's boat. I'd know it anywhere."

"Who the hell is it, then?" I asked her. "Patrick's at the house."

As we continued to watch, the boat headed straight along the shore towards us.

"It's some crew-cut white guy," I said. "I don't know him."

"That's Pancho," she said. "Or whatever his name turned out to be. Remember? From the Times?"

"Oh, yeah," I said. "He looked better as a Mexican."

He seemed to know exactly where he was going. He cut speed and turned in towards us. I let him beach it before we stepped out of the trees. He didn't see us until we were nearly on him.

"What the fuck?" he started. "Oh, it's you two." He noticed my gun. "Uh, I came to see Patrick."

"Why?" I asked him. "I thought you were in jail."

"My old man made bail," he said.

"I thought it was a million dollars," Morganne said.

"Yeah," he said, "The Prodigal Son and all, you know. I guess they want me in the family business. We're fabric importers, if you ever need any."

"I'll remember that," I said. "You just here to tell Patrick the good news? We can give him a message."

"I need to see him," he said. "And tell him they dropped charges against him."

"How about the others?" I asked.

"You mean the Poet and Lance?"

"And Lila," I said. "And Aaron."

"No," he said. "Just Patrick. I think his family's lawyer knew someone."

"You stay here," I said. "We'll go get him."

When we were out of earshot, I said to Morganne, "I don't want any of the others to know until Patrick's gone. Except Aaron."

"You think Patrick will leave now?" she asked me.

"Of course," I said. "He has no reason to stay."

"He and Aaron are old friends," she said. "He'll at least stay and help get the Orca back."

"I'm not counting on it," I said.

I motioned Aaron outside and told him the situation. He went back in and called Patrick out.

I told him.

He broke into a broad smile. "I knew they'd come through," he said.

Aaron went with him to the boat. Morganne and I acted like

there was nothing unusual. A little while later I heard the speedboat start, then disappear to the south.

"Where's Patrick?" the Poet asked as soon as Aaron came back without him.

"Gone," Aaron said.

As far as our raid went, Patrick's loss didn't require much of a change in plans. The real problem would come when we sailed. We'd need every hand we could get then, and he was our most experienced sailor.

The Poet freaked out for a while, but finally was reassured.

"I never trusted the rich bastard anyway," he said.

We considered the possibility that they would turn in Aaron for the reward, but the consensus was that they probably wouldn't. "They don't need the money," I said.

The next morning it continued to rain. A few leaks had worked their way through my many-layered roof and everything in the house was damp. Water slopped over the tops of the buckets under the ends of my roof-drain.

Intermittent downpours trapped the smoke inside and threatened to put out the fire. If we had been going to stay I could have fixed it, but it didn't seem worth my time. I had rigged a small shelter inside so that Maria and Do stayed dry. I figured the rest of us would survive.

About noon, I stoked the fire at the sweat, heated rocks for my afternoon ritual. Gerard came up the path towards me, tried a smile.

"You're from Eastern Washington, right?" he asked me.

"Some God-forsaken place," I said.

He shielded his face from the rain with his hand. "They said you lived up in the mountains," he said.

"I've been to the mountain," I said.

"Where would you go," he asked me, "if they had a warrant for you and you had some money and wanted to disappear?"

I looked at him. "You're running out too?" I asked.

"No," he said. "Not now. I mean after we're out of here. Where would you go?"

"You mean all of us?" I asked him.

"Uh, not really," he said. "I mean like if just one person wanted to hide out for a few years."

I considered the question. I was not going to tell him about Stehekin. I looked at his soaked polyester slacks and knit shirt with some fuzzy little animal where it should have a pocket, his muddy, low-cut loafers, his distorted eyes through thick glasses, and I nearly laughed out loud at the thought of him in some remote cowboy town. That gave me an idea. I tried to think where he would be most out of place, somewhere someone would kick his ass the first time he showed his arrogance. I had the perfect spot.

"Chesaw," I said. "It's in Okanogan County. Nice peaceful little cow town forty miles from nowhere."

"Chesaw," he said. "That's a weird name."

"Only place in the state named after a Chinese cowboy," I said.

He didn't seem to know whether to believe me or not. The Poet came down the path and Gerard didn't have a chance to question me further.

Morganne went in the sweat with me. When we came out we played naked in the freezing rain and sea until we both shivered uncontrollably. We put her sleeping bag inside of mine and both of us squeezed in until we warmed up. Lila teased us and the Poet glared.

By sunset, the rain abated and we built up a large fire to dry everything out. Cree came in with the evening tide and brought us fresh bread and a bottle of red wine. Nobody seemed to mind that the wine was wrong for our clams and roasted potatoes.

The rain resumed in earnest the next morning. The steady drumming of it on the sailcloth began to irritate me. I went outside barefoot and headed for the sweat. There were no major leaks in the little shelter, so I tied the flaps open and sat inside, looked out across the sea into the many shades of gray. Only the slight shift from blue-gray to gray-green distinguished between sky and water.

Under the water, of course, it was just another day. No change in temperature - a little less light, but that mattered only to creatures who had to try to swim with their eyes. The Orcas and the others would just go on about their business.

Eddie had told us that many biologists believed that heat drove the whales to water. Some combination of crustal shifts and carbon dioxide cycles had created a greenhouse effect that lasted millions of years. The ancestors of whales had moved gradually into the water to escape the heat. Over the millennia, limbs became flukes, breathing patterns changed. But buried deep inside those streamlined water-bodies lurked a land animal not that different from ourselves.

It was a great strategy until man came along. For all those millions of years they had suffered no challenge upon the seas but each other. And now, in no time, they might all be gone. Maybe it already was too late for them, and what swam around us were their departing spirits. And who knows what element they now adapted to.

My Grandfather taught me that the Earth was a great shapeshifter, an endless transformation afloat in time, a flower in the dry barrens. The ground beneath our feet can move ten feet in one shrug of the continent. So much for surveys and maps. Time ripples across the planet like wind over a dune, makes little changes this way and that.

Change is a problem only for individuals. And aren't we glad that all our ancestors had to suffer considerable change in their times. If they hadn't, we'd still be scurrying around dung heaps.

Even our language drifts and shifts and swirls into new dialects. In funny little backwaters, in the mountains and on the islands, thrive languages declared dead centuries ago. Linguistic doldrum centuries are lashed by storms of slang-driven revolution and artistic efflorescence.

And through it all, we move as though we dream with eyes wide open. And in our blindness, reality becomes, to us, the dream. Only in the extremes of death, accident, childbirth, love and fear does the world break through, though later we deny it and describe it, in retrospect, as dreamlike.

Our drama here, our little band of dreamers, like all the old forgotten tribes, would leave no mark, no moldering monument to another dream that died here on this sad western strand. And when we took our curtain call, the somber sea alone would slap it's grand applause against the shore.

In an hour or so, the rain eased and I decided to walk. It was too wet in the woods even for me, so I stuck to the beach, let the foaming waves wash my feet. I wondered if we too could adapt to that watery life. Clearly we had to go somewhere or die. If we started the children young and the grandchildren younger.... But I knew I belonged to the mountains. I ached for the sound of the wind through pines and the feel of fresh water flowing across my feet.

I heard someone call to me through the fog. It took a minute for me to recognize the Poet's voice. He came through the mist like some lost Caliban wailing my name. I didn't answer, but he saw me anyway and ran to catch up.

"I've been looking everywhere for you," he said. "No one knew where you were."

"No one ever knows where I am," I said.

He looked at me for a while. "I'll never understand you," he said.

I didn't argue. I was used to being ambivalent about people, but my dislike for the Poet had grown constantly over the months. There was something misshapen about the way he looked, the small, round Dutch face surrounded by thick red hair, the pale, undistinguished Irish eyes and obsequious grin, the lumbering gait. All of it seemed to reflect his insides, anxious and confused.

The story I had heard was that he was the illegitimate son of a Lynden farm girl who had run away with and been deserted by an Irish truck driver. To her Dutch Reformed parents, she may as well have made love to a wild man from Borneo as a Catholic from Ireland. They put her out in her fifth month when she began to show, and she had struggled on as a waitress and maid. It didn't seem that exceptional a story to me.

I often wondered why we tolerated him. True enough, he was determined to follow us around, but if we really had wanted to, I believe we could have gotten rid of him. But there was something there we all identified with in spite of ourselves. His permanent tenderness and desperate need to belong reached all of us, like something we hid deep inside but rejected only at peril to the whole.

Still, I didn't have to like him. "Did you want something?" I asked him as I walked.

"You have to help me," he said. "I've got to get out of here. Linda needs me, and the baby. And I have to correct the proofs of my book of poetry. It's called The Flamingo Dance," he said proudly.

I thought of film I'd seen of flamingo courtship, the tiny, reptilian head and neck writhing like a rose-colored snake while the gaudy body was thrown about in various awkward positions which the male bird believed were beautiful and seductive. And sure enough, there were female flamingoes with equally tiny brains to appreciate them.

"You have to help me," he repeated.

"How can I help you? I don't seem to be able to help myself," I said.

"You could leave if you wanted to," he said. "I think you're here because you like Maria. You think Aaron will blow it."

"Wrong," I said. "I'm here because I'm here."

"Well, I wish I wasn't," he said. "Lance talked me into it."

"I don't let people talk me into things," I said. "It makes life simpler."

"I have to correct my galleys," he said. "It's my first book. Being a poet is important."

"Don't care for it myself," I said.

"I don't think you care for anything," he said. "My problem is I care too much."

"Who told you that?" I asked him.

"I do," he insisted. "I care about everyone. That's how poets are. I'd like to stick my dick out the window and fuck the whole world."

"So that's what poets are into," I said.

"Poets have a lot of pain," he said. "I studied with Logan Johnson, the greatest love poet of our generation."

"I remember," I said. "But the greatest love poet of my generation is Bob Marley."

"I don't like that Black music," he said. "Too primitive."

"I've noticed you don't seem to like Black people much," I said.

"I can't help it," he said.

"Why?" I asked.

"I can't tell you," he said.

"Good," I said, "because I'm sure I don't want to know."

"I will tell you," he said. "I'm strong enough now."

He stopped and I kept walking. He ran to catch up.

"When I was a little kid," he said, "about three or four, I caught my mother in bed with a n-... with a black man. I watched them fuck for a while, then he saw me.

"He yelled at me, 'get out of here you ugly little honky bastard.'

"I started crying and he started laughing, then my mother laughed, too. I ran out in the street and she put her clothes on and came after me. Spanked me right in front of him and sent me to my room. Then I could hear them doing it again and laughing."

His voice was halting as he finished and I expected tears, but he got hold of himself.

"So now you don't like Black people." I said.

"I can't help it," he said. "It was very traumatic."

"We all have our burdens to bear," I said.

"Well," he asked me, "are you going to help me?"

"No," I said, "but I am going to tell Aaron."

"I'll pay you," he said. "Linda has money."

"Not that much," I said. I turned to walk the other direction and he didn't follow me, was soon lost in the mist.

I hated to bring the news to Aaron. A couple more defections and our enterprise would become difficult in the extreme.

But the trend was clear. The fortunate of our generation had gotten tired of being freaks, of boldly going where none had gone before, and had rediscovered that middle-class obligation to take the bribe when it came.

They crowded into the sell-out line, like so many sheep on the killing floor. Whether by inheritance or marriage, tenure or treachery, they all intended to get theirs. Just in case things got tight. Besides, they were bored. And it didn't make sense to be the last on the market. The good jobs would be gone.

I walked slowly up the path towards the house, let the mud ooze between my toes. The Poet had gotten there ahead of me and there were several loud voices. I burst in, asked Morganne what was going on.

"Gerard's gone," she said.

CHAPTER 49

I couldn't get a fire at the sweat that afternoon. Everything was drenched. Even the deeply buried coals were drowned. The floor inside was mud from water that seeped through the soil. I watched for Cree, felt the fog flow in from the sound with the tide.

I heard a motor start somewhere up the beach. It coughed and caught and revved just as always when Lance started his boat. I heard his voice, then the Poet's. Lance had warmed up the boat at least once a day, so I gave it little thought until I heard it pull away.

Maybe he would take advantage of the fog to give it a little work. But the sound faded to the northwest and I heard him come up to full speed when well out. I decided not to tell Aaron until I was sure they were gone for good.

I heard the Wigit long before I could see it. I caught the line from Cree and tied it.

"We have to move Maria and the baby," I said to her. "It's too wet."

"They can stay on the Wigit with me," she said.

Maria didn't like the idea, but everyone told her it was best.

"We'll see you every day," Morganne said. "And it won't be for long.

"Come with me Aaron," Maria pleaded.

He looked at her for a long time, held her and the baby.

"I can't," he said.

"I know," she said. "I guess I have to go."

"Not yet," Cree said. "I want to hang around for a couple of hours."

Maria smiled at her. "I'll be ready," she said.

She and Aaron and the baby huddled together until it was time to leave. I didn't hear either of them say a word until Aaron and I carried their stuff to the boat.

They held each other on the bank. Do began to cry and Aaron looked away.

Maria pulled his face back so he looked at her. "Good-bye my sweet dream," she said.

Cree finally said, "Come, Erzulie," and took Maria's arm.

Maria followed her as though entranced.

It was dark when they went out. I wondered, as the Wigit slid into the murk, if I ever would see Maria and the baby again.

I think Aaron wondered that too. From that point on, he didn't seem to care. There was something unnaturally smooth about the things he did, as if it all had been rehearsed long ago and now he carelessly walked through the motions.

Morning was a little less gray. Only a fine mist fell and we hardly noticed that anymore. Cree came in and Aaron spent some time on the Wigit with Maria and Do. Cree wanted to talk to me.

"I heard on the radio," she said, "that someone stole a Zodiac from the house. They asked all fishermen to be on the lookout for it."

"Must have been Gerard," I said. "I wondered how he planned to get off the island."

"They think it was Aaron," she said. "They didn't say his name, but the description was obvious."

"Sounds like Eddie's work," I said.

"They'll probably search the island," she said.

"Choppers can't fly in this weather," I said, "and there wouldn't be a trail a dog could follow. I don't think they'll come in here on foot."

"They might," she said. "They really want Aaron."

"I can't figure that out," I said. "We're just small potatoes. Everyone from the Colombians to the bikers to the CIA is doing a hundred times what we are."

"Aaron would make a good example," she said. "It doesn't scare White people when you put someone dark or strange in jail."

"But why Aaron? He wouldn't hurt anyone, really," I said. "There are White guys that are real criminals."

"People with power hate him," she said. "He's a renegade. He has the intelligence and education and style to be one of them, but he refuses. They can't stand that. It makes them wonder about their own choices."

"We could move sooner," I said. "With this muck, the moon won't make any difference."

"Let's talk to Aaron before I leave," she said.

Aaron was resigned to it. His smile became a grimace. "At least there won't be time for anyone else to split."

"They may already have," I said.

"Who," Cree asked me.

"Lance and the Poet," I said. "They took off in Lance's boat just before you came in."

Aaron walked along the beach to where the boat had been hidden. It was gone. He looked at the spot for a moment, then shook his head.

Cree was anxious to head out before the tide dropped further, so Aaron went back on board to kiss Maria and the baby. He and I walked back to camp and he sat silently in Maria's area. I told Lila and Morganne about Lance and the Poet.

"I'm just as glad," Lila said. "We don't need either one of them."

"We need the hands," I said.

"Not those hands," Lila said.

"We're going to go earlier," I said. "Gerard stole one of the Zodiacs from Eddie and they think Aaron did it. They'll come looking for us."

"Why here," Lila asked, "if they think he stole a Zodiac to get away?"

"They'll want to see where he was hiding and if anyone else is here," I said. "At least, there's a good chance they will. They know for sure someone was still on the island."

"Like, when are we going to do it?" Morganne asked.

"Tomorrow," I said, "or the next day at the latest."

The next morning, Lance and the Poet showed up as if nothing had happened.

"Where the hell have you been?" Lila asked them.

"LaConner," the Poet said. "I had to correct the galleys on my book, The Flamingo Dance."

"The Flaming Gonads," Lila said. "That fits."

"Great artists are used to jealousy and derision," he said.

"So now the whole country knows where we are, I suppose," Lila said.

"No one saw us," he said. "Except Robin. He had my galleys."

"I'm surprised you came back," Lila said.

"I almost didn't," he admitted. "I called Linda and she wants me back. Even with all my problems." He looked at me. "Problems aren't all bad," he said.

"So why did you come back?" Lila asked him.

"The police are looking for me," he said. "Linda said they call her every day."

"Fine!" Lila said.

"Robin said the publisher thinks my book will be a best-seller," the Poet said. "They're going to promote me as the 'Fugitive Poet.' Robin said Robbie Lerner... you know, Pancho? He already has a book deal. People are into us romantic types now."

"God, help us," Lila said.

"Well, it's a good thing we went," the Poet said. "To find out what's going on."

"So what did you find out?" Lila asked him.

"Only that the Feds think there's a million dollars hidden on the Orca. Robin says they've been tearing it up to find the money."

Aaron and I exchanged glances.

Lance noticed. "How much money is there?" he asked.

"Some," Aaron said.

"They won't find it," I said.

The rain came hard again and I was glad that Maria was with Cree. With the tide, they came in and we all went to visit them. Cree hadn't seen anything out of the ordinary or heard anything more on the radio. We relaxed a little.

I had grown used to sleeping damp, but I got chilled in the middle of the night, had to get up and walk around outside to get my temperature up. Not being able to get thoroughly warm once a day in the sweat wasn't good for me.

While I walked I heard a motor, just offshore, then saw a light sweep across the trees behind the sweat. It searched the beach and once passed right over me, but I held completely still by a tree until it went on.

When I felt warm again, I went back to the house, but I couldn't sleep any more. I built up the fire and watched them all, listened for any intrusion.

I could not believe that I had known all of them only a year. They had become part of the architecture of my thoughts. I looked at Aaron's face in the unsteady light. Even in sleep, it showed concern, even love, I thought.

I had asked Lila once, when I first knew them, what his secret was.

"He sees things," she had said. And he did. Things the rest of us never saw. Things we will probably never see. But he thought we all saw them, when at best, we had intermittent glimpses of shadows and reflections.

But even that was not his hold on us. The powerful part of Aaron was the part of him that was nothing, a void into which we all projected our ideal image, or a mirror which reflected back what we wanted to see.

He was the focus of the group's need for authority and discipline and the symbol of our power. Somehow we confused him with ourselves. He did not provide that clear, hard-edged boundary of self. He was amorphous, opaque, spongy, a hologram you could look at from all sides and not know that it wasn't real. But it felt different to us than to him.

I remembered, long ago when he'd recruited me for the voyage from Santa Cruz, I asked him why the boat was named the Quest instead of the Holy Grail or the Pot of Gold.

"The Holy Grail," he had told me, "is only an illusion, a magnet that keeps the compass constant. Salvation is in the questing."

I could see now that his chimerical goals were only magnets for the compasses of others. The rest of it, the drugs, the danger, the money, is just what passed for magic then.

That's all most people want, some friends, a little magic, someone they think knows where the hell they're bound. He had become the magnet for all our compasses. He was our North Star, our storm anchor.

The weak dawn came as to some dim world beneath the sea. The fire sputtered and smoked and I decided to put it out so the smoke wouldn't be seen in the daylight. That fire had burned on our hearth constantly all the time we'd been there and I hated to extinguish such an old friend.

The hiss and rush of the steam woke the others and we sat together and ate salmon and potatoes left from last night's dinner. I waited until Lance and the Poet found an excuse to go outside for a toot, then told the others about the searchlight.

"You'd better carry what you don't want to lose," I told them. "We might have to leave in a hurry."

The weather broke about noon and the sky showed patches of blue. Within an hour, the helicopter came. It was much larger than the one the sheriff had used to search before, and it was painted in camouflage. It flew ponderously up and down the beach, made one pass to the far side of the island and back. Then I heard it land some distance to the south.

"Let's get out of here," I said.

Everyone grabbed what they could. I passed out the guns, everyone stuffed their pockets with ammunition. The Poet shook so bad I thought he would drop the .38. Lance took on that calm I'd seen other combat veterans assume under pressure. I didn't like the look in his eyes.

Aaron stuck the .357 in his belt and carried the 30-30. Lance had the M-14. Gerard's .380 was in my belt and I also took the twelve-gauge. That left the other two automatics for Lila and Morganne. I was surprised that Morganne seemed more at ease than Lila did.

I stopped, went back inside and got my boots. I had tied them together with a thong, so I slipped my belt through it and the boots bumped against my hip as I walked. We struck inland, intersected the trail that led to the big house.

"Stay here for a few minutes," I told them, "I'll take a look."

"Be careful," Morganne said.

"I'll go with you," Lance said, looked at me narrowly.

We circled the low-lying ground towards the old village site, then crept up a small slope to the south. Near the top I dropped to all fours and Lance followed suit. We had to crawl around a bit to find a spot with a clear sightline to the beach.

The chopper sat quietly, engine off, and several men in Navy uniforms clustered around it. One of them seemed to give directions. A group of them headed up the beach towards the sweat, while two others took positions on either side of the chopper and watched the trees. Those two had rifles.

"I could pop those two from here," Lance said.

"That would do a lot of good," I said.

We slipped out of sight then walked rapidly back to where we'd left the others.

"This is it," Lance told them. "It's the Navy."

The Poet blanched. "I've got to get out of here," he said.

"We've all got to get out of here," I said, "and the only way we can do that is together."

"How about you, Aaron?" Lila asked him.

"I agree," he said.

"I know a place," I said. "I don't think they will find us."

"Where is this?" Lila asked.

"The big house," I said. "They'll never look there."

"How about Cree?" Morganne asked. "And Maria?"

"Cree won't come in until after dark," I said, "because of the tide. They will have that chopper out of here before dark."

"He's right about that," Lance said.

"What if they leave someone?" Morganne asked.

"I'll be here to meet Cree," I said.

We walked quickly. A few yards before the short cut I turned the wrong direction, walked a circle through tall Oregon grape where we left no tracks, then we stepped back over the main path and I led off down the slope.

The Poet tripped and fell, wouldn't get up.

"Come on," Lila said. "Let's go."

"I'm not going," he said.

"What's the deal?" Lila asked him

"I don't know," he said. "I just don't like it down there. I feel weird."

"Ridiculous," Lila said. "Get up off your ass. This isn't kindergarten."

"We'd better move," I said.

He followed us reluctantly and I turned often to look at him. The slope grew very steep and we dropped to hands and knees to clamber down. At the bottom I had them wade the stream for several yards, then turned to climb the slope.

""This can't be right," Lance said. "This is the way we came. If we just follow this creek, it's heading straight for the house."

"You don't want to do that," I said.

"I think we'd better follow him," the Poet muttered.

I took a couple of long switchbacks up the slope, followed trackless paths. In what seemed like minutes the grade lessened and dipped, then we stood looking down at the back of the house.

All was quiet. There was no boat at the dock and no sign of life. The Orca was in her usual place, just beyond our grasp.

"They're gone," the Poet said. "Let's go."

"We'll watch for a while," I said. "Make sure no one is there."

"I'm cold," the Poet complained.

"Don't be a pussy," Morganne said to him.

The clearing had been temporary and rain came steadily again. I knew none of us could stay still very long without getting chilled. After about fifteen minutes, I said, "I'll scout it."

"I'll do it," Morganne said. "No one wants me. If anyone is there, I'll tell them Patrick dropped me off to look for some stuff I left."

I couldn't think of an argument against it. "Be careful," I said to her.

"You'd better come back," the Poet said.

"I'm not you," Morganne answered.

She circled around to approach the house from the front. We saw her walk across the lawn as if she had come to visit friends. She disappeared and we waited.

"She won't come back," the Poet said. "Why should she?"

"She'll be back," I said.

Aaron was very quiet. He seemed content to follow my lead. I think it was a great relief to him. A few hours of the responsibility weighed on me and he had held it all together for years. I understood why sometimes, in the wan light of dawn or dusk, his face looked so old and tired.

In about ten minutes, Morganne appeared at the back door and motioned us down.

"They're gone," she whispered as we approached.

"Take your shoes off," I said, "we don't want to leave tracks for them."

"How about you?" the Poet asked, pointed to my muddy bare feet.

"I'll put mine on," I said.

While they took off their shoes on the steps, I washed my feet as much as possible under the rain gutter and wedged into my boots. I checked the soles, and they were smooth and dry.

The Poet started to go through the kitchen cabinets.

"Stay out of there," I said.

"Fuck you," he said. "I'm hungry."

"Cool it," Aaron said.

The Poet glared at me, but he stopped.

Even with no heat on, the house seemed hot. We stayed off the carpeted areas, sat at the kitchen table as we often had done in the past.

"Deja vu," Lila said. "Too bad there isn't a line stretched clear across the table like the old days."

Lance and the Poet glanced at each other.

"Eddie probably has some," the Poet said. "I'll go find it."

"Forget it," I said.

He looked at Aaron for confirmation, sat back down.

"So what do we do," Lance asked Aaron. Aaron shrugged.

"We can't swim out there," Lance said, nodded towards the Orca.

"We have to find Cree," Morganne said.

"I'll talk to Cree tonight," I said.

The Poet looked at me hard. "He's probably going to run out on us," he said. "Split with Cree and Maria, let us take the rap."

"Bullshit," Morganne said.

"I could have done that long ago," I said.

I thought about taking one of them with me, but I decided I could move faster by myself. Besides, they could all use some rest, but I'd had enough.

I pulled my boots off, strung them on my belt again, let my feet sink in the cold mud. I hadn't reached the top of the first rise when I heard the airplane. It was almost too dark to see it.

Lee came in low, under the overcast and made a bumpy landing outside the cove, struggled against the low chop to taxi around the

Orca to the dock. I started back towards the house, but saw Aaron and the others come out and struggle to get their shoes on quickly. They came up the trail towards me. I saw Eddie and Suzette get out of the plane. Eddie nearly went in the water as a wave tipped the pontoons.

As soon as Aaron saw me, I led away, watched for the short cut. When I came to it and turned off the trail, the Poet stopped.

"What the fuck?" Lila said as she pushed her way around him.

"I'm not going," he said. "We'll get lost down there in the dark and never find our way out."

"I know the way," I said.

"I'm going back," he said.

"Eddie can't take care of you," Lila said. "You'll go to jail."

"The sooner I get it over with the better," he said.

"You asshole," Morganne said. "I'll be glad to be rid of you."

"The feeling is mutual," he said.

He looked at Aaron. "I won't tell them what you're up to, boss," he said. "I owe you that."

Aaron only nodded.

"You owe him a hell of a lot more than that," Lila said.

"Fuck you, bitch," he said and started back down the path.

As he walked, Lance raised the M-14, aimed at his back. Aaron reached over quietly and pulled the barrel down.

"Let me do it before he has a chance to talk," Lance said.

"No," Aaron said. "It isn't worth that."

"He isn't worth anything," Lance said. "I know him. He'll tell them everything he knows."

"No," Aaron said.

Lance looked at him. "I don't know, man," he said. "I'm beginning to wonder if you know what you're doing." He looked at me. "Traipsing back and forth across this damned island isn't doing any good."

"What would you have done?" Lila asked him.

"Get the hell out of here," he said. "Let them have that damned sailboat. It's nothing but bad luck."

"How about the money?" Lila asked him.

"We could do runs again," he said. "Make the money back in six months."

"Not anymore," Lila said. "Colombians make all the money now."

"Well, I don't like this," Lance said. "It isn't the kind of leadership we need."

"And you could do better?" Lila asked.

"Well, I would have the guts to kill someone if we needed to," he said.

"We aren't going to kill anyone," I said.

"How about the guards?" he asked. "What if they put up a fight? What if there are ten of them waiting for us."

"We'll make sure there aren't," I said. "We'll do it tonight, before they can get anyone else out here."

He glared at me, but followed.

It seemed like only a few minutes at a brisk walk when we crested the slope and started down towards our camp. I assumed that the Navy was gone for the night but we approached carefully just in case.

No one was around, but they had found our house. Everything was torn apart and the parachute and sailcloth had been pulled back to let in the rain.

"I suppose my boat's gone too," Lance said.

"Let's find out," I said.

We left the others in a partly dry corner of the house and went down to the beach, found the boat more by feel than sight.

"I can't believe it," Lance said.

"The tide will be in soon," I said. "And so will Cree. This can still work."

"I don't like it," Lance said. "We should just take off."

"How about the money?" I asked him.

"Fuck the money," he said. "It isn't minc."

"It will take all of us a long ways," I said.

"I don't trust Aaron anymore," he said. "He's losing it. I think he's burned too many brain cells."

"He still has more than any of us," I said. "He's just tired. We need to help him out."

"Sometimes a man just has to help himself," Lance said.

"No one gets very far that way," I said.

"This is a new world," he said. "Nobody believes in that hippy shit anymore. Americans have to reclaim their individualism."

"Individualism is an illusion," I said. "Nothing is ever done by one person."

"Maybe not," he said. "But one person can damn sure get all the money."

"Money isn't that big a deal," I said.

"That's easy to say when you have a bunch of it," he said. "I know you made a lot of money and stashed it away somewhere."

"Someone's been telling you stories," I said. "My money is with Aaron's."

"So that's why you're still here," he said. "I thought it was Maria."

"I'm not after anyone's money or wife," I said.

"Well, you're after something," he said. "You've sure been throwing your weight around."

"Just trying to help," I said.

"Right," he said, "and I'm Santa Claus. Well I'm out of here."

"At least run us out to the Orca," I said.

"You're on your own, asshole," he said. He fingered the M-14. "Just don't mention my name." He began to clear away the brush and driftwood from the boat.

I thought about hijacking him, but decided against it. I didn't think any good would come of that.

"Well, have a nice day," I said, turned and walked away. I did not look back to see if he raised the rifle.

CHAPTER 50

There was a great splash offshore and I looked into the rising storm, saw nothing. Had it been the mountains, I would have found a place to hole up for the winter. My feet felt the way to our house.

"Where's Lance?" Lila asked me.

I shrugged.

Lila looked at Aaron. "That son of a bitch," she said.

He shook his head. "Right now we don't want anyone who doesn't want to be here." He looked in her eyes. "That includes you."

"Have I walked out on you before?" she asked him.

"Of course not," he said, "but this is different. This could be permanent."

"Life is always permanent," she said. "I don't have anywhere else to go, and if I did, it wouldn't make any difference."

He just looked at her for a while, then at Morganne.

I saw tears in her eyes, but she smiled at him and said, "Don't worry about me. This is my family."

He turned to me. "Don't ask," I said to him.

"What about Maria?" Morganne asked. "We can't take her and Do."

Aaron didn't answer at first, then slowly looked up. "No, I guess not," he said.

"Cree could take them somewhere," I said. "Before she follows us."

"Where?" Lila asked. "Who would take care of Maria, the way she is."

"One of us could stay with her," Morganne said. "But not me," she added.

"She doesn't have any family she can trust," Lila said.

"Everyone we know is on the lam or in jail," Morganne said.

"Patrick," Aaron said. "Patrick would do it, and they won't find her in Port Townsend right away. As soon as we're clear, I'll come back and get her."

"I don't know about Patrick," Lila said.

"He'll do it," Aaron said. "We go way back."

I felt my way to the moorage. I could hear the Wigit, the sound of the engine rose and fell with the waves. I flashed the signal and immediately Cree flashed it back. She came in closer but stayed at the wheel, shifted from forward to reverse to forward again to hold her position. There was no way in the rough water for her to get in close enough for me to go aboard.

I shouted to her from the bank. "Lance and the Poet split. We have to move tonight."

"I hear you," she yelled back.

"At ten," I said. "Watch the lights."

"I'll be there," she shouted.

We crossed the island again in almost complete silence. They followed my lead through the tricky part of the short cut without comment.

Lights were on in the house. We circled the familiar yard, watched for a while from the darkness. The lights of the Orca jumped and swayed from the waves pounding into the cove.

The remaining Zodiac had been pulled further up the beach to make it harder to steal. Light from a window splashed across it. Aaron's watch said it was just after eight, so we had plenty of time to get ready.

We found a dry spot under a large cedar.

"Can we get out there?" Morganne asked as she looked at the water.

"Not straight out," Aaron said.

"If we could get all the way to the point, the waves would help us," I said.

"They wouldn't expect us to come from that way," Lila said.

"If we're going to do that," Aaron said, "we'd better start now."

We could not move the inflatable with the heavy outboard attached so Aaron and I found a tool compartment and got the engine loose, dropped it and the plastic fuel tank on the beach. We also got the canvas cover off and anything else that would lighten it. We wrapped the long guns in a small tarp and put them inside.

We managed to haul the Zodiac into the water, but each wave threw it back at us. We half-floated, half-dragged it along the beach and into more sheltered water to the east. The bottom was slimy there and we sunk deeper with each step.

Morganne got in first, then Lila. Aaron stayed until last, pushed us as far out as he could before he climbed over the side.

I took the oars. We also had found two paddles so Aaron and Lila wielded those at the bow. Morganne crouched in the stern and held onto the guns so they didn't roll around or go overboard.

We could make no progress into the waves, so we followed the curve of the cove, just far enough out to stay afloat. Aaron and Lila got out a couple of times to push us off the sand.

It took us more than an hour to make the quarter mile or so to a spot just short of the rocky point. We grounded the Zodiac in the quieter water there and I waded ashore, crossed the neck of the point and looked to the north for the Wigit but could see nothing.

"I don't see her," I told them when I came back, "But she'll be here."

At twenty minutes until ten, we pushed off from the beach. We fought our way parallel with the waves until we were a third of the way across the mouth of the cove. When we turned, the chop came almost directly from the stern and carried us quickly down on the Orca.

Morganne scrambled to get the guns out, I tried to back-oar while Aaron and Lila braced for the impact. I gave up on the oars, laid them lengthwise and held on. So much for surprise, I thought, when the bow bumped noisily into the Orca's side, bounced and bumped again.

We swung around and I tried to fend off the next blow. I stood and managed to grab hold of the ladder as we slid past. I could not hold the Zodiac, my feet broke free and I swung from the ladder, got my knees onto a rung. As they slid past the other way, Aaron passed the end of the bow line to me and I got a double hitch around the bottom ladder rung before it tightened. When the line slacked I tied it and got up the ladder out of the way. As soon as Lila came up, I got on my belly and reached down for the guns. Morganne passed them to Aaron, who clung to the ladder and he handed them up to me then followed. Morganne clambered up behind him.

I hoped we didn't need the guns, because I wasn't at all sure they would fire, drenched as they were. I couldn't wait to worry about it. Aaron was beside me and I handed him the 30-30. I checked the shells in the shotgun and we moved into the shadows of the passageway. I saw Morganne messing with her automatic. Lila's was still in her waistband. I touched it and she looked at me, drew it out.

The Zodiac thumped against the hull with each wave. Still we saw no one. The three of them stayed by the wheelhouse while I scouted the main cabin. The lights were on in the dining room, but no one was there. Then I saw movement through the glass in the galley door and the shadow of one of the guards sat down. They were at our old crew table.

I told the others. We whispered quickly about it, decided to sneak through the dining room even with the lights on, because they could not see us from where they were.

The heavy door was unlocked and I opened it just enough to slide through. Morganne followed, then Lila and Aaron. He slowly closed the door.

I didn't hesitate, kept near the wall and crept to the serving line. We crouched below the round ports in the double swinging door. I noticed that the lock pin was down on one door, pointed to it. We lined up behind Aaron on the other side and he burst through.

I raised the shotgun, saw Lila's fat friend and a younger marshal stare wide in surprise. They each held a glass and between them was a bottle of Jack Daniels from the ship's stores. They put down the glasses and raised their hands without being told. I wondered if they practiced it at the academy.

"Please don't move," Aaron said.

"You won't get away with it," the fat one said.

"Quiet," I said.

Aaron looked at Lila. "Get the guns," he said.

"I'll do it," Morganne said.

I think her hands were steadier than mine as she approached them. She unsnapped the fat one's holster, took out the .38 with her left hand. She held her automatic well away from him and her eyes did not leave his face. She handed Aaron the revolver, went around the table for the other.

"Stand up," I said to them when she was clear. They stood and I had them take off their coats, throw them on the floor and put their handcuffs and keys on the table. The fat one had a small radio and I had him push it across the table to me. I made sure it was turned off.

The young one was beginning to tremble. The fat one looked at him with disgust.

"They aren't going anywhere," he said, "not in this weather. They'd need a tugboat to get clear of here tonight. Tomorrow morning our relief comes and here they are like fish in a barrel."

"Shut up," I said to him, let him look into the twelve-gauge.

"I'll search them," Lila said. She patted the pockets of the young one, then up the insides of his legs.

"Hi, sweetheart," the fat one said to her when his turn came.

She ignored it, went through his shirt pockets, threw some folded papers and lifesavers on the table. When she touched his leg, he bumped his pelvis at her.

"Touch me there again, sweetheart," he said.

Lila stood and kneed him hard. He gasped, started to grab her. I gestured at him with the shotgun and he doubled over, Lila backed away.

Aaron took the handcuffs and key rings from the table, tested the keys. He snapped one cuff on the young one's wrist then led him around the table, looped the chain around the bolted-down table leg then motioned for the fat one to lower his arm for the other cuff. He refused at first, but I cocked both hammers on the double barrel and he cooperated. Aaron pocketed the keys.

Lila and Morganne stayed with the prisoners; Aaron and I went to the wheelhouse. I hit the switch for the running lights, three times, then twice. In a minute I repeated it. I waited a couple of minutes, flashed again. Aaron cranked the diesel and it caught, but it was ragged, had to be re-started.

I stared out into the sound, saw no lights at all. I signaled again. "What about the anchor?" I asked Aaron.

"We'll have to cut it," he said. "All the batteries are down and it's pretty rough anyway."

"There should be a hacksaw in the forward tool locker," I said.

"Spare blades, too," he said. "You'll need them."

I had to get a flashlight from the galley, heard the marshals' voices. I stuck my head around the corner.

"Don't put up with any bullshit," I said to Lila and Morganne. "You can always shoot one of them if you need to."

The fat one glared at me.

Aaron continued to flash the signal. I found the hacksaw and a package with two spare blades. I had to hang from the deck, work upside down. The pitch and roll kept the chain moving and me hanging on. At first it seemed like it would never cut through at all, but gradually a thin groove showed in the flashlight beam.

A large wave nearly tossed me overboard. I broke the saw blade in the process. I put in a new one and continued to cut. Peripherally, I saw lights flash, knew it was the Wigit. Cree had come around into the cove to approach from the quieter side. I put down the saw and went to the ladder.

Cree stayed ten or twelve feet off our side. I pointed to the anchor chain, made a sawing motion. She turned her stern to our rail and quickly came back and tossed me a line, returned to the wheel. The Wigit tugged against the line when I tied it.

Aaron attached another line to a pin thirty feet up the rail and threw the end onto the cabin of the Wigit. Cree scrambled up, ran the line through and used it to pull herself alongside. Aaron and I put over our longest fenders and Cree already had hers out. The two craft banged together as they rode the waves in parallel while we talked.

"We'll have to tow her out of here," Aaron said.

"No problem," Cree said. "I have a cable ready." She pointed to a dark coil of two-inch hemp.

"We have to take Maria and the baby to the house," he said. "I have to call Patrick."

"I'll stay here," I said. "Get things ready."

"Just cut half a link," he said. "We don't want it to give early."

I nodded. Aaron climbed down into the Wigit. I saw Maria's face, pale and frightened, as Aaron went into the cabin. She clutched Do to her breast.

Cree engaged her prop and I cast loose the bow line and the Wigit turned stern-to. I ran along the deck to let go the other line and they headed in towards the dock. There still was no sign of life at the house.

I went back to the anchor chain and sawed at the heavy link. I was more than half way through the one side. I worked at it for several more minutes, nearly through, when that blade broke. I put in the last blade and carefully sawed again.

The Wigit bounced at the dock as Cree waited for Aaron. The yard lights came on and a few minutes later I saw Maria and Aaron go into the house. As I broke through, the link made a groaning sound and partly opened. I wondered if I had gone too far already.

The waves mounted, came from one quarter then the other, swung the Orca like a twisting pendulum against the chain. Water came over the midship rail on one side then the other. The bow plunged up and down, worried the damaged chain like an anxious dog.

I looked in the galley. Lila winked at me.

"Under control," Morganne said grimly.

The prisoners did not look happy.

It seemed a long time before I saw Aaron come out of the

house and run towards the dock. I went to the ladder and waited for them.

Aaron climbed up carrying a half-inch line that was tied to the heavy towline. He pulled over the large line and I helped him drag it up the deck as Cree slid forwards and maneuvered out around the anchor. I passed the line over the anchor chain while Aaron secured it. I waved the flashlight at Cree and she took up the slack and pulled gently.

The tug of the towline lessened the tension on the anchor chain. It moved around a little more but that was not as bad as wondering whether it would suddenly snap and a chunk of steel zip through my head as I hung over the side.

I sawed as fast as I could. The link began to open and I ducked. The loose end of the chain whizzed past my ear as it shot through the hawsehole. The anchor-end of it hissed into the water.

As our full weight hit the towline, it snapped taut and pulled the Wigit backwards. Cree opened the throttle. Slowly the momentum changed and the Wigit began to move us, a motion you could feel but not yet see. Cree drove straight into the waves and the slight headway made the Orca wallow less. I felt a shudder through the hull as Aaron engaged the diesel.

I climbed to the wheelhouse. You could just see the Wigit as our bow lights swung back and forth. Aaron steered towards the fishing boat as though it were the point of a compass needle..

We began to make noticeable progress out of the cove, and soon we were clear of the point. The water was even rougher, but at least we wouldn't go aground before we started. Between the two engines we moved right along.

When we were in mid channel, clear of the south end of Defoe, Cree turned us westward and strong waves slammed into our starboard bow. Aaron fought with the wheel.

"Once we turn Cape Flattery," he said, "we can fly on this wind."

There was no point in trying to raise any sail with the wind so much against us. Cree swung us south, well clear of Victoria Harbor. A fishing boat towing a fancy sailboat through this storm would surely attract attention. I hoped we would get beyond the Victoria-Port Angeles Ferry lane before daylight.

Morganne made coffee and I carried some up to Aaron. It was impossible to guess how much actual progress we made. There were no visible lights or landmarks. I knew we must be somewhere south of Lopez Island.

With the downward pull of the tow line on the bow, the Orca's bowsprit disappeared into each oncoming roller past the cat-head, scooped water and flung it back to run down both sides of the deck and cascade over the break. And with each dive, the prop broke free of the water, let the diesel race. I worked the throttle while Aaron steered. I calculated local time from the chronometer and we had been under way just over an hour.

I checked on Lila and Morganne. Lila wanted to talk to Aaron, so I took her place. The shotgun seemed to make the marshals nervous.

"He won't shut up," Lila said, nodded towards the fat one as she went out.

"Bring some rags from the engine room," I said. "We'll gag him."

"I'll remember you, buddy," he said. "No spick punk with a bunch of women gets the better of the Service. We'll make sure you have lots of fun in the joint when you go down."

"We could move you outside," I said. He shut up.

I spelled Aaron at the wheel a couple of times as the night wore on. Steering was mostly a matter of holding the rudder still so the Wigit could determine our direction. We considered lashing the wheel, but thought our small corrections probably contributed to net miles.

Aaron had the radios on. All we heard was broken up routine chatter. Every half-hour, he would depress the mike button and say, "clear." Cree would repeat it back to him.

They said nothing else.

CHAPTER 51

Eventually there was a slight lessening of the darkness around us and we could see a small circle of water. The waves were smaller and more from the west, which meant we were coming into the lee of Vancouver Island.

The vibrations of both engines ran back and forth through the tow cable, used the deck for a sounding board. I didn't like the feel of it through the soles of my feet, so I put on my boots which damped it some. This mechanical grinding against the wind was far different from running before it. I would be glad when we made that turn into open ocean.

Midday looked no different although a light meter might have said there was more light. Everyone was tired except the marshals, who napped by turns at the table. I was concerned that it would give them an edge.

They said nothing more except to ask for coffee or food, but they constantly watched whoever was with them. If they hadn't lied about their relief being due today, someone would have missed them by now.

I took their radio up to the wheelhouse and we turned it on, but had no idea if it was on a good frequency. The storm was our friend for now. Even if the Navy could fly, they probably never would see us. And the cutters should be tied up at the dock or out on rescue missions.

Cree swung us more to the southwest. Aaron said it was to

clear shallow water off Beachey Head. She stayed on the Canadian side, not that it was any great protection, but we hoped their response might be a little slower. Our success could depend on whether anyone believed we were desperate enough or stupid enough to try for the open sea in this weather.

There were bright patches towards evening, but never any true clearing.

When I checked in the galley, the fat marshal said, "I want to talk to the bossman."

"I'll see if he's interested," I said. I went up to see Aaron.

"It can't hurt to talk," he said. "If they think I'm listening, they'll be less likely to do something stupid."

I took the wheel and followed the silhouette of the Wigit into the last faint color of sunset. I was surprised, in a way, that we had gotten as far as we had. I assumed that Eddie had called the authorities soon after Aaron left the house. At best they must have been looking for us for at least twelve hours. I was used to seeing ahead, but there was nothing beyond the moment that seemed real.

We talked about what we would do if we did get away but it was all like something I'd read somewhere, only real if I put quite a little effort into it. The calculable reality was simple: as soon as the weather cleared, they would hunt us down with airplanes and radar and armed ships. They were not going to forget about their two comrades.

When Aaron returned he chuckled grimly. "They never give up," he said. "They want to negotiate a plea bargain: we give ourselves up; they'll forget about the kidnapping charge."

"What did you tell them?" I asked him.

"I'd think about it," he said.

"We've got to get rid of them," I said.

Aaron stared at me.

"I mean turn them loose," I said. "Cree could take them somewhere."

"I don't know if we'd hold our own out here," he said, "without the tow. Someone would have to go with them for a guard - and they'd run to a telephone before she got back to us."

"We could let them take the Wigit," I said. "Cree would do it."

He didn't say anything for a while. He looked into the red light of the binnacle glass as though he studied his own face. "We'd never make Cape Flattery," he said.

"What if we didn't intend to," I said.

"We can't get around the end of the island and head north," he said. "But if we came about and ran before the wind...." He thought about it. "Maybe we could get back around Victoria in the storm," he said. He looked at me. "It might work. We could try to slip past through the Gulf Islands and go north, try to make Bella Coola."

"Cree would like that," I said.

"I can't think of anything better right now," he said.

"You need to talk to Lila and Morganne," I said. "I'll go send them up."

"Watch this snake," Lila said to me. "When I went to the toilet he offered Morganne immunity."

"He doesn't have anything I want," I said.

When Lila and Morganne were gone, the fat one looked at me closely. "You could get out of this," he said.

"I intend to," I said.

"We could help you," he said. "You're in the perfect position, assistant to the boss. You know everything, but it really isn't you we want."

"No thanks," I said. "But I might be able to help you."

"How?" the young one asked. The fat one looked exasperated.

"I could get them to turn you loose," I said.

"For what?" the fat one asked.

"Forget you saw any of us." I held onto the edge of the table while a large roller pitched us up then down. The heavy light fixture groaned against its cables.

"That would be a little difficult," the fat one said.

"Maybe you didn't see anyone," I said. "They wore hoods,

came out of the shadows, blindfolded you. Maybe you heard them speaking Spanish, smelled like Colombians. Maybe they thought there was money on board."

They looked at me.

I waited while another wave passed beneath us.

"That's all?" the fat one asked.

"That's it," I said. "We're all kind of in this together. Maybe we can all survive it."

The young one had begun to look relieved. The fat one was more suspicious, but then I was a dumb spick.

"How do we do this?" he asked me.

"We'll give you the fishing boat," I said. "You go one way, we go the other."

"I'm no boat jockey," the fat one said. "Someone will have to go with us."

"No way," I said.

They looked at each other for a moment.

Aaron came in. The fat one waited until Aaron wasn't looking, then caught my eye. He nodded his agreement.

"Hey, man," I said to Aaron. "Let's turn these guys loose. We don't want a kidnapping rap."

Aaron looked at me as though surprised. "What did they offer you?" he asked me.

"It was my idea," I said. "We turn them loose in the other boat, and they'll say they don't know who we were."

"Right," Aaron said. "How do you enforce that?"

"Trust each other," I said.

The fat one watched us closely.

"You don't trust cops," Aaron said.

"It would work for us too," the fat one said to him.

Aaron turned. "Okay?" he asked.

"It would look better for us if we were hijacked by a gang of Colombians," he said. "Not some hippy with a bunch of women. And we'll take half the money."

"What money?" Aaron asked.

"The million," he said. "We know it's on here. We'll find it sooner or later. Unless you want to split it with us now."

"There's no million dollars," Aaron said.

"How much?" the fat one asked.

"A hundred grand," Aaron said. "Maybe a little more."

"Chump change," the fat marshal said.

"It's all I've got," Aaron said. "Take it or leave it."

"Fifty grand," the marshal said.

Aaron considered it. "We need enough time to pass the cape," he said. "A day, at least."

"Okay," the fat one said, "no problem. We'll get lost for a while," he laughed, "do some fishing."

Aaron looked at me.

"Sounds good to me," I said. "I'll tell the others."

Lila and Morganne both had hold of the wheel, one on each side. Spray beat against the glass constantly. Water poured in behind me. I told them about the deal with the marshals.

"You can't trust them," Lila said. "They'll call in their buddies the minute they can."

"How about the money?" I asked. "It would be hard to explain if one of us started talking about it."

"It's just cash," Lila said. "And not very much. It can disappear fast."

"Anyway," I said, "We aren't going south. While they watch for us at Cape Flattery, we'll run the other way and disappear up the Inside Passage. With the money."

"How much money is left?" Lila asked.

"Over a hundred thousand," I said. "Even after we pay them. With mine and what Aaron has left. We can all split it."

"I have money there, too," Morganne reminded me.

"Go talk to Aaron," I said. "Play along with whatever he says in front of them."

"They think we're stupid," Aaron said when he came up.

"They don't know the difference between stupid and crazy," I said.

"I'd rather take the Orca down," he said, "than let them have it."

He motioned for me to let him have the wheel. "We'd better get the money up here," he said. "Can you do it?"

I nodded. "Be right back," I said.

He handed me a card with the combination. "It's a cipher," he said. "Seven up, then seven down."

I got the hammer and a pry bar from the forward tool locker, grabbed a couple of screwdrivers. I slipped past the galley doors and down the steel ladder to the hold. It was moving around more than I was used to. I had to lie against the bulkhead to keep my balance.

With the flashlight I could see where they had torn open ventilating ducts and smashed in sections of heavy bulkheads as they searched. I went down the short second ladder and crouched my way into the lower compartment. The floor was sound, but there was water above the floor boards that sloshed one way then the other with the pitch and roll. It had the dirty-tea color of bilge water.

I felt for the screws under the filthy water, worked quickly with the screwdriver. I could probably have pried some of the boards up, but I didn't want to take the time to find out. Working alone, it must have been more than fifteen minutes before the last heavy screw yielded and I could get the bar under the edge of the jigsaw shaped false floor. I was soaked and I was sure the water already was deeper than when I had come down.

The boards had swollen and gave way slowly as I pried on one side then the other. When the section came loose, water sucked under it momentarily, then welled up as the Orca rolled back. The safe was underwater.

I felt for the dial and could turn it, but got only intermittent glimpses of the numbers through the brown water. I turned the flashlight on the card, added seven to the first number, waited until the water drained to the other side and turned the dial. The second number took two rolls, but I was careful not to go past it. The third was just a few ticks back, then the last required a double revolution of the dial and a precise stop. I felt a faint thud as the lock fell open.

I stopped. There was no way I could get the door open and the money out between rolls. I resigned myself to diving for it. I turned the handle and pulled just as the water started down. It did not budge, so I pocketed the flashlight, waited through a swing back and forth, pulled with both hands, and it opened.

I reached in, felt my moneybelt and pulled it out, draped it around my neck. Akbar's film cans floated up as water poured in. I got several out and tossed them away. I reached in for Aaron's money. He had said it was in several bundles, each wrapped in brown paper. I had to put my face into the water to reach to the bottom. I tasted petroleum and other worse things. I tried to wipe it off with my sleeve and managed to get some of it in my eyes.

I felt several notebooks. I grabbed one, hoped it was mine. I located several of Aaron's bundles and a large one I thought was Morganne's. I got them out, held them between my knees. The next roll nearly submerged me in the filthy water. I waited for it to flood back and reached in for several more bundles.

I made several trips, put the bundles and notebook up through the hatch into the main hold, then climbed the ladder. I sat until my eyes didn't burn so much, then looked for some way to carry the bundled money. I didn't want to make two trips. I finally took off my jacket and shirt and tied the sleeves of the shirt at the cuffs. This made a good set of pack bags to replace the moneybelt around my neck. I put the moneybelt where it belonged and slid the wet notebook into my pants.

I got up into the main passageway and past the galley and climbed to the wheelhouse. I dumped the shirt on the map table.

I took the wheel and Aaron laid the wet bundles out. I tossed my money belt over with them.

"How do we split it?" he asked me.

"I don't care," I said.

"Let's give them their fifty thousand first," he said. He counted out five of the muddy bundles, broke them open and checked them. The money wasn't that wet under the oiled paper, just around the edges. In each bundle were ten thinner, rubber-banded bundles of a thousand each, all fifties and hundreds. That was less than half of what he had.

"Let Morganne have hers," I said, "and we'll split the rest with Lila and Cree."

"It works for me," he said. He dumped the money from my belt with his and started dealing the stacks of a thousand into four piles.

"Not a bad hand," I said when he showed me my pile. It must have had twenty-five or thirty of the thick stacks of bills. "Stick mine back in my belt."

He put it in, snapped the belt closed and handed it to me.

"I'd better go deal with our passengers," he said.

Aaron came back smiling. "They think they have us bamboozled," he said. "By the time they figure it out, we'll be long gone."

At the next half-hour mark, Aaron picked up the microphone and said, "Talk." There was no immediate response. "Talk," he said again, held the button down an extra second.

"Talk," Cree's voice said from the speaker. "How about the line?"

"Drop it," Aaron said.

"Roger," she responded.

I could tell from the change in the deck vibrations that Cree had slacked the line, and Aaron sent me forward to drop it. Cree came in close, matched our speed. I took the wheel so Aaron could go down and talk to her.

Without the Wigit to stabilize her, the Orca wallowed and yawed and I couldn't seem to do anything about any of it. I centered the wheel and held it as still as I could.

Aaron was back in just a few minutes. "She likes it," he said. "They'd get both boats anyway."

"How are you going to get those two on the Wigit?" I asked him. "I don't think they walk on water."

"We may have to hog-tie them and use the cargo boom," he

said with a grin. "Just hold her as steady as you can. I'll make them walk the plank."

When I could see them in the light by the ladder, it appeared they had changed their minds about leaving. They argued with Aaron and he gestured at them with the 30-30. The young one held onto the rail and puked down the side. The Wigit bobbed in and out of the weak light a good twenty feet off our side. I could hear the fat one holler, but the words were lost on the wind.

Aaron got them to the head of the ladder and Cree drifted closer, maneuvered her bow rail near. The fat marshal took two steps and jumped, rolled out of sight on the Wigit's deck.

The young one didn't want to do it. Aaron threatened him and finally he perched half way down the ladder and Cree came close again, held it for many seconds, but he wouldn't go. I saw Aaron lean down and say something. The Wigit bumped against us and he jumped, fell against the cabin with a howl.

We wallowed along for a few more minutes, then the Wigit reappeared, came at us at an angle, bumped against the Orca forward of the ladder. Cree stepped up onto the rail and jumped to the ladder as the Wigit slid past. I could see the fat marshal at the wheel, very pale. I couldn't see the other one. The Wigit bumped away and was left behind, quickly bobbed out of my sight.

I met Cree at the ladder, climbed behind her to the wheelhouse.

Aaron looked at her.

She grinned at him. "Where we goin'?" she asked.

CHAPTER 52

Cree used her sleeve to wipe some of the mud and oil from the map table and rolled out some charts. Aaron started to come about. As the waves caught us on the beam, the Orca rolled violently. High up in the wheelhouse as we were, we got thrown around pretty good. Cree and I grabbed the wheel on each side of Aaron.

As we came on around and began to move with the following seas, the roll and yaw were less, although each wave pitched us up and then down and shoved us back the way we had so laboriously come.

Morganne and Lila came up and shivered as the water poured from them.

"Do you think they'll make it?" Morganne asked.

"Who? The marshals?" Cree said. "They'll be okay if they can follow orders. I gave them a downwind heading straight for Port Angeles. The Wigit will take care of them."

"We want them to get there and report," Aaron said. "Hopefully, they'll look for us in the Pacific.

I took the wheel so that Aaron could help Cree plot our course.

They discussed the variables, considered the form of the island and how it would funnel the wind through the straits. Cree called the new heading to me.

"Let's get some sail up," Aaron said.

I kept the helm while the others struggled with the foresail. In the deck lights I saw canvas flap and ropes snarl. Cree went up to untangle the mess. Aaron turned a spotlight on her for a moment and the tangle came loose. They hauled on the line while Cree hung from the mast and guided the peak. They stopped with less than half the sail out.

The lines snapped taut and the canvas ballooned. The boom swept around, bowed as it took the strain. I could feel the Orca heel and bound forward. Aaron came up to cut the diesel, then helped the others haul out the main.

They unfurled it even with the top of the foresail, swung the boom out so we were wing and wing. She leveled out and I held the heading, about three points off the wind. We pitched less with the greater speed, but the roll was heavier with the sails out.

The marine radio remained quiet but we could pick up a Bellingham station on the AM. Morganne turned it up to hear the Eagles' "The Long Run." The newsbreak came on and the announcer said that Ronald Reagan had just announced his candidacy for President.

"President Ray-Gun," Lila said. "That's enough to ruin your day."

"He'll never make it," Morganne said. "He's too crazy. He was Jim Jones' buddy, remember?"

"That's what they all want," Aaron said. "The messiah."

We ran without lights, a shadow that fled through the storm. Cree adjusted the sails now and then, and Aaron took the bow, said, "Hello," over the intercom.

Each following wave tipped up our stern and hung us at a steep angle, prepared to plunge us into the unseen depths. Then just in time the bow would lift high for a brief glimpse of the clouded heavens.

We flew along so well that Aaron decided to raise the main all the way and set the jib. Both operations went smoothly. Cree came back up to the wheelhouse, Lila and Morganne went to the galley to make coffee and see if the marshals had left anything edible.

"White bread and bologna," Lila said as she came up with a bag of sandwiches. "Seems about right."

Morganne balanced a full carafe of very black coffee. "They left our coffee alone," she said, handed it to Cree. "There are a bunch of empty jars of instant."

Cree took the wheel while I ate. After less than half a sandwich, I decided she was right to have turned down the food. No one could get it down. We laughed about that and Lila and Morganne did a few steps to "Takin' it to the Streets." When they stopped dancing, they continued to hold hands then Lila put her arm around Morganne. They stared forward, into the darkness.

I noticed a tendency to roll. Any slight heel started her rocking, and she would pass center several times before settling down. I nearly froze to the wheel, made as few corrections as possible. No one else seemed to notice so I suppressed the adrenaline that tried to erupt each time we heeled over.

I said, "Clear" into the intercom, waited for Aaron's response.

"Clear," was his only reply.

Cree returned from another tour of the rigging. "Jah has brought us a great storm," she said. She grinned. "If they see us on radar, they won't believe it." She looked at the speed indicators. "We'll pass Victoria before dawn if we hold it."

"That could give us a day or two," I said. "But if it keeps blowing we won't make any progress when we turn north."

"The wind will be less in the lee of the mainland," she said. "We can motor if we have to. Storms don't last forever." She studied a chart. "We could get weather out of the southwest next that will blow us all the way to the Queen Charlottes. We must believe it."

"This is November," I said.

"There is always a little April in November," she said. "Believe it."

In the window glass, I saw Lila's strained face turn towards us. "My heart knows it's November," she said.

There was a shudder forward and the Orca seemed to stick with her head down. The wheel spun out of my grasp, a spoke smacked the back of my hand when I tried to grab it. The wheel stopped and started back. I got hold of it and hung on, then let go as I realized the rudder was hard over and would only make matters worse, It spun back, slowed and I got control, guessed at center.

"...help with the sails...." the intercom squawked.

"Let's go," Cree said. Lila and Morganne came out of their trance and followed her.

I fought to stay on heading. I could not see what they did, but I felt the speed slack. That lessened the overall motion, but the steering was less definite and wandered. I made the smoothest corrections I could, held my breath each time we rolled.

Morganne came in. "They cut the jib loose," she said. "I have to go back. We're going to drop the main. Aaron said watch for her to heel over hard when we do, but it will stop the rocking."

"Ay, Captain, I'll be doing my best," I said. It made her smile and she came over, put her hand on my back.

"Remember," she said, "when this is over I'm going with you - to the mountains." Her hand trembled and she took it away.

"I remember," I said.

She went back down to the deck. I looked into the red light of the binnacle, held fast to the heading.

I could see movement just below near the mainmast but could make out no details. We began to rock again and the wheel jerked one way then the other. I braced and fought it.

We tipped too far to port, I was sure the rail was under. As she started to right herself I felt Aaron behind me. He grasped my shoulder.

"Let me have it," he said, reached for the wheel. I stared at him.

"Get out of here," he said, pulled me away from the wheel as we heeled far to starboard. "This is my ship to go down with." He pushed me towards the ladder then got both hands on the wheel. "Take care of Maria," he said.

I nearly fell down to the deck as the boat centered for a moment and I thought it would hold. Then it began the inexorable roll to port.

"Lucky," Lila called, "Here!"

I found them huddled. Hands reached out for me. The port rail was definitely underwater; the rush of it below us was louder than the wind. Masts and timbers gave off shrieks and breaking sounds. There were sharp reports of lines snapping. I saw stays go slack, then tighten.

"If we go down," Cree shouted at us, "Hold on to each other."

I felt Morganne shudder as though sobbing and Lila's icy hand shivered in mine. Cree took hold of both of them and we made a four-sided circle, like parachute jumpers.

I felt the stern go up and the Orca lay on her side. We partly jumped and were partly thrown into the water with a tangle of rigging and canvas. We had to let go of each other to struggle with the lines which, like tentacles, tried to drag us into the sea.

Although foundered, the Orca began to roll back as if she would right herself. The masts came out of the water. Lines jerked and whipped. One hit me in the back of the head and another burned across my arm. I heard Morganne scream but I could not find her.

I knew I had to get away from the wreck and I swam desperately into a trough, felt myself lifted and thrown forward by the succeeding crest. I felt myself dragged down by my feet and waist. I struggled to the surface, kicked off my boots and fumbled the moneybelt off.

I swam again, but most of my momentum was from the water. I relaxed as another wave passed, felt myself float just beneath the surface, like a dolphin. I turned on my back, gasped in air when my face broke the surface, then swam again.

I knew land should be about ninety degrees to port of the downwind direction so I turned, but was carried further by the waves and wind than my own efforts. I began to feel very cold and I wasn't sure if I swam or just thought about swimming.

My mind wouldn't concentrate, wanted to dream. I swam like a fish, at home in the water. Without effort, I floated and laughed at the cold. I remembered the mountains, the ice-jeweled streams. There was frost on bright berries; my breath became steam.

I smelled her and knew her. She rose up from below, the great head a sudden presence beside me. I rode with her up one swell and down into the trough. She bumped me in greeting as a dog nuzzles a rabbit. I started to swim, remembered her speed, her sonar and hearing. I lay quiet and waited.

Again she bumped me. Then she made a swift movement, turned to grasp me. I felt the great teeth close, smelled the rotten-fish of her digestive tract. I let go, surrendered, at last, to her world.

Foam flowers have blessed my aimless wanderings,
Ineffable winds have given me wings.
I've seen sidereal archipelagoes. Islands
Whose delirious skies open for wanderers...
True I have wept too much.
Dawns are heartbreaking;Cruel all moons and bitter the suns.

---Arthur Rimbaud

EPILOGUE

Do is a cheerleader and plays flute in the band. Granny is so proud of her she could bust. The two boys, Aaron and Morgan, drive Granny crazy, but she won't let us move. Lila, the baby, is as pugnacious as her namesake.

I bought the ten acres of orchard across the road and put most of it in produce. I farm it with horses. We eat pretty well and sell or trade the rest. I keep to my own business and make sure no one follows me. I finally got a computer and I've learned to use it a little.

I take the kids to the Stehekin every summer, show them the things my Grandfather showed me, as much as I can remember. One of the neighbors with a stock truck takes the horses up to Twenty-five Mile Creek and we ride from there. It's the best time of the year but the ghosts walk with me a lot.

Maria said it all was just a dream that she won't dream anymore. She doesn't talk much, but when she smiles at me it doesn't matter. Like some long-ago sea captain's widow, she may wait still for Aaron to return. I wouldn't be surprised to see Cree.

Neither of their bodies ever was identified. And no one I talked to had any idea what happened to the old fishing boat. I'll bet it could be found somewhere near Bella Coola.

I thought once that I saw Morganne, a few years back, a tired waitress in a donut shop, but it couldn't have been her. I was happy about that. She would have hated it.

The medical examiner from Victoria identified the body: "...white female, 25-30 years old. 5'5" tall, 100lb+-. Name believed to be Morganne Fahey," and "...Lila Eskinazi, 5'6"...." Lila would have hated them for giving her weight. The article I read went on, "...Thought to have been on board as well were Aaron Burr Adams or Adamson of Seattle, the registered owner of the schooner, Cree Craig, a fisherman, of Nanaimo, B. C., and an unidentified man believed to be Mexican or Colombian who may have kidnapped the others. It is believed that these three also perished, but their bodies have not been found."

I found Maria as she wandered the streets of Seattle with Do. Patrick hadn't showed up by the third day and Eddie had contributors due for a visit. It wouldn't do to have her wander around talking of Guardians and Whale Dreams. He bought her a one-way ticket on the ferry at Winslow.

She said she went to Frank Lewis' office but he wouldn't see her. His secretary brought back a note with the address for the Salvation Army shelter. The lady there said they had no room, try again in a few days. She had been able to beg a little food from vendors at the Farmer's Market.

She had thought that Aaron might look for her at the Greek place, so she hung out there for a couple of days. They acted as if they didn't know her and finally the matron asked her to leave. She'd gotten hassled for breast-feeding in public and wherever she tried to sleep, they kicked her out.

I called Granny. She chewed me out and wired me some money. I got a rent-a-wreck and we made it to old man Corkindale's. My mares were happy to see me. They both had large foals sired by his Percheron. Even Snake's geldings seemed to have some dim memory. The old man volunteered to keep Flea until he died because he was afraid the old mule could not survive the ride over the mountains. I think the two of them had gotten quite attached.

Maria and I and Do and the horses made it over Cascade Pass in fine shape. We went slowly so the foals could follow us. The snow held off and the days were bright and filled with color. I saw fresh bear tracks along the river and knew we had made it in time.

Maria's eyes cleared when we were in the high country and she even talked to me a little by the fire at night. I tried to tell her about the wreck, but I have never found the right words for it.

Granny didn't seem surprised at all that I showed up with a woman and child. She cleared her unused sewing room for them, then went out and bought a big stack of baby things. She has never asked me about that year and I never have told her anything.

I've never told anyone much. I'm not always sure I believe any of it, especially the means of my escape. I have gone over it many times. I remember those great teeth, the certainty of my death. But she took me in her mouth the way a mother moves a cub and held me out of the water as she swam through the high waves with ease.

As we neared the shore, she rode a breaker, then another. Foam and sand lashed my face, I choked and struggled but she held me firmly. She lurched heavily as she writhed her way onto the graveled bar.

As the great head moved from side to side I thought of film Eddie had showed us of an orca killing a seal on a beach, tossing it's broken body about like a great cat would a mouse. But she spat me out, nosed me forward into the shallows as though she put me back in my place.

I lay there and gasped for breath, struggled out of the mud. I could hear her drag her huge body back into the water, but I did not have the strength to look.

Doctor Edward Randé would insist that she did it for selfish reasons alone, that there was no chance that she felt sympathy for a fellow creature in distress. Whatever her reasons, she saved my life at risk to her own. And mine is not the only such case.

Before I would admit my experience, I wanted to know if it was unique. It was not. With a little research I discovered that there were hundreds of stories over the centuries of orcas or dolphins who rescued drowning humans, in Puget Sound, in the North Pacific and all over the world.

I have wondered much about that year which seemed a lifetime, have wondered which was my first step on that dark road downward towards that shadowed coast. It has occurred to me that I never went to the sea at all, but fell asleep in some snug den there in the mountains and dreamed it all. But that would not explain Maria and Do or the spirits that walk beside me in the dark of the moon.

Especially Aaron. Sometimes, when I first glance into a mirror, I see his face for a moment. Or my shadow, cast long and thin by the lowering sun, will move in a certain way and the hair on my neck will rise. And often, I hear his deep voice long into the night, hypnotic and entranced, enchanted and enchanting.

Sometimes, I think we dreamed him, all of us together - projected our need for a king, and he was just a shadow. We might not recognize him if we met him on the street. Sometimes, I think he dreamed it all, including us, and it was we who were fading creatures of his imagination. Most of us are only the dream creatures of the powerful among us.

There are other versions of this story, of course. Besides the newspaper accounts there have been several attempts at revisionist history.

There is Robbie Lerner's book, Ride the Wind, in which we all are committed and highly-disciplined international terrorists raising money for the revolution. He was secretly in charge, of course, and in contact with a vast network of spies and saboteurs. He deeply regretted the glorious deaths of his comrades and exhorted his readers to step into the breach.

Then there was Walt Gann's series of articles in Our Sound magazine. He claimed to know that the wreck was staged. We'd sunk the Orca and had gotten ashore with more than a million dollars. He was sure we had paid off the authorities to put out the story we'd all drowned. He had a section on each of us, speculating about where we'd gone with our share.

Lila had been seen in Anchorage, he said, running a first-class whorehouse. There were telephoto shots of a fat blonde woman leaning out a window above a sign that said "Supper Club."

Cree was painting in Paris, according to him, and Morganne headed a religious cult somewhere in the New Hebrides. The Dark Stranger, as he called me, had been a Colombian contact of Aaron's who had helped Aaron flee the country.

His finale was an interview with Aaron in Belize, where he and Maria now lived in luxury while Aaron directed the operations of an international cartel.

Here, where they call me by my given name, no one has heard of Lucky. If you come here to find me, you never will. And if you did, you would not believe it. I might pass you on any street, bump into your cart at the supermarket, and you wouldn't know it. Sometimes I think I'm a spirit, the way people look through me.

And you would not know which of the silent Mexican women who watch their children play in the park is Maria, or guess, when she smiled at you as you passed, that she hadn't spoken in years except to the children.

I don't talk that much, myself. As the elders say, "You need only a few words to speak the truth." My children, my garden, my horses, say all that is necessary.

I suppose my life has run on luck, but as much of it has been bad as good. In that sense, I suppose you could call anyone Lucky. Given that definition, it seems like luck is pretty much a neutral factor.

At night, some trick of light and shadow makes the trees around this old house seem to glow. Many have remarked on it.

I just say, "The air here is so clean that the leaves reflect the light from the Great Bear." Most of them think I'm crazy. I don't argue the point.

But my horses are fat. Each season I have truckloads of produce. And although she never says so, I know Maria loves me. And every year, here in the valley, there are more golden children.

About the Author

I am a Westerner, blood, bone and soul. I am more at ease on a horse than in a vehicle. I belong to the land, not the land to me. I am an outcropping in human form of the spirit of this wild, fierce, overwhelmingly beautiful part of planet Earth. I live on a ranch crossed by a creek lined with beaver dams and populated with most of the wildlife originally found here including an occasional wandering cougar. My family has horses and cattle and sheep and goats as well as the whole compliment of fowl. A flock of wild turkeys makes it's home with us and flies home to roost atop the chickenhouse every evening. We produce almost all our own food and usually have a year's supply stored around the place.

My white ancestors came west in covered wagons and lived at peace and mixed with the Native people they found here, so, in the parlance of Sherman Alexie, who comes from the neighboring Spokane reservation, I am from the "Little Bit Tribe" - I'm a little bit Indian. Among my children are two dark and beautiful half-Native daughters and I consider it an honor to be their father. It was not the people of the Earth, the farmers and ranchers who were driven to exterminate the elder peoples here but the urban people, the politicians and merchants who saw them as impediments to hegemony. To us they were our neighbors and relatives and still are. Almost half the population of our region is Native and the Colville Reservation in my home county of Okanogan is 1.3 million acres - a good-sized sovereign nation.

After seven years at the University of Washington in Seattle getting what my cowboy grandfather described as "more education than a person needs," I returned home. I am the Executive Director of the Upper Columbia Group, a salmon and environmental recovery organization which works with landowners to design and fund restoration projects in the Upper Columbia River Region. We work closely with the Colville Confederated Tribes and the Yakama Nation in Washington State and the Okanagan Nations Alliance from British Columbia as well as the farmers and ranchers of the region. For me, this is not a job but a great honor and opportunity to work with my people.

My writing reflects my intimate association with the physical world. The environment is not a background for my human characters but an active presence. My characters are drawn from the people I have known in my life in the west and you would not be surprised to bump into one of them on the street but there is more to these people than you may have imagined. There is much in my writing of the Earth-centered wisdom of our Native elders but my novels are not "preachy." I have often been told that my stories are "too real" to be fiction which I take as a great compliment. They are fiction, but fiction that grows out of real life lived by real people in real places. Yet sometimes that reality is not the same reality that most of us see around us every day, but a reality imbued with the natural magic that flows from the heart of our mother, the Earth.

Printed in the United States
1275400007B/31-36